In the National Interest

In the National Interest

A Work of Fiction

*To: Shirley
Harry Currie*

Harry Currie

Copyright © 2018 by Harry Currie.

ISBN:	Hardcover	978-1-9845-3552-8
	Softcover	978-1-9845-3551-1
	eBook	978-1-9845-3554-2

All rights reserved. No part of this book may be reproduced or transmitted in any form or by any means, electronic or mechanical, including photocopying, recording, or by any information storage and retrieval system, without permission in writing from the copyright owner.

This is a work of fiction. Names, characters, places and incidents either are the product of the author's imagination or are used fictitiously, and any resemblance to any actual persons, living or dead, events, or locales is entirely coincidental.

Any people depicted in stock imagery provided by Getty Images are models, and such images are being used for illustrative purposes only.
Certain stock imagery © Getty Images.

Print information available on the last page.

Rev. date: 06/14/2018

To order additional copies of this book, contact:
Xlibris
1-888-795-4274
www.Xlibris.com
Orders@Xlibris.com
778826

CONTENTS

Acknowledgments ix
About Famous Historical Quotations And Our Book's Title xi

Chapter 1   In The National Interest 1
Chapter 2   The Presidential Declaration 17
Chapter 3   Cia Involvement 20
Chapter 4   The President 35
Chapter 5   First Assignment—El Salvador 47
Chapter 6   En Route To El Salvador 61
Chapter 7   San Salvador, El Salvador 65
Chapter 8   The Company Problem 73
Chapter 9   Senor Pico's 93
Chapter 10   The Embassy 96
Chapter 11   The Colonia Plant 107
Chapter 12   The Ambassador's Residence 115
Chapter 13   The Rhinoceros 124
Chapter 14   Colonia Showdown 132
Chapter 15   In Chambers 139
Chapter 16   The Embassy 150
Chapter 17   Two Safe Rooms 168
Chapter 18   The Shit Hits The Fan 189
Chapter 19   Home Sweet Home 201
Chapter 20   Home And Campus Issues 214
Chapter 21   Whoops, El Salvador Again 227
Chapter 22   Kpp Field Teams 238
Chapter 23   Kpp Agent Gear And Kit 240
Chapter 24   Bomb School 243

Chapter 25 The Balloon Goes Up 254
Chapter 26 Balloons 2 And 3 277
Chapter 27 A Reckoning 294
Chapter 28 The Ultimate Reckoning 304
Chapter 29 Home Sweet Home Again 320
Chapter 30 Kpp Fight School 329
Chapter 31 A Well-Deserved Break 339
Chapter 32 A New Day, A New Idea 347

DEDICATION

To "my band of brothers" who continue to accompany me in my life's journey from which this novel has drawn so liberally, if not literally.

ACKNOWLEDGMENTS

I wish to thank my wife, Johnette, for her support and encouragement in the rendering of this text; my son-in-law, Michael Wallace, for his help in instilling continuity and color; and my son, Shawn, for helping me keep track of the characters and keep continuity and flow. Additionally, I want to thank all of the above for their invaluable help in reading and editing the text and for the many insights that helped me supply a more readable, informative, and interesting book.

ABOUT FAMOUS HISTORICAL QUOTATIONS AND OUR BOOK'S TITLE

In 1805, the U.S. Marines—led by Lt. Presley O'Bannon—marched across the desert from Egypt to free U.S. hostages being held by Barbary Coast pirates in Tripoli, Libya, in what is known as the Battle of Derna. Again, in 1815, a fleet of five U.S. frigates was sent to tame the Barbary Muslim pirates to affect the return of U.S. captives and to exact significant monetary compensation for their efforts. And the Battle of Chapultepec, during the 1846–1848 Mexican-American War, was dubbed "the Halls of Montezuma." This led to the famous but chronologically inverted lines in the "Marines' Hymn" "from the Halls of Montezuma to the shores of Tripoli."

Another quotation related to the Barbary Coast excursions was "Millions for defense, but not a cent [penny] in tribute." It was originally made by Robert Goodloe Harper, a U.S. senator, in 1816 in response to the above two prior Barbary Coast pirate excursions by the USA, meaning that the USA would spend whatever was necessary to protect our assets but would never pay a blackmailer's ransom. This quote was picked up most famously by Pres. Thomas Jefferson, to whom most incorrectly credit it. However, the prior quotation—"From the Halls of Montezuma to the shores of Tripoli"—became the now-famous "Marines' Hymn."

The latter quotation, "Millions in defense, but not a cent in tribute," became the de facto foreign policy of the USA and is today commonly understood worldwide by all, friends and enemies alike.

In today's world, this U.S. policy is interpreted as the fact that the United States will do whatever is necessary to see to the safety and security of the U.S. military, diplomats, public employees, and assets and will not negotiate with anyone, terrorist or others, regarding them. With respect to protecting the individual citizen, a VIP, or the industry of the United States, this current policy falls woefully short. Protests, complaints, or strongly worded intergovernmental messages are the more usual response.

Accordingly, the framework of this book and others to follow is based on the suggested extension of this policy—acting against states, terrorists, or others who foster, promote, or give solace to those who will act against our people, our industries, and our assets. Such action will be like "an eye for an eye" and will be limited to the recovery of people, removal of threats, and restoration of the asset affected but not include the more tortuous exaction of the recovery of monetary compensation for the efforts required. All this is more in keeping with the current actions of the USA vis-à-vis the war on terrorism. This clarified interpretation based on that original quotation "Millions in defense, but not a cent in tribute" is clearly "in the national interest," the title of this book.

1

IN THE NATIONAL INTEREST

This president—James A. Knapp, tall as Lincoln—stood his full six feet four inches and scornfully stated that everyone understood that the USA would not negotiate with terrorists. Standing like this, one understood how this charismatic man had become president. His very presence radiated charm and determination. And stated so boldly, even the strong willed though somewhat shorter director of central intelligence (DCI), Bill D., felt moved by his will. However, the president's statement was actually a question, and Bill—a longtime associate and confidant—understood it as such.

"Yes, Mr. President, everyone understands that the U.S. will not negotiate with terrorists who kidnap U.S. diplomats. They understand that we will not give in to their demands to release prisoners or give them supplies or money for any such hostage taking. But"—he paused for effect—"they also know that with similar kidnap and extortion techniques, they can get significant funds or other largess from large U.S. international corporations, VIPs, and other U.S. citizens to expand and support their movements. This, in turn, effectively trumps our 'no negotiation' stance with respect to U.S. interests. And—no, typically, they can't get prisoners released, but they can fund their movement's needs for weapons and supplies. And with enough money, they can affect or force some few foreign releases that are most important to them.

"This suggested that a presidential declaration will allow the CIA to form a team to deal with these happenings promptly and effectively in a somewhat covert manner. It will put us on the offense against these actors. Although we cannot overtly claim such actions, effective results will demonstrate to the public that real action is being taken and will return us to an offensive position."

The president, leaning back in his comfortable Oval Office chair, turned and gazed out the window at a gardener raking up the last of the winter's dead leaves. The beginning of spring was in the air. He knew Bill was right; after all, this was exactly what he had asked of him. He knew positive action plans needed to be made to deal with this pressing issue. With some two years remaining in his first term of office, he believed they had time to make some significant action on this project.

His thinking done, the president abruptly turned to Bill. "This document is exactly what I need. You've spelled it out just as we've discussed earlier, but I'm anxious. I don't want this declaration getting public disclosure unless and until we're completely sure it is effective. We can't afford a backfire. You're the DCI. Keep it classified, damn it. And keep me informed—not in detail, mind you, but informed. Understand?"

"Thank you, Mr. President. With your input, we've worked hard to give this document the feeling you originally expressed to me and I promise to keep you fully informed. Let's code-name it 'Jennifer.' That way, if anyone stumbles into or overhears any talk, we can just say we're talking about that cute new girl the First Lady has as her Secret Service tender."

"Good idea, Bill. She is a looker, isn't she?"

With that, John M.—deputy DCI waiting in the anteroom—was brought in to witness the signing. The president's secretary, Julie, logged the declaration in and made copies for the president's personal file, the official White House file, and the CIA—all duly classified appropriately as "Top secret—Presidential/CIA eyes only."

"Julie, please notify the chopper we're on the way and that we're going straight to Langley."

As the DCI and his deputy boarded the helicopter for the short trip to Langley, Virginia (CIA headquarters), Bill contemplated the task before them. It was an important undertaking that was critical to national security. He knew, however, that he and the agency were up to the job. His career, spanning some twenty years in the Defense Intelligence Agency (DIA) and the Department of Defense (DOD), now seemed just a long preparation for this very assignment.

Safely ensconced in his seventh-floor office, the director commented to his deputy, "We've got the presidential declaration. Now we need to figure out how to accomplish the goals set out in it. Get Ops [the operations director] up here ASAP. I'll get Margo to clear my schedule for a while. You get yours cleared as well, John."

"Margo," he called, "John and I are going to be meeting with Ops for an hour or so. Please clear my schedule. No interruptions, OK?"

Shortly afterward, John announced, "Bill, I've got Ops here with me and have cleared my schedule for the rest of the day. You ready?"

"You bet, John. Come on in, Joe. Boy, have we got a story to tell you."

...

"Director, that's quite a story, but have you any idea how to pull it off?"

"No, but I hoped you might give us your thoughts."

"Well, Director, it just so happens that I do, but I'll have to talk it over with one of our chief scientists, OK?"

"It's not a scientific matter, but if you've an idea, go with it—soon. It's 'TS, eyes only.'"

"Gotcha. See you right after lunch, one way or another."

"Done. We'll both be here, Joe."

"No promises, but I'll see you then."

With that, Ops strode off in a purposeful manner. His height was near that of the president, and he towered both the DCI and his boss, the deputy director of central intelligence (DDCI). These characteristics, when added to his outstanding abilities, were key to his being chosen for the post of CIA operations director.

"Director, I talked with Marvin L. He's one of our best ops science guys, although that's not what's important here. What is important is that he has an overview of all the technical gizmos and operational elements and has a good way with people and solving problems. Just recently, he told me about the exploits of one of our outside technical groups that relates directly to the problem at hand.

"I talked with Marvin, and he agreed that one of our contractor groups in Dallas seems perfect for this operation. Oddly, they are already running a program much like the one we need but just in defense of their own company's people and interests. They'll need some additional funding and training, but I think they might be our best bet of putting a team together that can handle this problem. They have technology by the tail and are can-do people. Also, they will give us some standoff space since they are a nongovernmental organization, just in case we or they screw up and we need deniability.

"Let me fill you in on my thinking, and then with your approval, I'll get to work on it. Marvin is already their contracting officer and technical representative [COTR] on several technical items. Assuming Marvin agrees and they check out, the chain would be their team leader to Marvin to me to you two. From there, it's up to you."

"From us to the president, 'eyes only.' OK, I'm on it."

The next day, after an early flight to Dallas, Marvin drove to the Exlite Inc. corporate office and, using his COTR company badge, was able to walk in on Max, the Key Personnel Protection System (KPPS) team leader, unannounced.

"Hi, Max."

"What?" Max looked up, surprised. "Why, hello, Marvin. Long time no see. What's up?"

"Max, I need your help in a big way. I need to tell you I've upgraded your security for this. This is a 'top secret—eyes only' problem. Let me talk it out, and if you're amenable and you think it can be done, we'll go from there. It'll take your company's top management approval, but with our history, I think they'll go for it. If you do, the agency will pay the freight, but we need deniability, so it'll be a black operation. The company will make a standard operating profit margin on all your operations, but they will have to relinquish control to you and me on the classified stuff. I hope you're amenable."

"Sounds like a tall order. But of course, if you need us, I'll do everything I can to help. As you say, we'll have to clear it with top management. My team has always been dedicated, but this sounds like it's over the top from anything we've done for you before. Normally, our interface has been on the development of technology items only."

"Yes, Max, but it's directly in line with the kinds of things you guys have been doing for your company's security over the last couple of years. And Exlite would benefit from the results of the efforts as well."

"OK, but should I get a couple of my people in to hear you out?"

"No, not yet. You can take care of that later. First, let me go over the whole thing with you. Then let's see how you respond. But again, this is top secret. Let's go to your most secure area and get lunch sent in."

"Done. My office here is the most secure we have for now. Let me tell Kathy to hold my calls and others, OK?" Over the intercom, Max said, "Kathy, no calls except for absolute emergencies. Please order lunch for us. I'd like you available, so order for yourself as well. Notify all who report directly to me to stand by in the offices immediately after lunch until I release them, and have them notify their staff to plan to be in the office tomorrow for an important briefing. Notify anyone in the field to tie things up and plan to return to Dallas ASAP. And, Kathy, find out the availability of Bob Briscoe [Exlite security manager], Raymond Thornton [the executive vice president {EVP}], the president, and the chairman. Let me know as soon as you can of their availabilities and when all notifications are complete. Thanks.

"OK, Marvin, I'm all yours."

"First things first, Max. Sign this nondisclosure security agreement. Tear off a carbon for your file. Store it. And here are a few blank copies for anyone you might brief. Keep a list, and keep me informed of all on it. I'll send you more forms when I get back to DC. As I said, this is eyes only, top secret, which is CIA-presidential."

"Wow! Marvin, this is important."

"Yes . . . yes, it is. And assuming this is a go with all, you will report to me and from time to time come to DC and brief Ops and whomever.

But most importantly, you must keep me informed. And we need to work on a 'tasking' basis for project and funding purposes. Again, this is all assuming you and the company agree."

"OK, Marvin, but quit beating around the bush, or we'll never get anything done. Get to the point."

"Max, we need you to form a quick reaction team for us, your KPPS team, to enable us to quickly and reliably track key items and people anywhere in the world, similar to the KPPS operation you run for your company. In fact, I need you to inform me more completely of exactly what and how you perform the KPPS function for your company. Then from that, I can tell you better what I have in mind for you to help us generally meld the two operations. Initially, we want to use your current team capabilities to serve your company needs and, as an offshoot, to help us out. Then we want to enhance your team's capabilities to serve our needs, with your company needs becoming secondary. Both would be served, and we would pick up the cost. Also, you need to recognize that the help you give us might often be for other companies, not just yours."

"Sounds good but complicated. Offhand, I see no reason the company would not want to go along as long as the ventures are truly national security in nature and not company competitive."

"Well, that's understood. But inevitably, there would be some conflict of interest. And we would claim the preference and would insist, for security purposes, that the need to know be severely limited. General information can be shared up your chain, but the actual detail would have to be eliminated because of classification."

"Marvin, I can't speak for Exlite at this moment, but I think we can pull this off."

"Max, it's important that we have a show-and-tell for a few key people in DC. OK, now how about some of those KPPS details?"

"OK, Marvin, as you know, KPPS is an acronym for Key Personnel Protection System. We categorize our operations around the world in three: sites where there is a real possibility of terrorist action with little or no notice, our highest priority; sites where there is possibility of terrorist action and that are difficult to respond to from Dallas, our next priority; and sites where there is less possibility of terrorist action, our lowest priority.

"We equip Category I sites and key personnel there with a communications system [comm] that includes the individuals their vehicles, and their homes. We harden their homes to a point. And we brief them extensively. We equip the key personnel with clandestine emergency location/rescue transmitters [ERT] and the metro-area/city/locality with an area-wide monitor [AWM] system that detects and triangulates the location of these transmitters when they are activated. We equip and train an emergency location team [ELT] with aircraft, vehicles, and handheld trackers capable of homing in on these transmitters individually at varying range.

"Category II sites are equipped with enough clandestine emergency rescue transmitters to cover all the key personnel. We stash enough aircraft-mountable, vehicle-mountable, and handheld tracking equipment for rescue should it become necessary. We train a few key security personnel to operate the equipment until our emergency response/rescue team [ER/RT] team can arrive on-site, if needed.

"Category III sites are equipped with enough clandestine emergency rescue transmitters to cover all the key personnel in that area. A key security person is trained in their use and distribution should they be needed.

"Finally, we equip and train a Dallas-based international emergency response/rescue team, which responds by specially equipped company jet aircraft capable of detecting, tracking, and homing in on our clandestine emergency rescue transmitters at up to 250 miles away. In addition, the teams are equipped with compatible comm and intercept equipment, some specialty ransom equipment, and other appropriate items.

"We have categorized twenty-two of our company sites around the world, and there are several in each of the above categories. In short, we have equipment and a few trained people in Japan, the Philippines, Singapore, Australia, the Netherlands, England, Portugal, Spain, France, Germany, Argentina, Brazil, El Salvador, Canada, and the USA.

"I'll be glad to give you details on all these—the equipment, personnel, training, and maintenance—later as you desire."

"Here's lunch now. Kathy, how's it going?"

"Fine, Max. Bob Briscoe is in town and says he'll be available at your call, give or take a half hour. The executive VP, president, and chairman are all in town for the next few days. They can be available at their offices within an hour or so of notification. All your guys are here and standing by. Their people are all available. Russ and Matt are in Italy and finishing up. They can be back in a day or two, if needed."

"Thanks, Kathy, check on the whereabouts of the company jets. Are they scheduled? Is there one in Europe now that can be used to ferry Russ and Matt home if necessary?"

"OK, will do."

"Marvin, is there any problem using our company jets to transport you back and forth as available? They're often in DC and are constantly coming and going. It would enable you to travel less visibly. We could charge you standard commercial airfare to counter any naysayers."

"Yes, Max, if we could work out some kind of ticketing thing, you could charge my American Express card."

"Good. I'll have our traffic department work something out."

"OK, Max, let's take a break. I'd like to go to the hotel and take a nap and a shower. We could convene again later this afternoon, if that's good for you."

"Good idea. That'll give me a chance to bounce this off Bob Briscoe and give him an early go at the EVP, president, and chairman."

"Good, Max, see you at about four. Bye."

"Kathy, get me Bob Briscoe."

"Bob, I've got to see you right away. Right, I can come there or . . . OK Bob, I'll be right over."

As Max drove over to the corporate office where Bob was located, he hurriedly organized his thoughts.

"Bob, I need to see you privately," Max said as he shut Bob's office door. Max reviewed the morning meeting between himself and Marvin. "Well, Bob, that's the gist of it. I see no problems at my end but suspect the situations will put us in some danger from time to time. However, that's the case with our KPPS operations now. Do you think we can sell this?"

"I don't know, Max, but I'll give it a try. Apparently, we are covered financially. Legal will bring up the liability issues."

"Yes, Bob, and it will increase our business, with our profit margin maintained. Additionally, we are sure to have a big upsurge in our capabilities and a substantial upsurge in equipment, team, etc., all at CIA expense. Certainly, we will have better intelligence and good support worldwide. However, the secrecy will be severe, and I'll likely be unable to brief anyone on our detailed operations. I'll get it fixed that you and I work as we do on our KPPS operations. You'll have to take care of our management."

"OK, Max, I'll check with the executives and get back to you."

"Good, I'll check back with any updates. Marvin's resting, but we'll reconvene at four this afternoon. I'm sure he'll still be here tomorrow morning. I'd sure like to send him home with a positive response then, if you can manage it."

"OK, Max, I'll do my best and get back to you with any questions from the principals. Good luck."

Max returned to his office and cleared away for the staff meeting. "OK, is everyone here? Kathy, I want you to stay for this briefing but need you to copy this nondisclosure agreement for everyone to sign. List them all down, and log this all in."

Max met with his KPPS staff and briefed them on Marvin's request and his discussion with Bob Briscoe. "Well, guys, that's the gist of it for now. Sign the nondisclosures. Kathy, you witness them all. I want each of you to give a short nondetailed briefing to your individual team members. Get them each to sign a nondisclosure, have Kathy witness, log, and file them.

"Vic, engineering, and Barry, manufacturing, I want you to be with me in the 4:00 p.m. meeting with Marvin. In the meantime, all of you, go think this through as best you can, and give me a list of your needs and to-do lists first thing in the morning. We'll have a general meeting at ten. At that time, I'd like your inputs on anything else you can think of that's pertinent. But I'd like those needs and equipment lists by 8:00 a.m.

"Kathy, call my wife, Gina, and tell her Marvin is in town and that I'd like her to fix a simple home-cooked dinner for us tonight. Marvin and I will retire to my study to talk business after dinner. We'll take a break and have a little dessert with Gina to break the evening. I'd like you to join us at dinner and for some of the conversation. If you can, tell Gina that. I'd like you to spend a little time with her and then take a few notes for me after we talk business."

"OK, boss. I can make it. I'll call Gina."

"Thanks, Kathy."

"Marvin, you are right on time. You look a little more composed. Got a little rest?"

"A little rest and a great shower were all I needed."

"Well, I met with Bob Briscoe, corporate security, just after you left, and he is meeting with top management about now. Too early to hear back anything, but I expect to hear either questions from them while you're here or possibly an OK by tomorrow morning."

"OK, Max, I've digested the info you gave me on KPPS earlier, and your current coverage assures us of a good expansion base. I'm surprised you guys are operating as widely as you are. I congratulate you. I know you've had excellent results in El Salvador and in Italy but had no idea of your spread elsewhere. This puts us in an excellent position to sell what we have in mind to any who might disapprove, although I expect little opposition at home since there will be little information released in-house about your operations. Can you pull together a presentation of the info you gave me with a little detail so that I can take it back with me tomorrow afternoon? I'll need to leave by lunch to get home tomorrow night."

"Sure, Marvin, I'll just clean up a recent presentation we made to the executive committee for you to take back with you. I'll give you a memory-stick copy for your computer. Here, let me pull this out now, and we'll go over it."

"Kathy, please transfer the presentation I gave to the executive committee last week on KPPS to my laptop."

"There, we've culled out the nonpertinent info, and I've stored it on this memory stick for you. We need some kind of code word for this whole operation. Any ideas?"

"Jennifer, Max. Call it Jennifer."

"OK, Jennifer it is."

Kathy stuck her head in. "Max, I talked to Gina, and she said OK. What time should she expect you, us?"

"Tell her 7:00 p.m. promptly. OK with you, Marvin?"

"Yes, yes."

"Thanks, Kathy. Warn us at six so we'll have time to pick up and get over to my house. I'll drive Marvin, and if you like, you can ride with us. I'll bring you back here and Marvin to his hotel when we're through."

The next morning, Max checked in with Kathy. "Good morning, I really enjoyed dinner with you guys last night and the visit with Gina. Your guys have their equipment and to-do lists on your desk. I've set up coffee and rolls for 10:00 a.m. That's when you wanted your morning meeting. Marvin said he'd be in at about eleven.

"Thanks, Kathy. Heard anything from Bob Briscoe?"

"No, nothing yet."

"Well, let me scan through these lists and see if anything makes sense."

Shortly thereafter …

"Max, Bob's on line 1."

"Thanks . . . hello, Bob. How'd it go?"

"Unusually well, Max. They had a few questions that I presumed to answer. We can go over them later. The short answer is they approved. You're to report to me or the EVP, my boss. He or I will report to either or both of them. A KPPS executive committee is to be formed. Members are to be you, me, the EVP, the president, the CEO, and Sid Wormler, a working board member. This will keep it all legal. You should brief them all at an appropriate time, whenever you're ready and they're available. They can sign nondisclosures at that time. Otherwise, unless you run into some difficulty, it's a go."

"Thanks, Bob, that's nothing short of a miracle. I worked out with Marvin last night a way to 'projectize' this whole thing with work orders by task. He will issue a general contract through our regular channels and fund it annually and with quarterly add-ons as needed. He'll then issue work orders by number, which we will document with one to two pages of general info for identification and funding purposes. We will write classified reports for the agency and make presentations as required. Our in-house projects will follow the same format with internal reports to the KPPS executive committee. A summary of all agency work will be done financially only to this committee. Finally, I am likely to need some exceptional capability to obtain in-house funds from time to time to keep things rolling. Our financial reports of all work done will show all activity and clearly state coverage of all costs and our respective profit margins. Also, I need the ability from time to time to commandeer our jet aircraft for special operations just as we do for in-house KPPS."

"OK, Max, I will arrange that."

"Bob, since the board is aware of KPPS and its merits, I think all our efforts either for ourselves or the agency should be handled under the guise of our KPPS operations."

"Agreed."

"We'll need to grow some to handle more extensive operations worldwide, need some additional equipment, all of which will be funded by the agency. Finally, some of our people, especially field people, will have to have some special training. The comptroller will need to be briefed so that funds will be available and the capital committees directed to respond appropriately."

"Max, I'll take care of that through the EVP."

"I'm sure Marvin will be willing to meet with the executive committee from time to time if absolutely necessary to answer their questions. But I'm sure he would rather stay in the background, if at all possible."

"OK, only if absolutely necessary."

"Of course, Bob, in every case, I'll keep you abreast of all our activities and needs. And thanks, Bob. I'll depend on you, and you can trust me."

Shortly thereafter, Vic and Barry arrived in Max's office. "Well, guys, I've reviewed your equipment and to-do lists, and I feel that they need much more thought, but we need to talk much more about the vision I have of our new operations so that you'll be able to do that. Otherwise, everything you've listed, I'm in agreement with. You need to prepare the appropriate capital requests and get them on the division agenda. Bob

Briscoe will take care of seeing that the capital committee responds to these requests. Thanks."

On the intercom, Max said, "Kathy, what about the Learjets, Russ, and Matt?"

"One Lear is in Europe and can divert to pick up Russ and Matt at Rome Fiumicino this afternoon. The other Lear is here in Dallas at Love Field and not scheduled."

"OK, Kathy, please contact Russ and Matt and tell them the details. Get the European jet to pick them up and bring them home. Schedule the Dallas jet to take Marvin to Washington National at noon. Have them phone Bob Briscoe for approval, if necessary. Bob is arranging for us to have this scheduling authority in the future."

Marvin appeared at 11:00 a.m. "Hi, Marvin. I've heard from Bob Briscoe, and everything is a go. They've formed an executive committee composed of myself, Bob, the EVP, the president, the chairman, and one working board member who is already read-in on our agency interaction. This keeps all our board actions legal.

"I've scheduled our Learjet to take you to Washington National at noon. I'll brief you on the details that we've set up at corporate while we drive to Love Field. This trip is on us. In the future, if available, we'll fly you either or both ways at commercial airline rates as agreed on your American Express card. This will only be available when it is convenient, that is, a Lear is available or happens to be in or going to a vicinity. This should lessen your visibility coming and going. OK?"

"OK, let's go."

2

THE PRESIDENTIAL DECLARATION

TOP SECRET (1/2)
PRESIDENT/CIA—EYES ONLY
(Exempt from automatic reclassification or downgrading)

THE WHITE HOUSE
WASHINGTON, DC
January 14, 20XX

NATIONAL SECURITY DIRECTIVE NUMBER 21

NATIONAL SECURITY DIRECTIVE ON PROTECTION OF KEY U.S. INTERESTS AND CITIZENS

The U.S. policy regarding the protection of our ambassadors and other government employees and representatives has been a mainstay in our fight against terrorist action against these persons and assets. The long-term policy has been that the USA has not, does not, and will not negotiate terms with anyone with regard to the safety of government personnel or assets. We will make every effort to protect these personnel, but in the event of hostile action against them, no ransom of any type will be negotiated. If necessary, we will take military action against anyone who would take hostile action against our people. (U)

Fortunately, this long-standing policy is known and understood by those who oppose us. And by and large, hostile parties do not take action against our people in an attempt to extort or negotiate a ransom of any sort. In those few cases where they have failed to note our policy through ignorance or otherwise and have kidnapped or otherwise attempted to subvert it, we have been firm in our resolve regarding this policy, and such action has been unsuccessful whenever any such attempt has been made. (U)

Unfortunately, hostile actors have been successful against our industrial and civilian population where kidnapping and extorting ransom, supplies, and other goods from our citizens and some of our large multinational companies have been accomplished. These monies, supplies, etc., have been of significant help to those who act against us. From this source, they have been able to fund and equip their forces to fight us and our interests around the world. (TS)

Accordingly, in the national interest and in accordance with the intent of the original Jeffersonian policy of "millions in defense, but not a cent in tribute," we do today extend and enact this policy of protection to counter any such hostile action against the peoples, holdings, and country of the USA. In further support of this policy, the following directions are given: (TS)

TOP SECRET (2/2)

1. Create a clandestine security system and emergency action team under the direction of the director of central intelligence to counter offensive moves anywhere in the world against U.S. citizens, corporations, and other holdings. (TS)
2. Provide equipment and training to these team personnel to enable prompt and effective action. (TS)
3. Provide such support to this team as might be necessary from time to time by the Department of Defense, Homeland Security, or other departments of the U.S. government. (TS)

4. Generate economic support from Congress to fund such efforts (estimated $200 million as a current FY supplemental). (TS)
5. Have an agreement to use $50 million of the president's emergency budget and $50 million of the Central Intelligence Agency emergency budget of this FY to fund immediately. Reprogram such additional funds as might be required to enforce this action effectively. (TS)
6. In time, generate an ongoing presidential executive order to authorize and fund ongoing efforts thereafter. (TS)

James A. Knapp
President, USA

**TOP SECRET
PRESIDENT/CIA—EYES ONLY
(Exempt from automatic reclassification or downgrading)**

3

CIA INVOLVEMENT

The DCI called Marvin in to tell him that his principal responsibility, as of now, was as team director of the CIA Emergency Response Team and that he would be a member of and report to the executive committee, that is, the DCI, DDCI, and Ops. "Marvin, this briefing on the capabilities of the KPPS Group in Dallas was just the good news we needed to hear. I can hardly believe the capabilities they've accumulated, and that story of a foiled extortion plot in El Salvador was nothing short of phenomenal. If it hadn't been for that simple boggle when all their support went to breakfast and then Max short-circuiting it and recovering in time to catch the culprits and roll the whole gang of bad guys up, I'd think you'd made the whole thing up. Please give Max my regards and tell him that I'm looking forward to meeting him sometime in the not-too-distant future."

"Thank you, Director. I'm sure that he will be thrilled to meet you and tell you some other stories of their exploits. And I'm gratified that we could get their corporate agreement to allow the KPPS group to expand their capabilities and goals to hopefully accomplish similar successes in our domain. I think their current coverage around the world will allow them to come up to speed to fill our needs quicker than anything we could accomplish otherwise."

"I agree. Get on with it. You need to get the contract, work authorizations, and tasking in place so that we and they can be ready to respond as our needs arise. Hopefully, we'll have a little time to grow this up some before something explodes on us. I'll brief the president that we have a plan and a small group already trained and ready to respond. He doesn't need to know the details yet.

"As you know I already have $100 million in authorization, but don't get carried away. Let's limit the expenditures severely to start with. Keep me informed, but get out there and get going. I'd like to meet with Max sometime, but that's not a necessity. Let's keep it at your level. And pray that nothing pops up too quickly. I'm concerned that we could get some really bad press if anything goes wrong. But again, this KPPS group gives us an arm's-length standoff from any finger-pointing if things do go wrong. God help us and be with these guys.

"Thanks again for the quick action and turnaround, Marvin. Leave these viewgraphs and a copy of the presentation they sent up, and I'll use them to brief the DDCI and Ops as soon as they are available. Keep to the chain of command, but don't hesitate to contact me if you need to. And congratulations, Mr. Deputy Director."

"Thank you, Mr. Director. I appreciate your confidence and will keep the committee in the loop and not bother you personally unless absolutely necessary."

"Good, Marvin. Good luck and Godspeed."

"Yes, sir."

Back in Dallas. "Russ and Matt, good to have you two back. How was Italy? Did my summons keep you from finishing your tasks there?"

"Things were going well, boss. We were surprised at the sudden summons and the unexpected airlift you provided, but our inspection and maintenance chores were finished there. We were just saying our goodbyes and buying a few dinners when the call came."

"Well, guys, I've good news and bad news. They're both the same. Our successes have been recognized, and now I need you to read in on a new security clearance."

Being "read in" is a security term for signing a statement of understanding that specific classified issues are being disclosed, of which only those others listed are aware. Typically, it includes the reading of the file on the specific matter disclosed.

"I need to quickly brief you both on the other side of our house, the non-Electronic Apprehension System (EAS)/Key Personnel Protection System (KPPS) security side. In short, we work as a concept, design, development, and production base for certain types of equipment for the CIA. That's the last time we'll openly use that name. Normally, we refer to the agency as Dad. Mom is, of course, our company. Our group is actually the product of them both. Dad funds us and keeps our technology going, but Mom feeds us and directs our day-to-day activities. That's been it until now. Now Dad has come and asked us to bring our KPPS capabilities to bear on his own KPPS-like activities worldwide.

"Accordingly, we'll need to grow and change but will continue our EAS and KPPS activities, only now for both Mom and Dad. The good news is that we will need a few more good people so we'll be better equipped and with the latest intelligence, not just our own homegrown variety. The bad news is that we will be called on by either or both Dad and Mom to fill their needs. We will be our own people, but they will control us, and we might have to work a little overtime in faraway places. Of course, that's nothing new to the three of us. I doubt the danger will increase materially. KPPS is already a dangerous sport, but now we will have a better legal base for what we do.

"It's time for our 10:00 a.m. meeting. Stay where you are, and I'll give you the new protocol in a few minutes when everyone else is here. Matt, will you ask Kathy to come and join us for this meeting?"

The whole group had gathered. "Good morning. Glad to see you all here. I know each of you has questions from the limited briefings you've had, but please hold them until I'm through. Each of you has now signed a more extensive nondisclosure agreement. Things are going to change, but our jobs are going to stay the same. Soon we'll have a few new people joining us to expand our capabilities. We'll be moving into more secure new quarters, and each of you will be expected to pitch in and help out no matter the occasion.

"In this regard, all our company rules will stay the same, but your compensations will be adjusted to match your job according to your specific assignments. Field team personnel will be paid on an increased fixed salary basis regardless of time spent or of venue. And typical overtime pay will not apply. I'll explain this in more detail in a moment. These new salary rates will be available to all field team personnel according to assignment.

"All home office personnel will continue to work a standard forty-hour workweek, but each will likely have required overtime assignments. Overtime will be paid to you on a +50 percent basis over your calculated base pay and +100 percent for Saturdays, Sundays, and holidays. Additionally, if you are called to be out of town, you will receive time off for the additional hours spent on travel. This time will not be counted as overtime. Whenever you are on assignment, you will receive time off when you return home equal to the nonwork (or travel) overtime spent. That means if you're out on assignment for twenty-four hours and have worked a ten-hour day, you'll receive straight time for eight hours, overtime at +50 percent for two hours, and additional time off when you return home for an additional six hours. Sleep time is sleep time regardless of where you are. There is no pay for the eight-hour night except and unless that time is required and then paid at 150 percent rate. All of you will be salaried. The pay factor is just a way of calculating your due.

"Finally, your base pay will be bumped by +15 percent if on nonlocal domestic assignment or +25 percent whenever you are on international assignment. And that means overtime is then +50 percent of base over that. In some unusual cases where I judge the risk as higher, the international base will be increased by an additional +25 percent. Additionally, there is some reason to believe that the occasion might arise that either Mom or Dad might wish to reward you or us further with a bonus should our efforts and results be outstanding. That bonus will be shared equally among all personnel involved on each one's salaried base proportionally.

"All this said, you need to understand that most of this time is honor based and that we will trust you to report your work hours honestly. It is a tenet of your employment, and I expect each of you to respect this. No BS. Any cheater will be promptly terminated and held legally liable."

"Above all, security is of utmost importance, and I expect each of you to report any breach immediately so that we can take proper precautions. No exceptions. I trust you. You trust me. Mom and Dad will be happy.

"I've asked each of your supervisors to brief you to the level of salary information you need to know and to answer any pertinent questions. Don't ask things you don't need to know. Don't speculate except as requested to do so. The organization chart will begin to expand and grow a little, and you'll each be kept informed and considered for promotion when and if. I've an open door if you need it. If not, don't abuse it. Take your questions to your supervisors. I'll deal with them as necessary.

"Last thing, if you've an idea of how we can do things better, put it on paper. And if not able, put it out there somehow. We need your help. I'll let you know about our move ASAP. That's all for now."

Shortly thereafter Bob Briscoe phoned. "Max, sorry to phone so late, but I wanted to tell you that I've briefed the brass on all we've spoken of, including hours, pay, etc. They said to tell you 'OK, but don't abuse it.' You've been given authority to spend the dollars you requested and to authorize Learjet travel and others. The comptroller has been briefed on your authority, and he will take the necessary steps with the capital committee. Finally, we've arranged a site for your occupancy. It's been recently vacated and renovated. Stop by my office, and we'll go see it together and arrange for the security you'll need. Oh, by the way, when do you expect to hear from Marvin and get the initial contract?"

"Don't know, Bob, but soon, I hope."

"Do you know an initial amount?"

"No, but I'll let you know when I hear anything."

"Max?"

"Yes, Kathy."

"Marvin's on the phone for you."

"OK, thanks. Kathy, tell Jimmy and Barry I'd like them to join me for lunch and a trip to Bob's office and a possible new facility . . . hello, Marvin."

"Yes, Max. I had a good meeting with the DCI, and he's approved everything at this end. He'd like to meet you but no hurry. I've got your initial contract here ready to go. It's funded at $10 million initially, and I've the ability to fund you additionally at that much a quarter if needed. If something hot pops, we'll get additional funding through work authorizations per task. Also, Max, I think it would be a good idea if you'd come up for a few days and let's talk over the ideas each of us has about how we proceed."

"OK, Marvin, but I'd like at least a week to get some plans together at this end, OK?"

"Sure, but don't take too long. I'd like you to meet my boss, Ops, at least on this trip, and then we can go up a level with each trip. You tell them some of the stories you've told me, and it'll keep this on the front burner. And my feeling is, in today's world, something is likely to pop anytime. Their support is essential in that case."

"OK, Marvin, I'll get back to you in about a week and arrange a visit a few days hence."

"Thanks, Max. Put on your thinking cap in the meantime."

"OK, bye."

And then …

"OK, guys, come with me in my van. We're going to Bob Briscoe's office and possibly a new site for us. I just talked to Marvin. The contract is ready. I'll go get it next week. We need to all be on the same page. Bob says he thinks he's got a place for us. I trust him. He's got our best interest at heart as you know. He's supported all our efforts in the past, and he is really behind this. He's our best friend and our key contact into top management."

They entered Bob Briscoe's office. "Hi, Max. Good you brought Barry and Jimmy with you. Boys, have I got a surprise for you. Let's go get in your van, Max, and I'll direct you to your new facility. Don't worry, it's perfect. You look it over and give me the go ahead, and I'll phone the comptroller to lock down the sale."

"The sale? The company is going to buy a new place?"

"Yep. Remember Barker College, that exclusive girl's college that moved out of the Highland Park area a couple of months ago?"

"Vaguely. Is that in Dallas?"

"Sure is, just on the border with Highland Park. Most people think it's in Highland Park. Just follow my directions, and we'll be there in a few minutes."

Then a few minutes later …

"Bob, is this it? My god, I thought this was some kind of walled-in Highland Park community."

"It is, just in Dallas, not Highland Park. Hold your breath. I've got the keys to the gate. On the way home, I'll brief you on the other changes the executives have in mind for you."

Upon returning to the lab, Max called another meeting. "OK, everyone, I've called you together to tell you about our new home. We'll move there in two weeks. So when we're through here, I need you all to go through everything and sort and discard the junk. Let's plan this move. Barry will be in charge of the move. All I've got at this time is a simple layout of the property. Tomorrow we'll have detailed layouts for everyone to see and to comment on. It will take us all to make this happen.

"Let me say that things are really going to change. We're to be dissociated from Exlite and become a wholly owned subsidiary known as the KPP Group. We'll report directly to the EVP, Raymond. Barry and I will meet with the company facilities manager to work on details tomorrow afternoon. But again, we're moving in two weeks.

"Our new facility was formerly known as Barker College. As some of you are aware, it actually moved to North Dallas a couple of months ago. It is conveniently located at the edge of Highland Park but is actually in Dallas. I had previously only known it as a walled community. It is that, but it was actually a walled girls' school for transforming young girls into young ladies. It was a finishing school of the old days. Anyway, it's now ours.

"As you can see from the general layout projected, the property is twenty acres. It is completely walled (fifteen-foot-high walls) with two front gates, one entrance and one exit. There is one back or service entry/exit. There is a main or administrative building. There is a dormitory and cafeteria intended to house and feed a hundred. There is a gymnasium and an Olympic-sized swimming pool with attached showers and changing room. There is a school or classroom building. There is a modern large, twenty-five-horse barn. And there are several other small support buildings. On the grounds are several interesting features, including a garden center complete with greenhouse, an archery range, and several scenic walkways. Notice that there is a two-story parking area across a dead-end street beside the rear of the facility.

"Well, as I said, it's all ours. There's a lot to figure out, but some things are clear. The admin building will be our office and engineering building. The school building will house our lab. They're both bigger than what we actually need now, but that gives us plenty of room to grow as needed.

"Again, I've asked Barry to work with me to handle the move. And I've asked Jimmy to help decide on our communications, transportation, and other needs. I've asked Russ and Matt to form three emergency response field teams and to come up with all their needs. Additionally, they will go through some additional training soon. Several more of you will be selected to take other jobs and some others to take some specialty training.

"Now to partially contradict myself, I've asked facilities if they can accelerate the move, if at all possible. With some luck, this could mean we might move before all the facilities work being done and just living with the construction problems in the interim. If they can do it, we'll get operational much faster. As you know, anything might pop up on us at any time. We need to get operational rapidly. Questions?"

"Max, what about our commercial EAS business?"

"Well, as you know, KPPS came from EAS, and the technology is entirely compatible. The company has agreed to let us keep and grow EAS from all Gross Product Margin (GPM) in excess of 25 percent. We currently operate EAS at about 60 percent margin. If we allow an error margin of 10 percent, this will allow us use of about half our margin for growth or whatever. Currently, with four cities operational in EAS, this means we can grow a new city operation every year. That means in about four years, we'll be able to grow two new city operations a year, but that's getting ahead of ourselves. Also, we have some new product ideas for EAS. Hopefully, these will enhance this growth. In short, we will continue to operate EAS as a commercial entity with only the natural new products that make sense added.

"Now on the other side, KPPS will be operated at 25 percent margin based on expenditures of Dad's money but at cost, 0 percent GPM, for Mom's operations. Dad will pay for all his needs, and Mom will pay for all of hers. Mom will front all expenditures, capital and otherwise. Dad will pay Mom back for his share of expenses at the 25 percent margin level continuously from funds distributed in advance quarterly. The first quarterly advance has been established at $10 million.

"All this is to say that we will operate EAS as a normal business, and growth will be self-funded from excess margin, and KPPS for the company will be operated at cost, and KPPS for Dad will be at a 25 percent margin. Dad has agreed to a 30 percent margin, which gives us an additional 5 percent benefit."

From the floor, Barry asked, "Max, does the new compensation package stand with both parties? And you need to comment on the new work month concept you and I discussed earlier."

"OK, thanks, Barry. The comp package is approved. Everyone will be salaried. But each of us will keep up with his overtime and out-on-assignment time on a time card basis for the purpose of our new compensation package.

"One new feature that I should explain is an idea I had. As a standard, we will all work a twenty-day work month based on five eight-hour days each week. There will be twelve such months each year. There will be thirteen paid holidays observed each year. These include New Year's Day, Good Friday, Memorial Day, Independence Day, Labor Day, a three-day Thanksgiving (Wednesday, Thursday, and Friday), a four-day Christmas (Eve, Christmas, and two others based on where the weekend falls), and each person's birthday (typically moved within the week to coincide with the weekend). Additionally, there will be two two-week mass vacation periods each year, one in the summer and one around Christmas. As soon as possible, I will publish an annual calendar that we will keep updated a year in advance so that everyone understands it. Additionally, everyone will have five sick days and five personal days each year. Vacation days and personal days do not carry over unless preempted by work. They are not cumulative from year to year except where they might be lost because of on-call or other business mandates. However, time off to compensate for out-on-assignment periods does roll over from year to year but do not accumulate.

"I know this sounds complicated and there will be a million questions, but let me say that it is a very good deal. In short, every month has from twenty-eight to thirty-one days. No day that is a twenty-ninth, thirtieth, or thirty-first will be worked except as designated as an overtime day. Please hold your questions for the schedule that I will put out. I'll attempt to explain it better after that time and after you have had time to digest it and discuss it among yourselves and with your direct supervisors. Again, in short, every third month, you'll have three days off—the twenty-ninth, thirtieth, and thirty-first. If any of these is a weekend, so be it. If they abut a weekend, then all the better, five days off. The best side of this is that most everyone will be at work five continuous workdays every workweek. The downside is that some of you who will have special wants and needs outside the above guidelines might be frustrated. We'll reevaluate this program in a quarter, again after six months, and again after a year. If the program survives over an extended period, it will be made permanent. Likely, there will be adjustments and some special circumstances, including customer special needs.

"That's it for now. I'm sure you've all lots to think about. Thanks for your attention."

Max returned to the office. "Max?"

"Yes, Kathy."

"Marvin on line 1."

"Thanks . . . hello, Marvin?"

"Hello, Max, I know you're not due here for a few more days, but something has come up. Can you get up here for an early meeting tomorrow morning with the director?"

"Sure, Marvin, how early?"

"Eight sharp."

"Hold on a moment, Marvin . . . Kathy?"

"Yes, Max."

"Can I get a Lear out of here late this afternoon or early in the morning to arrive at DC National by seven?"

"Don't know, but I'll check and get back to you in a couple of minutes."

"Thanks, I'm on the other line with Marvin. Just break in with an answer."

"OK, back soon."

"Marvin, I've just asked Kathy to check for a late flight today or early in the morning. I told her to break in on us when she knows the answer. So what's up?"

"Well, Max, the president asked the director earlier today how we can help make our people in the field feel safer when things get really hairy. When asked, I tried to explain what you guys did with the KPPS program originally to counter that very thing. I don't think I did a very good job, but at least I didn't bungle it completely because he asked me to get you up here right away, if at all possible, to explain it more fully to him and his executive staff. That includes the director, the deputy director, and Ops, my boss. Apparently, he wants me there as well. I seem to be the momentary technical guru, thank you very much. And I've been designated a deputy director."

"Marvin, you have apparently earned it. And hopefully, it's more than just momentary. Of course, I'll be glad to come and give it my best, if I can just get there in time. Fortunately, I've done this a number of times and have a pitch ready. I'll need a viewgraph or laptop computer projector. How much time will I have? And how much show-and-tell should I bring?"

"Max, I'd say you'll have a good thirty minutes and maybe as much as an hour. I think he has a meeting with the president at ten."

Kathy broke in. "Max?"

"Yes, Kathy, go ahead."

"There's nothing available this afternoon or tonight, but a Lear is coming in late and can get you to DC National by seven if you can be at Love Field at four thirty."

"OK, book it, and thanks, Kathy."

"Will do, signing off."

"Marvin, you heard that. Can you arrange a pickup at National at seven?"

"You bet. I'll be in the car, and we can talk a little on the way. We'll have no time to spare, but we can make it. I'll be sure there is a viewgraph projector and screen available for you. Thanks. I'll let you go and see you in the morning. Bye.

"OK, goodbye."

"Kathy, will you pull out the basic KPPS pitch for me? I'll need a copy on a plug-in memory and a set of viewgraphs. And tell Jimmy I'd like to see him in about ten minutes for a half hour. And ask Barry to come in for about thirty minutes when Jimmy leaves. Also, get me a travel authorization, Lear to DC, and an open commercial return. I'll need an overnight hotel in DC and a $500 travel advance. I need to leave here at about three o'clock today. Give me a warning, and thanks."

Max called home to Gina. "Hi, honey."

"Hi, what's up, Max?"

"I've got a four-thirty flight out of Love Field in the morning, so I'm coming home early. Be there about three thirty. Do you have any plans this evening?"

"No, I don't. I'm just going to the store to pick up something in a few minutes, but I'll be there when you get home."

"OK, good. I'd like to go out to the Sizzler for supper at about four thirty, if that's not too early for you. Then it's just home, pack, and to bed for me."

"OK, honey. Slow down. Don't go to fast. I'll pull out your bag and put out some clothes for you. It'll be easy for you to pack that way."

"Good, thanks, honey. See you in a bit."

"OK, bye."

Shortly thereafter, Max was on his way home and carelessly watching the traffic and lawns along the way. It was springtime, and Dallas was in bloom. He thought, *It's a great city, great life.* He thought of Gina, an early night, and smiles.

4

THE PRESIDENT

Washington, DC, National Airport, 7:05 a.m.

"Max, over here."

"Oh, Marvin, where'd you steal the golf cart?"

"Just borrowed one from airport security for a few minutes."

"Legally?"

"Yes, legally. Get in. We're just going around behind that hangar over there."

"OK."

"Wow! Whose helicopter?"

"Ours for now. The director just got in the office and let me use it to pick you up."

"Must be nice, Marvin. Why do you and I rate?"

"We don't, but the director likes to move fast whenever the president asks him to do something. Apparently, I told your story just right. He is impressed and appears to think your story could well be the answer to this particular question."

"Decisive, is he?"

"You bet, that's why he's the director."

After a quick ride ...

"We're here, Max. Jump out and follow me."

Director's entrance, CIA HQ, Langley, Virginia

"Max, we've got to stop at security for a minute. I've had a special badge made for you. The internal chip already contains your data and fingerprints from the files. They want to take new head pictures, front and profile, and do a retina map of each eye. It'll only take a couple of minutes. All this data is stored in your badge, and then our badge readers will compare your fingerprints and retina scans with that stored in the chip for a biometric ID confirmation. Oh, and they'll want to see your Texas driver's license in addition to my say-so to make this initial confirmation."

"Woof, that didn't take long. Now all this new data and the picture are digitally encoded in my new ID badge chip?"

"Yes, even if you lost it or someone stole your ID badge, your picture and all this data would be read from the chip and compared to the person using it to confirm or deny it is or isn't you."

"Wow! That's better than anything we have. Can we get this stuff?"

"Yes, and believe it or not, we can load an encrypted version into your laptop to allow you to use it on anyone's badge real time in the field. The only thing you'll need to add is one of those little electronic fingerprint sensors and a similarly small retina scanner. They're both very small and plug-in. But enough for now. Come on, hurry up. We're just on time.

"Damn, Marvin, that's quite a gantlet we've had to run to get to the director's seventh-floor office. I think I've already worn out this new badge we just made. I was really afraid it wouldn't work the first time I put it in the slot."

"Ha ha! I'll stick my head in first and see if he wants us here or in his adjacent conference room."

"He says come on in. I'll introduce you, and then we'll go on through into his conference room."

"OK."

"Mr. Director, let me present Max Curtis of the KPP Group of Dallas, Texas."

Max shook hands with the director. "A pleasure to meet you, Mr. Director."

"No, the pleasure is mine. Thank you for making yourself available to us on such short notice, Max. May I call you Max?"

"Yes, sir, please do. If you don't mind, I'll call you Mr. Director?"

"Ha ha! OK. I hope your short trip from the airport was OK."

"Unexpected and excellent. Also, the new ID badge is a surprise and the best I've seen."

"Thanks, Max. We worked on it awhile, and I think it is finally perfected. We are working on adding a DNA test to it, but no one likes the idea of sticking their finger each time they pass through a door.

We'd all be shredded in short order. Now I wouldn't mind spitting in a little dish. But then I guess we'd have to invent a new type of self-cleaning spittoon. Just kidding, but little jokes keep this place bearable at times."

"Mr. Director, we're going to get along fine. Anyone who can interject a little humor is my kind of guy. You must be from Texas."

"Ha ha! Thanks. No, I'm not from Texas. But yes, I think we'll get along just fine."

They walked across the office and into the conference room. "Max, let me introduce John M., my number one, the deputy director, and Joe F., Ops. Sorry, but we just use initials for our last names. That keeps our personal security better. I asked them to listen in because they're the chain down to Marvin, your COTR. Together, we're the CIA Executive Committee.

"Now let me say that Marvin thoroughly (*with humor*) screwed up his presentation of your ideas. Thankfully, we're a thoroughly screwed-up crowd and think we understood every bit of it. I'd like you to tell me all you can in a half hour about your KPPS concept and operation. So no more interruptions from us until you've told it all."

"Yes, sir. I think I understand what you want and have loaded my laptop with a memory stick of an outline of our operations. Additionally, I've got these viewgraph slides that I'll use.

"Our company has twenty-two major manufacturing operations spread around the globe, and the terrorist threat has been experienced at only two so far, in Italy and in El Salvador. But they were sufficient to alert us to the security need to both protect our key personnel and reassure them so that they can continue their functions. Let me interject. Because of the time constraint, I will not tell any war stories here and now, just the facts, what our philosophy is and how we implement it.

"We thought, through several scenarios, of how to classify the threat and discarded all but the simplest for a myriad of reasons. In essence, we classified all our sites into three easily understood and remembered categories." Max proceeded to discuss those three categories he mentioned previously to Marvin.

"The concept is that only very few sites would be Cat. I, a few more Cat. II, and the remainder Cat. III. And accordingly, as the threat at a site rises or falls, we would similarly recategorize and reequip that site appropriately. Then we decided to equip all sites in each category to assure their ability to counter or survive any action taken against our key personnel in the following manner.

"Cat. III sites—equip the site security manager with clandestine emergency location (rescue beacons) to protect key personnel assigned to that site. That includes spares, test equipment, etc. Train them in the use of said equipment. Help them define who the key personnel at the site are. Help them brief these key personnel, their wives, and their families (with appropriately fashioned briefing material for each). Perform a communications survey of the site/area for possible placement of an area-wide communications system, should it ever be required.

"Cat. II sites—equip the security manager with Electronic Location Beacons (ELBs), and train him and others as he might designate as in the Cat. III sites above. Additionally, equip the security manager with an electronic tracking system (ETS) adequate to enable him to track down any key person who might be taken or missing. Again, train him and his staff in the installation, operation, and use of this equipment. Help him brief key personnel and family members appropriately. Perform a communications survey of this site/area.

"Cat. I sites—equip and train all key personnel with individual ELBs, and train them in their use. Install the site with ETS equipment to enable tracking these. Train local site security team to operate this equipment. Help brief key personnel and family members appropriately.

Perform a site/area communications survey, and install an area-wide communications and beacon alert/tracking system, including area-wide communications for key personnel and their offices, vehicles, and homes and paging for family members. Equip each key person's home with a 'safe' room, an interactive security system, etc. Equip all their vehicles with communications and security/alarm systems. Evaluate the potential use of armored shuttle vehicles for transportation.

"We currently have twenty-three such sites categorized, equipped, and being maintained around the world. They are in the US, Canada, El Salvador, Brazil, Argentina, Britain, Holland, Germany, France, Portugal, Italy, Japan, and Singapore."

Max subsequently reviewed the following presentation for them ...

>Installation/maintenance team (I/MT)—equip and train a team of personnel capable of being deployed to any site to equip and train key personnel and family member, site security managers, and personnel in the operation and maintenance of all equipment. Additionally, schedule regular maintenance of all equipment and continued training of personnel.

>Emergency response team (ERT)—equip and train a team of personnel capable of being quickly deployed internationally to assure the location/rescue and safety of any key person who might be threatened, attacked, or taken. Additionally, this team is equipped with an area-wide communications system, general SIGINT equipment, and other items that might be expected of an action-oriented team of this nature.

>Emergency location/rescue beacons—an array of beacons clandestinely hosted by on-person devices that might normally be carried by a key person. This device

is a low-power (~100 mW) pulsed transmitter (100 ms at 30 sec. intervals) with an operating lifetime in excess of ten days. Other devices where size allows will also contain an individual ID code and a GPS location cell unit.

Emergency Location/Rescue Beacons

Pocket calculator*
Pocket picture holder/medicine holder/alarm watch
Pocket watch*
Wristwatch*
Vest pocket wallet and calculator*
Pocket ID/calculator case
Executive briefcase*
Commercial mint package*
Personal four-cigar holder

Depictions of all these devices --- Show key items (*) being worn by Max ...

Direction-Finding Location Equipment

Remote detectors—capable of being mounted throughout an area that allows immediate detection, remote alerting (to a central HQ site), and generally tracking the location of an ELB activated in the area and, when available, reporting the individual ID and GPS location of that beacon

Depiction of typical Remote Detector ...

Area-wide monitor—an HQ-located central alert monitoring computer/display

Depiction of typical monitor. ...

Vehicle trackers—capable of acting as single site location systems that can individually and precisely track down and home in on ELBs and as aircraft-mounting adapters to enable mounting these systems on light aircraft, jet aircraft, and helicopters

Depiction of typical Vehicle Tracker. ...

Handheld tracker—capable of medium- and short-range detection and tracking ELBs

Depiction of medium range Hand-held Tracker and of short range Hand-held Detector. ...

"We defined key personnel generally, that is, those officers, directors, site managers, or employees responsible for the conception and implementation of the company plan for that site and others who are put in a most visible position of authority, such as a comptroller who personally obtains or distributes cash payroll; human resources manager apparently responsible for hiring, firing, etc.; those who manufacture and test sufficient equipment spares and others to fulfill the current needs and to provide for natural growth; and those who manage the operation of the Key Personnel Protection System (KPPS).

"Mr. Director, that's the best I can do inside thirty minutes. Questions?"

"Yes, Max, but I want to delay them until later. I need to meet with my staff for a few minutes. Would you please wait in the outer office with my secretary?"

"Margo, will you come in, please? I'm going to leave Max with you for a few minutes while we chat, OK?"

"Certainly, Mr. Director. Max, if you'll come with me."

In the ensuing period, the staff conferred ...

"Well, Deputy Director, Ops, Marvin, what do you think? Marvin, we've talked while you and Max were in transit from the airport. I felt that if his presentation and equipment were as good as you depicted it earlier, we should immediately implement it appropriately but adjusted to our needs at all the embassies."

"Director, as your deputy, I feel that we should adopt that plan. Ops, how about you? Any reservations?"

"No, I agree. Of course, we need to study it a bit more and lay out our needs that are, of course, slightly different in nature than theirs. In fact, if El Salvador and Italy are Cat. I in their book, I suggest that we ask Max to cover our key people in those two areas immediately within his system. I think it unlikely that we could come up with as good a system in any reasonable time frame. And it appears that Max can cover them in quick order."

"Marvin?"

"God, it looks good to me. Ops, I think that is a terrific suggestion."

"Marvin, I told you before, when we're among friends, you can call me Director, not God. Ha ha! OK, I'm out of time. I'm going to take Max with me to and from the president's office and park him in the adjacent alcove until we're through. This will give me a little more time with him, and if the president is impressed ..."

"Marvin, you stand by in your office until we're back. See that Max has a place to stay overnight. He can stay in our guest quarters if you like. I know he's anxious to get back to Dallas, but tomorrow is soon enough. Ask him to not leave before midafternoon tomorrow. Have him into your office in the morning, and begin to work on his security and other needs."

"Yes, sir, Mr. Director."

"OK, Margo, I'm going to take Max with me. Call the pad, and tell them I'm on the way."

"Yes, sir."

"Max, come along."

Following along with the director, they moved quickly through the offices to the helicopter pad just outside. "I'm going to the White House for a quick meeting with the president. I'd like you to ride along with me so that we have some more personal time together. I never have much time, and I doubt that you do either when in your element. I'll park you in the president's anteroom for anywhere from fifteen to forty-five minutes, if you don't mind. Then you can accompany me back here, and I'll release you to Marvin. I'd like you to stay overnight. We have guest quarters. Marvin is seeing to that. I'd like you available until midafternoon tomorrow at Marvin's. Then you can go back to Dallas."

"Yes, sir, Mr. Director, that's entirely acceptable to me. I already have a hotel reservation, but I'm at your disposal."

"Max, cancel the hotel and stay with us, if you will."

"Yes, sir."

In the Oval Office anteroom, Max was introduced to the president's secretary. "Julie, I'll leave Max here for a few minutes, if you don't mind."

"Certainly, Mr. Director, he'll be just fine here."

"Max, can I get you something to drink or eat? People who get left here often haven't had sustenance for some time because they've been shuttled from pillar to post."

"Thanks, I really could use a sandwich and a Coke, if that's not too much trouble."

"No trouble for me." She summoned a girl from the next alcove. "Ruthie, could you come over and take Mr. Curtis to our chow hall? They've been starving him, and he desperately needs something to eat."

"Sure, I'll be right there."

"Oh, Julie, I didn't mean to be any trouble. Is it close so that I can get back quickly when the director is through? I don't want to inconvenience him."

"No trouble, it's close, and I'll be here to take you back on a moment's notice when he comes out."

"Thanks, Julie, you're a lifesaver. I haven't had a thing to eat since I left Dallas at four thirty this morning."

After only a short walk down hallowed halls, Max was ushered into a very nice eating area. And shortly thereafter, he enjoyed his favorite—a chicken salad sandwich, chips, and a Coke. "Ruthie, would you ask the chef back there if he could give me a moment?"

"Gladly."

The chef stepped out. "Hey, thanks for that sandwich you put together for me. It hit the spot. I really appreciate it."

"Thank you, sir, and you're welcome. Close to lunchtime, got to go."

"Max?"

"Yes, Ruthie?"

"The president."

Turning, Max saw the president and the director approaching and stood.

"Mr. President, I'd like to introduce Max Curtis, the KPP Group director out of Dallas, Texas."

The president extended his hand. "Glad to meet you, Max. Walk with us."

"Thank you, Mr. President. I'm certainly surprised and glad to meet you."

"Max, I've no time, but I want you to know that the director has briefed me to the best of his 'limited' ... *humorously* ... ability. And fortunately, that was all I was able to understand. But I wanted to thank you personally and ask that you extend your abilities and capabilities to include us. We'll certainly support you."

They approached the Oval Office. "Thank you, Mr. President. Of course, you'll have our support."

"Thank you, Max, and thank you, Mr. Director, for bringing Max along. Bye."

"Goodbye, Mr. President."

5

FIRST ASSIGNMENT—EL SALVADOR

"Good morning, Marvin."

"Hi, Max, had a good night?"

"Yes, the apartment was great as was the marvelous breakfast they brought in."

"Good, good. I met with the DCI, DDCI, and Ops earlier this morning. The director briefed us on his talk with the president and your meeting with him."

"It was hardly a meeting, just a walk down the hall. He was very gracious to see me. And I was truly pleased and excited to meet him. The director is just great."

"Good. He thinks the same about you. He asked me to give you his regards this morning. And a walk down the hall is all one gets with a busy president. You're lucky."

"Well, thank you, and give the director my best regards the next time you see him."

"OK, I will but now to business. The president has agreed with the director's suggestions that we style a program similar to your KPPS program. And the director asked me to get with you and develop an overview suggestion for the support of our embassies around the world."

"I'll be happy to. But how soon does this need to happen? I've got lots to do restructuring my offices into a new location in Dallas and building up the operation to support you."

"Well, you'll just have to learn how to delegate a lot of that. A question, what is the location and KPPS category of your El Salvador and Italian sites?"

"San Salvador is the El Salvador site, and it is Cat. I. There are two sites in Italy, Aversa and Rieti. They are Cat. II and Cat. I respectively."

"Well, Max, here's the deal. The director wants you to include the embassy key personnel into your San Salvador operation ASAP."

"You really mean ASAP?"

"Yes, and the sooner, the better."

"OK, I'll make a plan as soon as I get home and let you know when we can do it. You do understand that your key personnel must be identified, and they must be interviewed and briefed, including family members."

"Yes, and?"

"And then their dwellings and vehicles inspected, alarmed and communications assessed and made compatible."

"Yes, and?"

"And we'll have to figure out a protocol to interface between our company and the embassy."

"Right, how soon?"

"Let me get home. You get me the count and identity of key personnel, family members, dwellings, vehicles, etc., and I'll give you an answer. Marvin, I know you want this done quickly, but your embassy people are used to moving slowly. We don't. So we'll need their cooperation because when we get started, it will move very rapidly, no siestas."

"Yes, they'll cooperate. There's a presidential mandate, OK?"

"Marvin, next, I'd like to talk about some things we need that I hope you can supply."

"OK, get on with it."

"Number 1, we need the ID badge system you just introduced me to."

"OK, can do. I'll arrange for a disk or whatever for you to read into your computers wherever you need it. I'll see that you get a couple each of the fingerprint and retina sensors and the info and authority so that you can order more. I'll leave you for lunch with one of my people that you know and arrange this so that you can take it with you this afternoon."

"Number 2, we need a cell phone with an encryption system for communications between ourselves as well as between you and me. And get me a few satellite phones with encryption for out-of-range emergencies."

"OK, can do. I'll get you at least two of each to take with you and info and authority to order more."

"Number 3, I'd like to arrange whatever training you think our field people need. And I'd like that to include a bomb detection overview, self-defense, and a modicum of light-weapons training. By the way, I'd like to take the self-defense training myself. And I need for Russ and Matt to get training ASAP."

"OK, Max, I'll need to know how many people for each and their ID info from the badge system. I'll get back to you in Dallas and let you know what kind of schedule these might be on. Now let me get you lunch so that I can work on these. This afternoon, let's talk about reports, financial procedures, etc. You're scheduled to leave here at four for a plane to Dallas at six.

After lunch, they met again. "Marvin, I'd like to make a call before we get into the financials and others."

"OK, use line 1 on that desk over there. It's an outside line. You can call long distance direct."

"Thanks." Max called Dallas and arranged for pickup for himself and others when they arrived.

And then …

"OK, Marvin, I'm ready."

"Right, I've got a driver who'll take you to National in time for your flight. My secretary will give us the high sign when it's time to go."

Shortly thereafter, they got the high sign, and Max was chauffeured to National Airport by way of the Potomac River basin. Max had been to Washington and seen the cherry blossoms many times but none where they were in more beautiful display.

The next morning, in Dallas, Max announced over the intercom, "Kathy, let Barry know I'm in the office, and get Russ and Matt in here as soon as they're able."

"Will do, boss. Good trip?"

"The best. I met the president and saw the cherry blossoms. Get Bob for me."

"OK, wait one . . . Bob's on the line."

"Thanks . . . Bob?"

"Yes, Max. Good trip?"

"You bet. Let me fill you in quickly."

It only took Max a few minutes to fill Bob in.

Then . . . "Max?"

"Yes, Kathy."

"Barry's here for you."

"Thanks, tell him to come on in."

"OK, Barry?"

"Hi, Max, good trip?"

"The best. We're in like Flynn. I met with the director and his staff. And I met the president. He was very gracious, and we're on our way. Barry, how are things going on occupying the college? And how's our move planning progressing?"

"Good, Max, but slow. The deal's done. And all the power is on. We can occupy at any time. But getting facilities online and making the upgrades happen is a slow go. We need some priority."

"OK, hold on a minute . . . Kathy, get me Bob on the line again."

"OK, wait one . . . OK, line 1."

"Bob?"

"Yes, Max."

"I need your help. Barry says that the facilities group is dragging its feet. Can you get the EVP to get us a first-class priority? I need Barry to be able to get this set up and the move done without having to go through hell. Time is now a priority for us if we're to take on the tasks we're being assigned."

"OK, I understand. You don't have to sell me. Give me a few minutes. I'll get to Raymond as quickly as I can, and he'll get you the priority and have facilities phone Barry directly most probably within the hour. But first, I'll have to get Ray. Tell Barry to stand by. I'll get back to him directly if I'm delayed getting through. Otherwise, he'll be hearing directly from facilities very shortly."

"Thanks, Bob. I've got Barry here with me now, and he's overheard my end of the conversation. Thanks. Bye . . . OK, Barry, I think that should fix it. You'll hear directly from Bob if he has trouble getting to Raymond. Otherwise, you'll be hearing directly from facilities within the hour. Don't take any crap off them. But treat them nice if they respond well. I need you to push this ahead as fast as it can be pushed. Now if you've got some layouts there, I'd like you to go over them with me."

"OK, Max, thanks for the help. Here, let me lay these out on the conference room wall and tell you what the rest of the guys and I have in mind."

"Barry, I like everything you've planned so far, but I'd like you to add the following to your thinking:

1. Replace all our phone lines with fiber all the way outside the walls and to the nearest exchange, if possible.
2. Install a radio antenna on a building high point that's not offensive, that will reach all our people individually, and that will interface with corporate and security. Bob will arrange for their cooperation.
3. I want a secure operations center that includes communications and security control, most likely in the admin building. Does it have a basement?
4. The dormitory needs to be refurbished. Two apartments (with all amenities) should be configured to house married couples. Two or more rooms should be motel-like, with two king-size beds. The remainder of the rooms should be equipped as either single- or double-occupancy dormitory rooms with a bath for each two rooms. I'll leave the actual count of these rooms and others up to you according to the practical layout considerations. A washer-dryer set should be included on each floor, if possible. And if possible, it needs a gathering/TV room on dormitory floors. Include telephone and other things. It would be good to have an entry gallery.
5. If possible, I'd like you to set up an indoor small-arms gun range, nothing too big but something we can all train and practice on.
6. We need a serpentine jogging trail completely around the site and just inside the wall and if possible, along the way, fitness training stops.
7. Remove any and all trees outside the wall on our property that might overlook the interior of the site. We don't need any nosy onlookers.
8. Add large trees inside the walls where there are gaps in those now present that might allow onlookers.
9. Add and redo the gates to include double trap gates operated by the control center for both entry and exit and to disable tailgating. And the gates need to have metal added to disallow visual. And for exceptional circumstances, the internal ones

need to be able to be staked into reinforced ground sockets to disable ramming.
10. The wall needs to be topped with both external and internal razor wires.
11. We need a couple of golf carts for running around on the grounds.
12. The gym and pool need both male and female showers, changing rooms, lockers, etc.
13. We need an automatic emergency site power.
14. We need good AC and heating.
15. We need an outside patio and barbecue area.
16. We'll need a couple of vehicles—minivans, I think, and a small bus, about sixteen-passenger. We can get any large haul vehicle help from corporate.
17. Look at securing the next door parking site and possibly adding an overhead walkway to it.

"I know I'll have additional ideas, but that'll keep for our next meeting on this. You most probably have more and better ideas. Put them in to me for review. Let everyone that counts look at all this, and see what they can add that makes sense.

"Barry, this needs to be your baby. I'll be too busy. Run things past me, but don't let them hold things up. Keep Rick appraised of the cost estimates as you go. Let's move as soon as we can. We can just live with the construction mess as things finish up, OK?"

"You bet, boss. I'll get it done."

"Oh yes, Marvin has arranged for some special items for us. When you're ready to discuss security, see me. I've got some special software for you, and we'll have new ID badges, readers, etc. I'll try to get some of this moving without interfering with you. Thanks, Barry. I think Russ and Matt should be here by now. Tell Kathy to send them in."

"Hi, fellas, just a moment . . . Kathy, would you please get Cali from purchasing to come see me in about thirty minutes?"

"OK, will do."

When Russ and Matt entered, Max said "Well, here's the scoop. We are going to add the El Salvador Embassy key personnel to our system there. I don't know how many yet. Marvin will call with that data as soon as he has it. I need you to determine the status on the ground in San Salvador and prepare a list of all that we'll need to upgrade a typical family, including cost. Additionally, I'd like you to think through the problems of integrating these people into our system there. Put together a problems list so that I can get the issues dealt with chop-chop.

"I've given Barry the authority on the move and changes. Help him as you can, but basically, look over the layouts, ask questions, and make suggestions. He'll make the decisions. I still have a veto.

"Also, I'll need you two to go to DC for a week or so to take some training and to determine if they've any goodies that we need. We're getting personal cell phone and other communication devices with encryption so that we can converse anytime we need to. Also, we're getting special ID badges with biometrics.

"That's it for now. Tell me if you've any problems. Get back to me with what I've asked for ASAP. And thanks."

"OK, Max. Call if you need us. We'll get you updated on the status in El Salvador soon."

"Good. I'll call as soon as I get a key personnel count from Marvin."

"OK, bye."

Kathy, on the intercom, said, "Max, Marvin on 1."

"Thanks . . . hello, Marvin."

"Yes, I knew you'd want to hear about the key personnel count in El Salvador ASAP, so that's why I called."

"Good, go ahead."

"Well, initially, it'll only be two people, their ambassador and his military adviser."

"Families, Marvin?"

"Yes, both married with wives in San Salvador. They both have kids, but they are mostly all grown and married and one in college here in the States. The ambassador has one teenage daughter living with them in El Salvador. Both have leased homes in El Salvador."

"OK, Marvin, I'm a little worried about the interface details, but I'm sure we'll work it out.

"Oh yes, Max, I want you to know that we've attuned the ambassador to the priorities. And he's assured us that you'll have his and his staff's full cooperation."

"Thanks for that, Marvin."

"Anything else, Max?"

"Yes, what about that training?"

"I'm working on it. Get back to you soon. Anything else?"

"No, that's it for now. Bye."

In Dallas in Bob Briscoe's office, he asked his secretary, "Sherri, is Vic here?"

"Yes, Bob, he is."

"Get him to come into my office right away. Thanks."

After only a very short delay ...

"Hi, Bob, what's up?"

"Hi, Vic, sit down. We've got a problem in El Salvador."

"Yeah, what's that?"

"I just got a call from Chuck, the plant manager, and he says that there's some heing and sheing going on that he needs some help handling. I'd like you to go down and see about it. Can you?"

"Sure, Bob, right away."

"Good. Look, I'll get Sherri to work on a Lear for you for the first thing Monday morning. It's just a three-and-a-quarter-hour flight, but you better pack for a week or more. And I'll get a hold of Max, and he'll have someone equip you for a Cat. I site."

"Gee, do I need all that?"

"You bet. No telling what you're likely to run into."

"OK, boss, I'll get ready. Have Sherri let me know about the transport."

"Good luck, Vic. And be careful."

Bob addresses his secretary ...

"Sherri, get Vic a Lear to go to El Salvador Monday morning. Prep his travel papers and get him some cash too. And get Max on the phone for me."

"Max?"

"Yes, Bob."

"We've got a small problem in El Salvador. I'm sending Vic down Monday morning to fix a heing-and-sheing thing. I need you to send someone over here this afternoon to equip him to operate in a Cat. I site for as long as necessary."

"Sure, Bob, we'll equip him with an emergency location/rescue beacon at, say, level 2. And I'll give him a portable intrusion detector and remote alarm [PIDRA]. Just in case, I'll have him an earphone listening device and a small walkie-talkie on their frequencies. Anything else you can think of offhand?"

"Yes, one of those digital binocular cameras. What is the level 2 device for Cat. I?"

"Level 2 is a wristwatch with clandestine beacon. Tell him I'll get Matt out there with these things within the hour. And oh, I've just asked Russ to update me on the KPPS circumstances in El Salvador. Mind if he tags along with Vic?"

"No, that's a good idea. I'll tell Vic. And I'll add him to the jet manifest. I told Vic to pack for a week or more. Tell Russ. I'll have Sherri book them into the Camino Real in San Salvador. You take care of Russ' travel papers, dollars, etc.?"

"Right. Bye."

Then, turning to his secretary, Kathy, and changing the subject abruptly ...

"Kathy, see if you can find a source for immersion Spanish. Give Marvin a call and see if he can get us the State Department stuff on language learning. I'd like us all to start on Spanish."

"Us all?"

"Yes, us. I'd like us all to learn a couple of new languages. And I'd like to start with Spanish. We could get someone to come in once a week to help and use tapes or whatever the State Department suggests, and we could help one another. I know everyone won't want to, but everyone who goes into the field for us needs some language training. And you too."

"OK, it might be fun. We could use the tapes when we're coming and going to work."

"Good, that's the idea and on airplanes and others. Thanks. And get Matt and Russ in here for me right away."

Turning to Russ, Max adds the following …

"And, Russ, add an extra mini-stun-gun to your duffel for Vic. Take this new encrypted cell phone with you. Marvin gave me two, and I'm ordering more. You can use it to call me anytime. Also, take a couple of your field scrambler walkie-talkies with you for local communications between you and Vic in case he needs your help. No telling what you two might run into. Come home as soon as you're able. Put an open commercial return in your travel authorization with an adequate cash advance. Maybe you can hitch a ride home on the Lear when you're ready to come home."

"Max, Bob's on line 1."

"Hello, Bob . . . OK, he's here now. I'll tell him. Bye."

"The Lear for El Salvador will be ready to leave at eight Monday morning. Vic will meet you at Love Field. Before you go, I need you to put your right and then left index fingers in this electronic fingerprint device, then right and then left eyes to this retina scanner, and finally a full face and side view picture. Now off with you. Give my regards to your wife."

"OK, boss, see ya."

Then turning to Kathy ...

"Kathy, I need you to come in here and get this new ID stuff transferred to your computer and hook up these three items—the fingerprint scanner, the eye retina scanner, and the digital camera. This is our new ID device. Marvin's sending us the chips and ID card printer. We need to order at least three more of these for our new operations center. Thanks."

6

EN ROUTE TO EL SALVADOR

On Monday morning, on board the Lear en route to El Salvador, Vic and Russ were airborne about thirty minutes, and a phone rang. "Hey, Vic, that's my new phone ringing . . . hello? Yes, Max, I can hear you just fine . . . OK, you say this is encrypted? Yes, OK, Vic's here with me . . . yes, stand by a minute. I'll put this on speaker so that he can hear . . . OK, I've got my pencil and pad. Go ahead."

"Russ, I want you to meet with the ambassador and the military attaché, and they'll scan you and issue your new ID badge. Then you give each a KPPS briefing; survey their offices, their transportation, their homes; and interview and brief their wives and include the ambassador's daughter. Then will come the hard part. I want you to interface with their embassy security staff and determine their security protocol with respect to these men, their wives, and the girl. Then try your best to determine how we can best interface with their security and the protocol we'll have to use to include them in our system. Our mandate is to include these two and their wives into our KPPS coverage but not—I repeat, *not*—include us in theirs. Now that is likely to be a complex problem, but it's not for you to solve, just to evaluate and bring your best info home to us to solve. Savvy?"

"OK, boss, I understand."

"Vic, any comment?"

"Yes, where do I fit in?"

"Just observe and give Russ your best advice, and he'll do the same for you. Oh, yes, I've packed two X-ray-proof false-bottom film kits, one for each of you. The pilot has them and will give them to you when you're through customs in El Salvador. Use the contents judiciously. Good luck, and check in when you can. I'll try to get you some more stuff down there by Lear if there are more flights planned while you're there. Bye."

"Bye, boss."

"Russ, what does he mean about stuff in the film bags?"

"Well, my guess is guns and ammo."

"What?"

"Well, we don't advertise it, but sometimes we need more than just a stun gun to protect ourselves. We've obtained a special gun developed for the CIA and had special ammo developed for us. It's a mini-.380-semiautomatic, six-plus-one capacity. The slug is a hollow point that is shaved down a bit, filled with a bead of mercury, and sealed over and pointed up with a Teflon jacket. The shaving allows the addition of the Teflon. Together, the Teflon and the pointed tip assure penetration even through Kevlar vests. After initial penetration, the mercury in the slug explodes into the surrounding tissue, and the hollow point expands dramatically, assuring a large diameter exit, if any. It's small, lightweight, and easy to conceal. Needless to say, it is very powerful and accurate up to fifty feet. It's called the Mini-mite."

Then Vic says, "Russ, the colonel is meeting us at the airport and will take care of getting us and our gear through customs and others. He'll stay with us until we're in the Camino Real Hotel. I plan to tell him what I'm here for but don't know what you plan to tell him. You know the colonel is our outside man in security in El Salvador and is to be trusted. But I expect you know that from your past acquaintance with him."

"Yeah, let me think this through."

And in just a moment Russ replys, "I think I'll just tell him the truth. I'm here to see that we add the U.S. ambassador and the military attaché to our KPPS security as key personnel. Maybe he'll have some ideas of how to actually accomplish that."

"Russ, this is the pilot. You said to tell you when we approached El Salvador. Well, we're there."

"Thanks. Vic, I know this is your first trip to El Salvador and thought I'd show you the iconic view. Look out the window to your right. See that? A large squat, flat-topped mountain adjacent to a taller pointed top one. That's the view. The flat-topped one is El Boqueron and the pointed top one is El Picacho. They're both volcanoes. El Boqueron blew its top off thousands of years back. The flat-topped effect in profile is because it is an open-pit volcano. The opening is about two miles in diameter, and the hole is about a mile deep.

"Actually, the inside of the hole is almost completely wooded. There's a walking path down into the volcano that takes several hours to traverse, and there's a small farm down inside about halfway down where there is a shelf. In the center is the caldera with a small ash-walled minivolcano shape at the center. You can actually walk up and down this mini to the very center. The volcano is not active but is alive. There's no smoke or opening to the inside. Max and I have joked with the natives how pretty it must be in the winter with all the snow and all. Max suggested that they might line the inside and use it as a giant water source when the snow melts. Of course, it doesn't snow in El Salvador. This is the equatorial zone.

"The capital city, San Salvador, is at the foot of El Boqueron, but El Picacho is only a few miles down the road. El Salvador is roughly fifty miles wide and one hundred fifty miles long. They generate twice the power they need in the whole country in two projects. In the far north, there is a large dam that generates enough power for the whole country. They actually use only half that power and sell the other half to their northern neighbor, Guatemala. In the south, they have a geothermal operation and sell the other half of the power generated there to their southern neighbor, Nicaragua. In short, between the two, they keep half the power and sell the other half and get their own power for free. The half they sell pays for the projects that now generate the power and their maintenance. I suspect they make a fairly handsome profit as well."

7

SAN SALVADOR, EL SALVADOR

As Vic and Russ stepped off the plane, they were met by the colonel. Born and raised in El Salvador and the product of a military background, he rose in rank to colonel and then exited the military to become a security consultant about the time Exlite decided to put a plant in El Salvador. He became the principal security consultant to Exlite at that time.

"Hi, Colonel."

"Hi, Vic. Welcome to El Salvador."

"Hi, Colonel."

"Oh, Russ, welcome back. I didn't know you were coming. Bob briefed me on Vic's arrival and basically his mission. Are you helping him out?"

"No, Colonel, I'm here on a different mission. I'll brief you on that while en route to the hotel."

En route, Russ explained, "Colonel, I'm here to vet the U.S. ambassador and the military attaché and see how to add them to our KPPS key personnel list here. So I'll need your input because I suspect we'll have some trouble with their existing security. First, I will need your initial input with respect to that."

"OK, Russ, but I'll have to think about it. How about we meet first thing in the morning and discuss it over breakfast?"

"Good. Make it 8:00 a.m."

"OK."

En route, they passed the Flower Clock, a beautiful display in a traffic circle about thirty-five feet in diameter. In its center, a slanted clockface of live flowers displayed the time. Further on, they passed the straw market, and they all turned to view its wares. It was always the same and always different. The locals had a way of ferreting things from all over to the market. Once, a year earlier, Max and Russ had spotted boxes full of straw hats. The boxes had arrived with them full of equipment just two hours earlier.

"Here we are at the Camino Real Hotel. Russ, you remember Fernando? He's still the doorman here."

"Good old Fernando, he's been a friend of ours for a while."

"Colonel, will you arrange for a car for each of us?"

"Sure. Any preferences, Vic?"

"Anything with air-conditioning."

"And you, Russ?"

"Yes, I'd like a VW bug from the battery factory—you know, the one run by the judge. I like that old rhinoceros. Tell him it's for me, and he'll give you a good one.

"He'll be glad to hear you're in town and will want to know when he can see you."

"Tell him I'll be available for lunch Wednesday, if it pleases him. Just let me know, and I'll plan to meet him at the factory then."

"I'll do it. And if he asks me to join you?"

"Say yes. And please plan on it. If he's otherwise tied up then, set another time, and you and I and Vic will plan to do lunch instead, if that's OK."

"OK by me. You, Vic?"

"Sure."

"OK, guys, I'll drop you with Fernando. Call if you need me. That cell number that you just programmed into your phones is good 24/7."

Then, as they approach at the entry to the hotel, Fernando appears. "Hi, Fernando."

"Senor Russ, long time no see."

Russ and Fernando exchanged pleasantries while being ushered into the hotel. They checked in, and Fernando had them lodged in good rooms with a view. Then as they parted in the hallway, just doors apart, Fernando said, "Russ, I'm tired. I think I'll have a shower and a nap before dinner. See you then."

"Good. See you at about six for drinks in the bar, if you like. Otherwise, see you at about seven in the restaurant."

"OK, see you then."

At breakfast on Tuesday, Russ greeted, "Good morning, Colonel."

"Good morning to both of you. Russ, what's your schedule?"

"Well, I talked to Max last night after Vic and I had dinner. He said that you and I should be at the U.S. Embassy for a 10:00 a.m. appointment with the ambassador and the military attaché."

"OK, have you got a plan?"

"Yes, I think we will get the amenities out of the way and then tell them the details of our plan B operation here, including the response mechanism. We should brief them on the other key personnel. Now about whether we put them in our comm net is an open question that has to do with their present communications setup. And we'll just have to determine how we can fit a plan B response into their security setup. However, we will have to insist that we be allowed to inspect their current personal setup at home and in transit. We're likely to hit some opposition there from their current security people. Likely, their setup is adequate or superior to what we provide, but we'll just have to determine that. When all's said and done, we'll likely have to appeal direction of a plan B response. But in any case, we won't allow them to access or dominate our plan B security here."

"Sounds good to me. Is Vic going with us?"

"No, Vic needs to get on with his own task of separating the *hes* from the *shes* at the Colonia plant."

"Well, I've got you both cars out front. The judge says hi and that Wednesday for lunch is fine. He did ask me to come also."

"Good. You need to dial Vic in on that lunch too. Let's go ahead to the embassy now in your car."

"OK Vic, I'll check in with you whenever we are through or near so for the day, or you check in with me, whoever's through first."

"OK, I'll bill the meal to our rooms. You and the colonel go ahead."

U.S. Embassy, San Salvador, El Salvador

The drive to the U.S. Embassy was very nice. Russ enjoyed seeing the myriad of trumpetlike blooming flowers everywhere. Spring here was just like spring in Dallas, only more foliage. It was not hot yet, and that was good. When the heat would come, it would dry out, and the roads would become dirt and dust. Finally, the embassy. They were welcomed and issued into a security room.

"Good morning, gentlemen. The ambassador's expecting you. However, Russ, I'll have to ask you to come into security and be scanned for a new ID badge that's been sent down for you."

A few minutes later after these chores are accomplished ... "OK, that was painless. Both your fingerprint and retina prints have been confirmed, and your new badge will be ready in just a minute. We've checked your associate's ID, and he will be allowed as your visiting guest. He'll wear one of our visitor's badges and might be stopped from time to time as you proceed in this facility. So stay close. He's your responsibility."

"Fine, thanks. Does my new ID badge allow unlimited access?"

"Yes, sir."

"Thank you."

Inside the ambassador's office were the traditional portrait of the sitting president and a U.S. flag. "Mr. Ambassador, I'm Russ Talbot, and this is Colonel Marin, our outside security man here in El Salvador."

"Glad to meet you two, gentlemen. I've heard about you, Russ, from your boss, Max, in Dallas. We are generally familiar with the colonel and his activities here. This is Mr. John Jones, 'JJ,' our military attaché and the CIA station chief. You'll meet the head of security for the embassy a little later. Russ, I'd like us to get right down to business. I've another appointment in a half hour."

"OK, Mr. Ambassador, let me just jump in. I've been directed by my boss, Max, and he by your bosses in DC to add the two of you to our plan B security here in El Salvador. Is this your understanding as well?"

"Yes, it is. I've received those directions from the State Department, and JJ has received the same from his HQ."

"JJ, I've been instructed by Max that Marvin sends his regards."

"Thank you. I don't know Marvin well but have met him, and I hold him in great regard because of his reputation. Thank you warmly for his regards."

"First, I'd like to say that we categorize our international sites by risk factor as I, II, or III. Cat. I is the riskier. El Salvador is a Cat. I site. At such a site, we install and operate an area-wide communication system that is repeater based and equip our key personnel with home, vehicle, and office comm units. Additionally, we equip each of their homes, vehicles, and offices with a sophisticated intrusion detection and alerting system. I assume, at this point, that you do the same and would not need to be included in these features. However, for us to assure that your security in this regard is up to or exceeds our standard, we will need to inspect your offices, vehicles, and residences accordingly.

"Finally and more importantly, you will be fully briefed and included into our plan B system. Plan A is that nothing untoward ever happens to you or is covered by your own security. Plan B is our response to the fact that plan A might fail, and you or yours might be extorted, kidnapped, or taken as a hostage.

So inclusion in our plan B system means that you will be equipped with one or more of our clandestine electronic location/rescue beacons.

You will be thoroughly briefed on the units available to you, and your selection will be honored. Each beacon is a personal item that anyone would expect that you might carry on your person, for instance, a wristwatch. It will work normally as a wristwatch but also contain a microtransmitter that when triggered by a simple operation will transmit an ID and location signal that can be sensed and tracked to its location by aircraft at distances of 250 miles, by remote detectors located on buildings throughout the city/area at distances of 15 miles, and by ground-based tracking vehicles at ranges of 3 miles. This watch will transmit this very short, 0.1-second signal every 30 seconds for a continuous period of ten days. Of course, you will be able to simply activate or deactivate this signal. Its removal and fiddling with by another will activate it. But a more complex manipulation is required to deactivate it. Typically, there is a telltale sign to alert you if you have accidentally activated a unit.

"We have installed a countrywide detection, ID, and location system for these transmitters. Additionally, we have aircraft equipped to launch and home in on these. We have a small team locally who can operate and maintain all this. And finally, we have an emergency response/rescue team in Dallas that will immediately respond to such an emergency and are trained and equipped to locate and rescue anyone so held. I think we're out of time, but I'll be glad to continue to brief JJ since you have to go."

"Wow, Russ, I had no idea. I know that you're likely to run aground with embassy security while attempting to add us to your system. But let me say that we both appreciate your efforts, and I'll be glad to help however I can to grease your path with our security people. Thanks again. Yes, I must go but am anxious to get back with you as you progress and to see and select from those items you have intriguingly put before us. Bye. Stay and continue in my office as suits you, JJ."

"Mr. Ambassador, one more thing."

"Yes, Russ?"

"Please speak with your wife, and let her know we'll be coming by to see her and the residence."

"OK, fine. I'll brief her tonight."

"Thank you, sir."

Max asks, "JJ, is it OK to call you that?"

"Yes, Max, please do. Everyone does."

"Thanks. Now let me fill you in a little more completely, and then I'd like some lunch."

"OK, Russ, would you like me to get some sandwiches sent in?"

"Yes, thank you, and then I'd like to check out this office and yours and then visit with your security director. Then we'll leave the colonel and your security director to go over details while I look over both of your offices, OK?"

"Sure, my time is yours."

"Thanks."

8

THE COMPANY PROBLEM

Vic met with Chuck, the plant manager. "Hi, Vic, I'm sure glad to see you. I hate things like this, and I'll be glad to have you handle it for me."

"Thanks, Chuck. Bob sends his regards and asked that they be forwarded to your wife as well."

"Thanks. She'll be glad to hear from Bob Briscoe. He's a favorite of hers."

"Yep, Bob's a favorite with all the women. He's a real charmer. OK, Chuck, fill me in."

"Well, my personnel manager's secretary, Silvia, has come to me with an accusation that her boss, Eduardo, is having an affair with Maria, one of the workers in personnel. I've tentatively skirted around this issue with both, and they both say it is untrue. However, I feel that Silvia is telling the truth because she is very mad about it. She seems to be a woman scorned. She's not very attractive, and Maria, well . . . of course, to complicate things Eduardo is married and has a couple of kids. I think that his wife is unaware of the affair but not certain. I've taken no further action or conferred with no one about this except Bob and now you."

"Chuck, I have a set technique to handle this type of problem. However, I need you to confirm that your policies here are the same as our corporate policy, that is, no heing and sheing between a supervisor and one he or she supervises."

"Yes, Vic, that's our policy as well. It's clearly stated in our policy manual, and every manager has been specifically briefed on all the issues therein. In fact, I had each of them sign a statement specifying this briefing. I was present and made potions of the briefing myself, and one of the items I covered was this. Additionally, they each, in turn, were responsible for briefing all their staff and employees."

"Good. I'd like a copy of the sheet that Eduardo signed."

"OK, it'll be a little tricky, though, because those records are kept in personnel."

"OK, no hurry, but I'd like to put this copy in the investigation record."

"Fine. What's next?"

"Well, I'd like to talk with Carlos, your security man, and set up a polygraph. I brought one with me. I'd like you to be busy elsewhere. I don't want you involved so that, if anything goes wrong, you can just blame it on me and be clear of any backlash yourself. Bob developed this technique I'll be using, and it's almost foolproof. Also, I'll need a private office to conduct my interviews with a little bit of a vestibule. Then I'll schedule interviews with the two of them individually, him first and then her."

"OK, give me a few minutes, and I'll set you up in an office. With a secretary?"

"Yes, please. I forgot that."

"OK, just stand by here in my office a few minutes. Yolanda, my secretary will get you anything you need."

"Thanks. I'll be fine."

A few minutes later, a lovely young woman entered. "Vic, I'm Yolanda, Chuck's secretary. Can I get you anything?"

"Yes, can I have a cold drink with ice?"

"Sure, you want a cola?"

"No, frankly, I'd rather have water."

"OK, but I'll make it bottled. Our water here is good, but let's just make sure."

"Great. Then make it two. I'd like to take one with me."

"OK, I keep bottled water in a cooler in Chuck's anteroom. Any time you want one, just stop in and get it. Don't bother to ask. Just take what you need. I'd suggest that you always take an extra with you as well. You never know when you'll be able to get good water when you're out and about."

"Yolanda, if it's cooled, don't bother with the ice."

"You sure?"

"Yes, thanks. If it's OK, I'll just follow you to see where this magic cooler is."

"Fine, come along."

Just as Vic returned with his water and an extra, Chuck reentered. "Vic, I've got you a conference room, and this is Maya, your secretary. She's

Salvadoran and speaks English fluently. I guessed you were deficient in Spanish."

"Good guess, Chuck, I'm inept at languages, although I learned some Japanese while in a Japanese POW camp for a short time during WWII. Didn't enjoy it and don't like the language. Think that's what has kept me from attempting other languages as well."

"God, Vic, I had no idea. It must have been terrible."

"Sometime if you get me really drunk, I'll tell you about it. Yolanda is great. She gave me free rein of your personal anteroom water bottle stash."

"Good, feel free. Take all you like anytime. Just leave a note with her if it runs dry."

"Thanks again. This office will do fine. Will you please ask Carlos to come see me?"

"OK, call if you need me. Otherwise, I'll leave you be."

Addressing her, Vic asks, "Hi, Maya. I'm Vic Visos from Dallas security. Make yourself comfortable at the desk in the anteroom. I'll call when I need you."

"Si, senor, just buzz if you need me."

A large man in a security outfit entered Vic's new office. "Vic, I'm Carlos, plant security."

"Yes, I've heard lots of good things from Bob Briscoe about you. By the way, Bob sends his regards."

"Thanks. I like Bob. What's up?"

"Carlos, there's a reported heing and sheing between Eduardo, personnel, and one of his girls, Maria. I hear she's a looker."

"Yes, she is, and I've suspected a liaison there, but I'm not aware there's been a complaint."

"Well, there has been, and that's why I'm here to run an investigation with your help and as a training for you."

"OK, what can I do?"

"Let me get out this polygraph and show you how to operate it."

After unloading, setting up, and demonstrating the polygraph Carlos says, "OK, Vic, I understand. I'll take the polygraph down to my office and set it up. You'll send Eduardo down for me to hook up and ask the questions you've listed here and then bring him back up to sit immediately outside your office until you're ready for him. I'll give you the polygraph results then."

"No, just bring him back, and have him sit outside until I'm ready for him. I'll get the polygraph results from you later. Remember, don't discuss anything with him. Don't ask any questions other than those I've listed. Be very professional."

"Yes, sir."

"Good, thanks. And send Maya in as you leave."

"OK."

As she enters, "Maya, I need to discuss some things with you."

Then Vic asks, "Will you please send for Eduardo in personnel for me?"

"Yes, sir."

A few minutes later as he enters, "Eduardo, thank you for coming. I'm Vic from corporate security, Dallas. I've been sent down by Bob, who sends his regards."

"Thank you. I think Bob is very special. Do you work for him directly?"

"Yes, I'm his deputy."

"Oh, this must be important."

"Yes, it is. Frankly, there's been a complaint that you and one who reports to you, Maria, have been having an affair."

"No!"

"Wait, don't say anything yet. I want you to know that Bob, Chuck, Carlos, and I are currently the only ones who know of this accusation. Bob sent me to tell you that he doesn't believe it. Nevertheless, under company policy, it must be investigated. So I'm here to conduct that investigation. Once it is proven false"—he winked—"the person who entered the complaint will be promptly dismissed."

"Good. It's a lie, I swear it. Let's get on with it. Clear me and fire the bastard."

"Good, you understand. Now for the record"—Vic activated a small recorder—"this is Vic Visos, deputy director of security of Exlite Inc. of Dallas, Texas. I am here with Eduardo Maca, director of Exlite Inc., human relations, in El Salvador." Vic stated the date and time and had Eduardo proclaim that he had not been intimidated and was answering the following questions of his own free will and that all his answers were true.

"Eduardo, do you know a young lady by the name of Maria in the personnel department?"

"Yes, Vic, I know Maria. She's been a good employee, and she's worked for my department for the last two years."

"Eduardo, are you now having or have you ever had an affair with the young lady, Maria, while she has been an employee of the company and subordinate to you as personnel director?"

"No, Vic, absolutely not."

"Good, Eduardo. Now I must ask if you are willing to take a polygraph to substantiate these statements."

"Yes, just as soon as it can be arranged. Just let me know, and I'll make myself available."

"Well, thanks. I brought a polygraph down with me and have just finished training Carlos in its operation. You know, of course, that a polygraph cannot be used as evidence"—he winked—"in court because of its fallibility."

"Yes, I'm aware of that."

"Good. Eduardo, I'm going to ask Carlos to come and escort you to his office to administer the polygraph. He will ask you only a set of questions that Bob and I prepared in Dallas, none other. And I must ask that you speak to no one from the time you leave the office until after you return. At that time, I will interpret the polygraph results"—he winked—"in your presence against our prepared questions."

"Thank you, Vic."

Vic asked Maya to get Carlos. *Knock, knock.* "Yes, come in, Carlos."

"Vic, you called for me?"

"Yes, will you please escort Eduardo down to your office and administer the polygraph with the questions listed for you?"

"Yes, come with me, Eduardo."

"And, Carlos, Eduardo is to talk to no one until after he is returned to me, OK?"

A chair had been carefully arranged outside Vic's office door, and seated there was Maria. As Eduardo exited, he stared at her but can say nothing. Maria uttered his name and watched him as Eduardo was escorted down the hallway to Carlos's office.

"Come in, Maria. I am Vic from corporate security in Dallas. You are here as was Eduardo because you two have been accused of having an affair. I am here to conduct an investigation and discover the truth. Eduardo is now being subjected to a polygraph (lie detector) examination to determine this truth.

"I must ask you to be entirely truthful with me. I'm in your corner. It is not unusual for a man of Eduardo's position to use his position to seduce a young lady such as yourself and use her for his satisfaction and then later to discard and then dismiss her from employment to cover himself. I am fearful for you that you have become caught in just such a web. And it is my obligation to step in to protect you." Vic went on to brief Maria on the purpose of the recorder, and he entered her vitals, again asking the questions regarding coercion and others.

Afterward, Vic buzzed the intercom to Maya. *Knock, knock.* "Yes, come in."

"Vic, Carlos has given me this polygraph result for you."

"Thank you, Maya." Vic shuffled through a few pages of computer output and made marks on each page. "Well Maria, it's just as I suspected. The polygraph results from Eduardo confirm the accusations that you two have been having an affair, and knowing he has failed the polygraph, he has confessed the affair to Carlos. He has indeed taken advantage of you, and I've arrived just in time."

Maria, who had been sitting dumbfounded and much shaken, suddenly broke into tears. "Now, now, Maria, I understand. You take a moment to calm yourself. All I'll need is a simple statement from you. I don't want any details. I know this is an embarrassing moment, and I don't want to make it any worse for you. I just need you to confirm the affair and sign a simple statement, and I'll have Maya take you back to your desk. Then we can talk again later after Eduardo is appropriately disciplined. OK, dear?"

Maria, sniffling, nodded in *agreement*.

"OK, I'll need you to clearly state that you are and have been having an affair with Eduardo, who is a supervisor above you in the chain of command here. OK?"

Maria sniffled and wiped her eyes with a tissue Vic had supplied. "OK, Eduardo and I have been having an affair."

"Good, now sign this, dear." Vic produced a single sheet of paper that stated, "Eduardo, my boss's boss, and I, Maria, have been having an affair." Maria signed it and wept into another tissue. "Thank you, dear."

Vic buzzed Maya and had her escort Maria out of the office and back to personnel. This time, it was Eduardo who occupied the facing chair as she exited. Seeing him, she began weeping wildly again and hurried away. "Come in, Eduardo." Eduardo, taken aback and visibly shaken, entered the office.

"Eduardo, I'm sorry. It seems we were all wrong. Maria has confessed the affair and stands ready to offer up all the details should you not admit to it. In fact, should you not readily admit it, she plans to go to your wife and tell her. I think we can calm her and prevent this, but you must now admit to the affair."

"Oh shit, Vic, I admit it. I was weak. You saw how pretty she is. I just couldn't help myself. I'll do anything to make this up. You've got to give me an out."

"First, Eduardo, you must sign a simple statement admitting to the affair. Then we'll see what we can do to help." Vic slipped over a single sheet of paper that said, "I, Eduardo, admit to having an affair with an employee in my office, Maria, who is subordinate to me."

"OK, Vic, I'll sign. What can you do for me?" Eduardo signed the paper.

"First, I must tell you that you will be immediately discharged from the company with no benefits—no profit sharing, no insurance, nothing. You and your family will be discharged here in El Salvador."

"But, Vic, I was hired in Dallas and transferred here with a package guaranteeing my rights and return."

"That's dead now."

"No, Vic. Please what can you do for me?"

"No nothing, Eduardo. You, of all people, personnel manager, know that penalty."

"Wait, Vic, give me a minute."

"OK, one minute and counting." One minute had passed. "Done, Eduardo."

"No, Vic, I can give you something."

"What do you mean?"

"I know of something serious going on here that is worth a lot."

"What?"

"No, I need a deal."

"OK, you give me something, and I'll make a deal."

"How do I know you'll take care of me?"

"If what you have is big enough, I'll convince Maria not to go to your wife."

"Vic, it's much bigger than that."

"Eduardo, you need to give me an idea of what this is about."

"Vic, I know of a couple of inside guys who are running a scam that has cost the company big bucks and will cost even more in the future."

"Theft?"

"More."

"If so, it'll have to pay for itself many times over or no deal."

"Vic, I promise you this'll pay for itself many times over if you'll let me retain my rights."

"No deal. You've got to give me something more."

"OK, Vic, a big kickback/extortion that's been running for at least two years."

"Is Chuck aware or involved?"

"No, it's completely hidden."

"Eduardo, I'm going to go out on a limb and say I can negotiate a deal for you, if what you say is true and provable. If the scam is as big as you say, I'll get you and your family home and let you quit there. I'll even try to get you your profit sharing up until the start of your affair with Maria. And I'll try to talk Maria out of going to your wife. But, Eduardo, if this isn't all you make of it, I'll nail your hide to the door. In any case, you'll have to sign a full disclosure of your affair and your agreement to quit with only those rights I can negotiate for you."

"Oh god, Vic, that would be wonderful. I know I made a big mistake with Maria, but I'd be forever grateful if you can get me this deal."

"You've got my word. I'll try to get the whole deal on the condition your info works out. Deal?"

"Deal. Vic, give me another few minutes to collect my thoughts, and I'll lay it out."

Having finished thinking Eduardo begins explaining.

"Vic, the two inside people involved are Michael, production manager, and Torros, purchasing manager. They, at first, solicited kickbacks from two major vendors of ours, and that evolved into the formation of a company, unlisted, including the four of them that share equally in the scheme. That's really all I know. But I'm sure that they must have involved more vendors in the kickback scheme over time. Oh, yes, and recently, it appears that Carlos, plant security, has somehow become involved. I don't know how. They are more and more secretive and are unaware that I know as much as I've told you. I just happened to overhear a few conversations between Michael and Torros over a wide expanse of time."

"Eduardo, are you involved at all?"

"No, no, I swear."

"Then why didn't you report your suspicions earlier?"

"Well, I was going to tell Chuck what I suspected but then got the hint that Carlos was somehow involved, and that scared me off."

"Are you sure you weren't trying to deal yourself in?"

"Absolutely not. I've always been loyal, and my indiscretions with Maria were personal, not business related. I'm sorry."

"OK, Eduardo, I want you to write out a confession in long hand of your affair with Maria, no details, and sign it. Then I want you to separately type out your suspicions involving Michael and Torros. Be sure to include the suspicion that Carlos is involved. Be as detailed in this as you can. Do not sign this one. I'll leave you to this here in this office. Maya will supply you with whatever you need. But do not leave this office or talk to anyone other than Maya until you have turned these papers over to me. Then I'll direct you what to do next. You may go to the restroom, but do not talk to anyone in the meantime other than your wife. Explain to her that you have to stay late if it takes you overtime."

Vic buzzed Maya. "Yes, Vic?"

"Maya, I want you to tend to Eduardo, who is to stay in this room doing the write-ups I've required of him. He is to talk to no one other than his wife on the phone. If and when he does make any call, I want you to listen in and record the conversation on the recorder I hooked up for you earlier."

"Yes, Vic, anything else?"

"Yes, he is only allowed to go to the restroom. Have some food and drink sent in for him at mealtime. He is not to leave until I have received the documents from him personally. I'll approve your overtime and meals, if required."

"I'll see to it."

"Thanks, Maya. And call the number I gave you for me if anything comes up."

Then, "OK, Eduardo, you heard. See you later. Maya will call when you're through."

Vic left the office and talked with Maya. Afterward, he stuck his head into Chuck's office. "Come on in, Vic. I've just finished this up. Would you like something to drink?" Chuck called his secretary, Yolanda. "Get Vic and I a couple of colas with ice, will you?"

"OK, boss."

"How's it going, Vic?"

"Good. I've gotten written confessions out of Eduardo and Maria."

"You're kidding. That fast?"

"Yep. And I'll talk to Maria again later this afternoon. I'd like you to have the assistant manager of personnel stand by to dismiss her at that time. She should be relieved of all her company possessions and escorted out before quitting time today."

"OK, will do. And Eduardo?"

"Something else has come up, Chuck. Eduardo has told me a story about Michael and Torros being involved in a kickback scheme for over two years."

"What?"

"I know it seems incredible, but also, somehow Carlos is involved."

"No."

"Yes, we'll have to step lightly. For now, I want you to sit back totally uninformed. I'll start an investigation tomorrow morning and see where it goes. I've sequestered Eduardo to write up all he knows about it. I'd like you to arrange for Eduardo and his family to fly back to the States late tomorrow. Just say they have a family emergency. I'll send him home tonight to tell his wife.

"He'll be dismissed in Dallas, and he'll get his benefits up to the time of the beginning of his affair with Maria, if this proves up. Also, I promised to talk Maria against going to his wife. He will sign a disclosure that agrees to all this, contingent on his information proving up.

"Again, if this all proves up, you'll need to see that all their things are packed up and returned to them in the States but only when the investigation is complete. He is not to be involved or identified as the tipster."

"My god, Vic, I can't believe it. I'll do as you ask. Please keep me informed."

"I will, Chuck, but you must be outwardly uninformed and uninvolved. This might be quite sticky and could even be dangerous. I'll brief the colonel this evening."

"Are you sure the colonel's not involved?"

"Yes, trust me."

"Do you need anything else from me?"

"Yes, I'd like a list of the top ten vendors and the contacts you deal with locally. But be careful, and don't alert purchasing or manufacturing.

Make up an excuse, like you need the info for a presentation you need to make to Dallas."

"No problem, I already have that data in a presentation I made recently. I can give you the amounts we spend with them quarterly and annually over the past couple of years."

"Good, I need that. How soon can I have it?"

"Just a few minutes." Chuck called out to Yolanda. "Will you get Vic a copy of my last annual and quarterly reviews as regards our vendors?"

"Sure, Chuck. I'll have it for him in a couple of minutes. Want it as hard copy?"

"Yes."

Chuck turned to Vic, "OK, Vic, where are you off to from here?"

"I'll ask Yolanda to make some inquiries for me as I've got Maya tied up watching over Eduardo. She's likely to require some overtime and meals for them both."

"OK, I'll take care of anything she needs, Vic."

"OK then, I'm off after checking with Yolanda."

Exiting Chuck's office, Vic approached Yolanda. "Yolanda, I need to contact Dallas privately. Is there another office I can use?"

"Sure, use one of the small anteroom offices outside the personnel area. They're usually used by vendors. But they are private."

"No phone extensions for someone to listen in on?"

"Yes, but if you press star-star-1 after you reach your party, all extensions are locked out."

"Nice feature. Thanks."

"Here, let me take you and get you set up in one."

They walked down the hall and got Vic settled in one of the compartments.

"OK, Vic. Need anything else, just buzz me on no. 10."

"OK, thanks a lot."

Vic hooked a small box to the phone through the handset line and switched it off. He then accessed the long-distance line and, when hooked up, dialed through to Dallas and Bob Briscoe's office. Then he dialed star-star-1 to cut off any extensions.

"Hello, Bob Briscoe's office."

"Sherri, this is Vic calling for Bob from El Salvador."

"OK, hi, Vic, one moment. Bob has a visitor who is just now leaving ... OK, I'll put you through now."

"Hello, Bob?"

"Yes, Vic. How's it going?"

"OK, please turn on your encryption to key J."

"OK, key J ... done. You?"

"Yep, I turned mine on too."

"Good reception?"

"Yes, a little digital noise, but that means it's working. OK, Bob, good news and bad news. First, the good—I've gotten Eduardo and Maria to sign confessions. I'll dismiss Maria later today. I used your standard polygraph procedure. I used Carlos as the examiner. He was really surprised when I told him to discard the polygraph results. He didn't understand what had happened. I didn't inform him despite our plan to use it for training him because something else has come up that I think he is involved in. That's the bad news.

"Eduardo wanted to make a deal to save his past benefits and get his family home. He confessed to being aware of a large-scale kickback scheme among the manufacturing manager, the purchasing manager, and two or more vendors. According to him, it has been operating some two years and now has become a partnership between these four and maybe involves other vendors as well. Not clear yet but apparently, Carlos has become involved recently. I'll be ticklish, but Carlos might claim to not be involved but merely investigating. It's likely to take a few days, but I'd like to get into this and clear it up. It's very important to determine Carlos's involvement."

"You're right, Vic. Do you need anything? You need to do this personally, and I'll try to keep Chuck clear. He's not involved, is he?"

"No, apparently not. I plan to brief the colonel and Russ this evening when we meet. They've been over at the embassy all day today. Haven't talked to them yet."

"OK, Vic, good job. Don't' cut it short. Everything here is fine. Max and his crew are busy moving to their new premises and fixing them up. It looks like they'll have a regular country club over there. Ha ha! Anything you need from Dallas?"

"Yes, Bob. I'm having Eduardo and family shipped out tomorrow evening on a family emergency pretext. Will you handle him at that end? I promised him dismissal at that end with full benefits until the start of his affair with Maria here. I'll have him bring a copy of our agreement to be approved by you, if you approve. I think it's the right deal but contingent on how it works out here. His benefits should be held up until it's over here, and we'll arrange to collect and ship his household stuff then as well. That keeps him out of the informant spot and keeps him in check until after it wraps up here. OK?"

"OK, sounds like you thought of everything. Are you sure it's worth the information he's provided?"

"Yes, contingent."

"OK, I'll look it over and let you know if I see any shortfalls. Anything else?"

"No, lots to do. Oh, this encryption stuff Max's KPP Group worked out for us works well."

"Yes, it does. Goodbye."

"Goodbye and good luck."

Vic phoned Russ. "Hello, Vic?"

"Yes, Russ, it's me. I've made good progress but have turned up another more serious problem here. I just phoned to see if you and the colonel can meet me for an early dinner."

"Sure, Vic, but I'll have to check with the colonel. He's with the Embassy security man just now."

"OK, but convince him to come. It's important."

"Fine, Vic, I will. Let's not eat at the Camino. I'll break away as soon as possible and catch a shower and a quick rest. Let's meet at six at Senor Pico's. It's an open-air place up on Escalon just below the turnaround.

Escalon is that expensive area rising beside El Boqueron. Ask Fernando, the doorman. He'll direct you if you need it."

"OK. It's a plan. See you at around six."

"See you, bye."

9

SENOR PICO'S

At six, Vic parked beside Senor Pico's van and walked to the eating area.

"Senor?"

"I'll be joined by two others in a few minutes. In the meantime, *una cerveza, por favor (one beer, please)*."

"Si, senor."

Five minutes and one beer later, Russ and the colonel arrived. "Russ, thanks for suggesting this place. It's great. Colonel, I'm glad you could come too. The view from up here on the side of Escalon is beautiful. The whole city just opens up to you from up here. Also, I've been admiring the flowers everywhere. I never knew there were so many varieties of trumpet flower or so many colors. And just after I got here, there was a migration of small parrots that flew through. They were beautifully colored but awfully noisy."

"Vic, Russ thought you would like this location because of the view. And you know I'm always available for company business. Russ said it was important. Did you have trouble with Eduardo?"

"No Colonel, that went like clockwork. They both confessed readily. Eduardo wanted to make a deal. But first, I just ordered a second beer for myself. You two need to catch up."

"Waiter, *dos mas*. Gracias."

"Well, let me catch you up on Eduardo's revelation."

As they were waited on and then consumed a couple of beers apiece, Vic briefed them on his day's happenings. "Vic, do you think Carlos is really involved?"

"I don't know, Colonel. I'll have to proceed as though he is, but I'll have to tread lightly because he can scoot right out of it if I'm not careful."

"Damn, I was responsible for getting him that job."

"Don't worry, Colonel, maybe he isn't involved. It'll all come out soon enough."

"Well, just let me know so I can kill him if he is."

"Please, Colonel, no killing."

"I know, but I will certainly feel like it if he's involved."

"Vic, what's your plan?"

"Well, Russ, this evening, I'm going to go over the vendors list and amounts that Chuck got for me. Then I plan to approach the most likely vendor tomorrow and see if I can break him down. If so, I'll pressure him until he gives up the rest."

"OK, Vic, but is there anything we can do?"

"Yes, just be available on my call, in case I get my butt in too deep."

"You bet. The colonel and I will jump if you call and give you any backup you might need. Good luck."

"Thanks. What are you guys up to?"

"Well, we briefed the ambassador and the attaché, and the colonel has been working with their security man. Tomorrow we plan to visit the attaché's house and the ambassador's residence and brief their wives. If we can, we'll do a complete security analysis of their lifestyles. But who can tell how much they'll let us in? At the least, we'll give each of them KPPS devices and get them involved with the colonel. He'll have to figure out how to respond to any emergency and not step on or get stepped on by their security. It's a conundrum."

"Hey, I'm hungry. Are we going to order?"

10

THE EMBASSY

Next morning, Russ, the colonel, the ambassador, the attaché, and the security director met. "Good morning, all. I hope yesterday was productive?"

"Yes, Mr. Ambassador, we all got acquainted, and everyone understands the ground rules. Additionally, I inspected your office, anteroom, and conference room and found nothing untoward."

"Well, Russ, what do you plan next?"

"Mr. Ambassador, I understand that the colonel and your security director have more ground to cover. And I'd like to interview your wife and daughter and inspect your residence and personal vehicles with JJ, if you can arrange for that."

"Certainly, Russ. I briefed my wife and daughter last evening while we were in transit to a local party, and they both are available to you anytime today. I'll just phone ahead now and confirm an arrival time with them. When?"

"Well, Mr. Ambassador, I'd like to look over JJ's place first, but that should not take long. We should be able to be at your residence by about eleven. Would that be convenient?"

"I'm sure it will be. How long do you expect to take?"

"Don't know, sir. But the interview should take about an hour and a half for the two of them and the inspection of residence and cars about another two hours, I expect."

"OK, Russ, just give me a minute." The ambassador phoned his residence. "Julie, Russ and JJ will be there at about eleven. He thinks the interview of you and Sally will take about an hour and a half and the inspection of house and cars another two hours . . . what? . . . Oh, yes, that's a good idea. I'll let them know. Thanks, dear. Bye."

"Russ, Julie says she'll have lunch prepared and ready for you shortly after noon. That way, you can eat just as you finish the interviews. And then you can get on with the inspections without delay."

"Well, thanks, sir, that's very gracious of her."

"I think you'll find her a very smart, gracious, and cooperative lady. My Sally, who's fifteen, is anxious to meet you. She's sure you're a first-class-spy type."

"Hardly, but I'll try not to disappoint either of them."

"Anything else?"

"No, we'll take our leave and let you know any results as we get done."

They departed the ambassador's office and continued in conversation among themselves. "Well, Colonel, JJ and I will excuse ourselves to our task and you two to yours. Let me know when you're done, and I'll do the same for you, OK?"

"Si, Russ. We'll see you later. Bye." They departed two by two in opposite directions.

At the ambassador's residence, Russ and JJ met the ambassador's family. "Hi, JJ."

"Hi, girls. Let me introduce Mrs. Julie Wilkins and her daughter, Sally, all of Ambassador Wilkins's family here. This is Mr. Russ Talbot of KPP Group out of Dallas, a wholly owned subsidiary of Exlite Inc. here in El Salvador but based in Dallas."

"Good afternoon, Mr. Talbot. Please call me Julie. All those other forms of formal address leave me cold."

"Thank you, Julie, it's a pleasure to meet you. And please call me Russ. Mr. Talbot is my father. Ha ha!"

"Thank you, sir. I understand that you are here to help the family, and that's my chief concern, not the embassy and all that stuff."

"Yes, ma'am, that's our chief concern, your family's safety and security."

"Thank you, sir. This is my daughter, Sally. She's a bit precocious but our pride and joy nonetheless."

"Hi, Russ. I've been anxious to meet you ever since my dad told us about your mission last night."

"Hi, Sally. And, Julie, it's good to know I'm expected, and I'm delighted that we have common interests."

"I hope James told you about luncheon plans."

"Yes, he did. And it is most gracious of you to make yourself available to us on such short notice. The lunch is an unexpected bonus."

"Follow me. We'll meet for your interviews in James's conference room."

"No, if you don't mind, I'd rather we conduct the interviews outside in that lovely garden I saw off to the side as I entered. I hope there is somewhere we can sit comfortably there."

"Yes, Russ, there is, but that seems an unusual place to meet."

"It is, but I have my reasons. Please?"

"Yes, of course. I can have some drinks served?"

"No, in fact, I'd like you to make sure the area is cleared of any staff or gardeners."

"OK, as you say. Give me a couple of minutes. Sally will direct you, and I'll join you shortly."

"Thanks for your indulgence."

"Of course, no problem."

"Sally, while we're waiting on your mom, let me start by asking you a few questions, OK?"

"OK."

"You're fifteen?"

"Yes, I'll be sixteen in a couple of months, August."

"How are you schooled here?"

"I go to the American school set up by the embassy. It's just a few blocks from here."

"Describe your typical school day."

"Well, I get up about six forty-five, dress, eat with mom and dad, and then depart for school."

"How do you get to and from school?"

"Most days, Dad shuttles me to school at eight, and Mom picks me up just after three."

"And those days you don't go and come with Mom and Dad?"

"Sometimes Dad sends an embassy car, and on others, I walk the few blocks with friends."

"Ever deviate your route or go to another's house immediately after school?"

"Yes, my best friend, Tanya, lives about halfway. And when Mom arranges it, I sometimes stop there with her, and we do homework and girl stuff until Mom picks me up at about five thirty."

"Do you always know in advance when you'll be walking or staying with Tanya? And who is Tanya?"

"If not in advance, Mom calls the school, and they send a note to the room. And Tanya is the daughter of the embassy communications officer."

"Thank you, Sally. How about boys? A special one?"

"No. Mom says I should wait until we're back in the States to start dating because I'll be older then. But yes, I like boys. And I like Junior the best. He's Tanya's brother and a year older. He often helps us with our homework when we have trouble with it. Also, he is very fluent in Spanish. He had been taking it in the States before his dad was assigned here. He's a big help, and I like him a lot. If he were to ask me on a date, I'd beg Mom and Dad to let me go, but—"

"That's fine, Sally. Here's your mom now."

"OK, Russ, I've made assignments that will keep any staff away from this area. Has your time with Sally been productive?"

"Yes, it has. She told us all about things she'd never confess to you. Ha ha!"

"Yes, I'll just bet she did. Did she tell you no dates until we get back to the States?"

"Yes, first thing. She's a lovely young lady, and I like her a lot." He gave a sideways glance and winked at Sally. "Now, Julie and Sally, I need to brief you on why I'm here. I'm sure you've all used the term 'plan B' and know that it means a backup plan when your original or all other plans have failed. Well, we're here to give you a definitive plan B. I'm sure you've been briefed and, I hope, updated regularly on your personal security issues. Each of you have different issues. The ambassador is the most visible and, accordingly, has the largest security profile, but you two have different security profiles as well. In short, your individual plan A is to be safe and secure as you live your lifestyle here with as little security aggravation as possible. I don't know or necessarily need to know the details. But I do know that you each have a plan A.

"Again, I'm here to provide you a plan B should your plan A not work out. Just like a slick spot that causes an unavoidable accidental fall, sometimes plan A just slips out from under your feet and causes you to fall. So what is plan B when that occurs? I know you have contingency actions that you can take, but what happens when all that fails? What happens if one or more of you is taken captive or hostage by a criminal or terrorist group?

"We've set up an extensive location and recovery system for our key company personnel here in El Salvador. We've been asked to include the ambassador's and military attaché's families in it as a plan B to the State

Department's security. This means that the ambassador; you, Julie; you, Sally; JJ; and his wife, whom I haven't met yet, are to be included. This network also includes five key personnel company families. We'll cover who they are later. Likely, you have met some, if not all, of them already. The kids all go to the American school with Sally but are of differing ages. In total, there are about twenty people involved. There is no need for you to know one another or meet, and we prefer that involvement in this program never be discussed except with family. That especially means the kids. However, we do think it is a good idea that you each know who all the others are.

"OK, here are the basics. Each key person—and that means you—will wear or carry one or more personal items selected from a number of items that I will show you. Different items might be worn or carried on different occasions to suit the occasion or dress. These items include, among others, a variation from a locket to a wristwatch or medication dispenser. I think you'll like the selection, but I'll show you all these items later. We've selected and designated them to be either useful or decorative and hopefully nonintrusive to your lifestyle. For now, let me explain their purpose.

"Each device has a clandestine or hidden transmitter inside it. Each device performs the normal function expected of it, in addition to being a clandestine emergency location and recovery rescue beacon. In other words, a watch tells time, as well as performing its location function. Each device has its own unique activation and deactivation switches integrated into its normal functionality. These devices are easily activated by the user or anyone else who might fiddle with it but has a combination to keep it from being too easily deactivated. These beacons, when turned on, emit a unique signal that includes the user's ID. These signals are only on for one hundred milliseconds (a tenth of a second) every two minutes. In this manner, we can ID a person in trouble and their continuous location with a signal that does not alert others. Longer or more frequent signals might be detected by various detectors, AM or FM radios or TVs. Ours is not.

"Throughout San Salvador, we have stationed special remote detectors that can detect your signal as soon as it is activated. In a special security area at our main plant site, we have a computer-based display system that will track these signals as they move throughout the area. We have vehicles that can individually track down or home in on these signals at distances of 3 miles. And a light aircraft is equipped with similar equipment able to track these signals at ranges up to 25 miles as they might travel outside the San Salvador area into the countryside. Finally, were such an eventuality occur, we immediately dispatch a special team from Dallas that can be here within three hours with a Learjet similarly equipped and able to home in on these signals from as much as 250 miles away. This team is equipped with a wide array of other equipment to enable the safe recovery or rescue of any one or more of our plan B key personnel.

"Of course, there are accidental activations, but these are mostly when they are first introduced to a new user and until the person is more familiar with them. There's a short break-in period for these new users. Although we take all activations seriously, we do make allowance for the occasional accidental activation. We carefully check that the person in question is indeed missing before we activate the full force of recovery and dispatch of our Dallas team.

"Now I've brought this case of inactive devices with me to show you and to allow you to discuss and pick the ones you'd prefer. Don't worry, you can always change your mind and select another at any time. Although he's not with me now, Colonel Marin—our outside security man—will be your contact here in El Salvador. He is in charge of our detection and response squad locally. I'll have JJ introduce you tomorrow or the next day, and he will come and deliver the devices you pick from the array I'll show you today. But remember, you can change your mind at any time. Oh yes, the colonel's wife is a local doctor, if you happen to have a need for one.

"OK, let me show you these. I'll also show you how they are turned on and off and how you can determine that they are indeed in the state you select. Each unit has a unique ID, and the ones you select are coded to your name in our computer. In that manner, we'll know who has activated a device either purposely or accidentally. If accidentally, we'll contact you so that you can turn it off and schedule you for a rebriefing on your unit."

"Russ, shall we stop for lunch now? It's time."

"Yes, thank you, Julie. I'm through with the interview unless there's something you'd like to add from your viewpoint. I would like to know how your typical days go, including weekends."

"OK, let me have lunch brought out, and then we can talk through that as we eat, OK?"

"Great."

The colonel was in the embassy's security office. "Tell me, Ron, is your office secure?"

"You can tell by the combination lock on the door and the safe built into my desk."

"Well, it looks good. Do you have security conferences in here?"

"Yes, but only with my men."

"OK, will you fill me in on your procedures vis-à-vis the ambassador, the military attaché, and their families?"

"Sure, I'll run it all down for you."

"Also, please include their intercommunication techniques with one another and your office."

"Sure, let me get out the schematic that shows these interrelationships, and I'll sort of make a checklist on it as we proceed with all their procedures."

"Thanks, Ron."

Russ was still at the ambassador's residence, with lunch completed. "Well, Russ, what next?"

"I'd like a tour of your residence, focusing on the office and conference room but including the bedrooms and any inside and outdoor storage areas or sheds."

"I'll get a little layout of the premises and then leave you to tour as you like. Sally and I have a little shopping to do, so we'll leave you to it after I've shown you the layout. JJ is familiar with the residence."

"Good. Thank you. Please feel free to be about any shopping you have to do. This has been a very pleasant experience, and the lunch was delicious. Sally, I've enjoyed meeting you. Hope it wasn't a disappointment?"

"No, sir, it was great. Bye."

"Russ, I'll leave you with this layout and be on my way. Take your time, and thank you for your concern with the safety of my family and giving us a very good plan B."

"You're certainly welcome. And I'll leave my contact numbers and those of my boss, Max Curtis, in Dallas. Anytime, have no reservation, and contact us to discuss any concern, OK?"

"OK, and thanks again. Who do I really have to thank for this?"

"The president asked us to include you in our key personnel plan B profile personally."

"The president of the United States?"

"Yes, ma'am, personally."

11

THE COLONIA PLANT

"Chuck, I reviewed the data you gave me, and it is clear that the two outside vendors involved in this scam must be Julio Cesar of Parts Unlimited and Dumo Foscia of Circuits Ltd. Both are based here in San Salvador. I'd like you to arrange for Michael, manufacturing, and Torros, purchasing, to go into conference with you from about nine today until noon. And allow no interruptions and therefore absolutely no outside contact for them. Dream up some emergency session that you must prepare for corporate regarding manufacturing status.

"Additionally, I need you to phone these two vendors and arrange a meeting with me at the Camino Real at about nine thirty. I need to assure that there will be no contact between your two and my two before or during our meetings. Tell them I'm a corporate manufacturing person from Dallas who is interested in setting up a new plant in the Far East and wants to talk to them about outsourcing, if they are outsourcing to the Far East or at least help me understand the process here so that I am able to set up a system over there."

"Can do. It's almost eight thirty now. Let me call the meeting with my two guys first, and then I'll call your two just before nine and let you know if they'll be able to join you at the hotel."

"Think you can manage to get them to come to the Camino?"

"I'm sure of it. Whenever I call, they always bend over backward, not wanting to spoil their nest egg here."

"Good, be persuasive. I'll leave you to it and go on to the hotel. Phone if there's any snafu."

"OK, bye."

After a while, Vic's cell phone rang. "Vic, this is Chuck. I've arranged both meetings. Julio and Dumo both have agreed to meet you there at the Camino in about thirty minutes, maybe a little later if there is traffic."

"Thanks, Chuck, and good luck. I plan to be through before noon. But I'll call you when I'm through so you can end your meeting."

"Good, thanks. I'll be waiting on your call. When it comes, I'll just tell them the Dallas meeting was cancelled and to be scheduled later. I'll just ask them to better their data in the meantime."

"Good idea. Bye, Chuck."

Later, Chuck met with Michael and Torros. "Hi, guys. Let me explain what's up. Corporate in Dallas has asked for me to come up and review with them the complete history of our manufacturing and purchasing operations. They're only interest is in expenses versus product output. They're not on a witch hunt but are looking for our product unit cost history and our current status. I think they're fixing to open another plant in Asia and are going to use our data as a rough outline for their projections. They're in a hurry, so I suspect someone has planned a trip to Asia and wants to be armed with profile data.

"With a little luck, we should be able to wrap this up by lunch. In any case, I've asked Yolanda to have lunch prepared for us and sent to my conference room at about eleven thirty. If we finish earlier, you can just return for lunch and my thanks."

Vic's meeting happened at the Camino. "Hi. I'm Vic Visos of Exlite Corporate, Dallas. Which of you is which?"

"Hello, Senor Vic, I'm Dumo of Circuits, and this is Julio of Parts. I'm limited and he's unlimited. Ha ha!"

"Good to meet you. Please let's all sit down. As you can see, I've had snacks and drinks put out. Please avail yourselves of them. I'm glad you've a good sense of humor. I think you're going to need it. You see, I'm not as advertised. Actually, I'm from corporate security in Dallas. I've asked you here for a specific reason.

"Let me say that I'm aware of the scam you two have been running with our local manufacturing and purchasing guys, Michael and Torros. And I know it's been going on for the last two years. I've got all the documentation here in this folder. Please feel free to scan through it. It clearly lists in detail most of the kickbacks and payment made over these past two years. It's been very profitable for all involved, just not for Exlite. I want you to know that Michael and Torros are going to be fired and prosecuted to the full extent of the law. They will serve a major part of the remainder of their lives in prison here in El Salvador."

"Senor!"

Vic spoke forcefully. "Shut up, damn it. Don't either of you speak again unless I ask you a specific question. I hope you both saw the police vehicle parked out front as you entered. In the room next door are special police with warrants I've sworn out against both of you. At my signal, they will enter, arrest you, and take you directly to jail. And I assure you that no bail or other arrangement will be allowed. I am a personal friend of Judge Santos. I'm sure you've both heard of him. In our parlance, he is known as the hanging judge. In your case, I'm sure he'll be glad to let you both rot in jail before you're ever brought up on charges, much less tried and found guilty. So sit there and hear me out, or I assure you, you're gone." Both sat down, nodding their understanding.

"Although we have all the evidence we require to prosecute both of them and both of you, I want to know all the details of how this got started and any and all involved in your companies and ours. And if you're entirely truthful and give me the information I require here today, then I will limit your prosecution and not destroy your companies and families, if it is not deserved. Understand me?"

"Si, senor," in unison.

"If the details warrant, I'll spare the innocent and not destroy you. No, wait, I'll get you two a deal that you can live with. Otherwise, I'll hang it all on you and see that you get the maximum. Your families will be the big losers. You'll go to jail, and they will suffer complete loss as we go about recouping our losses and inflicting punitive damages. I'm going to record your comments. Now you may speak."

Julio and Dumo exchanged a meaningful glance. "Senor?"

"Yes, Julio?"

"Will this recording be shared with Carlos in security here?"

"No, absolutely not. Why do you ask?"

"Senor, Carlos is involved."

"Thank you. I assure you that Carlos will not hear this tape, and if involved, he will be fired and prosecuted as well." Vic, again, spoke forcefully. "Speak up right now, or I'll fetch the *policia*." Vic moved toward the door to the connecting room.

"No, wait, senor. We will tell you all you wish. We are guilty. We have profited, but we are not to blame. About two years ago, we were called in to the Exlite offices by Michael and Torros for a meeting about supplies for production. They threatened to drop all our contracts and force us out of business with Exlite, our major customer, unless we cooperated in their new incentive program. They said that this program would assure us all the contracts for circuits and parts in our areas if we would agree to return to them 15 percent of all our contracts with Exlite quarterly in cash. This cash would then be split as 5 percent for each of them and 5 percent for us. This last 5 percent was to be our incentive. They would, in turn, see that we would win all such contracts at an amount to include this additional 15 percent. We were given one day to consider. We took the day offered, but there was little to consider. We took them up on their offer. We then both agreed to bank these funds separately and, should this day—today—ever come, to return the funds. We have kept records, and the cash is regularly deposited in a deposit box so that it might be returned to Exlite."

"Dumo, do you agree with this statement?"

"Si, senor. I confess too. But we have not used any of the funds. We will return them to you at once."

"No. First, I wish to see the records you kept. And second, what is Carlos's involvement?"

"I kept those records, and they are in the deposit box with the cash. I can get both for you inside the hour."

"No, when we finish here, I will have Chuck meet us to recover both the records and the cash. I'll want to review the records before I decide what to do with you."

"Si, senor."

"Now about Carlos?"

"Si. About six months ago, Carlos got us all together in a supposed security meeting and said he knew all about our kickback scheme. He demanded that the kickback should be increased to 20 percent with the increased 5 percent to be his. And he insisted that Michael and Torros expand the kickbacks to include the other vendors, not as partners, as we two were, but simply to retain Exlite business. The kickbacks for them were to be 15 percent and that we would not share in this."

"Is that it? Were any others in your companies or ours involved?"

"No, senor, not to our knowledge."

Vic activated his recorder and said, "This is Vic Visos of Exlite Corporate Security, Dallas, in San Salvador, El Salvador. This recording is the interrogation of two Exlite vendors here. It is 10:30 a.m., Wednesday, May 26. Those present are myself and the two vendors Julio Cesar of Circuits Unlimited and Dumo Foscia of Parts Ltd. They have both confessed to me of being involved in a scheme to defraud Exlite of funds through dealings with employees of Exlite El Salvador. The entirety of this session is recorded to allow Exlite to recover any and all funds extorted in a kickback scheme and to identify any and all personnel involved.

"I want each of you to identify yourselves and your companies, make a statement that you agree or disagree with the contents of this tape, and answer the question 'Were you forced to make any statements here today?'" In short order, with only a little prompting, both identified themselves and again confessed and insisted that they had kept accurate records and the cash separately in a deposit box for return to Exlite at the appropriate time.

"OK, it appears that you are telling the truth and that you were forced to abide by the rules of the situation thrust on you. Additionally, if the records you supply and the funds you return correspond to the information I have collected, I am ready to make a deal with you.

"Here is what I require of you. Meet with me, Michael, and Torros of Exlite tomorrow morning when I confront the four of you with the details of the conspiracy that you have supplied me here today. They will be unaware that we have met and that you supplied this information. I want you to witness their protestations and later clarify to me any situation to which they might refer. We three will meet with Carlos separately tomorrow afternoon and take him down then. I want you to agree to be witnesses against these three in their prosecution. And I want you to personally submit reports to the American Embassy through a cutout, to be identified later, of any and all subversive activity of which you might be or might become aware.

"Again, assuming all this, here is what I will do for you. First, I will recommend against any prosecution of you in this incident. Second, I will recommend that your companies continue as suppliers to Exlite. And third, I will recommend that you each personally be treated with respect. Is this acceptable to you?"

"Si, senor. And thank you for your understanding."

"OK, give me a few minutes to dismiss the *policia* and to call Chuck to meet us. Where is the deposit box?"

"Banco Salvador, senor."

"OK, do you have the key, or must you fetch it?"

"I have it, senor."

Vic phoned Chuck. "Hello, Chuck? It's Vic."

"Yes?"

"I have all the data I need from Julio and Dumo. Apparently, they could do little about the kickback scheme but put all the funds they 'earned' into a lockbox against the day they were found out and kept a record of everything. I need you to meet me at Banco Salvador as soon as possible to recover the records and the cash. Two of us should be adequate to witness this event. They're going to keep shut and meet with me and your two in the morning. Make sure they're there early."

"OK, will do. We're just finishing our meeting here." And for those listening, Chuck added, "Sorry to hear the meeting in Dallas is cancelled. Do you know when it will be rescheduled? Not for a month or more. OK."

"They are there with you and listening?"

"Yes, that's right. See you soon. Goodbye."

12

THE AMBASSADOR'S RESIDENCE

Russ and JJ toured the residence. "JJ, is the residence visited by the sweep team?"

"The residence was swept originally when the ambassador moved in. But it has not been swept since."

"How long ago was that?"

"About two years ago."

"JJ, can you arrange for the residence and its environs to be swept regularly?"

"I can request a sweep by state but only about once a year, maybe twice, and even then, it might not get done."

"Not good enough, JJ. How often is the embassy swept?"

"Twice a year."

"Does that include the security office?"

"No."

"How often does CIA sweep your office and residence?"

"They sweep my office quarterly and my residence every other time so every six months."

"Not good enough. Can you arrange for them to sweep the embassy offices, your two residences, and the security office at least once a quarter?"

"I can request it, but it's not likely to happen without some muscle."

"OK, I'll get you the muscle. You make the request."

"Done."

"OK, let me get my gear, and then let's look over this residence."

Russ, goes to the car, collects his satchel of gear, and returns to JJ.

"JJ, I want to sweep the ambassador's home office first."

"OK, exactly what does your gear do?"

"Well, not nearly as much as a sweep team's gear, but mine is more related to detecting transmissions through the air and over the AC lines. Usually, when a surveillance is made, it's either wireless or over the normal AC supply lines. I'll tune this radio to some music station and let that be our source to look for. My receivers are not very sensitive but are able to look entirely over the frequency band at once. Here, you take this little handheld box, extend the antenna, and sweep it over the walls, floors, and ceiling. Concentrate on any hole or fixture, wall plug, wall switch, etc. I'll plug this little handheld box into each power socket."

"Russ, I'm getting a very faint tone and elevation of signal strength over here just above the wall socket."

"That's just the power line in the wall. Turn the sensitivity down a bit until the tone just goes away. A sudden jump in tone is more what you're looking for. That shows stronger signals."

"OK."

JJ and Russ proceeded to sweep over the entire room and all its fixtures. "JJ, come look at this. I've found something."

"What?"

"I don't know yet. Bring over the tool bag from my kit."

JJ brought over the toolbox, and Russ lifted a small box and cable from it. "Notice that the detector I've plugged in here shows a fairly large signal. That's a carrier frequency on the line.

Russ plugged in the new box, turned it on, and adjusted the sensitivity. "Listen, hear our music? Let me adjust the volume." The music from the radio placed in the middle of the ambassador's desk was clearly heard from the small receiver's speaker. "That's a bug."

"Where is it, Russ?"

"I suspect it's built into the wall socket itself, and the microphone pickup is likely behind the round ground hole in the three-hole socket."

Russ proceeded to unscrew the wall socket carefully and practically noiselessly and pulled it out from its mounting without disturbing the power line. "Here it is, just as I suspected. OK, let me put it carefully back in place. Then we'll finish sweeping the room. There is generally another on the other side of the room to obtain a stereolike effect and to assure that all voices in a room are picked up."

Again, they proceeded to sweep the remainder of the room. "Yep, here's the other one. It would be the last one tested. Now we leave them in place until we've done the entire residence to assure that the people bugging this do not know we've found it. It's likely to be put in place and monitored on or just off the property by some insider on their staff. Likely, it is voice activated and recorded, tape recovered/replaced, and then listed to elsewhere. The voice activation allows the recorder and tape to last a very long time. No voice, no recording. It might be replaced only every week or so."

JJ and Russ continued from room to room, first placing the radio music source in the middle of each room and then sweeping everything, with nothing else found. "This is really odd, JJ. No other bug of any kind is found elsewhere in the house, and then suddenly, two more of the same type are found in Sally's bedroom. What do you make of that?"

"I don't know, Russ."

"Wait, JJ, I know. They must be planning for a kidnap of the ambassador's daughter at some time and need any information she might give while talking to friends either in her bedroom or on her phone. That way, they'll know her plans and schedule."

"God, I think you might be right. But why didn't they just tap the phones?"

"Well, for one thing, their phone system is fairly complicated. And also, they already had this type of tap in the office. They could easily add on her bedroom to the existing system they had set up."

"OK, Russ, what's next?"

"Well, we must find the receiving end of this. Again, I think it's most likely on the grounds. If it were in the house, you would have picked up the recording bias signal with your wireless sweeper. So it must be elsewhere on the grounds. And if that's the case, it's likely in one of the gardening sheds."

"Russ, that means the gardeners are the most likely suspects."

"Right. We mustn't alert them. Let's see if the wife and the girl are about due back."

Phoning the ambassador's wife, Russ quickly found that they were about to return home. Russ asked Julie to dream up an excuse to get the gardeners off to pick up some flowers or supplies. Upon her return, Julie asked the gardeners to go to the supply store for her to fetch some fill dirt and fertilizer. She guessed that they would be gone for just over a half hour.

Russ then asked Julie to take Sally and absent themselves from the premises for at least an hour. He promised to call them when it was safe to come home. The girls left quickly.

"JJ, leave the radio and music in Sally's room on. And then let's search the main gardening shed first. It has a power line from the house and is the likely place for someone to stash the receiver and recorder or whatever."

JJ and Russ proceeded to the main shed and searched with the RF sweep receiver and visually. Suddenly, Russ announced, "JJ, I've found it. It's behind a false back to this workbench that they apparently use as a desk of sorts to pot plants on." Russ pulled the bench away from the wall so that they can see the items concealed on the backside. "See, this is the receiver, and here is the recorder. Give me the receiver, and we'll test this incoming line. Yep, listen, hear our music station?"

"I do, Russ, and here behind this panel are dated and new recording tapes. The dated ones are from the last two weeks, and the others appear not to have even been opened yet."

"JJ, stop the recorder a minute, and pop out the tape."

"Here it is."

"This tape is dated Monday and is only about one-eighth used. Here, date this new tape, pop it in, and press Record."

Russ dropped the used tape into his bag. "It's going. JJ, run in and turn our radio off and bring it with you. Remember, it's in Sally's room."

"OK, back in a minute." JJ hustled off, and about a minute later, Russ heard the music cease, and the recorder automatically stopped.

"Russ, here's the radio. But bad news, I think I heard the truck with the gardeners returning." JJ was watching for the returning gardeners when he was suddenly surprised to see them spotting him in their shed. JJ ducked back inside and warned Russ. They quickly decided to casually stroll out to meet the gardeners. "Hi, fellas," JJ said as they exited the shed.

The gardeners had both pulled out revolvers and quickly proceeded to shoot repeatedly at Russ and JJ from some distance. Both Russ and JJ ducked and clambered back inside, turned over a table, and got behind it. The gardeners continued shooting and got much closer. Suddenly, there was silence. "They're reloading, JJ. Have you got a gun?" Russ had pulled out his Mini-mite and freed up his clips. JJ showed a regulation army .45.

As the door of the shed was torn open, Russ said, "You take left." The two gardeners entered, firing wildly. Russ steadied his Mini-mite on the top edge of the table, rose to eye level, rotated the gun to the gardener on their right, and fired two shots into his chest. As he collapsed, Russ heard two earsplitting booms to his left and turned to see the other gardener pitch backward and out the door.

"You OK, Russ?"

"Yes, JJ, except maybe for my hearing. Damn, that's one loud gun."

"Yes, it is."

They approached, nudged, and examined their respective targets. Then they changed places. "Damn, Russ, look at the damage your shots did. Mine look clean and as you'd expect. But yours—what is that little gun anyway?"

"It's a special .38 automatic with explosive ammunition, JJ."

"Well, damn, my .45 knocked my man backward, but yours tore your man up. It's all liquid inside his chest. Where'd you get that thing?"

"It was developed by your people sometime back. We modified the hollow-point ammunition with a drop of mercury and then overcoated it with Teflon. It'll penetrate Kevlar at fifty-plus feet, and the mercury causes it to explode on penetration."

"Woff, don't shoot me with that thing. It's just so little."

"Five inches and a half pound with a little clip on the side that enables me to clip it in my pants pocket, which I've modified with a comfortable thin leather insert to clip the gun to."

"Maybe I'll get me one of those."

"It's a good second or ankle gun, if you really need the .45."

At that moment, a large marine guard came running out to the shed from the house. He quickly pointed his rifle at Russ and JJ. "Whoa, big boy," said JJ.

Recognizing JJ, he dropped the barrel. "What's up, JJ?"

"Well, you can see this one here. There's another inside. They have been bugging the ambassador's and caught us just as we found their gear. They came out shooting, and we were forced to return fire. Unfortunately for them, they weren't very good shots on the run. We were."

"What's your name Marine?"

"Blaine, sir. Sergeant Blaine."

"OK, Sergeant, contact embassy security and tell them what has happened. Have them send a team out. Your lieutenant is with Colonel Marin at the embassy. Have them both meet us here ASAP. Your lieutenant can notify the locals when he gets here."

"Yes, sir." The marine scampered away with rifle at port arms.

"JJ, let's recover our brass. I don't like leaving too much evidence." JJ and Russ went back to their places in the shed and searched the floor for their spent brass. It was found and tucked away in Russ's bag.

Russ picked a small digital camera from his bag and proceeded to photograph the two dead. He repositioned them slightly, took face pictures, and then returned them to their dead pose. Then he pulled a small kit from the bag and proceeded to fingerprint both men's right index fingers. He placed the fingerprints on a slide and photographed them. "I'd like copies of those, Russ."

"Sure, I'll make you a disc when I get back to the hotel."

About seven minutes later, the colonel and the lieutenant came skidding up to a stop just a few yards from the shed and jumped out. "Russ", the colonel asked, "you OK?"

"Sure, we're both fine, just a little debate. Our side won."

"The marine who called this in said you had discovered a bugging system and were, in turn, discovered doing so."

"That's right. They came on firing, and we had no alternative except to return fire. They weren't too good."

"OK, we've decided to call the locals in. You two need to scoot. Please each of you turn in a write-up first thing in the morning. Not too many details about what you found, just detail them starting it and you finishing it, OK?"

"Can do. We'll have to write it all up for home base anyway. They get the details. You get the description of events."

"Right, go."

True to his word, Russ called Julie, gave her the short version, and told her that it was all right to return home.

Russ and JJ proceeded back to the embassy. Once there, Russ went back to the hotel. JJ did a write-up of the entire circumstances for the ambassador, State Department, and CIA. He then made a phone call to the CIA headquarters in McLean, Virginia, to report in.

Russ, at the hotel, made a disc for JJ of the photos and fingerprints he'd taken. Then he made a detailed write-up for Max in Dallas and a simpler one for the embassy and the *policia*. He phoned Vic and made a date for dinner. Finally, he stepped into a welcome shower.

Out of the shower, he hooked up his encrypter to the phone and called Max, in Dallas, to give him the lowdown. "Russ, are you all right, and do you need more ammunition?"

"No, I've only fired two shots and don't plan on any more."

"OK, take care. Back Vic up until he's through, and then I'll see you soon."

"Good. See you soon, boss."

13

THE RHINOCEROS

Over breakfast, Russ related to Vic the remaining details of the confrontation at the ambassador's residence yesterday. "Well, Vic, that's the gist of my afternoon yesterday."

"Russ, is there likely to be any kickback from the police or government?"

"I doubt it. JJ's got that covered. What's with you today?"

"Well, Russ, I've got a meeting first thing this morning with Chuck to explain yesterday's happenings with the two vendors and then lunch with you, the colonel, and the judge at the Rhinoceros Factory. Lunch will take about an hour and a half, and then the meeting with the two company inside men with the two vendors is scheduled for 2:00 p.m."

"Good luck with that. I plan to use the morning doing revisions and more write-ups on yesterday for everyone. The colonel is meeting me here at the hotel just before lunch, and then after lunch with you and the judge, we plan to go over these for his edification and training in how we do write-ups. He doesn't like write-ups much, but who does?"

"OK, if that's all, I'll be going."

"No, Vic, one more thing, I'd like you to go to my room with me, and I want to equip you with a PIDRA."

"OK, but what's that?"

They retired to Russ's room, and he gave Vic a PIDRA and explained its purpose and use. "This is PIDRA, Vic. It's a portable intrusion detector and remote alarm we developed for our field people. There are actually three identical intrusion detectors and a pager. All are the same size. The first intrusion detector is for your hotel/motel room, the second for your vehicle, and the third for miscellaneous uses, like covering your rear or guarding an area where you might leave important information, equipment, etc.

"These intrusion detectors are composed of a miniature passive infrared motion detector, a transmitter, and some logic to perform its magic. Notice the unit has double-sided mastic with a cover sheet. You just zip the cover sheet off the mastic and stick the unit under a bedside table in your room, aiming it toward the door or entry area. Whenever you get ready to leave the room, just reach beneath the table, and snap on this little slide switch. There's a time delay of about five minutes to allow you plenty of time to gather up whatever you are taking with you and leave before the unit activates. Be sure to hang the Do Not Disturb sign up on the doorknob outside your room. You take the pager unit with you and clip it to your belt or keep it in your bag until your return.

"If someone enters the room while you are gone, the unit will detect the entry and transmit a special code to your pager. As you return to the hotel, turn the pager unit on. And if there has been an intruder, the little red light on the pager will turn on. If the intruder is still in the room, the pager will vibrate as well. All three of these units work alike and are coded to your pager only. In a car, you just hide the detector beneath the dash. These units are intended to warn you before you walk into something or before someone sneaks up on you.

"We've tested these thoroughly, and they work. I had one in my room on the twenty-second floor in San Francisco and purposely set it off and checked it with my pager as I went about business all over town. My pager could detect it everywhere I went with the exception of when I was in an elevator in a couple of the downtown buildings I visited. You don't need to leave the pager on. Just check it before returning to the hotel, car, etc."

"So what do you do if it says there was an intruder while you were gone?"

"Simply go to the desk, tell them as you approached your room you heard a commotion inside, and ask that they check it out. When they do and if no one's there, simply apologize and say it must have been next door. That's it. Any questions?"

"You say you guys developed this for your field use?"

"Yep, try it. You'll like it."

"Damn, thanks a lot. After your day today, I see why we need stuff like this."

"See you for lunch at the Rhinoceros Factory."

At lunch, the judge, Vic, Russ, and the colonel met. "Senors, the man with me is my associate and close friend, Judge Rodrigo. I thought you'd like to meet the other honest man in San Salvador who essentially sees things the way we do. I hope you'll feel free to call on him if I'm not available. I trust him implicitly."

"*Bienvenidos*, senors. I am glad to meet you. My friend Judge Santos honors me by saying he is my friend and that he trusts me. I promise you I will live up to that high honor. It is good to meet you. Senor Russ, Judge Santos has told me of your and Senor Max's exploits of last year here. I am honored to meet you."

"Russ, how is Senor Max? Well, I hope."

"Max is doing well and sends you his regards, Judge Santos. He's busy as a bee just now in Dallas. We are expanding our business in the States and in security areas throughout the world just now. It keeps him home, but I'm sure he wishes he were here with us now. If you like, I'll phone him before we leave and give him a chance to say hello himself."

"That would be nice but hardly necessary. I remember him fondly as I do you and your exploits with our little Volkswagen. I understand you're driving one of ours now. I told our maintenance department to give you the newest in stock and to make sure it was in excellent shape. I hope you have found it so."

"Yes, Judge, I have. Better than the last one. Ha ha!"

"OK, Russ tell us the story. What happened with the last one?"

"Yes, Senor Russ, what happened?"

"Well, OK. Before I had met Judge Santos, I came here and rented a VW. It was convenient to get around in and attracted little attention. After driving it around for a week, Max and I had to go up the mountain to check a repeater system we were putting in. You know there are a dozen or so switchbacks and all dirt road to the top. Well, on about the fifth or sixth switchback, we encountered a muddy spot and got stuck. Fortunately, there were some coffee pickers coming down the mountain on foot. We persuaded them to help push us out of the mud. They did with no trouble, and I paid each of them about five colones for the help. Well, that's twenty colones total, about US$8.

"Max joked with me at the time as we continued up the mountain, questioning how I would put this on my expense account since there was no receipt. The funny thing is when we got back to the States, my expense account was kicked back for that very reason. Max wrote a note and drew a picture of four pushing a VW and explained that they had nothing but their shorts, a rope, and their machetes, no receipts. Of course, accounting took his word for it, and I did get my expenses approved. Now accounting always questions something in hopes of getting another one of Max's notes, depictions, and stories. Anyway, that was our first experience going up that trip.

"Our second experience was that, when we got to the top and got out of the VW, we saw a wet trail following us. Upon inspection, it was a trail of brake fluid. The right rear brake line was positioned against a shock, and it had worn a hole in the brake line. Of course, we had to fix it, or we couldn't get back down the mountain. We had very few tools, so our solution was to pinch off that brake line to the right rear wheel and to refill the brake cylinder but no fluid. After much thought, Max concluded that the only fluid available was urine. Fortunately, I had enough to fill the master cylinder.

"After finishing our inspection of the repeater site, we cautiously made our way down the mountain and to this plant. Here, we told them what had happened, and they set about draining, flushing, and refilling the line and, we thought, repairing it. During this process, we were introduced to Judge Santos, who was, as always, taking his ease during the siesta with a little lunch and a little tequila. He invited us to take our ease with him, and we became fast friends over a few drinks that early afternoon.

"It was only later that week, when we turned the VW back in as we prepared to return to Dallas, that it was found that the brake line had not been repaired but that we had been going along on that crimped line all the remaining time. They had reordered a new brake line, and it had finally come in. They were glad to see us return the VW so that they could finally replace that brake line. Before we got too mad, the judge intervened, and we all laughed about it over a few more drinks. Oh, yes, he promised it would never happen to us again and now always gives us the best he has. No more stories, let's eat."

"OK, enough storytelling. Judge Santos, I need to tell you what happened at the ambassador's residence yesterday and seek your advice." Russ told of the finding of bugging devices in the ambassador's residence and of the attack and subsequent shooting of the two gardeners by Russ and JJ at the residence. "Well, I've made a full written report for the *policia*, the embassy, and my bosses back in Dallas, but I'm wondering what, if anything, I might do to forestall any action against myself and JJ by the local government authorities, who are sure to investigate further."

"Senor Russ, let me apologize for these hostile actions by my countrymen against the embassy, its personnel, and yourself. I'm sorry that the occasion necessitated your killing both of your assailants. And I'm sure that the local *policia* and likely the government will wish that formal legal inquiries be made.

"However, I feel you can forestall these by making a formal statement to the courts regarding the events leading up to and including the shooting of these two culprits. In this regard, although it is complicated by the actions having taken place on the property of the ambassador and including a formal employee of the embassy—namely, JJ, the military attaché—and yourself, an employee of Exlite. As you know, the embassy and the residence of the ambassador are protected under the formal relationship between our two countries. Unfortunately, not many completely understand this relationship and the fact that these two places are actually U.S. territory and that they just happen to be in El Salvador and are subject to special treaty protections.

"Specifically, I suggest that you and JJ appear before my court in chambers and make a full disclosure of this event. The sooner you do this, the better. I would suggest as early as first thing in the morning. I will make myself and the court stenographer available to take this information, and I will ask the state's prosecutor to be on hand as well. In this manner, we should be able to reassure anyone in the government that the case is in hand and being handled appropriately.

"There is one problem. You will be making a statement in English, and the court records must be in Spanish. Could the embassy lend a hand in this regard?"

"I don't know, Judge, but I'll contact JJ right away and see if the embassy can send over a stenographer and translator to enable the information to be recorded in both English and Spanish for the court. Can I get back to you this evening? I should be able to determine if we can put this all together for first thing in the morning. What time?"

"Eight o'clock would be perfect, *mas e minus* [more or less]."

"OK, give me a number to contact you, please."

"We'll both give you ways to contact us at the office and otherwise. If you're going to go about doing your business, it's likely you'll need one of us from time to time. Oh, by the way, I saw Senor Reitmann yesterday and told him an associate of Senor Max was in town. He said he'd be glad to see you if you have time while you're here. In any case, he asked that I send his regards to Senor Max."

Senor Reitmann was one of the oligarchy and a personal friend of Max's through an original friendship between Max's mother-in-law and Reitmann's daughter. Max always visited with Reitmann whenever he was in the country. Reitmann had extensive holdings in El Salvador, including an entire mountain where coffee was grown at the top, pineapple fields in the middle slope, and coconut palms at the base. A stream fed down the mountain and was used for irrigation, into a lake, and to the Pacific.

Shrimp swam up into the stream, bred in its fresh water, and returned to the ocean. The baby shrimp were seined from the stream at a size of about sixteen to the ounce and dumped into the lake. They were fed dry dog food in the lake and seined out at a size of about sixteen to the pound. They were a delicacy in that they had never been in salt water and therefore had not developed the tough skin under their shells that saltwater shrimp had. One of the restaurants in San Salvador served these as a specialty item, and Max always took guests there. Whenever Reitmann heard that Max was taking someone there, he saw to it that they were not charged. Reitmann always insisted that Max and any guests he might have come and dine with him at home where everything that was served was grown or raised on Reitmann's finca (farm). Russ attended one such treat while visiting in El Salvador with Max last year.

"Thank you. When you see him, please tell him that I will give his regards to Max. Again, Judge Santos, I thank you and will call you later. Judge Rodrigo, it has been a pleasure to meet you. I look forward to seeing you in the future. I appreciate your contact information because, from time to time, we in security attract trouble."

"Senor, it is my pleasure."

"Well, we need to say our goodbyes. Vic has an important meeting to attend, and I've reports to write and the embassy to contact about the translator-stenographer."

14

COLONIA SHOWDOWN

Vic was at Exlite, Colonia. "Hi, Vic. Chuck said you wanted to meet with us? I'm Michael, productions, and this is Torros, purchasing."

Shaking hands with each in turn, Vic said, "Yes, glad to meet you. I've also asked your two principal suppliers to meet with us as well. This must be them now."

"Yes, it is. This is Julio Cesar of Parts Unlimited and Dumo Fascia of Circuits Ltd."

"Good to meet you, Limited and Unlimited."

"Si, senor, glad to meet you. What's up?"

"It's a security issue that has come to my attention."

"Well then, shouldn't Carlos be called in?" asked Torros.

"Not yet. I have asked him to join us a little later. First, I'd like to address the issue with you two, Michael and Torros."

Nervously, Torros asked, "What's the problem, Vic?"

"First, I'd like to make a statement uninterrupted. Then I'll address questions. OK?"

Nervously, Michael and Torros both said, "OK."

"Certain information came to my attention after I arrived that concerned me. I asked Chuck to furnish me with some detailed data that I have here." He showed a folder of papers. "And it clearly states that the two of you, Michael and Torros, have been obtaining kickbacks from several of your suppliers, including Julio's Parts Unlimited and Dumo's Circuits Ltd. over a period dating back two years."

"No, Vic—"

"Shut up," Vic said menacingly. "I'm not through." He continued. "Additionally, this data shows that you have allowed significant overcharges to these two while cutting out any aspect of competitive bidding by others."

Again, both suggested they wished to reply; and menacingly, Vic said, "If you know what's good for you, you'll shut up until I finish. I want you to understand that this is not a negotiation. This is a proven accusation. I intend to see that you two are fired with prejudice today, jailed immediately, tried to the full extent of the law, and sued for damages to the extent that your companies and families are left destitute. Now you may speak. If there are other collaborators in this, I want to know. This is the only thing that can possibly alleviate our vengeance for these acts against the company. Anyone? Speak up, anyone?"

"Si, senor," Michael begins to speak.

Carlos, who had been listening outside the door, came plunging in. "Shut up, Michael!" he bellowed.

Surprised, Vic said, "Carlos, I've been expecting you. Do you wish to confess your collaboration with these two?"

Carlos, furious, snatched a machete from its wall hanger and charged Vic, who stumbled backward, clutching for his Mini-mite pocket pistol. Torros and Michael backed away while screaming invectives in Spanish at Carlos. Julio and Dumo simultaneously exclaimed *Madre de Dios* (Mother of God) and scrambled to escape toward the doorway.

Carlos, screaming, took a swing with the machete at Vic, who simultaneously fell backward while firing his Mini-mite from the hip. Carlos, hit in the chest, crumpled on top of him. Vic, who took a glancing blow from the machete and under the weight and momentum of Carlos's charge, hit his head on a two-drawer file cabinet and was stunned. They ended up a twisted pile on the floor.

Hearing the gunshot, Chuck ran from down the hall and called to Yolanda for the nurse, an ambulance, and security. Yolanda, two security guards, and the nurse all showed up shortly, and Yolanda announced that an ambulance was on the way. Chuck put the four who remained standing under guard and had them removed to Torros's office, which was nearby. Then he rolled Carlos aside and saw that he was dead. He quickly saw that Vic was bleeding from a small machete wound to the head and that he was barely conscious. He ordered the nurse to treat him without moving him. It was clear that he was slightly concussed from hitting the file. Then he picked up and pocketed Vic's Mini-mite pistol.

Chuck had the area cleared—a couple of guards to keep it that way—and phoned Russ. Russ, the colonel, and the ambulance all arrived at the same time, although it was clear from their relative braking distances that Russ was driving the fastest. It took him less than five minutes to travel from the Camino Real to the Colonia plant, some five miles distant. "What's Vic's status, Chuck?"

"He's coming around. He took a glancing blow to the head from a machete wielded by Carlos at the same time he shot Carlos dead with this little gun," Chuck said as he took the Mini-mite pistol from his pocket.

Russ said, "I'll take that." He pocketed it. "Vic, are you OK?"

Vic—still stunned and held in place by the nurse, who refused to let him rise—said, "I'll be just fine if someone will get Nurse Cratchet off me."

"Hold still a bit longer, Vic. Let me make an assessment. What happened?"

"Carlos obviously was listening at the door, and when they were about to disclose his part in the plot, he charged in, picked up a machete, and charged me. I toppled over backward, avoiding his swing, and took a fall. The file cabinet did me more damage than he did. This nurse has already patched me up. It's all on my little pocket recorder, if you can find it."

"Here it is, Vic," said the colonel. "It obviously was knocked off the desk, and I found it under this cabinet. I've turned it off, but all the audio should still be on it."

"Colonel, you go see to Torros and Michael. Don't let them turn Dumo and Julio. I'll get over there as soon as I can. You get their statements. Do you have a recorder?"

"No."

"Here, take mine. This turns it on, and this turns it off."

"OK, watch after Vic."

"Chuck, I want to take a few pictures, and then you can have the ambulance take Carlos's body to the morgue." Russ took pictures and then released Carlos. "Chuck, can you handle the *policia*, or should I call in JJ from the embassy?"

"I'll call it in, but you should get JJ anyway. We'll likely need him before it's all over."

Russ called JJ and gave him a quick overview. JJ said he was on the way with his security man.

"Russ."

"Yes, Colonel."

"Julio and Dumo are all right. I took their statements separately on your recorder, and they are both the same. I've put them together but separate from Torros and Michael. Torros is hot about the whole thing and is not holding it together very well. I just stepped away to tell you this. I'll return now and get their separate statements."

Russ took Vic's recorder and, sitting next to Vic, began the playback of events at double speed. In this way, he could listen to the whole set of events in half the time but, with concentration, not lose anything. Vic was sitting up by the time Russ finished listening to the tape of events, which included the colonel finding the recorder under the cabinet. "Vic, your color has returned, and that bandage on your head makes you look better as though you had more hair."

"Ha ha! I feel better. The nurse did a good job and gave me a pretty good painkiller as well."

Suddenly, there heard a commotion from Torros's office. Russ said, "Vic, you stay put." And he ran off toward the commotion.

The two guards were standing just outside the office, uncertain of whether to enter or not. Russ brushed past them and burst in. The colonel and Michael were tussling, and Torros held out a revolver toward the colonel. When he saw Russ, he turned the gun in his direction. Russ jumped behind the door and hit the floor while pulling his Mini-mite pistol. The revolver spoke twice, and two shots penetrated the door at normal chest height but well above Russ's head. Russ rolled out from behind the door and fired two quickly aimed shots at Torros, one in the chest and one in the neck. Torros fell like a wet sack of cement.

Simultaneously, suddenly threatened, the colonel kicked Michael in the crotch. Michael grabbed himself and began to double over as the colonel brought his hand up in uppercut fashion but with his palm extended. The heel of his hand caught Michael in his brow. His head snapped back, and he collapsed unconscious.

"Well done, Colonel."

"Well done yourself. I was in a pickle until you showed up."

"I guess they didn't want to give you their statements."

"You got that right. They doubled up and suddenly got the drop on me. I thought I might not get out of that one."

"Well, you did and quite nicely, I might say. Where'd you learn that blow to the brow?"

"I learned that from Max just last year. He used it quite effectively with the very same effect when we got in a tight place."

"I'll report that you are a great student. Now let's see about wrapping this up and letting Chuck handle the locals. Or do you think you need to stay?"

"I'll need to stay. You take Vic back to the hotel. I'll call my wife and have her look in on him. You just get him to bed. I'll check back with you when I'm through here. You clean up, get some sleep. I'll see you in the morning, OK?"

"Done. I'll check out with Chuck. I called JJ at the embassy, and he is bringing his security man to help out here. Let me know if you need me."

15

IN CHAMBERS

At 8:00 a.m. in Judge Santos's chambers, with the local prosecutor, were the judge's stenographer, Russ, JJ, Vic, the colonel, the embassy legal counsel, and an embassy stenographer and translator. All the amenities/introductions were taken care of. "Good morning, Judge Santos."

"Good morning, Russ. Shall we begin?"

"No, not yet, Judge, if you don't mind. I'd like to preface all this with a short description for you. Your stenographer should likely take this down. It might be important to you later."

"OK, Russ. Deidra, you may begin your recording of this session. Preface it normally, that is, date, people's names and associations, etc. OK, Russ, let's start with you once she suggests she has the preface set up. Each of you, give your name, citizenship, association, reason for being here, etc."

"Ready, Judge."

"OK, Russ, you first."

"My name is Russ Talbot."

"OK, Russ, give your preface statement."

"First, Judge, I'd like to break this into two parts. The first part involves my purpose for being in El Salvador this time. I was performing a counterintelligence sweep of the U.S. ambassador's residence, and just after we discovered a recording apparatus, the two gardeners descended on JJ and myself with revolvers, each firing rapidly but from some distance. We quickly retreated back into the gardening shed, and when they burst in shooting at us, we each returned fire and killed them at the entrance. The residence marine guard showed up immediately thereafter. That's the end of a brief description of the first incident.

"Next, Judge, I'd like to briefly describe the second incident, which took place yesterday afternoon after we had lunch with you."

"A second incident?"

"Judge, pardon me. James Querin, the U.S. legal counsel in El Salvador."

"Yes, Mr. Querin, go ahead."

"I just need to point out that we are here at the insistence of Russ and JJ. But you do understand that this first incident, as explained, is our jurisdictional matter, not yours."

"Yes, Mr. Querin, I agree on jurisdiction under the terms of our treaty, but I am here to hear out Russ and these others at their specific request. Despite international legal jurisdiction, there are likely to be parties, misunderstandings, etc., that are local in nature and that might need explaining through our court system. Specifically, they and you are here seeking my help in explaining to the government of El Salvador that the incident circumstances are entirely rational and legal within the confines of their understanding regardless of treaties. Further, it is my intention here to hear you all out and to rationalize the events and incidents within the Salvadoran court's understanding. Finally, it is my intent to solve a problem before it occurs—and it is the reason Senor Russ has asked me to intervene before any local *policia* or governmental misunderstanding occurs—and to assure your government of the understanding nature of our government in light of the events that have occurred."

"Thank you, Judge. In light of your statement, I will sit quietly in the background and trust in your stated intentions."

"Russ, go on. A second incident yesterday afternoon?"

"Yes, sir. Vic is actually here on a separate mission from mine. Actually, he came to investigate an infraction of our company policy and to chastise and removed the perpetrators from the employ of Exlite. However, in the midst of that action, he came upon a long-term collusion between two company personnel and two local contractors that came to include our internal Salvadoran security manager." Russ went on to describe the incident in some detail.

"And as I charged into the office, Torros fired two shots through the door at me. I returned fire, and he was killed. Well, Judge, that's the second incident. To me, it seems no different than the first, although the first involves a dedicated terrorist plot against the embassy. The second incident seems only to be a theft."

"Understood. OK, I understand the issues. We will treat these as two separate issues. I'll swear each of you in and have you detail your involvement in the incident we're dealing with at the time, that is, incident number 1 or incident number 2. Again, Russ, we'll start with you."

"Yes, Your Honor."

"OK, Russ, will you please make a statement giving all the details to which you were a witness regarding the incident at the U.S. ambassador's residence? Do not speculate. Just relate those events that occurred truthfully."

Each, in turn, was sworn in and testified to their involvement in each incident. "OK, guys, that's all."

"Thank you, Your Honor."

Afterwards, in chambers, the judge addressed Russ. "Russ, this has become a very complex problem. As you know, I and Judge Rodrigo are actually the judges appointed by the oligarchy and kept in place by the ruling government. We keep our skirts clean with them and the oligarchy, but from time to time, we get bumped around rather sharply by the government autocrats. I'll do the best I can with this information and get it into the government through our regular channels, but if there's a troublemaker somewhere in the system, it might be difficult to keep you clear of being arrested and tried. So in the meantime, I suggest that you keep a low profile and plan to return to the States if things get sticky. I'll keep you informed if there are troubles in sight. I'd like to ask the prosecutor here, Senor Salvos, his opinion."

"Judge Santos, I understand the details that have been explained here in these depositions, and I believe that I can report up my chain that things are in hand. However, as you mentioned, sometimes someone in power might make trouble. If that is the case, then arrests will have to be made and trials held. This double situation, the embassy and the Colonia plant, make the problems the more possible. However, since Russ, Vic, and JJ have been so cooperative and given their depositions before you and me, I have a fair to good chance of short-circuiting any backlash from above. In any case, should there be backlash, I can promise to alert the judge in time to avoid a confrontation of any sort. Of course, the embassy case is special, and your counsel will be able to prevail with the government, JJ. Nevertheless, this might aggravate the Colonia plant problem."

"OK, guys, that's our best effort. Good luck and goodbye. I've cases to try."

And the group said in unison, "Thanks, Judge."

As the group departed, Russ said, "Before we separate, JJ, come to the hotel with us, and let's have lunch and a strategy session."

"Fine, who all do we need, Russ?"

"I think you, JJ, Vic, the colonel, and I will suffice."

After lunch on the hotel patio, Russ announced, "I appreciate all the judge and prosecutor said. However, we need to make an escape plan should things go bad. Also, we need to talk about the implications of the bugs we found at the ambassador's residence. Let's talk about the escape plan. Vic?"

"If we can, we'll just fly out commercial. Or if we can't, maybe we can fly out by company Learjet."

Russ said, "If we're being sought out, neither of those would work. So first, Colonel, set up a southern escape route into Nicaragua. You can drive Vic's rent a car. Then I'll set up an escape route to the north, using Fernando to drive my VW. Finally, JJ, you set up a boat getaway to sea." He paused. "Any or all of these can be used for real or as a ruse to distract whoever if it gets close."

He continued. "Now I'd like to talk about the embassy and the ambassador's residence. After the bugging at the residence, I'm convinced that there's a terrorist plot to either assassinate the ambassador or more likely to kidnap the ambassador, his wife, or even more likely his daughter. Accordingly, JJ, you need to see to the ambassador's protection, that it's in place appropriately. Also, you need to see to the security of the residence. And last but not least, by any means, they need to look to the protection of the wife and especially the daughter.

"Let's get our emergency location/rescue beacons on them. Let's be sure they understand and use them correctly, and let's get our response team on the ball with their coordination efforts with embassy security. Additionally, after talking with the colonel regarding the security at the embassy, I'm concerned that the security office in the embassy might be bugged."

"What makes you think that, Russ?"

"Well, I'm convinced the daughter is the target and that the security office in the embassy is the command post for all security assignments and action plans. The ambassador's office and conference room is regularly swept as is the security encryption area, but the general security office itself is not. Any response or action by security in the defense of a kidnapping of the ambassador or a family member is responded to by that security office. I want to sweep it personally, JJ, as soon as possible.

"Finally, I suspect the terrorists are likely to target the Colonia plant because that's Chuck's base and possibly in response to our actions of the other day in breaking up the extortion apparatus. It might have well been a side issue with the terrorists. So far, they've left it alone because two or more of their brothers were involved. Also, I suspect that the terrorist threat against that plant might well now move up on their action list. We've got two transportable temporary safe rooms ready to ship from Dallas. Does anyone see a need here for either or both?"

"Russ, I don't know what the safe room is."

"Well, JJ, it's an eight-by-ten-foot room made up of armored panels that can be put in place almost anywhere as a safe room that will house two to four people and withstand attack for a prolonged period. It could, for instance, be built up inside a room adjacent to an office as a sanctuary if attacked. My suggestion would be to place one inside the ambassador's home adjacent to a bedroom or his office there. Or in the case of the Colonia plant, I would place it in the conference room adjacent to Chuck's office. His house, as the embassy, already has a built-in safe room. JJ?"

"I don't know. This is a lot to swallow. Let me talk to security and to the ambassador first."

"Good, but don't take long. If we need it, we need it soon. Vic?"

"Well, let me talk to Chuck."

"OK but, again, soon. In each case, I think we can get it funded. But first, we'd have to make our case. I'll start that anyway through Max in Dallas this afternoon. I have to make them understand the threat."

Later that afternoon, Russ was on the encrypted phone with Max, in Dallas. "OK, Max, I think that's all. Do you agree with my assessment of the threats here regarding the ambassador's daughter and the Colonia plant?"

"Yes, Russ, I do emphatically. Let me hang up for now and talk with Bob and Marvin. I'll call you back ASAP. Get Vic, and don't go anywhere. Stay put and await my call back."

"OK, boss. Bye."

That night, Vic joined Russ in his quarters for a room service dinner. "Well, that's almost verbatim what I told him. He said he was going to talk to Bob and that we should stand by here and await their call back."

"Russ, I agree with everything you've said. At first, I was skeptical. But once I thought it out, I am in agreement. Say, Russ, you paused earlier when you were making alternative escape plans as though you had something else in mind. I don't think anyone else caught it, but I did. What's up?"

"Glad you brought that up. I think any one of the plans I outlined might work well, especially with the others creating a ruse. However, I have a real alternate in mind that would trump the bunch."

"Yeah? What's that?"

"Stand by and listen. I need to make another call."

Russ picked up his house phone and dialed a number from his little book. "Hello, *do you speak English?* Yes, good. May I speak with Senor Reitmann? . . . Si, gracias."

After a short wait, he said on the phone, "Senor Reitmann, this is Russ Talbot, an associate of Max Curtis of Dallas . . . you say Judge Santos told you I was in town? Good. I've got a problem I was hoping you might be able to help me with . . . thank you, sir. I appreciate that, and I'm sure that Max will as well. Would it be possible for me to meet with you later this evening or tomorrow morning? . . . Yes, this evening would be fine. However, I am awaiting a personal call from Max in Dallas now. May I call back and set a time with you when that is done? . . . Good, thank you, sir. I'll call you later. Again, thank you. Goodbye."

"Russ, who is this Reitmann?"

"Vic, you remember the judge mentioned he was a close friend of Max's and a member of the oligarchy?"

"Yes, I recall now that his name was mentioned. He owns a mountain?"

"Yes, he does, and I think his help will assure us of the perfect way to exit the country if things get bad."

Max and Bob were on an encrypted conference call with Russ and Vic. "Russ, is Vic there?"

"Yes, he is, on the speakerphone with me."

"Well, I've got Bob on a conference line here. Ready?"

"Yes. Yes, sir."

"OK, here it is. We are both in agreement with your assessment of the situation there. I spoke with Marvin, and he immediately authorized a safe room for the ambassador's residence. You need to carefully plan its placement to assure its usefulness to the three family members. Remember, it is seven thousand pounds, so it must have adequate support."

"Right, I understand."

"Marvin is informing JJ through their network. I expect JJ will contact you as soon as he gets that communiqué. As for the Colonia plant, we agree with that as well but have figured out an alternative to the safe room there. Of course, you'll have to discuss it with Chuck and examine the area to assure that it will work, but here's our idea. If you cut a hole in the front wall of Chuck's conference room to the outside and install a roll-up door, then Chuck could park his armored Jeep Wagoneer in that area, that is, a mobile armored safe room. It's immediately adjacent to his office and would be quickly accessible. Then if the outside fence across the roll-up door is modified to break away from the inside only, he would have the best of both worlds, the safety of a safe room and the mobility of his armored vehicle."

"Yes, yes, Max, I see. Additionally, we could make a slide-out portion of fence to cover the broken perimeter after he crashed out to resecure the area."

"Right, do you think that will work? He could just enter and leave the site normally but park his Jeep in the new mobile safe room area."

"Damn right, it will work."

"Good, Russ, this is Bob. Vic, do you understand as well?"

"You bet. It's a good, cost-effective solution."

"Right, and Marvin agrees that they will fund this whole venture, including the parts you've already cleared up. He's anxious to report all this up his chain. That is exactly what they intend our team to do in cases of this sort. It's right on the ball and fits well within the strategy they had in mind. He is tickled pink that our first venture is working out so well. Also, your escape plan looks good from here. Hope it's not necessary. What does the judge think?"

"He feels he can handle it but has reservations. That's why we came up with these alternatives. Speaking of which, I have another."

"Yes, the others sound feasible, but what's this one?"

"Well . . ." Russ explained his plan in detail.

"You're right, Russ. I'll call Mr. Reitmann tomorrow morning if I hear from you that you two have worked it out. Good plan. Bob?"

"Excellent plan, Russ and Vic. Vic, how are your wounds? Russ said they weren't serious."

"Right, Bob, although Russ likes the bandage on my head. He says it looks like I've got more hair. Ha ha! I'm fine, don't worry, no problem. If there's nothing else, we'll say goodbye until morning."

"OK, goodbye."

Russ called Senor Reitmann and set up a meeting in an hour. Russ and Vic motored over to the Reitmann estate. "Senor Reitmann, I am Russ Talbot, and this is Vic Visos, our credentials."

"Yes, Senor Russ, I remember you from a dinner we had downtown here with Max last year. Let me introduce my son, Jaime. Drinks?"

"Yes, I'd love a margarita."

"Vic?"

"Yes, I'll take the same."

After a few amenities, the drinks arrived. Of course, they had to explain Vic's head bandage and the exploits of the past couple of days. "In case things go wrong, we'll need a foolproof escape route. I've already set up the following." Russ explained the north, south, and west sea routes. "But I feel all these three need to be used as ruses. What can you suggest?"

"*No problemo*, senor. Here's what we can do for you." Senor Reitmann and his son, Jaime, pitching in, explained their plan.

"That's perfect. I'd hoped you might have something like that in mind."

"And here's how you can contact Jamie or me if the emergency arises."

"Thank you. We should not keep you any later."

"Senor Russ, it's not late. Have another drink. I've had snacks prepared to offset the effects of the alcohol. Sit back. Stay awhile, and let's discuss the state of the world and our solutions to its problems."

"Thank you. We will."

16

THE EMBASSY

"Good morning, JJ. I hope this is a good time to look over the security office. Is the lieutenant in?"

"Yes, he's expecting us. But the ambassador would like to see you first."

"OK, lead the way."

"Good morning, Ambassador."

"Good morning, Russ. Let me say with all gratitude that my family appreciates what you did for us the other day. These people somehow got through our security net and had us set up—and at home, of all places."

"Yes, Ambassador, and no thanks needed. I was just doing my job."

"I know, but still, our thanks."

"OK, but I'm sure JJ has explained to you the fact that I feel that the locals were targeting your daughter, if not all of you."

"Yes, and I'm anxious to know you're thinking on that. It seems unlikely to me. The State Department's security system says that, in Catholic countries, families are not targeted. Rather, I myself must have been the target."

"Yes, sir, I'm sure you have been targeted, but you are a hardened target. Your wife and especially your daughter are softer targets. The State Department security and threat analysis was correct a few years back but is way out of date today. The current terrorists might be ill equipped, but they are unusually well informed. They have no big guns but lots of small ones. And they obviously have bugging capabilities as well. This means their intent is serious. The simple fact that your daughter's room was bugged and your bedroom was not shows they were collecting data on her and most likely listening in, at least on her end, on all phone and cell phone calls originating there. I'm sure she talks to her friends in private from her room by both these means. That way, they would know her plans, maybe even in advance of your knowledge of them.

"Sir, I have forwarded my recommendation that we install a safe room in your residence in a manner that all of you have access to it. This morning, I received affirmation that I should do this forthwith. I understand that the State Department will communicate this to you ASAP."

"OK, Russ, if you think it prudent and it's authorized, you certainly have my approval. I'm sure my wife will approve. She's crazy after the shooting the other day."

"Thank you, sir. JJ and I will look over the house plan and go over our recommendations with you later today."

"Good. I'm sure to have the confirmation from the State Department by then."

"Thank you, sir. But one more thing, can we borrow your conference room to study the plans and to coordinate with your security?"

"Yes, of course. I have a meeting out of building in a few minutes. You can have it all day unless something urgent occurs."

"Again, thank you. We'll talk later, sir."

"Thanks again, Russ. You have my every confidence."

"Yes, sir."

Introducing himself while entering, "Sir, Lt. Michael Henry, embassy security, to see you."

"Yes, come right in, Lieutenant Henry. I'm sure you remember me from the other day at the trouble I must have caused you."

"Yes, sir, no trouble at all, sir."

"OK, Lieutenant, you can call me Russ. And if you don't mind, I'll call you Lieutenant. It'll save us all time and trouble. OK?"

"Fine, sir."

"Russ?"

"Fine."

"I asked to meet with you here for two reasons. First, I'm concerned over the fact that the sweep team hasn't given your office adequate attention, and it might be bugged. It's an obvious source of information that they would need if they decided to take any action against the embassy, the ambassador, or his family and residence. Second, I'm concerned that the local terrorists are planning to kidnap the ambassador's daughter based on our discoveries the other day. Taking her would put more pressure on the ambassador and this embassy than any other single person, including the ambassador. And if this is true, information directly from your office would be critical to their action plan. I wish to sweep your office myself without any advanced notice and without any hoopla. Will you cooperate?"

"Yes, Russ, I'll do anything you recommend."

"Well, I'd like to go sweep it right now. But I'll need your help. First, I'd like you to take all the people present in the office aside, one at a time, into the hall or back here and tell them what we'll be doing and that they are not to change their routine or comment that we are even there. Then stand by the door and stop and brief anyone who tries to enter similarly. JJ and I will do the sweep. It shouldn't take more than an hour. But it must be kept a secret to those outside your area."

"Done. Give me twenty minutes, and I'll have everyone briefed individually and outside the area. I'll come back and let you know when the area's ready for you."

"Thanks. In the meantime, JJ and I will be going over the ambassador's residence plans as regards the installation of a safe room there. I'd like your input on this, but we'll pick up on this after the sweep of your area."

"OK, I'm gone to brief my people."

"JJ, I know you are not familiar with the kind of safe room we have, but help me understand these plans, and I'll take you to view the safe room in Chuck's house. Here, let me take a moment and check that we can go to Chuck's and see it this afternoon." Russ called Chuck and got permission to view the safe room setup there in the afternoon. "Chuck says his wife will be there to show us around."

"OK, let's look at these plans."

The lieutenant returned and announced that he had briefed each of his people in private and that the room was ready to sweep now. He explained that the adjacent encryption room was already a safe room, an anechoic chamber where his encryption communication equipment resided, and that they cannot enter there.

"OK, JJ, same drill as the other day. I'll inspect the area and sweep it with my passive RF testers. You take the AC checker and check all the power sockets. If you find one fully used, signal the lieutenant, and he'll get you an opening by turning something off and freeing a socket. All wall sockets, OK?"

"I understand."

"Lieutenant?"

"I understand."

"OK, let's do it."

Russ visually inspected the entire area carefully, including closets, shelving units, light fixtures, switches, etc. He then took out his testers one at a time and carefully moved them over every wall, panel, etc. He signaled a couple of times to turn an equipment off. They were turned off and then back on as he suggested. The end result was no radio frequency transmitters active in the area at this time. He knew that if a sweep were evident or announced, it would become known outside the area, and any remote-controlled transmitter could have been turned off for the duration of his inspection. However, since his sweep was unannounced, it was unknown, and any such action would not have been taken.

Near the end of JJ's inspection of the power sockets in the area, he discovered a "hot" one. Russ said that he should inspect another socket almost directly across the room from the hot one, another hot one. Russ knew that, usually, at least two such bugs were placed across the room from one another so that a stereolike effect occurred, and audio not normally available to one input would more likely be available at the second. Also, two or more people talking to one another were typically facing in opposite directions, and lower-level voices not picked up by one mike would more likely be picked up by the other or maybe even enhanced by the stereo pickup effect.

Russ carefully unscrewed each of the two suspect electrical sockets and eyeballed the insides. They were identical to those that they had found at the ambassador's residence. He put them back in place and placed a simple radio noise source in the center of the room between the two.

After leaving the security area, Russ said, "The pickup has to be nearby. Let's look."

A few feet down the outside hallway in a marked and locked janitor's closet, they discovered a small box on the rear of the topmost shelf. Otherwise, the closet contained normal cleaning supplies, a map, and a bucket. Russ examined the box and its contents, careful not to disturb anything, and pointed out to the lieutenant the tape recorder and its tape status indicator. He stooped and picked a PIDRA detection unit out of his case, placed it out of sight behind and at the other end of the shelf containing the recorder, and activated it.

"Lieutenant, I just planted a detection unit that will suggest if anyone enters the closet. It will transmit a signal to this pager whenever detection is made. The pager red light will illuminate only when this detection is made. However, an internal vibrator will show the continued presence of anyone in the closet. It should first light up, and then the vibrator will come on and stay on as long as the intruder is present. If the vibration stops, it means that the intruder has left the closet and likely closed the door.

"Whoever set this up has it set for replacing tapes every week. It appeared to be more than halfway through the tape, so the likelihood is that the tape will be collected and replaced maybe this Friday afternoon, tomorrow late. You need to discreetly determine the cleaning schedule and stay away from the closet until there is an intruder.

"If the intruder is legitimate, that is, simply fetching cleaning supplies, you need to keep him under surveillance and investigate the closet to determine if the tape has been changed out. If so, it means the intruder has recovered the old tape and put in a fresh one. That's your man. Detain him, search him, and recover the tape. Hold him for interrogation, and let me know. You need to be careful not to alert a legitimate intruder to what is going on because he might indeed be our man but merely doing his normal job at the moment and not recovering and replacing a tape at that time. Savvy?"

"Yes, I understand, even with your Texas accent."

"That's not Texas, that's 'Merican with a capital 'M.' Lieutenant, if you cannot be in the building continuously, you must brief and assign another. We can't afford to lose this opportunity."

"I savvy, Russ."

Then JJ said, "OK, Russ, let me take you to lunch at one of my favorite spots, and then we can go up into Escalon and see Chuck's safe room."

"Great, JJ, where is this place?"

"You'll see. You like fish?"

"You bet."

After a short drive, "We're just about there. It's a motel and restaurant just above Lake Ilopango, just beyond the military air base."

"Oh, what's the specialty?

"I told you—fish. There's a beautiful view from their patio some five hundred feet above the lake. It looks down on the lake the fish come from. The lake is actually a dormant volcano that is full of water."

"Oh, freshwater fish?"

"Yep, don't know what kind, but they're great. Here we are."

After ordering and savoring their meal, "Well, they were great fried fish. I just never had really whole fish where their eyes stared back at you while you ate them. Also, they were very ugly."

"That didn't seem to slow you down any, Russ. You ate every scrap but left the heads."

"Yes, well, so did you. Saving them for dessert?"

"Not me. Now where to in Escalon?"

"Just take us up past Senor Pico's and the circle, and I'll steer you to the house."

Again, after only a ten minute drive, "Here we are."

"Where, this house?"

"No, the house behind this one. Go to the gate on the right of this house, and press the button below the speaker box."

Shortly after pressing the button, "Hola?"

"Hello, this is Russ. The Mrs. is expecting us."

"Si, Senor Russ, we've been expecting you. Drive through the gate as it opens, and stop in front of the second gate."

After the first gat opens they drive through, "Russ, this is something. We're trapped between these two twelve-foot walls with the gate closed behind us and another closed in front of us."

The second gate wouldn't open until the first closed. From a speaker by a video camera on the wall, they heard someone say, "Senors, will you both turn your heads toward the camera on the wall? Thank you. The gate will open momentarily." And it did.

"JJ, the garage door will not open until after this gate closes, but we don't want to be in there. Just park out front here under the alamo trees. Notice there's another set of gates like those we came in on the other side there. They work the same way, one at a time but in reverse order to let us out."

A guard approached from the guard shack integrated into the house and just outside the front door. "May I please see your IDs? Thank you. You may now present yourself at the front door."

Russ rang the bell and was answered immediately by Anita, Chuck's wife. "Hi, Russ."

"Hi, Anita. I've got JJ, the military attaché from the embassy, with me."

"OK, one moment. As you know, the outer door will let you into the vestibule, but you'll have to wait for the outer door to close before I can open the inner door."

"Sure, I remember."

"Hi, again, Russ."

On entering, "Hi, Anita. This is JJ from the embassy. I've brought him to see the safe room set up here. We'll be installing one in the ambassador's residence. And we'll be adding the ambassador, his wife and daughter, JJ, and his wife to our key personnel list here. When they're fully integrated, I've asked JJ to introduce you to them all, and I think a little get-together here might be appropriate to get you all acquainted."

"Good. I've met the ambassador and his wife but don't know them personally. Look forward to it. What's the reasoning for adding them to our list?"

"As you know, Key Personnel Protection is global but, in the past, only with Exlite. We've taken on a wider range of activities under the direction of the White House and are including States people where under threat."

"Lucky you, JJ. Our minds have been much easier knowing these guys are out there thinking about us and caring for us as they do. Seldom do we experience a problem that they haven't already thought about and built some kind of equipment or offered techniques to help us. On the rare occasion we bring up a new problem, they are very prompt in their response—and very gentlemanly, I might add."

"Whoa, Anita. Now you've gone too far. We try our best, but she's just appreciative."

"I am."

"OK, thanks for that, but now I'd like to show JJ the house and then the safe room and our approach to using it. Would you lead the way?"

"OK, JJ, I won't state the obvious. We'll look through the first level of the house that contains living room, study, dining room, kitchen, laundry, and prep area that contains our emergency supplies. We have a large outside patio half covered by the upstairs patio. There's a step-down lanai and then, a couple of levels lower, a swimming pool and pool house with changing rooms, two small bathrooms, and all the pool accessories behind the pool house proper. We'll just walk all this out. Of course, we're completely surrounded by that tall wall as you can see."

"I notice that you have a large emergency power generator outside the prep area."

"Yes, and our water supply, trucked to us every other week, is below that level in a cistern. The cistern is also equipped with a water softener that also purifies the water. The cistern is supplied through valves at an opening out on the street near where you entered the first gate. As backup, there is a separate pump that will allow filling the cistern from the swimming pool via the water softener or vice versa in an emergency."

"Very impressive."

"Thank you, but it's all because of them," she said, pointing out Russ. "They constructed this place just for us and for complete independent survival. You'll notice that the only access to the property other than the double-gate entranceways is from the cliff at the rear of the property. It's a good three-hundred-foot drop to the street below.

"Now let's go upstairs, our living quarters with five bedrooms. At the top of the stairs is a door with a simplex lock. It allows us security and quick access but closes automatically to deter anyone from following or chasing us. Here we are in an upstairs den or lanai as it opens onto the upstairs patio. Beautiful view, isn't it? Four bedrooms with two baths adjacent are to the right through simplex locked doors. Our master bedroom is to the left through a simplex locked door. Again, security yet quick access.

"And again, the door automatically closes behind us. Notice that the bed is between two doors. The door on the left is my walk-through closet and dressing area into the bath. The one on the right is Chuck's walk-through closet and dressing area into the bath. Notice the strap from the ceiling on Chuck's side of the bed. Were we chased upstairs, the idea is that the upstairs door would delay an intruder as would the door to our bedroom. We would round the bed quickly and pull this strap, which pulls down a set of stairs that lead into the attic as a distraction. Then we would quickly step into Chuck's closet and dressing area, closing the door behind us, and push his clothes aside, and a small simplex locked door is exposed. See?

"Now for my favorite part, we quickly slide down the fireman's pole into a hidden room below, back on the first floor. Careful, we do this weekly just to keep in practice, but this is your first time."

They all slid down the pole individually. "Notice this area we landed in is just a vestibule with an open safe room door. We enter the safe room and slam its door shut. The safe room is armor plated to Level IV+. I'm told that means it will withstand close-up hits from any rifle, that is, .30-06, Kalashnikov, etc.

"Now step in, and let's close the door. Note the slight sound of the exhaust fans. Incoming and outgoing air vents are hidden in the construction of a portion of the walls outside. Here's the security system with video and audio throughout the house and grounds with gate controls and tear gas releases at our fingertips. Also, we've got complete communications through our repeater system as well as ham gear to contact the States. There are supplies enough to keep us and a very few others for a week. The house itself has supplies that will keep twenty or so for a month.

"Well, that's it except for how to get out of here. Actually, that's quite easy. We open the safe room door. Unlatch several latches on the wall, and a bookcase slides out in our downstairs den. When we exit, the bookcase slides back into position, the inside latches reengage, and the safe room area is once again hidden. Any questions?"

"Yes, how do I get a pass to be a guest if things go bad? Ha ha!"

"Well, you'll have to ask Russ here. They control all that through Chuck."

"Anita, you've been a good hostess again. Can we get a drink and spend a few more minutes with you before we go? Maybe you have some questions for JJ regarding the embassy, its staff, or your needs locally or have anything you'd like to bring up with me."

"I'd love that, nothing for you, Russ, but JJ. I'd like to ask how we can set up a little get-together. Here, let's go in the den. Russ, you fix the drinks. You remember where everything is?"

"Yes, unless one of you has a preference, I'll fix something light."

"Anything."

"Yes, anything."

"Anita, I'll set you up with my wife, and she'll involve the ambassador's wife."

"JJ, I'll invite them over for a morning swim and light lunch. That'll get us introduced and time to discuss our mutual interests. We'll take it from there."

"Well, my name is actually John Jones, therefore JJ, but my wife's name is Janet, so she's JJ too."

"Oh, what a hoot. I look forward to hearing from her. Please have her phone as soon as possible."

"I will. And thank you for your hospitality. I look forward to seeing you again."

They said their farewells and exited the compound much the same as they entered, except through the exit portal on the other side of the courtyard. "JJ, drive me to the hotel, please. I need to write a report on how things are going and talk back to Dallas as well. And please let me know the minute you hear anything from Lieutenant Henry."

"Will do. Anything you need from me?"

"No, I think not, JJ."

"Oh yes, Russ, I meant to ask you. How can I get some of these gadgets you've trotted out, like the sweep stuff?"

"I'll see that you get a full kit of our special gadgets, JJ."

"Good. If necessary, I can make a request through channels. I need to make a report and talk back to DC anyway."

"No, not necessary. I think it is better they not know all our tricks just yet. But I trust you, and I see that you actually need PIDRA and a few other items. Don't worry, I'll get permission and get them to you before I leave here."

"Thanks, Russ, thanks a lot. Even though I'm the military attaché and station chief, I get very little in the way of support items."

"Well, JJ, we have trouble on the other side of the coin. From time to time, we cannot get a weapon that we need. Maybe you can help me with that sometime."

"Say, Russ, that little mighty mite of yours is one of the things I want. It looks like something we must have originally developed but don't have."

"Your people did originally develop it for a European operation, I'm told, but we added the Hg and Teflon touches. Again, don't worry, I'll get you at least one. By the way, what will you do with the weapons we collected from the two gardeners?"

"Well, we'll photograph them, print them, and dispose of them. Why?"

"I think the colonel could use them if you could get them for him. His people inside and outside our plant have a terrible time getting weapons for defense. I'm sure he'll try to get the one back that was used against us at the plant the other day, if he can."

"OK, I'll see what I can do. Maybe the lieutenant can help the colonel out with something out of his stockpile."

"I'd appreciate you're looking into it for the colonel. And by the way, I think it would be a good idea for you, in your station chief hat, to develop a relationship with him. He is a government insider. He can't get much in the way of support from them, but he gets a lot of insider intelligence."

"Thanks. I'll do it. Please speak to him in my behalf. He is a great contact."

"Will do."

After a ten minute drive to the hotel, "Well, here's the hotel. Talk to you tomorrow, JJ."

After freshening up, Russ called Max in Dallas on his encrypted phone. "Well, Max, it's as I suspected. We found two bugs in the security office of the embassy. We left them intact and undisturbed. We tracked down the recording spot, a box on a shelf in a nearby hallway janitor's closet. I left it tagged with a PIDRA unit and the pager in the hands of the security officer, Marine Lieutenant Henry. He's appropriately briefed as are his people. It appears that the tape is due to be changed out sometime late tomorrow. They'll contact me as soon as the culprit is in hand.

"I showed JJ Chuck's safe room setup, and we'll determine the right placement for the one needed to be sent down to the ambassador's residence. Do you have an ETA on it yet?"

"No, Russ, not yet. It's ready to go, but there's been a quibbling over whether it should go by plane or boat."

"Shit, Max, it needs to be here ASAP, not on a slow boat to China."

"I know, Russ, just a bit of politics. It takes a special plane. Marvin is arranging for one out of Houston tomorrow late morning. It's on a truck to Houston now."

"Oh, good. Thanks. For a minute there, you had me going. I've impressed on the ambassador and JJ how important it is for Sally's safety. It's important that the ambassador hears that through official channels as well."

"Good. I'm sure that Marvin has already arranged for that notification. He's sure to have gotten it today."

"Excellent. If the safe room comes out of Houston mid-day tomorrow, it will be here by late afternoon. Maybe we can get it placed over the weekend. Not sure what the construction problems will be on the residence, but I'll tweak the ambassador in the morning, first thing."

"Anything else, Russ?"

"Yes, JJ is asking for a few goodies, a Mini-mite, a PIDRA set, and some of our small sweep gear."

"OK, he can have Vic's Mini-mite and PIDRA when you leave, and you can leave him some of your sweep items. I'll see that they're funded. OK?"

"Right. That's it."

"OK, but keep me informed on what you get out of the surveillance of the embassy security office bug."

"Will do. Bye."

Russ called JJ. "Hello?"

"JJ, Russ here. I just talked with Max, and he OK'd leaving you items as we leave here, and he says the residence safe room is en route to Houston today. It will leave there about noon tomorrow and arrive here by late afternoon. You need to get your construction people together, and you and I need to meet first thing in the morning to plan its installation. OK?"

"You bet. That's fast. You guys must have some connections."

"We do, your guys. Better tell the ambassador that his house is going to get torn up in a hurry. I'll work on it tonight. See you first thing in the morning."

"Good. See you then. Bye."

Russ stopped by Vic's room. "Vic, I hope you talked to Chuck about fixing up his conference room for his armored car."

"I did. And we've already got the construction people working on it—well, not working on it actually but working on the layout plan and materials."

"Good. The residence safe room is arriving tomorrow late afternoon. I'll be working on that plan with JJ at the embassy tomorrow. We both need to expedite these things if we can."

"Right, you take the residence, and I'll handle the plant. But we each need to have a backup, a foreman, in case we have to jump and run."

"Great, we're of one mind. I think we'll need to have at least one between us—one mind, that is."

"Ha ha! You're right about that. You haven't heard anything from the judge, have you?"

"No, and no news is good news."

"OK then, anything else? How about a drink?"

"I could go for about two margaritas. How about you?"

"Yes. Here or downstairs?"

"Let's go downstairs by the pool, stare at the stars, and down a couple."

"Let's go."

17

TWO SAFE ROOMS

Russ went at the embassy early the next day. "Good morning, JJ. Anything out of the lieutenant?"

"No, but I'd bet on late this afternoon, just about or after the normal quitting time."

"Right, I hope so. Have you talked to the ambassador?"

"Yes, I called him last night. He got his orders from DC and is in agreement. His wife is alerted and expects us this morning."

"Well, JJ, I went over the diagrams last night, and I think I see how we can do this about like Chuck's house. If we usurp a little room out of the back of both the master bedroom's double walk-in closet and a little out of Sally's walk-in closet, they're back to back. We can make room for the escape hatch and fireman's pole there for the ambassador and his wife and Sally. If I'm seeing straight on these plans, that would put the fireman's pole near the back side of that very large den downstairs. We can chop that den down in size by about a third by putting in bookcases, and the safe room can be fitted there. We need to add a stout door with a simplex lock at the top of the stairs. We need to stiffen up the two-bedroom doors and add simplex locks. We need to overlay the windows in both bedrooms with those metal shutters like you use at the embassy. And we need a little construction in the rear of the two back-to-back bedroom walk-in closets with a fire pole and floor hatch. Then downstairs, we need to make a bookcase wall to partition off that oversized den and make one of the bookcases latch and movable. Insert and build up the safe room with communication gear, and that's it."

"OK, Russ, that looks good to me. This list you've made up is an adequate guide for me. I can get this done, in case you are called elsewhere. By the way, anything from the judge?"

"No, nothing. But it's only been a little over a day. We'll see. Let's get to the residence and look it over with the Mrs. and see if it works."

"No, Russ, you go ahead. I'll work out of my office to get a couple of work crews started in your direction. I'll follow you about lunchtime. You'll be ready to take a break by then."

"OK, I'm gone. Call if you need me. Check on Lieutenant Henry."

"Will do. Bye for now."

Russ proceeded to the residence in his little VW, and JJ got on the phone with another Fredrico (foreman of the embassy construction group.

"Well, Fredrico, I'll need you to see to the construction work we've just gone over for the modifications here at the plant. Give me your estimate of how you'll go about it."

"OK, Vic. First, I'll get a crew of about three to tear the hole in the conference room wall in the next few hours. We have a spare electrical roll-up door in our warehouse. I think we can get it installed late today. I'll have the teardown crew lay a small cement ramp from ground level to the floor level of the room. It's only about an eight-inch rise. I'll have them lay two short wheel ways the six feet to this drive that circles the plant. That will all be dry and usable by tomorrow morning. Then I'll have the grounds crew overlay the new drive with decorative blocks and generally decorate the area so that it doesn't stand out. Tomorrow morning, the paint crew will paint the new roll door to match the decor we work out. On the inside, I'll have the construction crew fit the office to the conference room door with a simplex lock and finish out the area around the new doorway. We'll install a switch to open and close the roll door and fit it with a remote control that Chuck can operate from inside his Jeep whenever arriving or departing.

"I have a special fence crew that I'll call in to make over the existing fence just across the new roll-up door into a breakaway from the inside but not from the outside. Again, I'll have two wheel way concrete ramps the ten feet from the driveway to the fence. It'll be overlaid and decorated to disguise its potential use as a quickie exit. Also, I'll have the fence guys design a slide-into-place fence to cover the exit, if it is ever used, to quickly resecure the site. I think we can get all this done by Monday morning. If you say so, I'll justify extra overtime and keep them on it 24/7."

"Yes, do it 24/7. I'll brief Chuck and get that authorized. The quicker, the better. If it could get done before the Monday morning shift at eight, then a minimum number of people would even be aware of the work. The less awareness, the more successful the venture. OK?"

"Done. Please excuse me. I've got a priority job to do. Let me get to it."

"Thanks, Fredrico. You need me, call. I'll plan to be here on the site most of the day."

Then at the residence, Russ met with the ambassador's wife. "Well, Mrs. Wilkins, that's about it. What do you think?"

"Very good. I like it. It makes me feel safer already."

"It's no panacea, but if it seems good to you, I'd like to authorize JJ to get started right away."

"Done. By the way, I heard from Janet Jones, JJ's wife. She has set up a swim and lunch for us tomorrow with Anita. She said you arranged it."

"Right, I want you to become acquainted and even friends, if possible. I'll talk to her and tell her we'll be installing a safe room here similar to hers there. I think she will be glad to show you theirs and how it works. That way, you'll get a better feel and understanding for it while we're busy tearing up your house."

"Russ, do you think you can act that quickly?"

"Yes, we'll move heaven and earth if necessary, but I want the work done ASAP. We'll have the crews working 24/7 but try to knock it off during your sleep time. The actual safe room will be here this late afternoon and brought out here this evening. I expect the whole thing to take no longer than a few days. But there might be a little touch-up paint and others to finish after that, not sure yet."

"Boy, you guys move fast, nothing like the State Department."

"Yes, we want to get most of it done this weekend to keep it less obvious. That's all I have. May I use the conference room awhile? JJ said he will show up at about noon to go to lunch. Would you like to join us?"

"My, no. I've tons of things to do, and the morning is almost gone. Make yourself at home. JJ knows the ins and outs and has complete access. You just get to it. And thanks for making our security your priority."

"You bet. That's my job. Oh, yes, has the ambassador talked to you about my speculation that your daughter has been targeted?"

"Yes, and that scares me to death. I've been thinking about sending her back to the States to her grandmother for a while until this blows over. What do you think? How long will it be before this blows over?"

"Don't know. Can't advise you, but remember, it's only my speculation. There's no proof yet."

"Do you expect proof?"

"Well, I'm not sure, but we have an operation ongoing that is likely to tell us something this evening. I hope."

"Well, please keep me informed. Our daughter is our most precious possession, and I wouldn't want to risk her."

"I understand and will keep you advised. If the proof appears, I'll let you know and even help you make whatever arrangements you need. What about yourself? My speculation could as likely be about your safety."

"I'll stay with my husband unless ordered out by the State Department. But if Sally leaves, I'd likely go with her to get her settled and then return."

"OK, good to know your druthers. See you later."

Enter JJ, "JJ, you snuck up on me."

"Well, I can see you were engrossed in what you were doing. What is it?"

"Well, Julie approved our plan. And I've made some measurements and laid out a list of actions that need to be taken to facilitate the prompt installation and construction work."

"Good, Russ, because I've thought it through as well and made up a list of things that can be done in parallel. My thought is work 24/7 and get it done."

"Yes, JJ, but there needs to be an eight-hour sleep break for the family in their personal area."

"You're right. Say, Russ, let's go to lunch and discuss all this. I expect work crews here in about an hour and a half. There's a lot that can be done before we assemble the safe room. Hopefully, it will be here at the residence sometime tonight."

"Great, you'll make a good foreman."

"No, but I've got a real construction man who will be. I'll just point my finger and fill in the gaps."

"Good enough. I'm at your disposal on this until we hear from the lieutenant."

"I talked to him, and nothing has happened so far. One of the maintenance men accessed the janitor's closet but just to retrieve the mop and bucket to clean up a spill. The lieutenant reset the PIDRA after he returned them. Now it's just a waiting game again. He agrees with you. He thinks it'll come around quitting time or maybe a little after. Since it is Friday, everyone likes to take off right on time to get in a full weekend. So quitting time is at four thirty. Maybe by five."

"To lunch. How about Senor Pico's?"

"Too hot at mid-day."

"I know, let's go to the Sheraton. They have a great lunch. It's not far away."

"Sounds good to me."

In his hotel room, Russ called Fernando, who was at the lobby door. "Has the colonel discussed a possible getaway plan with you?"

"Si, Senor Russ, he has. Do you need me to implement it?"

"No but maybe later. When you get a moment, come by my room and pick up the keys to the VW and get yourself a copy made. That way, you will be able to implement on a moment's notice, even if I'm not actually available. You understand that you might just be called on to make a solo trip as a ruse to distract others from my actual route."

"Si, senor, I'll be right up."

"Thanks. See you in a few minutes."

Knock, knock. "Yes, who is it?"

"It is Fernando, senor."

"Good, just a second . . . thanks for coming. Here are keys to both our VWs. Get copies made pronto, and get them back to me as soon as you can. And here's a little something for you."

"Thank you, Senor Russ, but it is not necessary. You know I'm always glad to help you and Senor Max."

"Yes, thank you. But if something comes up, maybe what little time I have will be to give you a call. One of us—Vic, the colonel, or myself—might give you the go-ahead. Or maybe nothing will happen at all. In any case, it's a sizable tip well earned in either case."

"Si, Senor Russ, it is sizable, too much. But thank you. Anytime you need my help."

"Yes, well, you remember JJ from the embassy?"

"Yes, he has eaten with you several times."

"Well, from time to time, he might need your services or a little intelligence. OK with you?"

"Si, senor, I'm at his disposal."

"Good, thank you. You're a big help, and we seldom get time to thank you appropriately. I'll see to that as soon as I get a little time."

"No need, senor. Goodbye."

Russ returned to the report he was typing on his laptop computer. The phone rang. "Hello. Yes, Judge Santos, this is Russ."

"Russ, I'm just checking in with you. I have nothing to report, but I am concerned with the reactions that the prosecutor is getting to his reports. If it ever reaches the top, I'm sure there'll be no problem. But there are parties in his chain and adjacent that are not reputable. They might be the ones causing him some concern. You should have a plan, just in case."

"I do, Judge, in fact, several, just in case. You have my cell number. If anything comes up, do not hesitate to contact me so that Vic and I can take the appropriate actions."

"Right, I'll do that. However, I do not expect anything to happen until Monday. No matter what, I'll call you Monday around noon, my lunchtime. We can make another judgment then."

"Thank you, sir. I really appreciate your help. Goodbye."

Later, Russ called JJ to check on his progress. "Russ, you wouldn't believe it. These guys who always are on siesta are actually responding. I stressed the importance and offered them a little extra including a 24/7 incentive and maybe a bonus. That did it. They're here. They've divided into teams. One team has torn out the back of both closets and are now building in the little escape hatches in both. They've also cut a hole in the floor and have just brought in a pole for the escape. The second team is building the bookcases. They'll be put in place permanently after the safe room arrives and is built up. They've a very clever plan for opening one of the bookcases into the den to get out of the safe room area. It will latch into place much as Chuck's does. Finally, I just got a buzz from the military airport, not the commercial one, that they have just received a large shipment for me or you. So I've dispatched a pickup for it."

"Remember, the damn thing weighs three and a half tons, JJ."

"Yes, I remembered, and the flattop dispatched has a very heavy-duty forklift attached. They'll be able to get it."

"OK, JJ, give me a call when it arrives, and I'll come right over and show you how to unpack it. It comes with special tools to transport the sections and hold them in place and a small lift to handle the ceiling."

"Will do. I expect it will take about an hour and a half at least to get it cleared, aboard the truck, and here. Then they'll take it down and bring it as close as possible. We plan to use the open space beside the big patio doors just outside the den."

"Right, just let me know when you get it, and I'll be right there."

"OK, see you then. Bye."

Russ called Vic to check his progress. "Hi, Russ. The teams here are moving like crazy. The wall's cut as I told you before. Now the electric door is installed and works well. The inside team has fixed the tie door between the new area and Chuck's office, and they're finishing out the inside of the new roll-up door. They still have to wire in the switches, but they've already tested it with a bypass. The grounds crew has already laid the entry ramp cement and runners to the drive around. Additionally, they laid the runners to the fence. They'll be good and dry by morning, and they'll pick up all the frames then and work on the landscaping. The fencing crew showed up and worked out a way to make the fence break away from the inside but not from the outside. They'll be back in the morning with the necessary pieces to actually make it happen. At that time, they'll also install a replacement piece of fence that can slide into place if the breakaway is ever used. All the landscaping is lying about in piles, and it looks like we could be through with all this shortly after noon tomorrow."

"Amazing, how did you get them to work so fast?"

"A little incentive. I bumped their pay up and promised a bonus if they finished tomorrow, and they will."

"Well, you wouldn't believe it, Vic, but the same is true with the project at the ambassador's residence."

"Great, any news from the judge?"

The pager on Russ's belt activated. "Whoops, hold on a second, Vic. My car PIDRA just went off."

Russ went to the window and peered down at the parking lot, where he had purposely parked his VW where he can see it. He saw Fernando sitting in the car, starting it up, shutting it down, getting out, relocking it, and coming toward the building. "No problem, just Fernando trying out the new key I had him make for the VW so that he'd have one if needed for the northern deception run. I had him make an extra key for your VW as well for the colonel and his deception run."

"Good idea, Russ. Does he know your actual?"

"No, but it's not important for him to know that detail. The judge said no action by anyone yet. But hold your breath, there appears to be a problem brewing aside the chain of command of the prosecutor. Maybe nothing to it. But the judge said that he didn't think anything would happen before noon Monday and promised me a call then. Otherwise, he'll call in case anything comes up."

"Right. No news is good news at this point. Call if you need me. I'll be going to the residence in the next hour or so. The safe room has arrived."

"Great. You call if you need me."

"Will do. Bye."

Knock, knock. "Yes, who's there?"

"It's Fernando, Senor Russ."

"Back already?"

"Si, here is your key. I tried the new key in your car before I came up. It works."

"Good. Thanks again. Bye."

"Bye, senor."

Russ's phone rang. "Hello, this is Russ."

"JJ here. The safe room is loaded and on its way. It will be here about the same time as you, if you leave now."

"OK, I'm on the way."

Russ pulled into the driveway at the ambassador's residence just as the forklift is pulling the safe room down off the truck. "Just in time, Russ."

"Good, where are you planning on putting the package down?"

"Over here, just next to the patio. I'm afraid the patio wouldn't stand the weight."

"That's a given. Good plan. "OK, first, you need to take the two large planks loose at the top edge of the package. They are the only parts that are not used. Then disconnect the several panels that make up the remainder of the top of the package, and remove the entire contents. Just line it all up along the lawn or the patio.

"Next, locate the flooring panels and the bolts and nuts. All panels are marked A B, C, etc., and interconnected by flanges with these bolts inside the room. These two items are used to help you carry the panels into place. Just take the floor panels into the den and place them side by side where you want them located.

"Next, locate the adapter joints and the wall panels. Four of them are different. There's the door panel, two window and gun port panels, and one utility panel. Locate the room adjacent and up against two walls. The remaining space will be the vestibule or entry area. Obviously, the door panel and two window panels go in this area because the other walls will be against the existing walls. The utility panel needs to go in the least accessible area, generally near the rear corner. So take a wall panel, carry it into place, and bolt it using this hold-up rod, one to an end midpanel and one to a floor panel. This rod will be removed and reattached to the new panel as each new panel is secured in place.

"OK, when you've gotten the rear corner panels in place with support rods, take in the utility panel. Before putting it in place, string the electricity, telephone, and water lines through the baffles in the utility panel. Then carefully attach the other ends of these utilities and raise and secure the utility panel in place, again supported by a support rod until the next panel is attached. Now put up the remainder of the wall panels, saving the door panel for last."

Russ's phone rang. "Hello, Russ here. Yes, Lieutenant, glad to hear from you. What's up?"

"Russ, we caught the outside help, part of the janitorial service, when he went into the closet to change out the tape. He's here in my office singing like a bird. We tried to get him to hold off until you could get here but no dice. He's scared to death that we're going to kill him. He heard that you killed the two at the ambassador's residence and just knows we're going to kill him too. Of course, we're not, but it doesn't hurt that he thinks we are. He's giving up names. We've got a professional interrogator on him now, but if you want in, you need to come right away."

"Lieutenant, it sounds like you are doing quite well without me. Find out everything you can from him before you include the Salvadoran government guys. You will eventually turn him over to their intelligence service?"

"Yes but not as long as he's performing. We're recording everything and have a stenographer in there as well. The plan is to let him sing his song as long as it lasts and then after a break to actually interrogate him. That way, we'll have the ability to review what all he's already said and to make sense of it, go back, and fill in the blanks."

"Good job, Lieutenant. You need to inform DC, and I'll tell JJ. He's here with me. He might decide to get involved, but I'm staying here. Please put aside a copy of the tapes and steno info for me. Oh, and, Lieutenant, you need to remove the two bugs we found and send them to the Camino marked for me. If it's not too much trouble, include the bugging stuff from the ambassador's house. Thanks, and good work. Bye."

Russ quickly related to JJ what the lieutenant said about catching and interrogating the janitor at the embassy. "Great news. I'll leave you to it here, Russ, and go join in and get the State Department and CIA informed on the preliminary results. See you later."

Russ returned to the work area. "OK, guys, now that you have all the wall panels secured in place, you can bring in the carpeted plywood floor to place over the floor joists."

That done, "well, that was the easiest step so far. Now set up this small lift to help with the ceiling panels. There is the air tank that powers this lift. That's it, attach the crossed feet and the crossed holder on top. Next, bring in the ceiling panels one by one, set them each symmetrically on the lift, and use it to hoist them into place. Bolt them in securely to the wall panels. And just keep going until done."

"Looks good, but you need to go back and add any missing bolts and tighten each and every bolt to secure the entire room. That'll take a while."

JJ returned later that night. Russ continued instructing the crew. "OK, all done. Notice the door has no lock from the outside but has the throw bar that throws bolts into the ceiling and wall panels to secure the door from the inside. It's actually lever activated so that it won't accidentally fall into place and lock you out.

"Next, bring in and assemble the bunks. The air mattresses go on them. Bring in the fold-up table and chairs. Set the porta potty in a corner with the necessary items. Notice it works like a diaper genie. It takes each flush into a long plastic bag and forms it like the links in a sausage. It's airproof and odor proof. Place the folding privacy screen across in front of this area. Set up the small bookcase, and attach the rotating fan. String up the electrical. Set up the batteries, lamps, etc. The first aid kit goes over here on a hook, and the shooter's earplugs go in little bags just below the sliding armored gun ports.

"Last, string this air tube with nose pieces from beneath the bunks up and around the bunks to the pillow portion of the air mattress. When through, place the air tank used to hoist the ceiling below the bunk, and attach it to this tubing. This will allow occupants critical air for a period should there be a fire in the house. If some gas is used, there are gas masks in this kit beside the first aid kit. And if there is a fire that reaches this area, there is a sprinkler system atop the safe room that is activated by this switch on the bookcase. This will also keep the room cool. You need to pipe in water to the electrical control valve at the top back corner.

"This room is impenetrable to small arms or rifle fire to beyond Level IV. But in case attacked, the gun ports allow retuning fire without risk to keep any attacker at bay. And the lift should be placed below the bunk as well. It can be used to force the door open if it is blocked from the outside either by the attackers or by debris left by a fire."

On inspection, "OK, everything is in place. It looks good. You understand everything, JJ?"

"Yes, it was actually quite simple, but it has gotten to be well after midnight. I think we can release these guys until morning."

"Right."

"What about the bookcase wall, JJ?"

"I've already informed those guys that they need to be here at 8:00 a.m. to put it in place. The finish out upstairs will happen at the same time. Once it is all in place, you and I should brief the ambassador's family, walking through all the issues with them."

"OK, let's go get some shut-eye. What time do you want me here, JJ?"

"Up to you, but if you want to sleep late, do so. I'll be here early. Why don't you plan to be here at about ten?"

"OK, will do. I think I'll go early to inspect the plant improvements and be here at about ten. Need me before that, just call."

"Will do, good night."

"Good night. Good job, well done."

Next morning at eight thirty, Vic and Russ arrived at the Colonia plant at the same time. "It looks just like the rest of the plant. Good job."

"Let's go in and walk it out, Russ."

"OK, lead the way."

And, just inside and around the corner, "OK, here we are in Chuck's office. That door with the simplex lock is to the new safety room, the old conference room, which will actually garage Chuck's armored car when he is in the plant. Notice the door automatically shuts behind us."

"Good."

"Here's the door switch." Vic checked with the crew outside, and they were clear. He activated the door switch, and it quickly, smoothly, and quietly rolled up. Vic picked up the remote control, and they stepped outside. He activated the remote, and the door rolled down into place. Standing in what appeared to be a garden area, they inspected the new landscaping and were barely able to spot the two tread paths that led to the double drive that surrounded the plant. Crossing the drive, they inspected a similar setting that hid the tread ways to the fence. They inspected the fence and saw how it would break away when assaulted from the inside by the armored car but stand fast should it be assaulted from the outside.

The fencing personnel were busy attaching a roller fence to cover the breakaway section. They would be through in less than an hour. "Russ, I'm going to stay until they are finished. I'll call Chuck once they're through to come out and run his Jeep through the course to assure that he is able to easily perform the maneuvers necessary. You noticed the suspended tennis ball in the room?"

"Yes, I assume it is to tell him when he is in position to close the door."

"Right, good eye. Russ, I know you are anxious to get to the ambassador's residence to inspect the progress there. It's almost ten. Go. I'll call once Chuck has finished his rounds."

"OK, thanks, see you later then."

Russ departed the Colonia plant and went to the ambassador's residence. "Hi, JJ. How's it going?"

"Unbelievably well. They just completed the upstairs finish-out painting and also the bookcase wall. It works smooth as silk. I'm ready to walk the ambassador and family through it all. Please go with us and fill in any blanks I miss."

"OK, glad to."

The Ambassador enters, "Good morning, Ambassador. How was your night?"

"Well, it could have been better, JJ, but some damn woodpecker kept me awake until after midnight."

"Sorry, but we got it done."

"No problem. The wife and daughter slept well, and that's all that counts. I often don't go to sleep until late. Are you through already?"

"Yep, I'd like to walk you all through it."

"OK, give me a few minutes. I'll gather them up. They're both anxious to get their clothes back in place in the back part of their closets. When can they?"

"After lunch should be all right. The paint and lacquer will all be touch dry by then."

"OK, that's good news. You'd think, with all the clothes they have, they wouldn't be so anxious about the few things that had to be taken out."

"OK, JJ and Russ, we're all yours."

"I'd like to walk you all through the whole thing as though you were being suddenly attacked but just in slow motion. I'll try to keep the narrative short, but a lot of it is necessary to be sure you each fully understand what's involved. OK? Russ had done all this before, and he's going to go along to make sure I don't miss anything."

"It's your show, JJ."

"Fine, first, let's assume it's daytime. Where are each of you most likely to be?"

"If I'm here, I'd likely be in my office," said the ambassador.

"I'd likely be in the kitchen or my little office off the kitchen," said his wife.

"I'd be in either my room or the pool," said Sally.

"OK, if the alarm sounds, it might be sounded by any one of you or a servant. Or if obvious gunfire or a clear break-in occurs, each of you should immediately run upstairs, abandoning absolutely everything, and access your individual living areas through the new simplex locked doors at the top of the stairs. Go through either or both of your rooms through the simplex on those doors. OK, Sally, you go through your room, and your mom and dad will go through theirs. Meet you at the little common area through the back of your closets."

They each proceeded upstairs and into their individual closets as instructed. Russ accompanied Sally, and JJ accompanied the ambassador and his wife. Each was instructed that inside each closet was a small door behind some clothes that can be moved aside. Again, all these doors—the one at the top of the stairs leading to each private area, the ones into each of their private areas, and the door in the closet—were controlled by simplex locks with the same code, which they might change from time to time, and would automatically close behind them to hopefully add more and more time, or distance, between them and any intruders.

The ambassador was instructed to pull the strap hanging from the ceiling at the foot of his bed. "Stairs into the attic automatically drop down to suggest that you have fled in that direction as a ruse. As you enter the little door in the closet, duck. Don't hit your head. Each of your doors enters this same small area. Promptly slide down the pole here, like a fireman."

"Fine, JJ, but what's this pull-down door into the attic for again?"

"It's just a ruse, a misdirection, to catch the eye of anyone chasing you and misdirect them to climbing the stairs and at least looking into the attic for you. It hopefully gives you more getaway time. OK, everyone, down the pole. Russ and I will follow you, so step aside when you reach the bottom."

"Good, now enter the safe room, and the last one in slams the door shut and activates the locking mechanism. Here, each of you, try that so that you are accustomed to the weight and energy it requires to close and lock the door."

"OK, everyone's in. Good, now here's the theory of the safe room." JJ carefully and thoroughly explained all the aspects of the safe room and the various possibilities available to them. "Any questions? Anything I failed to cover, Russ?"

"Nope, perfect job, JJ. You've got communications in here to call the embassy for help. We've put in video cables, and over the next week, the audio-video guys from the embassy will install cameras all over your residence and even outside. At your option, you can address anyone near these cameras. Being able to see what's going on is important. You can report developments within the residence that your rescuers might not be aware of. I hope you understand about the gas masks, air tubes, and the emergency lift that enables you to exit should the door get jammed from the outside."

"Perfectly done, guys, how can we thank you?"

"Well, let's take the last step. How do you get out? Pop the safe room door, and let's go into the vestibule."

"OK, over here is the back of the bookcase wall. Pull these latches, and this last bookcase releases and rotates outward into the den. You can exit this way. Now simply push the bookcase back into place, and it will relatch automatically. Hear the clicks. It's latched. From this side, there's no indication of a false wall and exit.

"There's no way to open the bookcase wall from this side. You must enter from your closets above. If something in the safe room area needs maintenance, you can block the bookcase open for that purpose. Otherwise, never prop it open. It will become a habit and shouldn't. Never show your safe room to others, unless they have a similar setup, like Chuck's residence. Any questions?"

"No, none."

"You're good to go, Ambassador. Any questions or problems that JJ can't answer or handle, you have Max's number in Dallas. And should you have to use the safe room and feel uncomfortable about your rescue, call us in Dallas. We're only just over three hours away. If necessary, because of an unusual situation, call, and we'll send our response team.

But likely between JJ and the colonel from our El Salvador operation, you'll have all the help you need or want. Well, we're through here. God bless and protect this house and those who live here. Let's go, JJ."

They called Vic, who was en route, and rerouted him to the hotel. They all went there and agreed to have a very big congratulatory drink, lunch, and more drinks. The remainder of Sunday was uneventful except for three slightly tipsy patrons who went to bed early to make up for the nights before.

18

THE SHIT HITS THE FAN

At nine on Monday morning, Russ's phone rang. "Hello, Russ speaking."

"This is Judge Santos. Good morning. Bad news, the government is, at this moment, putting out an arrest warrant on you and Vic. They are not including JJ. They will send a message to the embassy regarding him. Two bad guys we've identified in the Defense Ministry are responsible. We can contain them and even prove they are a part of the FARC, but it will take us a few days. We can reverse this, but again, it will take some time. In the meantime, you and Vic are at risk. You need to immediately implement an escape plan. Keep me informed so that I know if I need to intervene in your behalf, but it would be better if you could leave the country until we can get rid of these two and undo their warrants."

"How long do we have?"

"Unknown, but I'd bet that they will serve you within the next hour and a half. Good luck. I'll let you get on with it."

Russ called Vic down to his room urgently. "What's up, Russ?"

"We've got to implement an escape plan. Wait, here's Chuck on the line now. Listen while I explain to him. It'll save time. Then go pack and hurry. We've an hour at best."

"Well, that's it, Chuck. Please phone JJ at the embassy and explain to him. We might need him, but I don't want to involve him unless necessary. Thanks and goodbye. I've no time."

"Good luck to you two. Call if I can help. Goodbye."

"I'm gone to pack up. Back in a minute or two, Russ."

Russ hurriedly packed. It was an easy job since, except for his toiletries, he lived out of his suitcase. He called Fernando. "Fernando, I need you to implement the northern escape plan. But first, I need you to recover laundry for both Vic and me. And I need you to take us to the Sheraton in the VW before you set out for the north. OK?"

"You bet. I'll be up with your laundry in two minutes and have your little VW near the side door."

Less than two minutes later, Knock, knock. "Who's there?"

"It's Vic."

"OK, come in."

"Russ, we have laundry downstairs somewhere."

"Yes, I know. Fernando will be here any minute with it. He's taking you and me to the Sheraton before filling up and starting on his long trip north."

"Excellent. Here, I'll open my rolling suitcase beside yours on the bed, and we can just put our laundry in, zip up, and be gone."

"Vic, you let him in when he knocks and identifies himself. Put the laundry away and zip up. I'll be right behind you two on the phone as we go."

Russ dialed the colonel. "Colonel, this is Russ. The judge called, and the government has issued a warrant for Vic and me. We're leaving. Will you pick up Vic's car and run the southern getaway ruse route for us? The key will be at the desk in an envelope with your name. You know the car?"

"Yes, Russ, what else can I do?"

"Nothing for now, Colonel. Fernando is taking us to the Sheraton and then running the northern route. They're both ruses, but they won't know that until they track *you* two down. That'll give us time to run the real route. Thanks. Must go. Bye."

"Will do. Call if you need me. Godspeed."

"Will do and thanks."

Fernando had shown up during the conversation; he and Vic packed away the laundry and proceeded out the door. Russ was hot behind them. "All aboard?"

"Yes, let's go."

In five minutes, "I'll drop you at the Sheraton side door. Here. Now I'll scoot to the gas station, fill up, and be on my way. I've got a good cover story figured out for when they eventually stop me. Also, I've got one of my boys at the hotel watching for the *policia* or whomever they send. He'll call me as soon as they get there, and I'll call you so that you'll be able to gauge your head start. Goodbye, my friends. *Vaya con Dios*."

They sought a quiet place, and Russ called Senor Reitmann. "Senor, Russ here. The cat's out of the bag, as we say, and the government has a warrant out on Vic and me. I need to activate the dual escape plan we went over. Is that possible to do immediately?"

"Si, Senor Russ. My son is here for the noon meal. Where are you?"

"We're at the Sheraton to stay a jump ahead of the *policia*."

"OK, my son, Jaime, will pick you up at the Sheraton side door in five minutes. Be ready, OK?"

"We'll be ready. Goodbye."

Right on time, "Senor Russ, it's me, Jaime, and I'm here to get you."

"We're ready to go."

"My father has set up the first phase of the plan. Two men similar to you two will be seen in an hour or so at the pier on the ocean renting a small boat and setting out to sea. A larger boat flying a USA flag will pick them up just outside the three-mile limit. Our limit is actually twelve miles, but it is well known that the USA only recognizes a three-mile limit. They will then head directly out to sea. Eventually, if and when they are stopped, the men will very simply be seeking big game fish.

"I'll take you first to my father's house. He wants to apologize for our government and give you a few things of sustenance for your trip. Then we'll go up the mountain to my plane. From there, we will fly below radar through the mountains north to Belize. I understand you can make arrangements from there."

"Yes, thank you. What time do you expect to land in Belize?"

"It's a short flight, but my little plane is slow. But the flight time will be about two and a half hours. So, say, three and a half hours from now. It's ten thirty now. That makes our ETA at about two, if Dad doesn't keep us too long. He's hurrying up lunch, hoping that you two will eat with us."

"Well, I don't know how good our head start is, but your estimate should do the trick. We don't want to be ungrateful, but we will have to just eat and run, if it's ready."

"Oh, it'll be ready. Here we are now. Hi, Dad, I've got them."

"Come in. Sit down. Eat. I've got you an extra lunch packed in case you get delayed anywhere along the line. You will keep me informed of your progress? I'll keep my ear to the ground or toward Judge Santos. Go ahead, eat . . . eat."

Russ and Vic ate heartily since they had had no breakfast. They departed to the plane, a Cessna. "Well, there she is, a little plane, but I'm quite good at flying it in the mountains. There'll be no trouble."

"How much fuel do you carry?"

"Enough for a six-hour flight. I'm full, but I'll likely refill anyway before coming back. Ready to go. It's noon now, so we'll be there at about two thirty."

Russ called Max in Dallas and had a Learjet dispatched to pick them up in Belize. The Lear would arrive in Belize at about three. They can turn around instantly without refueling.

As they took off in the Cessna, Russ's phone rang. It was Fernando. He told them that his man at the Camino had just reported to him that the *policia* had just arrived with their warrants and were busy searching the premises for the two of them. He projected that it would take them thirty minutes or so to determine that they had fled the coup and then another hour to send out an alarm for the VW rent cars.

"It looks good. With a little luck, we'll be in Belize before they actually start the search for our cars, Vic."

"Phone Dad and let him know."

"Let's get a little distance behind us before we speculate on our complete safety."

"Sure, you're right."

About 30 minutes later, "Russ, we're clear of El Salvador's airspace. We're actually in Belize. We'll be landing in about thirty minutes."

"Good. When we land, I'll call your dad."

"Thanks."

"When will the Lear be in Belize to pick us up?" asked Vic.

"About three. We'll have about a thirty-minute layover."

"Fine, I could use a little more sustenance."

"Vic, don't forget the lunch Dad packed for you."

"Oh, yes, either of you care for some? Russ?"

"I'll take a sandwich or whatever and a piece of fruit."

"Jaime?"

"Same for me. Please unwrap it for me."

Barely two hours had passed and, "Done. This all looks as good as it did at your dad's houses. And it tastes even better. I think my adrenaline was so high I couldn't really appreciate anything until we got into a safe zone."

"There's the strip. We're there."

"That was a really good landing, Jamie. I notice you didn't file a flight plan and only just contacted the strip before we landed. Is that usual?"

"Not really unusual down here. I never file a flight plan in El Salvador. I usually fly below their radar anyway, and if ever challenged by radio, I just tell them my tail numbers. They're used to me flying about. Other than commercial flights and military flights, there is very little private activity other than me. They're used to me, Russ."

"Will you have any trouble going back?"

"No, I'll just return the same way we came. They cannot see anything when you fly low in the mountains. And they can't even monitor my little field up in the mountain on our finca. They'll never know I left or returned."

"So you are going to turn around and go right back."

"Yes, if you feel safe in Belize."

"Sure, we've only a half hour layover before the Lear arrives. You need to get back before dark. I know there are no landing lights in El Salvador."

"Oh, yes, I have landing lights at my little field. I'll just call ahead and have them turned on if it gets dark. It's the commercial airport that doesn't turn on their lights. They have them but don't use them."

"Well, so long, Jaime. We really appreciate your help and your dad's hospitality. I'll call him and tell him we've arrived and that you are on the way back. Do you need fuel?"

"No. Don't forget your things. I'll drop you just outside that little building over there that is used for privates. Then I'll just turn and taxi back to the takeoff lane. See ya. And good luck. Let us hear from you."

"Will do. And again, thanks. And wind at your back."

When they stopped beside the private flight building, Russ opened his door and dropped to the ground. Vic handed down their bags and followed suit. They walked away and turned just as Jaime gunned his engine, turned, and made for the access strip and then for takeoff.

As they entered the building, they were approached by an official and told how to officially enter the country. A golf cart took them to the main terminal and the immigration entrance. They entered and were escorted down the line and to an immigration official. "Good day, senors. What is the purpose of your visit?"

"Just a stopover," said Vic. "We'll be waiting on an arriving Lear from the States to carry us home in less than an hour. You should have their arrival flight plan. I'm sorry, but is it appropriate to tip? We've not come in this way before and know we are putting you out some."

"Si, senor, tips are acceptable."

Russ offered him a generous tip in U.S. dollars, and the attendant was impressed and seemed to hurry things along. They showed their passports and were quickly cleared with no mention of their not checking out through El Salvador immigration. After a quick and faultless customs clearance, they were directed to a transition waiting lounge and were told the Lear had filed a flight plan and was en route and that they would be transferred back to the private flight building just as soon as the Lear was cleared for landing. The ETA was three forty-five.

Russ dialed up Senor Reitmann and got right through. He reported on their eventless trip to Belize and the fact that Jaime was already on the way home and would need the runway lights. Russ thanked the senor profusely and received the same in return.

"Vic, how about a Coke? We've only got about a half hour."

"You bet. The clerk said they would come and get us when the Lear was cleared for landing."

"Good, I'm going to rest my eyes then."

"Me too."

At three forty, an airline clerk woke Russ and Vic and told them that the cart was waiting to take them to the private flight operations center; the Lear had just been cleared for landing. They jumped up, grabbed their bags, and went directly to the door and the cart. They could see the Lear land and taxi just ahead of them to the private terminal. As they got there, the Lear's hatch opened, the stairs were let down, and the pilot descended. Russ and Vic both knew him, Vic Anderson. Then immediately behind him came Max, Bob, and Marvin.

"Hi, guys. We came to rescue you two." They shook hands and hugged all around.

Bob said, "Boy, it's sure good to see you, guys. Vic, how's the head?"

"Oh, it's ok. I just took a glancing blow. It just looks bad with the bandage. It's really healing quite well."

"Hell," said Max, "I think it makes him look like he has more hair than he had."

"Yeah, and who are you to talk?" said Russ. "It's really great of you three to come down and meet us. You want to go in the terminal and have a drink?"

"No, the pilot said he would get us a little fuel. It feels good to just stand out here. Let's walk around a bit, and we can get our legs back. Three hours in the Lear, you know. And besides, you two need to begin to tell us about your recent exploits. Who did who, who do we owe, and how much?"

"Yes," Bob said, "and what is our status in El Salvador? Is Exlite in jeopardy? Come on, just start telling us everything."

"First," said Russ, "we need to introduce Marvin to Vic."

"Oh, sorry. Vic, this is Marvin L., DDCI. It's OK to say that, isn't it, Marvin?"

"Yes, just so Vic signs a nondisclosure and security agreement."

They decided to keep the debriefing until back on board and merely chat about the status of things back home while they walked about until the fueling was completed.

Back on board, "OK", Vic said, "I'll start, and you jump in, Russ, if I get offtrack or forget something important. And then you tell your part, and I'll jump in if required." Vic meticulously reviewed his entire visit in El Salvador. "Well, that's about it for me. OK, Russ, now it's your turn."

"Thanks, Vic. I hope I do as good a job as you did telling my part of the story. Here goes." Russ then reviewed his entire visit in El Salvador. "Well, that's it for the both of us. Let's cover questions next, and then we'll speculate on the terrorist problem. You first, Max."

"What's going to happen with respect to the warrants out on you two, Russ?"

"I think in a week or two between the colonel, Senor Reitmann, and Judge Santos, they'll spook out the bad guys in the government. In fact, they already know who they are. And then they'll get rid of them and make the warrants and whatever else is involved go away. Bob?"

"What about the impact on Exlite?"

"I think that'll go away as well. But there's still the terrorist threat to deal with. Marvin?"

"What about the impact on the embassy and its people?"

"I think that all this is terrorist related somehow. But for the moment, I think the embassy is safe, and the ambassador and his family feel quite secure."

"OK, guys. Now let's switch to the terrorist question. Russ?"

"First, both safe rooms are in place as we all decided. There were a few finishing touches, all paint related, when we got sidelined, but I'm sure they're all done now. Now the terrorist question, I think the FMLN or FARN, their subsidiary, is behind all this." FMLN is Labor Front Organization and FARN is Armed Forces of National Resistance, which are Salvadoran political parties.

"Very likely, there are actual members or even leaders inside our Salvadoran Exlite operations who would be very hard to identify. But I think we are as well off with them inside because Exlite is not, in any way, raping the country or its resources. Essentially, Exlite is just using the population to perform higher-class technical jobs. These jobs are above the level they normally work at. Exlite trains the people for a higher-class job than they can do otherwise at a fair pay without subjecting them to the asinine apprentice program that other local employers do. These others pay half wages to apprentices for up to two years and then fire them. We pay full wages and promote the worthy. We have almost no turnover. People on the inside know that, and that's a powerful weapon. Accordingly, they don't shut our plants down because when they do, all they are doing is hurting their own people, our employees, and themselves. We're really the good guy in this. On the other hand, the government is the bad guy because they allow this disingenuous apprentice program and for all the other obvious reasons. So the government and other industries are the main targets of the terrorists.

"I know Exlite gets a little hit or shut down for a day or two from time to time, but others are shut down for extensive periods. We just get a little of their action. I'm not saying that we should let down our guard and invite the terrorists in, but the few we can't find are most probably beneficial to us. They can't completely hold sway over the FARN or whomever, but they have a certain amount of control because of their self-interest.

"The embassy is, of course, associated with the government and is a likely target as the U.S. always is in such a discourse. We can't help that. It is best that Exlite dissociate itself from the embassy where they can, but they must be associated with it as a U.S. company. This works both ways for and against Exlite as the tide ebbs and flows in the terrorist movement."

"That's all very esoteric, Russ, but well said. The real question is, what, if anything, can or should we do in the face of these most recent events?"

"I think we've done all that can be done for now. Security at the plant and at the embassy is tightened, and the safe rooms emphasize the riskier areas. However, one point that we have been out of the loop on is the interrogation of the guy at the embassy who was changing out tapes where they listened in on events in the security office of the embassy. The lieutenant said that he was singing like a bird, and I assume that some good info was obtained regarding the terrorist and their plans. Additionally, the intelligence gained might indeed lead not only to other participants but also to their overall philosophy. Too much speculation on my part, but I'm an optimist."

The pilot called back that Dallas was in sight and that they would be landing in the next few minutes. "Get prepared, seat belts, etc."

Marvin said, "Very worthwhile trip. I'm off to DC almost immediately. I'll deplane and get a meal with you guys, if you don't mind, and then Vic says he'll take me to DC."

19

HOME SWEET HOME

Max called a meeting of key staff and disclosed the pertinent things from Russ's trip to El Salvador. He congratulated Russ and then proceeded to show him around the campus to view the improvements made during his absence. "Here in the old administration building, we've set up our staff headquarters, meeting rooms, etc. Barry has seen to the refurbishments, air-conditioning, heating, etc., as well. So almost anything you see as an improvement, tell him how much you appreciate it."

"Will do, boss."

"Now downstairs is the security setup that includes all the campus video monitoring and communications equipment. You most probably didn't notice it, but Barry and I cleverly worked in antennas for just about everything in the fairly ornate roof structure. When you get a chance, look closely, and you'll see why I say 'cleverly worked in.' They really don't show to a casual observer, and from as far away as the fence line, they don't show at all.

"Russ, your office is located in the field team headquarters. We're initially going to have three designated field teams. You will head up team 1, Matt will head up team 2, and a newcomer, Dave Ferrell, will head up team 3. Of course, team 1 gets the first assignment, team 2 the second, and so forth. But for the time being, team 3 will be the home team, man headquarters, and respond to the needs of either or both the other teams as they are in the field. In this manner, team 3 will get training through their direct responses to the others and benefit from the rest of us until I decide they are adequately trained. Then they will be integrated fully and take rotating field assignments with you, two others with your others sharing the home team assignment based on the rotation. Also, when we get enough additional sites in place, we'll set up a training and maintenance team to see to the various sites like we do in EAS."

"OK that sounds good to me, boss. I hope they get up to speed fast so that we get lots of R & R. Speaking of which, my wife wants me to take a little R & R right now."

"OK, Russ, take a week, but come back ready. Marvin has training assignments set up for the three team leaders. You're to train your groups when you get back. I don't currently know how long the training is to be. Marvin will give me the details while you're out. Take your phone. Don't expect a problem, but you can never tell. It's almost lunch. Have lunch with the guys in the new cafeteria, and take a quick tour of the rest of the place. See your office. Then get on home."

"Thanks, boss. See ya."

"See ya."

Russ departed Max's office as Barry came in. "Hi, Barry. What's up?"

"Oh, just the regular. I could use a phone call from you or Bob to the swimming pool contractor. He's slow as Moses. In fact, his name is Mose. Please get him on the ball."

"Will do. Give his name and number to Kathy, and have her get him on the phone for me."

"Thanks, boss, that's all."

Kathy reported that the contractor was out to lunch. Max told her that he was going to lunch and to get the contractor on the phone for him as soon as he was back. The cafeteria food was good. He hoped it kept up that way.

"Max?"

"Yes." About an hour later, "Mose, on line 3."

"Thanks, Kathy."

"Hello, Mr. Mose?"

"Yes, this is Mose, no mister, please. It makes me feel old."

"Well, Mose, this is Max Curtis of KPP Systems Inc. You're supposed to be refurbishing a pool for us?"

"Yes, sir, we are."

"Well, I understand there's some kind of holdup."

"No, sir, not a holdup. That's what you do at a bank. This is just a delay. Ha ha!"

"Well, Mose, what's the problem?"

"There are a couple of pumps that are in short supply that we need, and they are just now ordered and will be shipped from the Northeast tomorrow."

"How long before we get them, Mose?"

"About ten days. They're to be shipped UPS ground, and that takes a while."

"Why not by air?"

"Well, our contract says—"

"Mose, I don't give a damn what the contract says. You put everything on a priority basis and get those pumps air-shipped today for your receipt tomorrow morning and installation tomorrow afternoon. I'll pay the express charges."

"Yes, sir, sorry. I didn't know."

"Well, you do now. Anything else you need, just call, and I'll authorize it, including overtime for your crew. But be assured we'll audit you and put you in the slammer if you screw us. We can be good customers and bad enemies. Savvy?"

"Yes, sir, I savvy. Glad to meet you and know the ground rules. Everything is now priority on any project from you guys."

"Thanks. Glad to meet a man who understands how to do business. Any problems, let me know."

"Yes, sir, you're the boss."

Turning to Kathy Max asked, "Kathy, get me Barry."

"OK, hold on . . . here he is."

"Barry, I've just gotten off the phone with Mose. He's all 'yes, sir' and 'no, sir' and 'it'll be done, sir.' If he doesn't get the pumps installed tomorrow, let me know."

"Will do, boss, and thanks."

"You bet. You need it. You got it."

Next day, late afternoon, Barry was back. "What's up, Barry?"

"They got the pumps, they're in, and the pool is being filled. It had already been sterilized and new filters put in. They're diamond quartz sands out of Australia, top of the line. They back-flush automatically at about 1:00 a.m. when needed, and I feel really good about them. You should be able to swim as early as late tomorrow afternoon. It takes a while to fill it and assure a complete flush through the filters. Thanks for the help with the contractor."

"He just didn't understand and needed a little push."

"Well, it worked. He's as friendly as anything, and I think you should call him and thank him for his haste."

"Will do. Thanks for reminding me. Anything else?"

"No, not now. We should go over everything on the list in the next couple of days, and you should do a walk-through inspection of everything done. I can give you a list, as we go, of people to send thank-you notes to."

"Good, Barry. That'll keep them on our side, and I'll stress how much we appreciate their efforts for us. We might need the goodwill when we need them for maintenance or other chores again. Say, why not do the walk-through tomorrow? I'll give you the whole day if you need it."

"That's good for me. I'll prepare a list tonight and see you at seven for breakfast in the cafeteria. We could start there."

"Right, but make it eight, OK?"

"Eight it is. See you then."

"Right, see you then."

Max marked his to-do list appropriately. Next morning at eight sharp, Max turned up at the cafeteria, sniffing. "Boy, something sure smells good. Hi, Barry. Did you tell them the boss was coming and they made a special effort?"

"Nope. It always smells good in here. They do an excellent job."

"Well, bring me up to speed. Tell me all about our special chow hall. Who are the cooks and others?"

"First, let me say that we're preparing and serving three meals a day with a cook and two helpers. The new guy you hired, Dave, team leader 3—the cook is his wife, Lisa. You remember her from when you hired Dave. She was a chef up in New York, not at a big place but a small one. Well, it turns out she was totally burned out on being a chef in New York. She loves to cook and all but hated the rush of it all. She was delighted to get out of New York and didn't want a full-time job, but she wanted to do something. This worked out perfectly for her and for us. We're a small group. She can handle us easily, so I hired her. A couple of the other staff's wives wanted to help out also, so I hired them as her helpers."

"But, Barry, what about special occasions?"

"Hell, Max, you won't believe this gal. She can handle anything. She already had me pull a couple of things out of the kitchen and add a half dozen more. In no time, she's got the kitchen running like clockwork. The three women all get along well, and they do all the shopping. In fact, she has the suppliers all standing in line and saluting her. In short order, she had them cutting their prices and taking her to pick out those special things she needs. She's been magic."

"Can we afford all this?"

"I think so. I've got a budget here she made out for us, including their salaries. They're all part time. Also, she's suggested we do some special meals. Here, you look at the list."

M/W/F—full staff

>Breakfast, $3.50 (7:00–8:00 a.m.)—eggs or waffles, meat, toast, fruit, drink
>Lunch, $6.50 (11:00 a.m.–1:00 p.m.)—meat, veggies, salad or soup, drink
>Supper, $5.50 (5:00–6:00 p.m.)—special dinner, according to weather
>(poolside, patio, or fireside)

Tu/Th—alternating, 1 helper only

>Breakfast, $1.50 (7:00–8:00 a.m.)—sausage or egg biscuits w/ gravy, drink
>Lunch, $2.50 (11:00 a.m.–1:00 p.m.)—wrapped sandwiches, fruit, drink
>Supper, $5.00 (5:00–6:00 p.m.)—wrapped sandwiches, fruit, drink
>Sandwiches—ham, turkey, and chicken salad
>Fruit—as available
>Drinks—coffee, tea, soft/fruit drinks

Friday

>Supper—cocktails

Specials

>Summer: cold sandwiches or meat salads

>   Spring/fall: roasted sandwiches
>   Winter: chili, Mexican, etc.

Scheduling

>   Monday breakfast—for inviting vendors
>   Wednesday luncheon—for inviting Exlite people and others

"What about Saturdays and Sundays?"

"We haven't worked that out yet, but at this point, we don't need it."

"I understand, but I plan to have people stay over with us, and that counts weekends. See what she thinks. Maybe we have stuff catered in then."

After reviewing the info given, "Damn, Barry, she's a magician. I think it's important that we have this service. And even if we have to supplement the budget a bit, that's OK. Of course, I met Lisa at the time we hired Dave, but I haven't had any time with her since then. Please invite Lisa and the other two wives, her helpers, to our next staff meeting so that they can be properly introduced and so I can congratulate them for their excellent start and addition to our staff and our campus life."

"Will do. That's just a week away."

"Right, I'll add it to my agenda. OK, let's see the kitchen and your new additions. Then what's next?"

"Well, I would never have thought that two steam kettles and two convection ovens would cover that much cooking. But as you say, both these types of items prepare food in half the normal time. Obviously, the addition of that large double commercial icebox and double commercial freezer will keep our supplies so that they will last longer. And the addition of the pantry was well done."

"Barry, you've done an excellent job here. We now have the facility to feed people continuously. That's exactly what I had in mind. Again, what's next?"

"Well, Max, I think we should look over the quarters and see if that's as well done."

"Everything is complete or nearly so. There were a few things wanting a couple of days ago when I checked, just a few items that had been ordered and either not yet received or waiting for some construction to be finished or paint to dry. The old dormitories are just next door."

Then after walking over and entering the dormitory, "OK, Max, this is the first floor. We're in the entrance area, and adjacent is the downstairs 'family room.' It's a living room with couches, chairs, a large flat-screen TV on the wall, etc. It's a community room for the whole building. On the other side of the hall, there is a reading room and library. And adjacent to that is a room with two washers, two dryers, a tabled folding area with hanging rods, and an ironing area with two boards and irons.

"The rest of the downstairs is divided up into three full apartments. We'll just stop in the first one. They're all alike. Here, they each have a den, full kitchen, and two bedrooms, each with a bath. Each has its own entrance from the outside. There is an apartment on either side of the long central hallway, with the third apartment running transverse of the other two. The central hallway allows access between apartments and to the community area. We've only just completed the outfitting of the first apartment. I thought it might be a good idea for your wife, Gina, and possibly some other wives to join in on the bedspreads, drapes, and decorative effects. They likely can think of some of the little things we're missing, like toasters, cleaning tools, etc. They can help with this same stuff on all three floors, including the game and family rooms.

"On the second floor"—they climbed the stairs—"we've divided this up into ten motel-like large equal-sized rooms. They each have two king-size beds and the necessary accoutrements, including small fridge, cable TV, and Internet access. There is a full-size bath in each. And each bath has its own instant water heater. There's a hall down the full length of the building and stairways at each end. Additionally, there's a large game room at this end. Again, we've only outfitted the first room for your approval before we continue."

They proceeded to the third floor. "This floor is the dormitory floor. There are two large dormitory rooms with baths and showers at the far ends of each. The idea is that if we had a gang of people staying over, the females would be in one dorm and the males in the other. Again, we've only outfitted it with a couple of bunk beds and chests. With your approval and the help of the decorating ladies, we'll finish it out.

"In all, we could accommodate three families, five couples with a child or two, and thirty-two or more singles according to how it's appointed. That's a total of about sixty people, way more than is likely but, in an absolute emergency, even more."

"Barry, that's great. I approve of all I've seen, and tonight I'll ask Gina to pick a few other ladies to help with the decorations. She'll contact you directly and schedule the others to help ASAP. I'd like this all completed soon.

"Of course, I'm familiar with the improvements in the HQ building and am most impressed with the security setup, camera coverage, etc. Security is a most important thing, but I want our families to have access so that they can enjoy the appropriate facilities. It will mean a lot to keep them involved and contributing, as they can, when our teams are in the field. Again, the key areas they cannot visit are the security area, the training and equipment area, and the gun range. However, if some of the family members want or need gun training, we can arrange for that.

"I've already seen and experienced the gym and the pool. You'll need to work with the three team leaders to outfit the training and equipment area. But I would like to inspect and understand the operation of the supply zone and its gating system. That could be a vulnerable spot. Our front entrance/exit is well done."

"Well, Max, the supply gate is operated just the same as the entry. It's just larger but just as safe. Let's go look over the area."

"Barry, I'm very pleased with the job you have done. We need to finish up with the missing items as quickly as you can motivate the women with their decorative efforts. Oh yes, you might get them to look over our admin area as well. How much is all this costing?"

"I don't have a total yet, with the missing items still unknown, but I'd estimate that, when we are through, we'll have spent about $2 to $3 million."

"Wow! We better get back to earning some money. I'm sure that's all in our budget, but it's still a lot of money. Be sure to keep Rick in the picture. His is the big job of budgeting and accounting for it."

"I know, but we had a lot of renovation to do."

"Yes, I know, no complaints. Keep on keeping on. And thanks again. Keep me informed, and let's work out the kinks. Barry, for your information, Russ and Vic did an outstanding job in El Salvador. Marvin just informed me that they are going to cover the whole operation, including that involved with the Exlite plant. The plant threat was exactly the kind of thing they want us to work on. The embassy situation was just a bonus. It's not over down there yet. We've yet to see the opposition response to the setback we dealt them. As you know, we make a nominal profit on all our operations for Marvin, so we've been earning all along."

Max returned to his office. "Kathy, get me Marvin on the phone."

"OK, boss . . . here he is."

"Hello, Marvin?"

"Yes, Max, how can I help you?"

"I got your note that you were going to cover all the El Salvador operations under your budget, and I just called to say thanks."

"No, thank you. That's exactly what we have in mind for you. Of course, the embassy situation was more important to the State Department, but the Exlite plant situation was our charter. So good job, and that's straight from the director. Anything else?"

"Yes, one thing, do you have any good contacts with Cessna? I need to return a favor."

"Yes, what do you have in mind?"

"Well, you know that Jaime Reitmann—we call him Junior—and his little Cessna was our perfect escape route. And although he wouldn't admit it, it was at some risk. We didn't even pay for the fuel. Of course, his dad can afford it but nevertheless."

"Yes, I understand. What do you have in mind?"

"I don't know if it's possible, but is there an engine retrofit or something to give him more power or some ability for shorter takeoff and landings and more fuel capacity or range?"

"Max, I know just the thing. Cessna built a kit for just that purpose for us a while back. Let me call my contact, and I'll get back to you if it's possible with his plane. Do you know the specifics?"

"No, but I wrote down his tail number, and I'm sure that's how Cessna keeps up with them. Here, it's CX142."

"Good, either I or Jack Sevell from Cessna will get back with you. He's their ops manager."

"Thanks, Marvin. I hope we can afford it."

"Don't worry, if he can do it, I'll authorize it out of our budget, a thank-you to Senor Reitmann from a friend."

"That would be wonderful. Thanks, Marvin. Bye."

20

HOME AND CAMPUS ISSUES

The next day, Kathy called, "Max?"

"Yes, Kathy."

"Marvin's on 1."

"Thanks, Kathy."

"Hello, Marvin?"

"I've phoned to tell you I've got your team leader training set up. How many?"

"Well, I've formed three teams. Russ Talbot, Matt Smith, and Dave Ferrell are the team leaders. Dave is new. You haven't met him yet. But he comes with good credentials and a sound reference. I'll keep him as the home team guy following up on all the needs of the other two until he is ready to be fielded. I still need to flesh out his team, but that'll come in the next few months."

"OK, that sounds good to me. You'll be able to field two teams and still have one in reserve."

"Right."

"Good. Things are looking pretty scary out there, and I think we'll need all that help before long. But it's good to get the team leaders trained ASAP. Sure you can spare them all at once?"

"Who knows? For now, yes."

"Well, I've got them set up. First, they'll take bomb school training at the Point, where you took it. Then they'll take the FBI course on small arms at Quantico, just as you did. Finally, they'll take a hurry-up course in self-defense at the academy in Quantico. We're shoehorning them in with a graduating class of ours. We do that from time to time. The FBI's not crazy about it, but they're cooperative. You said you'd like to take that as well. Think you're up to it?"

"Hope so. How long will all this take?"

"The bomb school is just three days. The small arms school is a week. And the self-defense course is a week as well. It contains some conditioning stuff as well. That's the part that everyone hates but needs the most. I've scheduled these in sequence, so it'll all happen in three weeks' time. They start next week. Can you get them here?"

"Yes. Russ is out on R & R this week but will be back next week. They've all got a ton of work to do around here, but I think this takes priority."

"OK, Max, I'll e-mail you the schedules and the barracks assignments, and I'll be out of it."

"Thanks. I'll see that they're there on time and ready to go. Thanks a million. In fact, speaking of millions, Barry just gave me a rough estimate of $2 to $3 million for the campus fix up. I don't know who pays what, but I'll send it upstairs here and then to you with and for suggestions."

"Good. Of course, money is important, but don't spare it for your real needs."

"I won't, and you should plan to stay here when you're in town. We've fixed up the dorm very nicely."

"Look forward to it. Anxious to see what you've done with the place. Your descriptions sound very good. A girls' school campus, huh? Are there bidets?"

"Well, I guess if you need one, I could see about putting one in."

"Ha ha! No thanks. See you soon, sport."

"OK, see ya. Bye."

Buzzing her, "Kathy, get Matt and Dave up here for me."

"Will do, boss."

In just a few minutes, "Max, Matt and Dave are here."

"Show them in."

"Hi, guys. First, Dave, let me say that today I took an inspection tour of the campus and was very impressed with the job your wife has done in organizing and getting our cafeteria service up and running. Please tell her for me job well done. I'm very pleased. I'm anxious for our first all-campus and all-employee get-together. It's not planned yet, but I'd like to plan it as soon as possible. However, that's likely to be a month or more away, depending on our completion and work schedule. I got your schedules for training in the DC area today from Marvin. Classes start next Monday morning.

"Matt, will you see if Kathy or you can get Russ and pass the word to him? You'll need to ready his kit for him, Matt. I don't know if he's in town or not. Hold on . . . Kathy."

"Yes."

"Is Russ in town?"

"Don't know. I'll see if I can find him."

"Thanks . . . OK, guys. I'll join you for the self-defense training the last week. I've already taken the other courses. Keep your eyes and ears open for anything that might make our jobs easier. And any acquaintance you might strike up could be very helpful in the future. You're to be tagged onto a graduating class of newbies from the CIA. See Kathy for your travel details. She'll help you with flights, money, etc. Any questions?"

"Max, is all this really necessary?"

"You bet, Matt. You never know what might be in store for you in the field. You know that."

"Yes, but—"

"No buts."

"OK, boss."

"Check in with me Friday. I'd like to know how you're doing in equipping the teams. And, Dave, how are you doing looking for new team members? Maybe I can pick up some slack for you when you're training. Remember, soak it all in, but don't give anything away."

"OK, boss."

"You bet, boss."

Then interrupted by his secretary, "Yes, Kathy."

"Marvin, on 1."

"Hello, Marvin, what's up?"

"Things are heating up in both Italy and Argentina. This is just a heads-up. I know you have equipment in both places. It might be needed, or we might need you to expand to help our embassies out in both cases."

"OK, anything definite?"

"No, just a heads-up for planning purposes."

"Thanks. Anything else, Marvin?"

"No, that's it. Bye."

After buzzing her, "Kathy, get Win Manske for me."

"OK, hold on . . . here he is, line 1."

"Win, can you come down here a minute with inventory figures? I need to see what we have on hand that we can use in Italy and Argentina."

"Will do. It'll take about fifteen minutes to pull the latest stuff up."

"OK, see you then."

About twenty minutes later, "Hey, boss."

"Hi, Win. Have you got your data?"

"Yep, right here on this gigabyte chip. Let me set it up on your computer here, and we can project anything you want on the screen."

"Good. I just got a heads-up from Marvin, and it looks like trouble is brewing in both Italy and Argentina, I assume in areas close to where we have plants."

"OK, here it is, boss. As you can see, we have a pictogram projected on the wall for Italy. It shows in detail all the inventory on hand for Italy. There's a similar one for Argentina. We'll look at it next."

"Good. Let's see. We have a Category II site set up in Aversa and a Cat. I in Rieti, where we have manufacturing plants. Rieti is small and situated about 90 miles north-northwest of Rome in the spinal mountains of Italy. Aversa is about the same but situated about 120 miles south-southwest of Rome. Neither has the ability to extend their communication coverage to Rome. If Rome is the trouble spot, we'll have to set up a completely separate Cat. I site there. It could be manned at the embassy, and we'd have to determine the critical coverage area because Rome is awfully big. Also, the distance between these locations might well be a problem for communications between them."

"We'll likely need an inspection and evaluation to see if we need to set up one or two repeater sites."

"Win, do we have any extra equipment in either Rieti or Aversa?"

"Yes, see, here in the two lower corners are the lists of excess equipment at each location. But it's mostly spares. See, Rieti and Aversa both have a spare remote detector, a spare tracker, and a few spare beacons, three each. Also, there are a couple of spare vehicle two-way radios and a spare walkie-talkie at each site. All else are expendables. No, that's wrong, Max. There are also three PIDRAs and a couple of panic bugs at each site. They are not excess but are there to accommodate visitors."

"OK, I'll add those. Let's look at Argentina."

"Here is our site in Buenos Aires. It is really a giant city, and as you recall, we have it outfitted as a Cat. I site as well. The coverage is much greater, and there are a few more spares, but overall, it is similarly equipped as those in Italy. You can see the numbers in the lower left-hand corner."

"Right, I've got it, Win. Please get me a couple of copies of these two overview pictographs. I'll review them with Marvin. Is there anything unique to these three sites?"

"Well, the two-way radio frequencies are different from Italy to Argentina, but that's about all. Italy is VHF, and Argentina, as you will recall, is UHF."

"Yes, and I know you've heard the story of how I got the frequencies in Argentina. Damn near got blown up doing it. But at that, they were the worst off. They lost the whole top floor of their central post office building."

"Yes, I recall your story. Italy wasn't that hard, was it?"

"No, it was a breeze. They bent over backward to help me. Argentina was the bastard at first. Then after the explosion and my help replacing their FCC records, they made an about-face. Lucky."

"'Lucky' is your middle name, Max."

"Maybe, hope it holds. Thanks, Win. Do we have any of the crystals for the channels in Italy and Argentina?"

"We have crystals for Italy, in fact, quite a few. We actually have a few, maybe three of their walkie-talkies. However, Argentina is another animal. The radios and crystals are made there and not here."

"Can we duplicate them here?"

"Yes, at least Motorola can, but you'd have to interact with someone high up to get them duplicated here."

"How is our contact with the Motorola subsidiary in Argentina?"

"Good. It's Senor Stevens. You know him, and he loves you. You got the UHF market broken open for them down there. I think he'd do anything for you."

"Win, have you established a rapport with him?"

"Yes but not as well as yours."

"OK, how about you phoning him and asking what the turnaround would be on some more of our radios there? Preferably the walkie-talkie with the vehicle plug-ins. Tell him we're just testing the waters to determine the turn time. Then ask if they could stock up some crystals on our buck to shorten that period. If he gives you any bull, just patch me in. Otherwise, just keep me informed. It's likely we'll need him sooner or later, so don't antagonize him."

"Gotcha, boss. I'll get him as soon as possible."

"No hurry, but go ahead and do it. And thanks."

"See ya, boss."

Turning to Kathy, "Kathy."

"Yes, sir."

"How about checking with Russ to see if he's in town."

"He is, boss."

"Is he available?"

"Yes, sir. I'll get him. Hold on . . . here, he is on line 1."

"Russ?"

"Yes, Max."

"Sorry to bother you. You at home?"

"Yes, Matt got me the other day and said that we were due out Sunday night. I was coming home anyway. We spent a couple of days with each of our two boys and their families. But now I'm home, just fixing to go out to the pool. Need something?"

"Yes, how about coming in and going in the pool here? I'd like to talk to the three team leaders before they go on training for three weeks."

"Sure, I'll be there within the hour."

"I won't keep you for long, Russ, two hours. OK? You'll be home for supper."

"See ya soon, boss."

Buzzing her, "Kathy?"

"Yes."

"Get me Matt and Dave on the phone."

"Hold on . . . they're on line 1."

"Hi, guys. I've called Russ in for a swim. I promised him two hours max. He said he'll be here within the hour. Can you two join us for a swim? I'd like to quiz you three on what needs to be done on team 3's behalf while you're out of touch for the next three weeks."

"I'll be there, boss."

"How about you, Dave?"

"Sure, I'd just like to gather a few notes and be right along."

"Both of you hold off until you see that Russ has arrived. I've a few things to do in the interim. But I'll see you both inside the hour at the pool. Bye."

Again, "Kathy?"

"Yes, boss."

"Get light sandwiches and drinks for four down at the pool patio in an hour and a half. Maybe a few pieces of fruit as well. Russ, Matt, and Dave will be joining me there for a swim in about forty-five minutes."

"Can do. I'll see that lunch is there right on time."

"No trouble?"

"No, none. Oh, Win stopped by a minute ago and left these two pictograms for you."

"Good. Send them and these notes to Marvin from me ASAP."

Max called Marvin directly. "Hello, Max, what's up?"

"I just wanted to tell you the details on our Italian and Argentine setups. I've just had pictograms of our two setups in Italy, Rieti and Aversa, and the one in Buenos Aires sent to you. Kathy is sending them secure as e-mail just now. You should receive them as we are talking. I've made some notes she is sending as well. Rieti and Buenos Aires are Cat. I sites, and Aversa is Cat. II. Rieti and Aversa are too far from Rome to couple our communications, but we can make a judgmental set up in Rome to suit your needs. Our setup in BA should fit whatever you need unless it's in the boondocks. Although we only have a few spares and backups in all these places, we do have a few extra beacons in each. I've got a few extra two-ways in Rieti and Aversa and about three extras here in hand. I've taken the liberty of seeing that we have soonest possible availability of two-ways in BA. So we're as ready as can be from your heads-up."

"Good work, Max. I didn't mean for you to do anything yet."

"Nothing done yet. But with the three team leaders in training for the next three weeks, I thought it pertinent to have things as ready as possible for an emergency. If anything does come up, I'll have to jerk at least two of them back on an instant's notice. We have our secure phones, and they'll have them in hand. Also, we're all equipped with the new ID badges, thanks to you. We have two full teams here getting equipped and ready for anything. We're still acquiring the third team. As I told you earlier, the third team will be the Dallas home team until they are all trained and field ready. They'll be here to back up the needs of one or both of the other teams. Normally, I would hope that we had only one team fielded at a time. Then they could all rotate assignments—one in the field, one as home backup, and one on R & R.

"Also, I just finished an inspection tour of our facility here, and we're lacking only a few pieces and some decorations before being complete. It will all be in place by the time our team leaders are back from training. I think you'll like the setup. I know we've discussed it, but it is working out better than I had hoped. I'll have Kathy send you a layout and my notes on the details. As soon as possible, I'd like to have three little open houses—one for you and anyone you care to bring, one for the powers that be here, and one for the families of the employees. You and anyone you bring should plan to stay here with us. We need the visit to make sure everything is shipshape. You won't need a thing. We have a couple of vans, a couple of golf carts, and an incredible food service made up of staff member spouses."

"Max, I have the two pictograms and your data on Italy and Argentina. It just arrived."

"Good, I'll ring off now. Please call if you've any questions. Of course, we have a fairly large array of our beacons and other backup gear available here. Any problems, let me know. I can go if my men are still in training."

"OK, thanks, Max. I'll look this over. And don't worry, if anything comes up while your guys are here, I'll depend on you to make the right judgment of who to use. Bye for now."

"Bye."

Max proceeded to the pool area and his locker and suited up for a swim. He was joined shortly by Russ and then Matt and Dave. They swam for about thirty minutes and threw around a pool ball for another fifteen. They got out to towel dry and proceeded to the patio outside the glass wall at the end of the pool when their light lunch arrived.

"Hi, honey," said Dave as his wife set out the lunch from the cart.

"Hi, honey," Dave's wife said. Then she blushed and explained she was just addressing her husband.

"That's a quick save. Russ thought you were talking to him. Or was it Matt or me? No matter, I don't think Dave noticed anyway. Ha ha! Thanks for the service. I toured your kitchen yesterday and was very impressed. I like your menus, pricing, etc. I hope Barry passed along my regards and agreement with your ideas and the way you've staffed and set up the operation. I hope you're satisfied because all of us partakers are."

"Thank you, and yes, I'm very satisfied with the arrangement and the approval. But no, I was talking to my husband and not you other three. But I appreciate the compliment intended. I've got to run. This is Friday, and I've got dinner in a couple of hours with reservations for forty employees, spouses, and their kids."

"Good for you. Congratulations. Bye."

Max launched into his lunch and into deep conversation with the other three, discussing team to-dos during their upcoming absence of three weeks. "My plan is to join you three for the third week of self-defense training. Marvin tells me it's chock-full of personal fitness training as well. As you know, you'll all be housed in barracks for all three training sessions. You all now have your new IDs and secure cell phones. Keep them with you.

"There has been some indication of problems in Italy and Argentina. Also, we haven't seen any response from the terrorist faction in El Salvador yet. And one or another of these might erupt at any time. Call me if you need me, and I'll do the same. Take care. Don't get hurt. Watch for equipment or techniques we might use, and develop any contacts that we might need in the future. I understand the people you'll be training with are a recruit group just finishing CIA training. Their group and you guys make up one training team. If your wives or families have any needs, have them contact Kathy, Barry, Rick, or me as appropriate."

With that, they launched back into a discussion of needs that were outstanding for the field teams. Finally, just before parting, Max said, "Wind at your backs, guys."

21

WHOOPS, EL SALVADOR AGAIN

Max's phone was ringing in his office as he arrived in Monday morning. "Max, this is Marvin."

"What's up?"

"JJ, in El Salvador, just phoned and said there were significant movements over the weekend. He said that they had raided a couple of places based on the information they got from the informant your equipment helped identify at the embassy. In these raids, they recovered a couple of more key people and some written plans. These plans supposedly outline an attack on the Exlite Colonia plant as well as the kidnapping of the ambassador's daughter. The two picked up seemed to confirm that both of these actions were scheduled right away."

"Damn!"

"I know this is bad timing with the boys away at camp, but the director and I think we'd better take some more defensive actions in both cases. What do you think?"

"Don't know. Let me think about it and query the colonel in El Salvador. I'll get back to you by lunchtime, just after if it takes a little longer."

"OK, talk to you then."

Max took a few moments to think and make notes and then dialed up the colonel in El Salvador. "Hello, Colonel, this is Max in Dallas."

"Hello, Max, I assume you've just gotten the word about the information here. JJ said he would have it relayed to you."

"Yes. What is your assessment on the ground?"

"Well, JJ is off adding every bit of security he can to cover Sally, the ambassador's daughter. And I've been busy here buttressing up the security detail at the Colonia plant. I could use your clear head on this."

"Thanks, but my head is not so clear right now. Let me just think off the top of it. First, tell JJ not to overlook the ambassador's wife. She might become a deflected target if they can't get to the daughter. Also, they might both get picked off since the mother is likely to keep the chick closer to her. That's not to second-guess JJ but just in case he has overlooked it in the rush of things. Also, with all the security at the plant, you should not overlook the house, Chuck himself, or his wife. Again, not to second-guess."

"No, no problem. Any suggestion at this point?"

"Colonel, please send me a short bullet list of all the things you're doing, and ask JJ if he'll do the same. Maybe these will give me some other ideas. And, Colonel, keep in close touch with JJ and me. Don't wait for messages to be relayed. Call me the instant you have anything definite, and I'll be there within four hours."

"Anything else?"

"No, that's all. Bye for now."

Max calls out, "Kathy?"

"Yes, boss."

"Get Vic Anderson at the hangar or whoever is there."

"OK, I'll buzz you when they're on the phone."

"Thanks."

When the intercom buzzed, Max picked up the phone. "Hello, Max, this is Vic Anderson. What can I do for you?"

"Vic, there is trouble brewing in El Salvador. Don't know that I'll be needed, but just in case, I was wondering what your schedule was like if it should suddenly get hot."

"We've got a normal schedule, but as of now, we have lots of blanks throughout the rest of this week. Just call if you need us. You've got our emergency cell number to reach whoever is OOD when I'm out?"

"Yes, I do. And thanks, Vic. I'll give you as much notice as I get."

"OK, that's our job. Don't hesitate if you need us."

"Thanks again, Vic. Bye."

Kathy buzzes, "Max?"

"Yes, Kathy."

"I just got secure e-mails from the colonel and JJ in El Salvador. They're some kinds of lists. Looks like their lists of last-minute actions they've taken. I thought you'd like to see them right away."

"Yes, thanks. Bring them in. I'll need to study them awhile. And get Bob on the phone for me."

Soon, on the intercom, "Max, Bob on 1."

"Hello, Bob?"

"Yes, Max, what's up?"

"Well, I just thought I'd give you some heads-up."

"OK, shoot."

"The security people at the embassy in El Salvador pulled a raid this morning on two areas they got from the guy they snagged with our PIDRA in the embassy security area down there. They discovered some plans regarding action against the Colonia plant and the ambassador's daughter. Nothing specific, but they were confirmed by a couple of guys they picked up in the raids. I've already talked with the colonel, and he and JJ from the embassy have sent me their responsive action lists to this threat. I'll send them to you secure when we finish this call. I'd like to hear back from you anything you might think of additionally. I'll include my notes to them regarding the couple of things I thought of off the top of my head. If you have anything substantial to add, please do so ASAP, and we, if you prefer, can get them to the colonel and JJ.

"Additionally, the State Department has reported a hotbed of activity in both Rome and Buenos Aires. I think we'll get tasked soon to respond to this by adding some of their people to our KPPS program in each place as we did in El Salvador. BA is no problem, although there might be a delay in getting two-way radios. I've taken action to speed up our ability to obtain these if needed. However, Rome is a different nut to crack. Our Rieti and Aversa communication coverage does not and cannot include Rome. They are too far away. If this activates, we'll have to figure out a way to install an area-wide monitor with remote detectors for monitoring at the embassy in Rome. It can be done but not as fast, and the area to be covered is potentially huge. I'll start my staff working on a plan this afternoon. I need to stress that none of this is actual yet. It's just a heads-up."

"Well, Max, it sounds like you have this all well in hand. I'll look at the lists and see if I can come up with anything helpful right away for El Salvador. Thanks for the heads-up on the others. It'll give me something I can tell Raymond about how things are going."

"Oh, yes, I forgot to remind you that I'm short staffed at the moment because I've sent all three team leaders to DC for three weeks of training in bomb school (how to spot and quell them), weapons school (small arms training), and self-defense (and conditioning). They are joining a recently graduated CIA squad in these. I'm planning on joining them for the self-defense training on the third week because I've already taken the other schools."

"Boy, that sounds like fun and possibly some hard work. I'd love to do that but think I'm beyond the age that it would do any good. Besides, at my elevated position, they'd never let me go anywhere to use any of that."

"Bob, it must be nice to be at such an elevated position—the prestige, the money."

"Yeah, the money. Anything else?"

"That's it. If things get too hot in El Salvador, I'll go myself and take a team with me. That's it for now. Bye."

After asking her in, "Kathy, please have all the field team personnel on campus report to their training area in fifteen minutes. I'll meet them there."

"Will do. I think they're all here, Max."

"Well, I'm surprised. Their bosses are all out of town. I'd expect them to be handling personal chores."

"No, I'm sure they're all here. The team leaders left a long list of things for them to be doing the three weeks that they are away."

"OK, good. I'm going over there, if you need me."

"OK, I've paged them all. They are either there or on the way."

"Thanks. One more thing, since this is Monday, see if Gina would join me for supper by the pool here at six. Tell her I plan to take a dip before we eat and to bring her suit if she wants to join me."

"Will do. You want me to put a reservation in for you?"

"No, I thought I'd do that on the way to the team hut."

"OK, see you later."

Max enjoyed his little hike from the administration building to the cafeteria on his way to what he called the team hut. It was spring, and Barry had had nice beds of flowers put in around the area. Additionally, all the construction equipment was finally cleared away, and the large square helicopter pad in the middle of the compound was clear finally.

"Hi, girls."

"Hi, Max," they all greeted.

"I thought I'd stop in and put in my reservation for my wife and me by the pool tonight."

"Done, glad to have you. There'll be about twenty or so joining you from the list so far."

"That's good. You girls are doing a bang-up job. I hope it's going as good as you hoped and planned."

"Better, Max, but no time to chat. Things to do."

"Bye, girls, see you later."

Max proceeded through the breezeway to the team training hut. All the guys were there. "OK, guys, I need you to sort yourselves out for me. Of course, I know every one of you but want to know your current assignments and top two responsibilities with respect to the new team structure. First, I want to redesignate the team IDs. Team 1 will henceforward be known as the red team, team 2 the blue team, and team 3 the green team. That will help keep the numbers straight for each team member." Each of them nodded and put a note in their notebooks.

"Thanks, that is a help. I'm Jerry Avery, red team no. 2 member, and my major responsibility is to be the alternate for the red team no. 1 member, the team leader. This usually kicks in when no. 1 is off shift, that is, sleeping or not at the current field site. My second major responsibility is as security for the team in the field. As you know, the team is broken into two components, first and second shifts. The first shift team members are odd numbered, that is, no. 1, no. 3, and no. 5. And the second shift team members are even numbered, that is, no. 2, no. 4, and no. 6."

"Good, who is blue team no. 2?"

"I am Max Baker, blue team member no. 2. My responsibilities are the same for the blue team as Jerry's are for the red team, but I'll repeat them if you like."

"No need. Who is green team member no. 2?"

"No one is assigned that yet, sir," said Baker.

"Who are the team members no. 4?

"That'd be me, sir. I am George Winters, red team member no. 4. My major responsibility is communications on the second shift. My other responsibility is technical consult."

"Who's no. 4 on the blue and green teams?"

"I am Serje Resnikov, blue team member no. 4 with the same responsibilities. And there is no green team no. 4 assigned yet."

"Who are members no. 6?"

"I am Sam Froth, red team member no. 6, and my responsibilities are as technician and gofer, sir."

"I am Felix Esters, blue team member no. 6, and my responsibilities are the same. And there is no green team member yet assigned."

"OK, no. 3s and no. 5s, it's your turn."

"I am Mike Manske, red team member no. 3 with the same duties. And there is no green team no. 3 yet."

"I am Bill Windell, blue team no. 3 with the same no. 3 duties. And no green team no. 3 yet."

"I am George Rendell, red team no. 5, and my duties are beacons and trackers. And no green team no. 5 yet."

"I am Charlie Winkie, blue team member no. 5 with no. 5 responsibilities. There is no green team no. 5 yet assigned."

"OK, you noticed that I had my recorder on. I want to get this all straight in my synopsis. You guys are currently operating without your no. 1s. As you know, they are in training in DC for the next three weeks.

They are coupled with a small team of recent CIA training graduates to form a bigger class in training. When they get back, they will train you all in the things they have learned, only in half the time.

"In the meantime, we must go on. Accordingly, no. 2s, you are in charge of the three teams. The world has not slowed or stopped while your no. 1s are out. You need to accomplish all the things they have left for you and be responsive to any call we might get in their absence. If we get an urgent call, I will become the no. 1 for the red team, who will be fielded. The blue team will take on the home team responsibilities. Do you know what that entails?"

"Yes, sir."

"Obviously, the green team has only a no. 1 and still needs five more members to be fully operational. When those members are assigned, the green team will become the home team until such time as I decide they are ready to be fielded. When that time comes, the three teams will operate in rotation. If the red team is fielded, the blue team will become the home team, and the green team will be on R & R. This doesn't mean that you don't have to work. It just means you'll work at a reduced and more relaxed schedule. If and when a team is selected to be fielded—one or more of its members are indisposed by sickness or for some other serious reason—the next team in line will replace that missing member's number with its own. And that empty spot will be filled by the next team's corresponding member's number. Additionally, if we were to get another field assignment while one team is in the field, say the red team, then the blue team would be deployed, and the green team becomes the home team. Hopefully, we'll have a full green team by that time. If not, it will be filled by our own staffers here. Is that clear?"

"Yes, sir."

"You all know the rules for pay and others according to your member number assignment. Additionally, you all know the time off regimen and how it works. If not, ask questions of me or any of the administrative staff. For this complex system to work, you must be prompt in supplying your time records and your special expenses. The system is unlikely to be faultless. If you don't get your due, complain directly to me if necessary. Now for all the good side of the pay and time off, there is a corresponding requirement that you respond promptly to assignments, especially fielding ones. You give us your best, and we'll do our best for you.

"Now one last thing, there are three hot spots right now that I'm aware of: El Salvador, Rome, and Buenos Aires. The first two are in the Northern Hemisphere and have weather the same as ours, but BA is in the Southern and is the opposite season. Make yourselves aware of the seasonal needs for these sites so that you can respond accordingly, if necessary. According to the latest intelligence, the red team is likely to be deployed to El Salvador sometime in the next few days or weeks. That's my best guess. I'll keep you informed. No. 2s, you should carry a secure cell phone at all times until your no. 1 is back. The rest of you should carry pagers. If you're called, we expect you to check in immediately, be on site within two hours, and be ready to go according to the assignment.

"Now I want any suggestions of on-staff people who might fill out our positions on the green team. Or I'd like your suggestions of others we might hire to fill those positions. Any questions?"

"No, sir. Jerry, red team no. 2."

"Oh yes. Jerry, would you take on the added task of arranging an overall team board on this wall here? List each team with the names and numbers for all of us to see. And figure out a way for us to clearly state and change the current assignment of each. And put this on the computer so that we can all have access to it."

"Yes, sir."

"That's all. Thanks for your attention."

Shortly thereafter, Jerry had a mock-up of the big board on the computer and, a short while later, an order placed for the actual board to mount on the wall.

22

KPP FIELD TEAMS

RED TEAM

1 Russ Talbot *(Out, training)*
Team Leader

2 Jerry Avery
Team Leader Alternate and Security

3 Mike Manske
Weapons and Service

4 George Winters
Comm and Technical

5 George Rendell
Beacons and Trackers

6 Sam Froth
Tech and Gofer

BLUE TEAM

1 Matt Smith *(Out, training)*
Team Leader

2 Max Baker
Team Leader Alternate and Security

3 Bill Windell
Weapons and Services

4 Serje Resnikov
Comm and Technical

5 Charlie Winkie
Beacons and Trackers

6 Felix Esters
Tech and Gofer

GREEN TEAM

1 Dave Ferrell *(Out, training)*
Team Leader

2 unassigned
Team Leader Alternate and Security

3 unassigned
Weapons and Services

4 unassigned
Comm and Technical

5 unassigned
Beacons and Trackers

6 unassigned
Tech and Gofer

23

KPP AGENT GEAR AND KIT

Max and his KPPS crew had developed an array of gear and equipment that their KPP agents—that is, no. 1 through no. 6 field agents—used in the field to successfully and safely perform whatever job they were assigned.

H/Motel – six one-man rooms or three two-man rooms, no extras needed, all queen or king beds

Apartment/House – one three-bedroom, two two-bedroom, or three one-bedroom with two beds each, all queen or king beds

Apartment Trunks – a set of rolling trunks packed with all the needs when renting an apartment anywhere in the world for a full field team, that is, six people minimum. Each team has one of these sets.

Winter Weather Trunk Only – six quilts, three electric heaters

Tents – for outdoor camping, in water-resistant duffel bags

> HQ Tent – for gathering and eating for six, one each team
>
> Cook Tent – especially vented for cooking and food storage, one each team
>
> Misc. Tent – for equipment storage, washing, toiletries, etc., one each team
>
> Two-Man Tents (3) – for sleeping, in individual member backpacks
>
> Camp Tables and Six Stools w/ Folding Backs – used in camping situations, one each team

Backpacks (6) – equipped in pairs alternating tent storage with foodstuffs for a week and with special waterproof shipping and carrying covers. Complete camping backpacks, individual weight of <40 lbs, that provide for survival for a week or more, provided for each individual in a field team. Backpacks come in pairs, where one pack contains a two-man tent, and the other contains an equivalent weight in cooking gear and foodstuffs, labeled as A and B, respectively. Each team member has one of these packs, one each member.

Day Packs (6) – light equipped for an overnight, one each member

Belt Bags (6) – meds and others, one each member

Tracking and Detection Case – standard portable airborne adaptable tracking equipment with ID capability, one each team

Surveillance and Security Case – mini-audio-digital-recorder, mini-video-camera and digital recorder, binocular w/ digital camera, monocular Starlight scope w/ digital camera, compact digital camera, KPPS beacons of choice, PIDRA system (four-item kit), local intrusion alarm, Mini-mite .380 semiautomatic (two sets of three clips of ammo) – one of each for each member (plus one spare for Mini-mite)

Communications Case – mini-laptop-computer w/ encryption, cell phone w/ encryption, two-way radio w/ encryption, pager – one each for each member (plus six for pager)

Spares – batteries for all kit equipment, one set each member as appropriate

Other – a spare backpack, day pack, and belt pack

24

BOMB SCHOOL

Here were notes from the team's diary.

> Russ, Matt, and Dave were resting in their bunks in the bunkhouse to which they were assigned at Fort Point. Each little bunkhouse was composed of three bunk rooms with two bunk beds in each. One room was at either end of the building and one in the middle. The other middle room was the bath. It was **CLARIFICATION** composed of four lavatories, four toilet stalls, four urinals, and a set of four showers. A short central hallway interconnected the rooms. A small janitor's closet partitioned off a portion of the bathroom. There was only one way in and out, except for the windows, the front door. The three of us decided on one of the end rooms. We sorted our things and chose up bunks. We kept the top, fourth, for storing extras.

Russ was the first to start talking. "Well, guys, the last thing Max said to me was keep a diary at school. It can always be destroyed later, but it's likely to help us remember key names for later. I'll keep the diary on bomb school, and you two can select which of you keep the diary for the other two schools. I'll type my notes into the laptop and read it over each night to you and edit in anything you picked up or that I just forgot. OK?"

"Fine," the other two replied.

"Let's go do a little exploring. These little maps they gave us show us where we're not allowed, which is a considerable amount of the area. We can take a look at the chow hall and others. I like to know where I am with respect to things. You guys up for it?"

"Yeah. Let's go. But first, I'm going to set up one of our entry alarms in our room and close the door."

"Good idea."

> We left our room and the little house and walked quickly in the direction of the chow hall. It was what you might expect—equipped for about a hundred. Along the route, we saw a number of other small houses like our barracks. But there was hardly anyone around, except for the people working prep in the chow hall. We found that large portions of the grounds were forbidden to us and, since we had no reason, let them be just that. We did walk over to the boat-launching area and were amazed by the lack of activity for such a large and well-equipped area. The shadows began to get longer, and the wind stiffened from the inlet. It got downright chilly. Checking the time, we decided to return to our barracks for light jackets and get ready for supper. As we entered, we heard the rumble of others inside.

Russ was first to enter the room and found Dave's intrusion alarm blinking. He pointed it out to the other two and turned it off. At that moment, a big blond guy came in behind them and said that their group of eight had come in and looked about. He explained that they had stumbled into the occupied room; set off the alarm, which scared the bejesus out of them; and reset it. He'd noticed that it still blinked, suggesting that it had been set off, but was unable to reset that feature. "Sorry," he said.

> He then proceeded to introduce himself and the couple of guys who had followed him down the hall when we came in. They, in turn, insisted that we visit their rooms and be introduced to the remainder of their group. They were part of a larger group of sixteen. Their other eight guys were assigned to the next barracks in line, one that we'd seen earlier.
>
> We gathered in two of the rooms and talked awhile. They were in the most recent group of graduates from the CIA academy and were here to get fully informed on the areas in which they had not yet been trained. It appeared that we were the missing three, or four with Max, who would make up the class of twenty for the three schools scheduled. All of them were in their early twenties and looked to be in excellent shape. We three, on the other hand, were in our thirties, and it showed. Nicely enough, they seemed to show deference to our age.
>
> Later that evening, after dinner and a short briefing on tomorrow's schedule, we three talked and decided that we'd each begin by befriending one or more of the other group and then expanding that as the tenure with them lengthened. In this manner, we felt that we would best be able to learn from the others and perhaps forge a bond or so that might prove useful later. (That, indeed, would prove true but much later.)

The food was wonderful and plentiful. Stuffed and briefed, the day came to an end but not before we again set out an intrusion alarm but, this time, just above the entrance door to notify us if anyone came or left through the front door. Sure enough, at about 2:00 a.m., the alarm sounded and scared everyone in the house. Russ quickly covered the distance to the front door and, on the stoop, found one of the other group, Roy, lighting up a cigarette.

"Can't sleep?" Russ inquired.

"Nope," Roy said. "I've been trying to quit smoking but haven't succeeded until just now. I think maybe that alarm of yours cured me." They laughed and exchanged a few amenities and returned to their cohorts to report Roy's indiscretion. It took a while for all to get back to sleep.

Then sure enough, first thing in the morning at about six thirty, the alarm sounded again. This time, it was accompanied by a loud crash and female cursing inside the doorway. It was one of the cleaning ladies. She had tried to get an early start on the day and had assumed that any occupants had risen by six. Needless to say, she had spilled her bucket of mop water and dropped the few supplies in her other hand when the unexpected alarm had sounded right near her head. She apologized profusely for her accident and her language, but the guys apologized right back to her. "Sorry we scared you. But we did learn a few words we hadn't known before." Of course, that made her blush, and they all had a laugh as one of the guys told her the story of the 2:00 a.m. wake-up even earlier.

Anyway, they were all awake. And they all dashed for the bath—eleven guys and four facilities. After a friendly little arguing, they worked out a current schedule for access, another for the evenings and still another for the mornings they were to be there. They broke up into four-man shifts for showering and others, half in the morning and half in the evening. That proved to be a little less troublesome but not completely.

It was the first morning at class. "The first thing I want to acquaint you gentlemen with is the fact that bombs are dangerous. Unless you are an expert, you never want to even attempt to defuse one. Second is the fact that bombs come in very different packages. So the question is, can you even recognize one? Some, yes, Others, no.

"We all recognize old time bombs. They look like and act like bombs. They are usually contact bombs, that explode because they fall on their nose where the detonator is located. Their tail fins are to provide stability in flight. But if you remember the old WWII movies of bombs dropping, they actually tottered downward, the fins only stabilizing them in the horizontal component of their flight. Later, bombs like the snake eye had very large snap-out fins that deployed only after a drop to make them fall more vertically and stabilized that component of their flight. This made them more accurate."

"The fuses of bombs were improved from the impact or contact fuse to a radar fuse. Here, the tip of the bomb contained a miniature radar set that could be set to explode the bomb at some set altitude above the ground. This improved the effectiveness of the bomb. Contact bombs hit, and their explosive force was damaging, but the ground or target caused the majority of the blast to be directed upward in a conical form, and formed a similarly shaped crater. These are fairly useless against ground troops. The radar-fused bomb that exploded above the ground caused the blast force to be directed in a conical fashion toward the ground from the altitude of the explosion, much more effective against ground troops. The explosive portion of the bomb was then further improved by adding breakaway particles similar to those seen in the pineapple scoring of a hand grenade, another type of bomb. In this manner, not only the explosive force of the bomb was directed at ground troops but the fragments as well. Eventually, these fragments were even shaped to spin and give them an even more destructive effect.

"Well, enough about dropped bombs. The introduction of C-4 and other pliable explosive materials enabled the making of bombs molded to any size and shape. Then the introduction of extremely small detonators enabled what are today called letter bombs. In short, anything can be a bomb in today's environment. Our purpose here is to acquaint you with an array of different bombs and bomb types used by terrorists and for you to witness the blast effectiveness of each. We can't teach you to necessarily recognize a bomb and certainly not teach you to defuse it but rather to acquaint you with types and their effectiveness so that, according to the conditions you find yourselves in, you can possibly recognize the threat and shield or avoid the possible effect.

"You'll notice that we're next to a bunker from which you can witness each blast close-up and better sense the situation and effectiveness of the same. In each case, you will be given the opportunity to observe the bomb to be exploded before its arming. You will then be removed to the bunker. The scenario will be explained and the bomb exploded. The seconds, up to a minute, just after this will be the most dangerous to you because you will want to observe the immediate effects. But I implore you, do not exit the bunker until after I release you. In some cases, metal from the scene will rain down for up to a minute later, and you will be in jeopardy if you exit before I sound the all clear. Understand? I hope so. In a previous class, a guy from the State Department exited too soon and was hit by a falling car bumper. He survived but spent a month in the hospital recovering. Understand now? Well, I hope so, for your sake.

"The first exercise will be a car bomb planted in a van parked along the street. A victim car will be towed past the van. The van bomb will explode. It will be fifty yards distant from the bunker, but the blast will be directed in our direction, so don't go out until I tell you. Now let's go see the van and its bomb.

"OK, we slide the side door next to the curb open and see three bags of fertilizer stacked against the far wall, noting that the bags had been sliced open and some of the fertilizer has spilled onto the floor.

However, if you look closely, you'll see that the opened bags have been saturated with something. The fertilizer is all gooey. Over there, see the empty quarts of automobile oil. That's the stuff. Now notice that three primers have been stuck into the mass of the gooey fertilizer. They are not connected, but detonators are tricky, so don't reach out and touch them. An unintended static charge on your body and hand could cause them to detonate. See, a ground wire is attached to keep static electricity from the detonators, and the hot wires are unattached. Our people will carefully attach the wires and remove the ground as we return to the bunker. When we're all safe inside, we will call for the target vehicle to be towed past the van bomb, and I will remotely trigger the detonator. You watch and feel the effects at fifty yards of only three bags of fertilizer. And don't go out of the bunker until I give the all clear. OK? All right, let's return to the bunker."

"Just a few minutes later as the last entered, everyone in the bunker? Can everyone see out the armored glass slits? OK, they've given the signal that the bomb is armed. I want you to notice that two regular cars are parked just in front of and behind the van, simulating a normal street scene. Now see the cable stretch tight and begin to tow the target vehicle down the street and past the van bomb. There, it'll pass at 25 mph. Now I'll trigger the bomb. Five, four, three, two, one."

Boom! A great explosive scene emerged from a spectacular cloud of dust and particles. Several in the bunker ducked as particles were flung straight in their direction. Several pieces of shrapnel were heard to clatter off the sides of the bunker. The back of the bunker was open, and a reduced feeling of the blast was transferred to those inside. The earth seemed to shake, and everyone trembled a little with the feel of it. It was more than disconcerting; it was fearful.

Shortly, the scene became more visible. A couple of guys headed for the exit and were promptly called down by the instructor. At forty seconds after the detonation, several large car parts came pummeling down on the top of and around the bunker. All were amazed.

Finally, after a full minute, we were released to go outside and observe the scene without the restrictions of the narrow bunker slits. The oohs and aahs were palpable. Both the bomb van and the target vehicle were gone, and both the vehicles in front and rear were thrown forward and backward respectively, toppled upside down, and some twenty to thirty feet removed from their regular places. There were a plethora of torn car body and parts strewn from the scene all the way to the bunker and in all other directions, but it was clear that the most were in the direction of the target vehicle. It was extraordinary that the simple placement of the fertilizer bags had so clearly affected the direction of the blast. We even recognized some car outer body parts in trees, farther from the scene than we had been in the bunker. It was amazing. It was frightful. And it smelled of explosive residue, not at all like the manure of which it was made.

Back at the instruction area behind the bunker, the instructor pointed out things not obvious to us. There had been a small wedge-shaped piece of metal about the size a man could hide behind at a distance of only thirty feet from the blast. On a stool fixed to the ground was a wineglass with wine. It had been protected from the explosion by the wedge just in front of it, although about half the wine had sloshed out. It was pointed out that shielding or sheltering even in proximity to a blast might well affect survival in an emergency. It was even clearer to all involved that dramatically increasing the distance between the blast and oneself was a much more desirable thing.

At lunch, the entire group met and talked with the three-man group called KPP agents from Dallas. There was much questioning and little information flow from KPP agents to CIA agents, but there was the beginning of a bond forming. The fresh CIA guys were anxious for action of any type, and the KPP agents were old hands at action and didn't particularly want any unless absolutely necessary. In short, the CIA guys were anxious for field assignments that were still several weeks away.

The afternoon was spent in classroom exercises examining explosive devices presented and guessing at possible ways to recognize and defeat them. Recognition was the killer. Molded plastic explosives could take any shape. The classes were structured to have everyone recognize some and not others. Failures won the game because the goal was to sensitize the trainees to the real world and their actual inability to counter it in terms of recognizing and defeating terrorist bombs. Rather, the positive goal was to sensitize them to the possibilities and the avenues to escape them. Everyone tried their hardest at recognition, and they were shown that even trained bomb-sniffing dogs were easily defeated by a clever opponent—not that all the suggestions weren't valid and should be tried but first rely on evacuation and cover.

That evening after supper, the KPP agents, our guys from Dallas, allowed Russ time to type his notes and then attentively listened as he read them. There were a few additions from the group, but by and large, the notes accurately described what they had learned that day. At the end, each noted one or two names of the CIA guys they had befriended and their primary interests. It was clear that of the sixteen CIA, there were four (Tom, Andy, Bill, and George—promptly identified as TAB-G) who were leaders and would in the future become movers and shakers. The team decided to attach themselves to these four while watching the others for anything they might have missed. (Again, their senses were right; and in the somewhat distant future, those four CIA would become their good friends and very helpful.)

The next three days were almost boringly similar to day 1. They were introduced to six types of roadside and other bombs with vivid demonstrations in the mornings and school hall lectures in the afternoon.

Finally, on the last day, they followed the same schedule but with the smallest of letter bombs. A Steelcase desk and chair were set just about ten feet in front of the bunker. A dummy wearing a football or motorcycle helmet was placed in the chair and his hands outstretched and holding a standard letter. A similar one was passed among the students for examination. It appeared normal in every aspect, no heavier or thicker than a normal letter of maybe five pages. But inside was a clever array of one sheet folded over a thin piece of plastic explosive with a subminiature detonator embedded. One end of the explosive held two small, extrathin hearing aid batteries. (They were told they were lithium batteries). Then a very thin wire was run about the inside of the envelope. When broken, this became the switch that attached the batteries to the detonator. Of course, theirs was a dud, but the one sitting on the desk in the dummy's hand was not.

> The instructor activated the little letter bomb remotely, and—boom!—seemingly, it was as loud as any we'd witnessed; but of course, it was much closer. Same smoke and debris, but being so close, we could actually see the hole torn in the top of the desk as it scooted forward awkwardly. We also saw the head leave the dummy at a sharp, high angle and fly some thirty feet away. The chair and body of the dummy were lacerated and thrown over backward for about five feet. When we left the bunker, and recovered the dummy's head, it was destroyed and the helmet torn apart. This seemed an even eviler bomb than any of the prior because there was the semblance of a person involved.
>
> Afternoon classroom time was more somber than the previous ones. Each of us had something to say that

expressed our shock and anger toward anyone who would use such a device. The rest of the afternoon was spent viewing bomb detection devices and X-ray-type machines that could be used for screening.

That evening, the base personnel—mostly our instructors and their technicians—threw us a little party for graduation. Good food, good eats, but best of all were the frozen margaritas. They lived up to their name and froze a few gullets and a few brains.

Our final review that evening caused us to go over the entire week and make copious notes in Russ's diary to study with Max and our teammates at home in Dallas.

We had the weekend off and spent it touring the DC area. We enjoyed a tour of the White House, the Capitol, and all the memorials. Somehow the memorials were the more touching and meaningful.

Next week, FBI land and the weapons course for all of us.

25

THE BALLOON GOES UP

It was Monday morning, and the boys were away at camp, that is, in DC. Max's phone rang and was answered by Kathy. "Kathy?"

"Yes."

"Is Max in yet?"

"No, not yet, Bob. He should be in by eight, and that's just a few minutes away. Problems?"

"Yes, but it can wait a few minutes. Have him call me as soon as he comes in."

"Will do, Bob."

At eight sharp, Max came in and greeted Kathy. "Good morning, Kathy. Anything up?"

"Yes, you missed a good breakfast. Lisa and her girls turn out good food."

"Yes, I know, but I just can't do it on Mondays. Need to get things straight for the week at home first."

"I understand. Oh, I hope you're caught up on your schedule because Bob just phoned. Sounds like something's up."

"Oh, thanks. I'll call him back right away."

Max sat down at his desk and called Bob. "Hello, Max, the caller ID says it's you."

"Yes, it is. What's up? Kathy said you called and sounded like something was up."

"It is, Max. I just got a call from Chuck in San Salvador, and he said his wife appears to be missing. She went out to the market early and was going to fix him a big breakfast but hasn't shown up. He dispatched someone to the market to look for her, and they reported back that she wasn't there. Right now, he's checking all her close friends to see if maybe she got a good deal at the market and stopped by a friend's house to drop off something before coming home. He hopes she has just gotten in a coffee conversation and will show up soon. In the meantime, he's checking. He's concerned enough to call me, so I'm concerned enough to call you. What do you think?"

"Bob, I think I'll call the colonel and alert him, just in case Chuck hasn't already done so. Maybe he has heard something that might be pertinent. I'm going to put my red team on alert, just in case."

"OK, Max, but I thought that Russ was in DC. He is red team no. 1, isn't he?"

"He is. But I'll substitute as red team no. 1, if necessary. Bob, I'll get back to you as soon as I've alerted the team and talked to the colonel and, on second thought, to JJ at the embassy."

"OK, do that. I'll hold off telling anyone upstairs until after I hear from you. Thanks, Max, and bye."

Then on the intercom, Max announced, "Kathy, see if the red team is all here, and tell them they are on three-hour alert for El Salvador. Tell them I'll talk to them in an hour."

"OK, boss."

"And, Kathy, after that, get the colonel on the line for me. I'll be talking with my wife. Break in when you get the colonel."

"Will do."

Max called his wife. "Gina?"

"Yes, Max."

"I have to go on alert for El Salvador. Please get my list and pack for me and, honey, not a word to anyone."

"OK, what's up?"

"Not sure, but Chuck's wife might be missing."

"Oh no, I'll get your stuff together."

"Thanks, honey."

"No problem, that's the job."

"Good girl. I love you."

"I love you too, and good luck."

Kathy stepped into Max's office. "Max, the colonel is out of touch at the moment. I left word on his cell."

"Thanks. If we don't hear from him within ten minutes, call again. If that doesn't work, try his home and attempt to track him down."

"Will do. Oh, Max?"

"Yes."

"The red team is here, and they confirm *on alert*. Max?"

"Yes."

"What exactly does that mean?"

"That means they're checking their lists twice and packing up the necessary gear to go for a week or two or indefinitely."

"OK, anything else?"

"Yes, alert Vic Anderson and see if we can have a Lear here and ready on two-hour notice. Tell him it's an alert, but there is no certainty yet."

"OK, will do. Anything else?"

"Will you pull out my ready list and check over it? I think everything's on hand but just in case."

"Will do. You're going?"

"Yes, I'll take over as red team leader, no. 1."

About five minutes later, "Max, the colonel on line 1."

"Colonel, what's the status?"

"I've both put out feelers for her. I've got two men at the market showing her picture and waiting to get some response now. Wait, I'm putting you on hold."

Almost ten minutes later, "Max?"

"Yes, Colonel."

"My guys report back from the market that she apparently arrived at about 7:15 a.m. and bought a few things and left at about 7:30 a.m. One of the people in the market saw her get into her car with a man, no description on the man but a Salvadoran. Hold on, I'll check with Chuck to see if she took the gardener with her or someone else."

Again, a short wait, and, "No. Chuck says she was alone, and he says he's checked all her friends, and none have seen her. It doesn't look good."

"Thanks, Colonel. I'll set the clock at seven thirty as the last sighting and with a Salvadoran entering her car at the market."

"Right, Max. I've got lots to do before I'm willing to say she's been taken."

"I know, but I want you to put your response team on KPPS full alert and set up a KPPS HQ manned 24/7. Get out your gear and double-check it."

"Yes, sir."

"I've already alerted my red team. Russ is in DC, so I'll be the red team no. 1. Understood?"

"Yes."

"Colonel?"

"Yes, Max."

"I'll report this and put my red team on ready. We will proceed on a response, but I'll call you later to determine the situation before we depart. Right now, we're on a three-hour response alert, plus a three-and-a-quarter-hour flight time. It's about ten here. So we can be there as early as four fifteen, if needed. Tell Chuck to keep a stiff upper lip. You go and do what you do so well. I'll alert JJ in the embassy."

"Yes, boss. OK, with luck, I won't see you soon. Goodbye."

Max, calling out, "Kathy?"

"Yes, Max."

"Get me JJ at the Salvadoran Embassy on the phone ASAP."

Kathy calls out, "Max?"

"Yes?"

"JJ's on 1."

"Thanks."

Picking up the phone Max says, "Hello, JJ?"

"Yes, Max."

"JJ, we have a problem. Our plant manager's wife is missing. Maybe it's a false alarm, but it looks less and less so. She left home alone for the market at seven. She'd gone to pick up a very few things to fix her husband a nice breakfast. When she didn't return, he put out a call for her with no luck. She has a cell and our stuff. There's been no KPPS alarm yet. The colonel has sent men to the market to get details, and they report that she was last seen departing the market at seven thirty with a Salvadoran entering the car with her, no detailed description on him."

"Max, I'll check with the colonel and see if there's anything I can do to help determine her status."

"JJ, I'd hoped you might have some recent intel."

"No, nothing. It's been exceptionally quiet."

"That's troubling, JJ."

"Yes, I know."

"JJ, I've got my red team on alert now. I'll be their no. 1 and am transferring them to ready and then response status in the next hour. If things don't reverse, we'll be there just after 4:00 p.m. Can you pave the way?"

"Sure, glad to, Max."

"OK, I'll call you just before we depart."

"OK? And, JJ, thanks."

"You bet. Anything else?"

"Yes, JJ. I'm fearful that when things start to boil, they boil all over. Keep a close watch on your charges. This might be an all out."

"Wow, you think so?"

'No, but better safe than sorry. See you soon."

"OK, goodbye."

Max, on the intercom, "Kathy, please come in."

"Yes, boss?"

"Call Marv Lewis and have him prepare and deliver cash to us at the airport just before 1:00 p.m. I'll need $2,000 dispensed to each red team member—no. 3, no. 4, no. 5, and no. 6—as twenty $1s, twenty $5s, twenty $10s, twenty $20s, twenty $50s, and three $100s. And $4,000 to no. 2, same quantities and denominations except for twenty additional $100s. Finally, $8,000 to me, as no. 1, directly, same quantities and denominations as no. 2 except for an additional forty $100s. That's an overall total of $20,120. Tell him this is an official KPPS response allotment."

"OK, boss, will do."

Max dialed Marvin's private number in DC. "Hello, Max."

"Hello, Marvin. We've a problem in El Salvador. It appears that our plant manager's wife might have been kidnapped this morning about seven fifteen at the market. We're checking, but the first inputs say she got in her car at the market with a Salvadoran that she didn't take with her. I've talked to the colonel and JJ. They're both pitching in. I've put my red team on alert, with me as no. 1 because Russ is in school up there in DC. I'll put my team on a two-hour response in about fifteen minutes. Thought you should know."

"Thanks, Max. I'll depend on JJ to keep you informed so I don't have to take out time to report in several directions."

"Good idea."

"Let me know if you need anything, and take care."

"We aren't certain yet, but it does look like it will be a go. My second in command is my administrative assistant, Rick Maury. Feel free to check with him or Bob. I'll contact you directly if necessary. Kathy will notify the boys, and if things get tricky, I might have to alert the second team (blue team) and get Matt, their no. 1, to come down and help."

"OK, Max, take care, and wind at your back."

"Thanks. Bye."

Max to Kathy, "Kathy?"

"Yes."

"I'm going over to the team hut. Please start a clock and a diary on this alert. At 7:15 a.m.—Salvadoran time is the same as ours—Chuck's wife was last seen entering her car at the market with a Salvadoran that she had not brought with her to the market from home. Keep a running diary of all events there and here. I'll leave the team hut for home and then to the airport, if Vic has the flight ready."

"Oh, I forgot. Vic phoned while you were on the phone with someone just a few minutes ago and said a Lear would be ready on two hours' notice."

"OK, call him back and declare the two-hour response notice at 11:00 a.m. Call Bob and tell him the same. Additionally, tell him I'll call him if we leave as we leave and that I'll have checked with the colonel to confirm before departure. And thanks in advance for all the trouble you're going to have while I'm gone. Oh, damn, tell Rick he's in charge while I'm out. We will take off at one. Call the guys at camp and give them the details. Tell them to continue their training but to be prepared for a quick exit if we get in trouble. Again, thanks."

"Max, I did check your list and with your wife, Gina. Everything is ready for you at the team hut and at home. Good luck. Keep us informed and God bless."

"Thanks. Bye."

As Max entered the team hut, as he called it, he found both teams there and ready for him. "Hi, guys. Red team is on alert and, as of 11:00 a.m., on a two-hour response to the Lear at the airport. I will be your no. 1. Blue team, you will become home team and assume the on-site watch and response to meet any needs we might have. I understood you have my kit ready."

"Correct, sir."

"Everyone have their passports and others?"

"Yes, sir."

"OK, home team, pack up everything except for housing and camping kits. However, pack our day packs and our belt bags. Deliver it to the airport at twelve thirty. Be sure all the labels are in place, and pack it in the Lear. They'll have to know the exact weight. They have scales there. Anything missing?"

"Boss, we don't have any of the extended weapons we've been planning on."

"What weapons do you have?"

"We have .380 Mini-mites for everyone, and we have the new .380 breakdown rifles with scopes for everyone and plenty of .380 ammo."

"That'll be fine. OK, everyone, break. If you have to go home to pick up your personal stuff, as I do, then do it now. See you at the plane just before one. Oh yes, there'll be money waiting for us at the jet. Any questions?"

"Yes, boss, but they can wait."

"Good. Red team, see you just before one. Home team, keep the home fires burning, and be alert. The guys at camp will be notified and brought home if it hits the fan. Otherwise, get us what we need ASAP. Thanks and goodbye."

Gina was waiting as Max arrived home. He saw his rolling suitcase standing just inside the door. "Hi, honey. It looks like you've gotten everything ready for me."

"Yes, yes, I have. So you have to go?"

"Yes, Gina, the guys are in training in DC, and it's an urgent response."

"I understand. There's been no word on Anita?"

"Wow. Anita. I couldn't think of her first name for the life of me. Thanks. That's a big help."

"Ha ha! A big help you're going to be not even remembering names."

"Yes, I know, but when I'm rushed, I seem to not be able to drag up names."

"Well, come into the kitchen. I've fixed you some lunch, your favorite—chicken salad sandwiches, chips, and a fruit drink. Also, I've got your list in there all checked off. You can review it and see if there's anything else you might want."

"Gina, you're the best."

"Yes, I know. Now give me a big hug, you big lug. I'll miss you and worry about you, you know."

"Yes, I know. I'll miss you too and worry if you're doing everything right. Ha ha! But you know this is what I'm good at. So don't worry."

"Yes, but other people are good at things too. And I worry that you might bump into one of them, and they'll be the bad guys."

"OK, so worry. I love you."

"And I love you more, or I wouldn't let you go or do this job at all."

"Ah, it's mostly administrative, you know."

"Yeah, yeah sure, and it's mostly downhill, so you won't tax yourself either."

"Right, see, you knew all along."

"Right, anyway, be careful, don't do everything yourself, eat, sleep, and hurry home. And you could phone once in a while, but if not, pass along messages."

"OK, and you feel free to interrogate Kathy if you're anxious."

"OK, now I've a couple of things to do myself upstairs. You read over your list and let me know if you need anything else. Sit still a few minutes, eat, and relax. I'll just be a few minutes. How long have you got?"

"Just about another twenty minutes. Then I'll have to leave for Love Field and the Lear."

"OK, back in a bit."

Gina says, "All set, Max?"

"Yes, the chicken salad was great, and I can't think of a thing to add to the list. You packed it all in the bag at the door?"

"Yes, honey."

Max grabbed her up, gave her a big hug and kiss, and said, "Don't you yes-honey me. I've got to go."

"I know. Have a nice vacation, and think of me back here slaving at home for you."

"Will do. Should I bring souvenirs?"

"Just yourself. We'll take some time off to ourselves when you get back, OK?"

"OK, love you."

"Love you. Bye."

Max was the next to last to arrive at the Love Field hangar. He stopped in to say hello to Vic Anderson, the head pilot. "Hi, Max. All your gang here and ready?"

"Waiting on one. Should be here any moment."

"We're near max weight according to the weights your guys gave me. I've got the tip tanks on and full fuel so we won't have to refuel in El Salvador. Just touch down, unload, and come home. That OK with you?"

"Yes, Vic, and sorry about the short notice."

"No problem. Now let me finish this paperwork. Let me know when your last man's here. Maybe we can leave a few minutes early."

"Right."

One of his crew says, "Max, you need to get your money. The rest of us have already signed for ours, everyone but George. He's not here yet."

"Phone George and let him know we're waiting on him."

"No need, Max, here he is now. He's pulling his bag out of the car in the parking lot."

"Good, last call. As soon as George is in, load our personal luggage. And have him get his money. I'll go tell Vic we're here and ready."

Max says to the pilot, "Vic, last guy's here and loading his personal bag. Everyone else is making a pit stop. Ready when you are."

"OK, get aboard as you're ready. I'll be right there with my copilot, Vic Muranske."

Max addresses his crew, "Everyone, the pilot is Vic Anderson, and the copilot is Vic Muranske. Get aboard."

"Boss," said George, "sorry I was a little late."

"You weren't late, George. You were seven minutes early. We were just anxious for you. Never apologize. Just do your best, and we'll always understand even if you are late. You might take a ribbing for it though."

"OK, thanks, boss."

"OK, no more boss on this assignment. I'm your no. 1, and try to call one another by number. We don't want others to know our names unless necessary, OK?"

In unison, they replied, "OK, no 1. Ha ha!"

The pilots got on board and did their thing. After a short period, Vic stuck his head in and said, "Hello, guys, welcome aboard. Our flight time is three hours and fifteen minutes. We've got a full load. Have a good trip with us and a good assignment. Stay safe at your destination and do a good job. You guys are our safety net, and we know it. Thanks. On arrival, we'll taxi you to a special area, off-load you and your stuff, and take off. No need to refuel. Max, please let me know if you're going to use any electronics on board. We can handle it, just want to know. Don't use anything until we're up to altitude. I'll tell you when, and you tell me what. OK?"

"Yes, thanks, Vic. Let's go."

Shortly after take-off, "Max, we're at altitude. You can use your cell phone now if you like."

"Thanks. I'll let you know when I'm off."

Max dialed up Bob. "Bob, we departed at 1:00 p.m. sharp. Will you notify my secretary, Kathy? She's keeping the clock and diary. And notify the colonel. See if there is anything new to report. If not, don't bother to call back."

"OK, Max, good luck. God bless, and may the wind be at your back."

"Thanks, Bob. Bye."

Max addresses his crew, "Guys, Bob says, 'May the wind be at your back.' OK, Vic, I'm off. I don't expect any incoming except for emergency and will notify you if so."

"Thanks, Max."

"OK, guys, questions? Let's do a little planning and then try to get about an hour of sleep or at least rest."

Always able to sleep regardless of the circumstances, Max's nap was interrupted by Vic's voice. "OK, guys, we're coming into San Salvador now. I'll swing over in a moment and let you see the logo volcanoes, El Boqueron and El Picacho, on your right. OK, there they are. El Boqueron is the shorter flat-topped one, and El Picacho is the taller pointed one. Actually, Boqueron is not flat topped. The top just blew off a few thousand years ago. It looks like a hollow-point bullet. The hole in the top is about two miles across, and the depth is about a half mile. There's a cinder cone down in the center, but there are actually some small farms on the inside on the way down to it. It's a long walk, but I doubt you'll have time to make it."

In almost exactly three and a quarter hours after take-off, "OK, time to land this thing." He leveled out, slowed, and made a perfect landing. After a short taxi, they departed the plane.

"Hi, Colonel."

"Hello, guys, welcome to El Salvador. Can I help you unload?"

"No, Colonel, the guys will get it. As soon as we unload, Vic is taking the aircraft back to Dallas. No need for refueling."

"JJ's here and will be with us in a moment. He's clearing up your arrival and all. There will be no inspection. Between us, we managed that. I thought you might have some things that didn't need it."

"Right, thanks. This is the same little terminal that we used last year."

"Right. Let's go inside, and when your guys get the stuff in, JJ and I both would like to meet them."

After about a five minute unload, Max again addresses his crew, "Guys, this is the colonel, and this is JJ, the U.S. Embassy attaché. Now let me introduce the red team. Normally, Russ is no. 1, but he's in training just now, so I've taken over." Max proceeded to introduce the team.

"Max, I've gotten you perfect quarters. Senor Reitmann has a house for each of his grown kids. One of his daughters is away in the States. Her husband is doing his internship at a hospital there. The house is vacant, and he insists that your team use it as your quarters for the duration of your stay. The house normally has a full staff. It's quite large. But while the daughter is away, it is only minimally staffed. He is sending over a cook and another staff member to look after your needs while you're here. Of course, he wants to meet your team and wants you all to eat at his house ASAP but understands the urgency of your business here. And he will wait until you might have time anytime during your stay. He sends his personal felicitations. His house is only two blocks away from yours."

"Sounds good. What other surprises have you for us?"

"Well, the judge sends his best as well and expects a visit—anytime as he says. He said to tell you the prior warrants on Russ and Vic had been quashed and that there would be no repercussions, thanks to the briefings and depositions they gave him. He has readied six special cars for you with his best wishes."

"VWs?"

"Right on."

"Good. They are less conspicuous and easy to get around in. No news?"

"No, there's been nothing else. We've combed the town, of course, and we've questioned anyone who might have seen anything. The seven-fifteen sighting is the last."

"How's Chuck holding up?"

"OK, but he asked to be included as much as possible. He understands that his signature on the letter 1 and letter 2 documents mean you can send him to the States on a moment's notice. But he asks that he stay here. He also asks that you make his home, which you named the Alamo, your HQ. It's perfectly situated and has communications."

"Thanks, Colonel. Tell him that we gladly accept his hospitality as a HQ site. We're two three-man shifts, and at any time, those on shift might need to catch a little sleep there. But otherwise, we'll be housed at the other residence. Let him know that I am anxious to speak with him, and yes, he may stay, with no interference. We'd like nothing better than to keep him informed and up to speed. Also, he might well be of help in several circumstances. Otherwise, he is to attend to his normal duties here and to keep the rumors at the lowest possible level. There are likely FARN members on staff and used to feed back info on our progress. Let's use that but prevent its being used against us. Tell him I'll see him ASAP but that I need to get a few things in order first."

"Will do. OK, let's ferry you guys and your equipment to the residence."

Max spent the time during travel to the residence catching up on all the colonel and JJ had done during the day and asking lots of questions. The other team members just gawked like tourists as they rode along. Every few minutes, they would ask the colonel a question about a building, some trumpet flowers, or a waif along the roadway.

"OK, here we are. I've had keys made for each of you. Your vehicles are in the courtyard." And there they were—six brand-new VW bugs, each a different color.

The colonel acquainted them with the residence, its security, and its amenities. They all marveled at the size and view it commanded from the lower slope of El Boqueron. The area of town was known as Escalon, or upward slope. There were bedrooms for twice their number and baths as well. But the feature they most admired was the beautiful swimming pool and its view. There were three staff members present—the main houseboy or butler, the gardener, and a guard or *serrano*. The cook and her helper and housemaid would arrive before the evening meal.

The colonel released them all to pick their rooms and unpack as much or little as they liked. Few unpacked completely but just loosened their packs and stacked out a few things, like toiletries, that were used daily. They were told the house water was potable, and Senor Reitmann had installed a water softener system exactly like that Max had installed in the Alamo, Chuck's house.

Shortly, they were all back on the big patio over the pool, ready for instructions. "First, I want you to know that the house is partitioned, and the servants are locked out of our use area whenever we like but mostly at night. Additionally, each room—as you might have observed—is safety lockable from within and without.

"Now, number 3, I'd like you to lay out and distribute the weapons and ammo. Everyone is to carry a day pack for the needs of that day. Pick your vehicles and pack whatever provisions you think you might need in them. List anything you might want or need. Pack away your breakdown rifles and some extra ammo for them.

"Number 4, you need to set up communications here that will interface with the system we have in El Salvador. Each of you will have a walkie-talkie on their system, but don't lug it with you. Just keep it in your car. Set up our comm system here as a user. Everyone is to carry their comm unit and a spare battery in their day pack. Set up a charger for two additional batteries each here and one in each car.

"Number 5, break out our individual beacons and distribute them. Then set up to arrange for two Cessna aircraft trackers and two ground vehicle trackers. Set one up on your car. Hold the other for another vehicle to be designated. Number 6, help number 5 as he needs you, and pick up the lists, go to the store at the foot of Escalon, and get the supplies requested. Also, get ice chests and water for each vehicle. Add snack food and others. Look in the kitchen and see what additional supplies they might need there, that is, milk, eggs, etc.

"I'm off to the Alamo to see Chuck and get us started with a HQ there. Check in with me as you get done the items I've specified, others I've forgotten, or those that you think of. Oh, yes, we'll break up into two shifts. First shift will be noon to midnight, numbers 1, 3, and 5. As soon as you're through with your tasks, numbers 2, 4, and 6, I want you to hit the hay. Your shift will be midnight to noon. See you later."

Max arrived at Chuck's house, the Alamo. "Hi, Chuck. Sorry about your wife. We'll do everything in our power to get her back quickly and safely."

"Hi, Max. Am I glad to see you, guys. Sometimes you've been just a pain in the butt but not today. It's our fault, you know. Anita just never has taken security to heart except here at home. She just traipsed around town like she owned it."

"Well, Chuck, I'm sure after this she'll be cured. It might have happened anyway. Who knows?"

"Thanks. Max, thanks for the words of encouragement, and most of all, thanks for letting me stay and hopefully be of some help."

"You know more about El Salvador and have influence and savvy that we might need. We do need you to pay attention to your job and keep the speculation down. I can't brook any interference, but we welcome all the help we can get. Also, I know if it were me, I'd like to be hooked into the latest info, and you're welcome to that. Also, I accept your hospitable offer of using your house, the Alamo, as our HQ. We'll be adding a little comm gear but not much.

"Can we count on a little food too? I'll have at least one staff member, if not three, here all the time. And we'd like to commandeer an extra bedroom with a bath to take a nap in or to clean up in. I think your downstairs study or library would be perfect as HQ, and you show me which bedroom and bath to use."

"Fine, fine, we seldom use the library anyway. And you can use the first bedroom on the right at the top of the stairs. It has a full bath with it. I'll see that the house staff understand your need for privacy. And if you'd like, I'll have them make you a couple of sandwiches and some fruit right away."

"Thanks, Chuck. Then without adieu, I'll start right in." Max went into the library and began moving a few things around to make a more convenient work area. He closed the connecting door into the downstairs den and one of the doors to the private patio that stepped down to the pool some thirty feet distant and at a ten-foot lower level. He rearranged the patio furniture and stole a couple of chairs from the larger upper patio to fill out his perceived needs.

Max dialed JJ. "Elvis is in the room."

"Max, glad you are here. Where are you? Sorry I didn't get a chance to meet with you at the airport, but after I got your things cleared, I had a call from the embassy. Had to go. Where are you?"

"I'm setting up HQ at Chuck's house, and we're housed in an extra house of Senor Reitmann's about three quarters of a mile away. How are things at your end?"

"OK, busy but no indication of anything sinister. Can I come over?"

"Please. I'm just trying to fix things up here to work out of. Don't hurry. Just call first so that I'll be here to meet you."

"OK, it's almost six. I'll be there at about seven."

"Wait a minute . . . Chuck, can we have supper here at about seven thirty? Five and yourself."

"Done. I'll send out to the Sheraton for a takeout. They do a good job."

"Thanks . . . JJ, we'll plan to eat at seven thirty. You plan to eat with us."

"Will do. My wife is playing bridge this evening anyway."

"Perfect. We'll see you at about seven or slightly after. Bye."

Max dialed the colonel. "Colonel, this is Max. Could you eat with us at Chuck's house at seven thirty?"

"Yes, glad to. How's Chuck holding out?"

"Looks good to me. Anxious, that's all. In the interim, have you talked to my no. 5 about aircraft?"

"Yes, I have. I'm at the airport now, seeing to the charters. I've got two friends whom we can trust to fly for us."

"Good, keep that moving. If it interferes with dinner, let it. We need to get a plane up ASAP."

"In that case, it might interfere. I'm just now ready to call your no. 5 and have him meet us here. It's unlikely I can make your seven thirty. Sorry."

"No problem. First things first. Bye."

Max's phone rang. "It's number 2. Max, we've gotten all our assigned tasks done, and I've released my shift to rest until midnight. Number 3 is done and has been helping numbers 4 and 5 with their tasks. Number 5 says he is awaiting word from the colonel regarding aircraft outfitting."

"Good, I just talked to the colonel, and I'm sure number 5 is on the phone with him now. Take off and rest up. Tell number 3 to come to Chuck's and bring his HQ gear with him. You're going to be caught short for sleep when it's your shift."

"Don't worry. We'll be fine. Most of the work and worry happens in the daytime anyway. Oh, by the way, the cook and her helper have arrived and are bustling about, putting up the supplies that number 6 bought.

I told her our schedules and that we didn't need any supper tonight. She was perplexed by our schedule but seemed to understand. Bye."

At seven thirty promptly, Chuck told Max the meal was set. In the interim, JJ had arrived. Max told Chuck that his number 5 and the colonel would likely be very late, if at all. They proceeded to eat a very nicely laid-out meal. They had a few drinks as well, but Max and number 3 each had only one. They exchanged pleasantries, mostly over the meal. The serious discussions didn't get started until afterward on the patio while number 3 set up some comm gear for the HQ function.

At about ten, the colonel and number 5 arrived and told about their setup of the two planes and briefing, test flying, and checking out the airborne trackers. The first flight was set to start at midnight, with refueling every four hours but with a capacity of six hours. Then there was to be a shift change at noon to correspond with their schedule. Coverage would not be present during the refueling and at shift change unless there was call for it. Number 5 explained the spiraling-up-and-out search pattern that would cover the entire country and beyond in just a few short hours.

At about eleven, the group parted, and Max checked out number 5's work. Then the three of them drove separately back to the residence and found the others had just gotten up and were in various stages of readiness. They cross-briefed one another, and the second shift departed for HQ at Chuck's at about eleven forty-five. The first shift opted for a quick swim and bed.

The night was silent except for the *serranos* all over town blowing their whistles and some firing a shot to let everyone nearby know they were there and on the job every hour. That was something to get used to.

The KPPS search aircraft flew two tanks of fuel and covered the entire country at varying altitudes. But no KPPS signal was present.

26

BALLOONS 2 AND 3

At 9:00 a.m., about an hour into the third flight, a KPPS signal was received by the pilot. He was electrified. He couldn't believe it. He'd flown for eight-plus hours with nothing and then suddenly, out of nowhere, a signal. He flattened his flying as instructed and turned into the signal. Each time he turned, he lost it. But when he flattened out, he regained it. The plane in a bank was blocking the signal from the antennae beneath the plane, just as they told him it would.

Following instructions, he went to maximum altitude, supposedly ten thousand feet, but he knew it was a little less. He then tracked in on the signal, which was coming from the opposite side of El Boqueron. There was almost nothing there except forest. He flew dead over the signal and could tell because the direction went from front to rear. He pressed the GPS location indicator and received a readout. He quickly noted it down.

He flew for some time and distance in a spiral so that, when he turned back into the track, he was crossing his original path at a right angle. As he passed over the signal, it again stated a front-to-rear indication as he passed over it. Again, he pressed the GPS locator button, and it read out a location almost identical to the first. He flew for home in a circuitous path so as not to alert anyone who might have seen him pass over. That was unlikely since he was at almost ten thousand feet.

The pilot picked up the communicator given him by number 5. "K-Air to K-Ground, K-Air to K-Ground, over." And he said again, "K-Air to K-Ground, K-Air to K-Ground."

Numbers 4 and 6 nearly stumbled over each other trying to get to the HQ communicator first. Number 4 won. "K-Ground to K-Air, we read you loud and clear, over."

"I have a signal. I repeat, I have a signal. It occurs every thirty seconds for about two seconds. Its ID readout is J-102. I have tracked it at max altitude twice at right angles. The readings were latitude 13°46'59.49" N and longitude 89°19'54.98" W, over."

"We read you, and there is no need to repeat. We have that. Please proceed to airport and land. Someone will contact you soon, over."

"Roger, over and out."

"We got her, number 2."

"Great, I heard. Get the map out, and let's pinpoint it."

Fetching the map, the points are compared, "There it is. The two points are practically the same. It's on the other side of Boqueron. Right, there appears to be a little village there. It's unnamed here, but someone has to know it. There are only a couple of roads stated here as leading there, one from around the southern base of the mountain from Santa Tecla and the other from much farther around northern Picacho and Boqueron from the other direction. Here, there also appears to be a third road westbound from the top of Boqueron. And if there's a connection down this side into Santa Tecla, that would be the shortest way but likely most dangerous and least likely. What time is it?"

"Almost ten thirty, number 2."

"OK, here's what I want you to do. Number 4, I want you to go to the airport, get backup there, confirm all this, and then go back here. Number 6, I want you to get a tracker on your car and go to Santa Tecla and then up Boqueron. See if you can find a way around to the other side on top and a way down the other side. If we lose comm with you, you will likely have to relay through our plane. He is down from time to time for less than an hour to refuel. Get the colonel to have someone go with you. And stop in Santa Tecla for supplies and a full load of fuel. Go. And good luck."

Number 2 dialed the colonel. "Colonel, sorry to bother you, but we have a signal. It's coming from the back side of Boqueron. I'm sending number 6 on a chase up around the top and down, but I need someone to go with him. Can you get someone to meet him at the Esso station in Santa Tecla within the hour?"

"I'll go myself if necessary."

"No, Colonel, but we do need you here at HQ when convenient. We need some map-reading and town-naming skills. And I'm sure that number 1 will want you here when he arrives. It's now only about an hour from shift change."

"OK, I'll detail a guard from the Colonia plant."

"Out of uniform would be best."

"OK, can someone pick him up?"

"I'll detail number 6 to pick him up and then proceed to Santa Tecla. Will he be ready right away?"

"Yes, his name is Pablo. I'll call him and be right there. Oh yes, he does speak English quite well."

"Thanks. Goodbye."

Number 2 rang Max. "Hello, number 2, what's up?"

"I'm sorry to bother you but wanted you up. Shift change is in an hour, and we've got good news. The aircraft got a signal from Anita's emergency rescue beacon at about 9:00 a.m. He located it precisely at maximum altitude and then left. The ID is correct, the PRF is correct, and the pulse width is correct. He got two precise GPS locations at right angles, and they are practically identical. The signal is coming from the back side of Boqueron from an unnamed minivillage. There are three ways in and three out. One is around Boqueron from Santa Tecla, the second is up and around the top of Boqueron and back down, and the third is the long way, around Picacho and Boqueron. I've taken a number of actions but thought, with shift change so close, you needed to be notified and get on in here."

"Good news, number 2, I'm sure you've done the right things. I won't try to second-guess you. The others are already up, and we're just now eating. The cook understood her instructions, and she's good. She understands that you'll want more of the same when you get here in about an hour and a half. See you soon."

Numbers 1, 3, and 5 showed up about twenty minutes later. They sat quietly while number 2 briefed them on all his actions.

Max immediately got number 6 on the phone. "Where are you?"

"Just at the foot of Escalon. I picked up the guard, Pablo, and am ready to head for Santa Tecla and fueling."

"No, come to HQ. Your shift is up. Trade cars with number 3, and he'll take your route. You were short-shifted on your rest time. Time to rest."

"OK, boss, but I can do it."

"Thanks, but no thanks. No telling what we're likely to run into. I need you rested for your shift tonight."

"Yes, sir. Be there in just a few minutes. Bye."

"Number 3, you heard?"

"Yes, sir. I'll go to Santa Tecla with the guard, Pablo; pick up supplies and fuel; and attempt to find the way up, around, and down the other side of the mountain. Then what?"

"First things first. Find your way."

"Right, boss. See ya."

Max called number 4, who was with the plane, getting fuel. He reversed his orders as well. "You understand number 5 will be there promptly to replace you?"

"Number 5, do you understand?"

"Right, number 1, I understand."

"Go to field. Fly and double-check the signal and sight without alerting anyone."

"Right, off with you."

Just then, the colonel arrived, and Max quickly briefed him. The colonel began studying the map and said he did not know the name of the village but would make a couple of calls, which he proceeded to do. Max called JJ and reported the good news without the details.

It was now 1:00 pm. Anita had been missing for about thirty hours. There was nothing at 2:00 p.m., and then at 3:00 p.m., HQ comm received a call. "Number 1, this is number 5, over."

"Yes, number 5, I read you loud and clear, over."

"I can confirm the prior data received. All numbers are good. I'm coming back."

"Yes, do that, over and out."

At three thirty, HQ comm was alerted again. "Number 5 to number 1, over."

"Yes, number 5, I read you five by five, over."

"We are coming into your area now and have received two—I repeat, two—new signals. They are R-106 and R-108. We have not had time to locate them yet, over."

"OK, stand by, over and out."

Max quickly consulted his log book and found that the two signals were listed as belonging to the ambassador's wife and daughter. Max quickly called JJ. "JJ, this is Max. We just picked up signals from the ambassador's wife and daughter. I hope they are just testing them. You need to check right away."

"OK, I'll call you right back."

The colonel's KPPS alert center called HQ and reported the receipt of two signals, one from R-106 and the other from R-108. There had been no test or accidental alert called in. "What action should we take?"

"We have registered this and are presently checking. Stand by and record all such alerts with time and others. Go ahead and alert your ground-tracking crew and have them stand by."

"Colonel, did you hear?"

"Yes, I hope this isn't an all out."

"Me too, but the circumstances suggest it. Have your ground-tracking crew attempt to home in on the signal as reported from the plant KPPS station. If they locate it, tell them to report immediately here and stand off and observe."

Incoming Radio transmission, "K-Air to K-Ground, we are tracking the double-signal vehicle from a distance, and it is moving out of the northwest corner of the city toward open countryside, over."

"Ground to Air, keep on it. We have no confirmation yet. Will get back to you when we do, over and out."

Incoming radio transmission, "KPPS central to HQ, over."

"Go ahead, KPPS central, over."

"We have the double signal reported beginning to fade toward the northwest, over."

"OK, continue to monitor. Report any dramatic changes. Have you a report from your ground tracker? Over."

"Yes, we have directed the van to proceed to the extreme northwest of the city as quickly as possible, but they are yet to report a signal, over."

"Good, keep on it. Over and out."

Max addresses the colonel, "Colonel, spread out the best maps we have of the area. Do we have a topographic map of it?"

"What's that?"

"A topo map is one that shows the ground elevations throughout the area. It also has roads and major landmarks. However, it mostly is to show elevations above sea level."

"We don't have one, but I'll put out an urgent call for one."

"Good. Do we have a name yet for the little village on the back side of Boqueron?"

"No, not yet. My call back should be anytime now."

Max's phone rang. "Hello, this is number 1."

"Max, this is JJ. Bad news, the ambassador's wife and daughter have been taken from the front of the residence. Two marine guards were killed. One attacker was shot and is in bad condition. We are rushing him to the hospital as we speak."

"JJ, were either of the girls hit or hurt?"

"No, not according to the guard who held on just until I got there. He died before he could be transported. Max, please tell me you still have a track on their beacons."

"Affirmative. Our air spotter has tracked them to the northwestern part of the city and said they appeared to be out into the countryside. We have our KPPS track van from the plant rushing to that area but with no signal yet."

"Thank god."

"You're welcome."

"Max, that's blasphemous."

"Yes, I know. Just get over here ASAP and help the colonel and me with our analysis and tactics."

"I'm en route."

Time for an update review of resources, "OK, Colonel, JJ's here. We need to review our stance. JJ, you, I, and the colonel need to review our resources and current stance and set up some tactics.

"First, we have two trackers committed to airborne. We need to keep them that way and direct both pilots to conserve their own reserves so that we can keep one in the air at all times. Number 5 is with them and will be until midnight. He'll train them in airborne tactic.

"Second, we have two ground trackers committed to the field, one trying to find a route over Boqueron, the second heading northwest in an attempt to catch a signal from the double-signal vehicle. There are two additional trackers available to us. One is the KPPS site spare and the other our spare. I suggest we commit them both ASAP. I'd like to commit them to two armored vehicles.

"Colonel, I'd like you to call Chuck and get two from him. JJ, I'd like you to commit six armed marines to those two vehicles. I'll commit my number 5 as driver for one and, if I can get him back, my number 3 as driver for the other. Is this doable? Colonel?"

"Max, I'll peel off and get Chuck on the line right now."

"JJ?"

"I'll get you the marines. They'll be anxious to go with the loss of two of their comrades."

"OK, you two work on that."

HQ comm received a call. "Number 3 to HQ, number 3 to HQ, over."

"Go ahead, number 3. This is number 1, over."

"I've found the route. We didn't go all the way down the back side, but I know we can. Also, I got the signal on the back side and can confirm it. I've returned to the summit to contact you. What do you want me to do? Over."

"Number 3, can you project a time from HQ to the signal via your route? Over."

"Yes, it takes about a half hour up, a half hour around, and I suspect another half hour down so an hour and a half total, over."

"Does your companion know the route? Over."

"Yes, and he's very coherent, over."

"OK, number 3, I want you to come to HQ ASAP, over."

"Will do, over and out."

Max gives out new assignments, "Colonel, I want you to take number 3's place and with his companion, the guard Pablo, retrace the route and get within a close but safe distance from the holding. When number 3 arrives, have him outfit you with appropriate arms. I'll need you at the scene to take control at the appropriate time."

"Sure, Max, but there's no need for the arms. I have my own."

"OK, but I want you to have one of our .380 breakdown rifles with scope and with a communicator. I'll have to depend on you on the far side of the mountain, if our communications break down. You'll need to take the lead. Savvy?"

"OK, I savvy and will do. I'll take off a bit and equip myself with provisions and arms for the two of us."

"Thanks. Get the answer from Chuck about the armored vehicles, and then take off."

"Max?"

"Yes, JJ."

"I've arranged for the marines, two teams of three. Each team will be standard equipped with sidearms and M16s. The third will be equipped with a sidearm and a BAR. Where and when?"

"Stand by, and I'll see."

"K-Ground to K-Air, over."

"K-Air, go An incoming radio transmission."

"Number 5, I need you here ASAP if you think your pilots can handle continuous coverage without you, over."

"They can. I'll have the second plane in the air immediately, and we will hand off the track when he acquires. That will take about fifteen minutes. I'll be there in thirty minutes, over."

"No, I'll have you met at the field when you come in. It'll be two of the armored cars with the KPPS spare trackers on board. I need you to fit out both as trackers and proceed to the embassy to pick up a team of three marines for each car. Come directly here, and I'll have number 3 drive the second car. I'll give you directions then, over."

"Yes, I understand, over and out."

Now for another input, "Colonel?"

"Yes, Max. I've just gotten off the phone with Chuck. He says 'OK and will do.' When and where?"

"Tell him and your KPPS station that the spare tracker there is to be picked up by one of the armored cars and transported to the air field and turned over to number 3 when he lands in about thirty minutes. He can drop the delivery person off at the Colonia plant."

"OK, I'll tell him, and then I'm gone."

"Good. And, Colonel, may the wind be at your back. Before you go, I want you two to note that there are now two additional items being put in place. An armored tracking vehicle driven by number 5 with three armed marines, one with a BAR, will be dispatched to go south around Boqueron. An armored tracking vehicle driven by number 3 and three marines similarly armed will be dispatched to follow on the embassy beacons to the northwest. JJ and I will stay here to help coordinate the rescues. Note it is now 4:00 p.m."

Max dialed Bob in Dallas. "Hello, Bob?"

"Yes, Max."

"I've got a moment and am reporting in." Max proceeded to brief Bob on everything that happened so far. "Well, that's a summary of our current standing. I'm going to phone Marvin next and give him the same report."

"Good report, Max, and I think you've got everything covered. I'll report the same upstairs."

"Thanks, and please make the same report to Kathy at our campus."

"Will do. Good luck, and may the wind be at your back."

"Thanks, Bob. Goodbye."

Max dialed Marvin in DC and made the same report with much the same response. This had left everyone equally anxious but hopeful.

Max then dialed Chuck at the Colonia plant. "Chuck, everything we have is in play and working. Why don't you come on home and at least listen in on the action? No hurry. I expect things to take a few hours to develop."

"Thanks, Max. I'll be there within the hour. I'm making sure the armored cars are stationed and full of fuel and some provisions."

"Thank you, Chuck. See you soon."

About an hour later, the colonel and number 3 arrived and essentially changed places. Only minutes later, number 5 arrived with six marines in two armored cars. After a quick briefing, number 3 became the driver of the second armored car. Both quickly departed in the same direction, but at the bottom of Escalon, number 3 went northwest, and number 5 went southeast.

An incoming radio transmission, "K-Air to HQ, over."

"This is HQ, go ahead, over."

"Back in the air and northwest of the city. The dual-signal vehicle is moving more rapidly now and appears to be veering more to the west, over."

"Can you give me a GPS reading, over?"

"Yes, the vehicle is near latitude 13°49'39.01" N and longitude 89°15'54.77" W, over."

"Stand by one."

Max quickly translated this into longitude and latitude on his laptop and looked up the reading on his map. "K-Air, over."

"Still here, over."

"Stay with it, but keep out of sight, over and out."

Max' analysis, "JJ, it looks like they might be on this road that circles around behind Picacho and even later behind Boqueron toward the same little village where the first signal is located. It's too early to tell, but they might be going to the same location."

"Max, that makes sense. We need to concentrate our tactics on that area and make ready for a rescue."

"Right, but again, it's too early to tell."

"What else might they have up their sleeves?"

"Well, JJ, they haven't made any ransom demands yet."

"No, they haven't, but as you point out, it's early yet."

"Nevertheless, JJ, we need to break out our ransom case, and you need to see about availability of cash for a ransom. Also, we need to estimate the time required for any of the bad guys to leave the village and return to a point where they can report to someone in the city, their bosses, by phone. This could be an important delay in their communication cycle that we can take advantage of in the ransom cycle."

"OK, Max, I'll look into the money. You prep the case and estimate their approximate communication delay."

Max's phone rang. "Max, this is Russ. Don't mean to interrupt, but we're anxious to know how things are going."

"Russ, I don't have much time, but I will say we have signals from all three beacons and are narrowing down. We are just now formulating our strike plan when things stabilize. Everything is working well, and everyone is busy. Wish you guys were all here as this narrows down to a finish, but all is well in hand. However, you understand the anxiety as this comes to a climax. Thanks for calling. Your team is performing up to spec. Tell the guys hello for me, but goodbye for now."

"OK, thanks for the update. Bye."

An incoming radio communication, "KPPS to HQ, over."

"Yes, KPPS, over."

"The signal from the extre, me northwest has been coming and going, but we haven't received it for the last five to seven minutes, over."

"Thank you, KPPS. Have you heard anything from your ground track team?"

"Yes, sir. Wait, stand by one . . . we have just heard from our team. They are receiving the dual signals and are closing on the source. The source apparently took the road to the west around El Picacho, and they are in chase, over."

"KPPS, tell them not to close too much. They should just follow them but at a distance of about one half their maximum range. Tell them to keep in touch and explain that we have dispatched an armored car with marines to follow behind them. However, you are likely to lose communication with them once they round the mountain. Do they have one of our small communicators? Over."

"Yes, sir, they do, over."

"Tell them to keep it on. The follow-up car, our aircraft, or someone atop one of the mountains will communicate with them with further instructions shortly after you lose communication, over."

"Yes, sir. I'll let you know when we lose communication with them, over."

"Good, I think their destination is a small village on the backside of El Boqueron, over."

"Yes, sir, that would most likely be El Gato, over."

"The cat? Over."

"Si, senor, I was born and raised there, over."

"Excellent. When you lose communication, I want you to turn over your job there at KPPS to another. Is someone available? Over."

"Yes, senor, Pablito, another guard, over."

"Good, I want you to come directly here to HQ when that occurs, understand? Oh, and what's your name? Over."

"My name is Alto. I understand and will be there soon, over and out."

An incoming radio transmission, "HQ to van B, over."

"Go ahead, HQ."

"When you get out of town to the northwest, you need to turn west around Picacho road and understand you are behind our KPPS van, which is equipped with one of our communicators, over."

"OK, will do, over and out."

A new radio com, "HQ to van A, over."

"Go ahead, HQ."

"It looks like both teams north and south are going to converge at the same village, El Gato, over."

"The cat? Over."

"Yes, over and out."

A new radio com, "K-Air to HQ, over."

"Go ahead, over."

"I heard those last transmissions. Am back in the air and heading between the peaks to pick up the signals, over."

"ETA? Over."

"I expect to be in range of all signals within fifteen minutes, over and out."

An outgoing com by Max, "HQ to Colonel, over."

Nothing.

27

A RECKONING

"JJ, we need to strategize a bit."

"Right, let's set out our resources again:

VW-1 with Colonel and a guard – unknown, going down the mountain east of El Gato
Arm-1 with number 5 and three marines – circling Boqueron on the south toward El Gato
K-Van with guard – north of El Gato and following dual signal
Arm-2 with number 3 three marines – approaching Picacho turnoff
K-Air1 – up between the peaks
K-Air2 – on the ground, on standby."

At that moment, they received a call from the HQ guard. "Sir, a plant guard, Alto, is here."

"Thanks, please let him in."

"HQ to Colonel, over."

Nothing.

A new outgoing com by Max, "HQ to K-Air1, over."

"K-Air1, go ahead, over."

"I need you to act as a relay to the vehicles on the far side, over."

"Roger, over."

"Call for VW-1 on Boqueron and determine his location and ETA to El Gato, over."

"Roger, over and out."

Max turning to the newcomer, "Alto, glad you're here."

With that, Max showed him how to work their radio and instructed him to brief the colonel via their airborne relay on the details of the village El Gato and possibly set up points therein. Alto quickly went about a prolonged and relayed conversation through the circling aircraft to the colonel.

"Done, senor."

"Thanks, Alto. Please stand by out on the patio, and thanks."

"OK, JJ, we need to confirm all their locations and ETAs for El Gato."

A new radio com by Max, "HQ to K-Air1, over. Request a location and ETA to El Gato for all units, over."

"Right, will relay, over and out."

An incoming com, "K-Air1 to all units. HQ requests your individual ETAs to El Gato, over."

One by one the individual field units check in over a period of but a few minutes.

"Go ahead, VW-1, over."

"Go ahead, Arm-1, over."

"Go ahead, Arm-2, over."

"Go ahead, K-Van, over."

The individual check-ins are confirmed to HQ, "K-Air1 to HQ, over."

"Go ahead, K-Air1, over."

"VW-1 says they are in the vicinity of El Gato now and assessing their best standoff location. Arm-1 says their ETA is about forty minutes. K-Van says they are on-site. Arm-2 says their ETA is about one hour, over."

"Thanks, over."

"Roger, over and out."

About twenty minutes later, "K-Air1 to HQ, over."

"Go ahead, over."

"We are receiving three signals. Have not identified individual signals, but all are from the same area, over."

"OK, relay any comm for HQ, but otherwise, let them communicate directly so as not to add confusion to the scenario. Please relay to VW-1 that he is in immediate charge, over and out."

Max' instructions are relayed to the field units, "K-Air1 to all field units. VW-1 is in immediate charge. Communicate among yourselves as you see fit. We will relay appropriate communications to HQ, over and out."

"OK, JJ, let's recap and get a time line.

> VW-1 with Colonel in charge – on-site
> Arm-1 with number 5 and three marines – forty-five minutes out
> K-Van with guard – on-site
> Arm-2 with number 3 and three marines – one hour out
> K-Air1 – over area and relaying comm."

At that moment, Chuck walked in. "What's up, Max?"

"Hi, Chuck, you're just in time for the action. Just stand by with Alto there. He was born in El Gato and has just gotten off the radio with the colonel giving him the layout. You can see our status of forces on our pictogram here.

"JJ, it's now five thirty. At about six thirty, all will be on-site and ready for orders. In the interim, we need to make a sketch of the area, sight unseen, and place the vehicles in their relative positions as they sort themselves out. We should be ready to strike at about seven. What's the light going to be like?"

"Well, it's summertime, so it will be light until eight thirty or nine. Also, they are on the west side of the mountains, so the light will be with them, Max."

"OK, when we get their setup, we need to have the least obvious chase through and locate the exact building and repositioning points. We should observe for as long as makes sense. And then at the least populous moment, strike."

JJ called the ambassador and asked him to come to HQ ASAP. The ambassador along with two marine guards showed in a very few minutes. "Ambassador, glad to have you. Your guards may stay on the large patio or as they perceive their duty. Things are going to pop soon. JJ will brief you and Chuck, who just arrived. Feel free to stay in here with us, but you might be more comfortable on the little patio here." The ambassador, Chuck, and JJ moved onto the little patio adjacent to the HQ area.

At seven, they received communication. "K-Air1 to HQ, over."

"Go ahead, over."

"The guys are all at El Gato and have taken up standoff positions. VW-1 reports that they are minimizing air traffic and that they have reconnoitered the immediate area for new attack positioning. In the interim, they are watching and counting people in the vicinity and in the small house where the hostages are being held. They request any orders, over."

"K-Air1, have VW-1 describe their setup and attack plan, over."

"Will do, over and out."

Max alerts the HQ team members, "JJ, get in here."

"K-Air1 to VW-1. HQ request description of current positioning, preattack positioning, and attack plan, over."

"K-Air1 to HQ, over."

"Go ahead Air, over."

"VW-1 says that they have been counting people in and out for the last hour and that the count is at a low of one or maybe two now, over."

"Tell VW-1 to initiate his attack plan now, now, now. Do not hesitate, reposition, and attack, over and out."

Max relays the attack order, "K-Air1 to VW-1, the HQ order is execute attack plan now, now, now, over."

In the village of El Gato, VW-1 announced, "VW-1 to all field teams, HQ says go."

"VW-1, repositioned within a half block and has the front doorway in my scope. K-Van, repositioned within a half block and ready for pickup. Arm-1, marines disbursed, BAR positioned to defend attack, and vehicle ready to reposition defensively on command. Arm-2, positioned defensively, marines disbursed, BAR positioned to defend attack, and vehicle ready to position defensively on my command. Go, go, go."

Suddenly, all donned bright red caps brought from the States to identify the red team and friendly combatants. All four marines sneaked around the two sides of the house and peeked into windows. Two lobbed flash-bangs in through these windows while protected by the other marine at their side. Then two quickly went to the back door and two to the front door. Both armored vehicles raced to the front porch area; two armed men came out the front door, firing at the vehicles. Both were promptly shot dead by double shots fired from the .380 rifles scoped in on them from the colonel, number 3, and number 5. Two marines dashed in the front door while two more forced the rear while shouting, "U.S. Marines, drop to the floor!" One additional kidnapper inside the house, just recovering from a flash-bang, raised his weapon and was shot dead by two of the marines. All three women were located and freed from their bonds. They donned bright yellow caps given by the marines.

Both armored vehicles quickly moved into a defensive V formation just outside the front door. First, one marine in his bright red cap appeared, followed by three others, each shielding a smaller female hostage wearing bright yellow caps. Suddenly, two men came charging from across the street, firing at the armored vehicles, and were promptly cut down by BAR fire from the two other marines hidden close by.

All three hostages were quickly put into Arm-1 with an attendant marine. The other marines jumped into Arm-2 and, led by VW-1, sped away toward the south end of the village. The BAR marines were picked up by the K-Van. The double-back doors were locked open, and the two BARs were steadied on stands and trained out the back to subdue anyone who might follow.

The whole entourage proceeded on the south road around Boqueron, with VW-1 leading and K-Van trailing. The colonel radioed their circumstances to K-Air1 for relay to HQ. Of course, the first of the string of messages was that all three of the hostages were recovered safely and unharmed.

Back at HQ, everyone was jubilant. Chuck was dumbstruck at the rapidity of the rescue action and the report that his wife was OK. The ambassador was just the opposite. He danced about the area and shouted, "They're safe and free!"

Only moments later, a message was delivered to the Alamo. The message was a ransom demand for US$3 million. If agreed, the answer was to be communicated through a local priest. Apparently, some lucky bad guy had been detached once all the captives were safely tucked away in El Gato. That someone sent the message to someone else, a boss, in San Salvador, who phoned in the ransom demand. Neither of them was aware that the hostages had been freed and their comrades lay dead in the streets of El Gato.

Max drew JJ aside, and they quietly made a plan. JJ went to another room and got on the phone. "HQ to K-Air1, over."

"Go ahead HQ, over."

"Tell the colonel to contact me on our secure channel as soon as he clears the mountain. Also, exercise complete. Come on home and release your pilots, over."

"Will do, HQ, over and out."

Max orders new contact info, "HQ to K-Air1, over"

"Go ahead, over."

"HQ wants you to contact them on your secure channel as soon as you've cleared the mountain, over and out."

Max turned to Chuck and the ambassador. "Ambassador, do you have a doctor and nurse on call at the embassy?"

"Yes, Max, we have two doctors and four nurses on call. One of the nurses is on call at all times at the embassy."

"OK, I think you need to get at least one doctor and maybe two nurses here to see to the women as soon as they arrive. I know they were reported well and unhurt, but they might be scraped up a bit and definitely will need some Librium or something of the sort to ease their nerves. Can you see to that?"

"Yes, immediately. Uh, and, Max, thanks from all of us."

"You're welcome. That's what we do, and the wind was at our backs."

"Max?"

"Yes, Chuck."

"Thanks from me too. I was too stunned at the rapidity of the action to assimilate what had happened. Thanks from the bottom of my heart."

"You two need to save it for the real heroes who rescued them. Chuck, as soon as they arrive, I'll disburse my troops and the marines. Maybe the ambassador will want to stay the night. I'm sure that the women will be running on high once they get checked over and the doctor and nurses leave. What say we plan a little party for all involved here at the Alamo in a couple of days? That'll give you all time to recover and plan your thank-you for the troops."

"Good idea. You'll go back to your quarters then."

"Yes, and we'll all catch up on a little rest. Besides, by then, my shift will be over. Ha ha!"

At eight thirty, they received a call. "VW-1 to HQ, over."

"Colonel, we've received a ransom note. The terms are clear and should be answered early tomorrow. So come here, and we'll disband. Meet me at my quarters, and we'll go over a plan JJ and I have lain out. I won't keep you long. And, Colonel, good job. The wind was at your back, over."

"Thanks, number 1. Our ETA is nine thirty, over and out."

Max addresses the HQ team, "OK, guys, their ETA here is nine thirty."

"Max, the doctor and two nurses say they'll be here at about nine ten."

"Perfect, Mr. Ambassador."

JJ pulled Max aside and told him that everything was set up for about eight thirty in the morning. "Good, JJ. I just talked to the colonel. He'll meet us at my quarters just after we all disburse from here. Hopefully, he'll be able to arrange the appropriate resources to help in the morning."

Promptly at nine twelve, the doctor and two nurses arrived and were badged and escorted in. They conferred with JJ and Max quickly, and they and their equipment were moved to one of the bedrooms upstairs. An adjacent bedroom was opened for them as well. The group continued to chatter among themselves uncontrollably.

Max dialed Bob in Dallas and told him the hostages had been recovered in good shape and were on the way to HQ now. He promised to call back shortly after they arrived and were inspected by the medical staff assembled. Finally, he asked Bob to notify his campus team. Max then dialed Marvin in DC and repeated the same to him.

At nine twenty-five, the convoy arrived. Several vehicles had to be rearranged in the courtyard to allow for all, but it took no longer than the entry procedure required. Everyone spilled from their vehicles, all still in bright red caps. The last to alight were the hostages in their bright yellow caps. Chuck grabbed up Anita, and the ambassador grabbed up both his wife and daughter. JJ saw to the marines and Max to his numbers 3 and 5. The colonel saw to his guards from the van. They all proceeded inside.

Max announced the agenda. "First, yellow hats to the medical facility upstairs. Second, thanks, everyone. We'll have a proper thank-you party in a couple of days so that our hostages have time to recover. Everyone, let's leave them to it."

And the group disbanded and went their separate ways. The marines were shuttled back to the embassy by numbers 3 and 5 and returned to their quarters. There were a few vehicles in the wrong hands, but there'd be plenty of time to sort them out after tomorrow.

Max, the colonel, JJ, and number 2 all retired to a far corner and discussed the next morning's tasks and how to accomplish them. The colonel had the best ideas; it was his turf. Finished, Max went to bed knowing that number 2 could handle things over his shift.

28

THE ULTIMATE RECKONING

The second shift began at midnight, and their tasks seemed to be straightening and cleaning up. In short, especially after the action of the prior shift, it was downright boring. Well, there were guns to clean, ammunition to account for, etc.

The real job of this shift was to sketch out pictograms of the upcoming day's plans. Max insisted on these pictograms, as he called them, as both communication tools for those about to go into action and, when corrected, historical documents to depict the actual happenings of a series of events. Number 2 carefully lettered on the pictograms the date and description of the events depicted. Max had left about three, the sequences of the exciting events of the day of rescue. He knew that Max would want to resketch and correct them, as well as add considerable comment to them, later. Accordingly, he carefully folded them and filed them away. Then he changed the tape in the HQ recorder. It held the audio of the prior shift that occurred within range of the HQ area it surveyed. This too he carefully labeled and filed for later review.

All this was done as numbers 4 and 6 proceeded to clean up the area and see to some refreshments and snack foods for their shift. They cleaned the weapons left out for them and inventoried the ammunition used. Then they set about checking all four of the vehicles equipped for tracking. They were then cleaned and readied for the day. Additionally, each was carefully spin-checked in a nearby parking area and refueled. They then refreshed the ice chests in each and resupplied their snack bins.

All this took most of the night hours. Around sunrise, they arranged themselves a sumptuous breakfast with the HQ cook. They then had her plan a nice luncheon for all at noon. Finally, they had her set out fruits and other snacks for the remainder of their shift. They notified the cook at the Reitmann house that she was to fix no lunch. Then at about eight, they tested the ransom kit and arranged for its easy access for later use.

At around nine, the colonel showed up and checked in with them. He saw the preparations they had made and discussed strategy with number 2, who in turn reviewed the pictogram of the plan they had discussed the night before.

The colonel then put in a serious phone call to the office of the president of El Salvador. After a little haggling, he spoke to President Marcos. They spoke for several minutes, and then the colonel hung up.

Shortly after, JJ came into HQ with several bags of money. It was divided into three parts but was all in Salvadoran colones. The first portion was small and fit neatly into an envelope, 200 bills of one-hundred-colón denomination, that is, 1,000 colones. (Two and a half colones was a U.S. dollar, so it was $4,000.) The second batch was placed in a paper bag and contained 1,250 bills of twenty-colón denomination, that is, 25,000 colones ($10,000). The third batch was also placed in bags and contained 25,000 colones of one-colón denomination, that is, 25,000 colones ($10,000). Bills in the two packages were banded together in sets of one hundred bills.

A small beacon was planted in one of the packages of bills at the bottom of the first larger denomination stack. A small magnet was planted in one of the packages of bills that would be adjacent to the beacon and in the second package. The removal of the first package would remove the magnetic field from the beacon, and it would activate. A second beacon was placed in a pack of bills at the bottom of the ransom case. There was a magnet buried in the ransom case itself that would keep it turned off until that package was removed from the ransom case. The ransom case was a rich leather model of vendor catalog case. The ransom case itself had a third beacon secreted in it. Another magnet piece was placed outside the case in concert with the feet of the case. It kept that beacon turned off until lifted off that magnet.

Each of the three beacons in the case was set to a different PRF or pulse repetition frequency. The signals emitted by these beacons were modulated each at a faster rate. The lowest rate was the case itself, and then they increased in rapidity as the money packets were removed. The team would be able to monitor these emissions and tell the stages of removal of the money from the case. Additionally, they would be able to track each of the packages of money and the case itself individually.

At about 10:30 a.m., the colonel left HQ, proceeded to the Catholic church, and told the appropriate priest that the ransom demand would be met later that day. The priest told the colonel that he had been instructed to tell him that the case was to be delivered to the priest in a given confessional at 3:00 p.m. during Mass being held in celebration of the patron saint of El Salvador. There would be many in line at the confessional, and he should stand in line and wait his turn. Additionally, the priest told him that the envelope at the top of the case was the church's payment for this service. The colonel returned to HQ and reported this discussion immediately.

At noon, numbers 1, 3, and 5 arrived at HQ and were briefed on the activity of their shift while enjoying the repast prepared by the cook. Number 5 immediately called the pagers of both pilots. K-Air1 responded first. "I need you in the air above the city, circling at 3:00 p.m. The vicinity in question is St. Lucas Catholic Church downtown."

K-Air2 called in promptly thereafter. "I need you on standby, ready to go at 3:00 p.m." Both responded positively.

Numbers 3 and 5 double-checked the tracking vehicles and found them neatly in a row and freshly supplied with fuel and snacks. All was in readiness. At around one, the colonel showed up in VW-1 and assured them that it had been refueled. Nevertheless, number 5 carefully checked it out and refreshed the snack supplies. At one fifteen, the K-Van driver showed up and was briefed and his van and supplies checked. Immediately thereafter, four of the marines showed up in battle fatigues and were carefully briefed. They would ride shotgun, literally, in each of the tracking vehicles, armed as before—two with BARs and two with M16s.

The group departed at one thirty for the church area and set up on a four-quadrant basis, selecting their parking spots to enable their quick movement, when necessary. Their comm gear was all double-checked, and at around two thirty, K-Air1 checked in when beginning his takeoff. He would be in position inside fifteen minutes. At two forty-six exactly, K-Air1 reported in position at altitude above them.

They were all ready when the colonel exited his vehicle, parked a half block away from the church with the ransom case. When he picked the case from the floor of the vehicle, it left the turn-off magnet and immediately began to radiate a low PRF radio signal that was out of the normal communication bands. All four trackers reported that signal to number 1 at HQ. Max and JJ waited there anxiously.

There was a crowd, and the colonel had to wait in line outside the confessional he had been assigned by the priest earlier. The line moved slowly, too slowly for everyone, but finally, the colonel entered the confessional. He communicated his presence to the priest, and a small door on the floor below the confessional window opened to allow the colonel to slide the ransom kit through. The priest blessed him, and he left the building. Then he went around the side of the church and reentered through another door. He positioned himself where he could watch the confessional.

Confessionals were set up in twos on either side of the priest's hole. He was then free to turn one way and then the other to hear confessions one from the left and then the right, thereby speeding up the process. While one person was leaving one side and being replaced by another, the priest can hear the confession of the person on the other side who had just entered. All this was good for the priest and good for the process, but just now, it made for two lines of people coming and going for the colonel to watch. There were just too many people.

Suddenly, he thought he saw someone leaving from the confessional side opposite the one he had used, carrying a bag. Was it the ransom bag? He couldn't tell. However, not to take a chance, he reported it as possible. Not a minute after, there was a report from a tracker that the case was on the move. The colonel hurried back to VW-1. And none too soon, he observed the movement of the case on his tracker. All vehicles were reporting the movement and were edging out onto the streets to follow.

It moved very slowly at first, and then in a few minutes, it picked up speed. The case was now in a vehicle and moving quickly southward. All vehicles were in pursuit except Arm-1 with number 5, the most experienced tracker; he was in front of the target and tracking him to his rear. K-Air1 reported the movement on the ground and his inability to do much tracking because it was so slow compared with his speed in the air. He could cross back and forth but would be of little help unless the target got up to road speed and left the others behind or avoided them by stopping. Then he could put the hounds back on the track by crossing over it and pinpointing its location.

Max told JJ that it was luck that number 5 was in front. He was the most experienced tracker and able to track as well in a leading manner as the others followed. They paced the room and listened intently to the comm traffic between the trackers. Once, Max told them to keep off the air unless they had something significant to report or lost the track but, otherwise, to use it to coordinate their tracking tactics only.

In short order, the target was determined to have turned into the parking area of the Salvadoran Ministry of Defense. Two vehicles went inside and determined the vehicle to have gone into a secured executive area. The case then was determined to have gone into the building and, some minutes later, was determined by number 5 to be in the northwest corner of the building at a high angle, that is, an upper floor. All four vehicles took up positions at escape lanes from the building and waited.

Once the track had turned into the Ministry of Defense, Max ordered the colonel to make his contact as they had worked out earlier. Max and JJ jumped into a car and quickly made it to the ministry. They met with VW-1, and the colonel stepped out. In short order, a long black limousine arrived. The colonel opened the door of the limousine and helped the president of El Salvador out. The colonel saluted and greeted him and then turned and introduced JJ and Max to President Marcos.

Four armed guards arrived on the tail of the president and exited their vehicle. The president ordered them to stand and wait for him in the vestibule just inside the doors to the ministry. He then turned to the three and said, "Let's go do it."

As they entered the ministry, a call from Arm-1 told them that the first package had been removed from the ransom case. They quickly went directly to the top floor and the northwest corner of the building as determined by the trackers earlier. Max opened a panel in the briefcase he was carrying and turned the unit inside on. It issued a low-level signal that intensified as they approached the office of the deputy minister of defense, Sandoval. Two guards were at the door but, distracted by El Presidente, did nothing to hinder them. At the door, the case was turned first one way and then the other. The indicator pointed directly through the door of the office. All four, especially the president, suggested that they understood the significance. Max turned the unit off and handed the case to one of the distracted guards, who sat it down behind a chair just beside the office door.

The colonel knocked twice rapidly and opened the door. The president strode in with the other three behind. "Wha—" Deputy Sandoval exclaimed. And then suddenly, he snapped to attention and saluted. As they entered, his aide was seen at a table in the corner by the window quickly covering something bulky with a large cloth. "El Presidente, I am honored. I didn't know you were at the ministry. What can I do for you?"

"General Sandoval, I am here on a special mission with these gentlemen. I think you know Colonel Marin, a member of my special staff."

The general stepped forward and shook the colonel's hand while mumbling, "I had no idea."

"And I assume you know the U.S. military attaché, Mr. John Jones."

Again stepping forward, the general shook JJ's hand and said, "Yes, certainly. How are you, Mr. Jones?"

"And this gentleman is Max Curtis, a member of the security staff of Exlite Inc. in Dallas, Texas, USA."

Once more, the general stepped forward, shook Max's hand, and mumbled, "So glad to meet you. This"—he pointed at the aide near the window—"is my aide, Major Duserte." The major stood at attention and saluted the assembly while attempting to shield the table's contents with his body. The president and the general returned the salute.

The general asked those assembled to sit. And as he strode back behind his desk, the president and JJ selected comfortable chairs and sat down. Max, however, pulled a small device from his pocket and turned it on. It began a low, slow buzz. As he advanced toward the major and the table, the buzzing became higher and higher pitched to a whistle as he was within a stride of it. The major stepped between Max and the table, but Max shoved him aside and placed the now whistling device on the bulky lump covered by the cloth. Max jerked the cloth aside, and where there had been a lump was now the ransom case delivered to the priest. It was open, and lying beside it was the first package, opened and with several packets of the twenty-colón notes sitting beside it.

The major went for his holstered gun, but Max turned swiftly, his right arm outstretched, and slammed the edge of his hand into the major's windpipe. The major grabbed two handed, gun and all, at his windpipe, choking for air as Max drove his left hand into the major's solar plexus. The major doubled over as Max went into a deep squat. He came out of the squat with his right hand flattened, its heel pointing upward. It connected with the major's forehead just as he bent double from the plexus blow, and his head snapped back with a loud and awesome clicking of his neck vertebrae. He was out cold as he crumpled to the floor.

During this melee, the general—unseen by all but the colonel—opened a desk drawer and pulled out a .45 automatic pistol. But before he could raise it, the colonel—in one continuous movement, using the president's chairback—was on the desk and kicked the general squarely in the face. Blood squirted out of his nose, and he dropped the pistol and grabbed his nose. The colonel quickly pulled his .380 Mini-mite and held it on the blubbering general.

Through all this, beginning with the exposure of the ransom case and money, the president was at first mumbling and then loudly exclaiming, "Bastardo, bastardo, bastardo!"

Max and JJ pulled their weapons and dropped to a knee, facing the door, in case there was more trouble to come. And come it did. The commotion drew the attention of the guards just outside the door, and they burst in with their weapons pointing wildly about. The president motioned to them, and they quickly lowered their weapons, thereby saving their lives. Max and JJ were on point and ready to fire.

The president, regaining his composure, sent the two guards to fetch his personal guards from the building's foyer. When they had left, he quickly spoke to the colonel in Spanish. The colonel turned and told Max to gather up the money and ransom case and that the three of them should leave and depart the grounds quickly. And this they did, passing the now six guards in the hallway as they rushed back to the president.

Max called off the entire tracking entourage and asked all to meet ASAP at HQ. He and the colonel climbed into the car Max and JJ had come in. JJ, the marine, and the ransom case went to the embassy to return the money and expense the 1,000 colones for the priest.

En route through town toward HQ, Max diverted to the church and went in with the colonel. There, Max cornered the priest that the colonel pointed and presented him with ten bills, US$1,000, for his honesty and help. They then returned directly to HQ. While en route, Max called number 2 and told him to rouse his team and meet him at HQ. Shortly thereafter, all including JJ were present.

Max gave a fairly rousing talk to all, thanking them for helping free the girls, as he called them, and for routing out the general, the leader of FARN, and a traitor within the government. This was likely to be a blow that FARN could not recover from in El Salvador. Certainly, it would cause the president to redouble his efforts against them. This all broke up into an eating and drinking match.

There was much work still to be done and verbal and written reports to be made. Max began by phoning Bob in Dallas and having him get Marvin in DC on the line for a conference call. All on the line, Max proceeded to tell them in short fashion all that had happened in the past two days. Bob and Marvin were both overjoyed and offered almost unending congratulations. Max said he was just doing his job but that it helped to have the wind at his back. He promised them both a detailed written report and summary ASAP. Then he asked Bob to send a Learjet to pick them up early after a day's rest in place.

Number 2 was picking through the rough pictograms when Max joined him. This would be a hard job to resketch and put detail on. They spent several hours doing just that. Additionally, number 2 carefully inventoried the audiotapes of all HQ activity in that area. Also, he packed up the laptop computer they used at HQ for recording all activity.

Number 3 picked up all the weapons and saw to their cleaning and servicing and inventoried ammunition. He was amazed at how few rounds were spent. He returned the weapons and three clips each to the team members.

Number 5 gathered up all the comm gear and broke down the HQ comm setup. He tested and packaged each item carefully so they would be ready for their next use.

Numbers 5 and 6 spent their time removing trackers from vehicles and packing them carefully away for their next use. They dismantled the aircraft trackers and packed them as well. They paid the wet rental rate charged for the two aircraft and put in an extra $100 as a tip. Having gotten additional money from Max, they paid the two pilots $2,000 each. Their actual bill was about $1,000 each, but Max had instructed the overpayment. Additionally, they returned the VW fleet to the Rhinoceros Factory and thanked them profusely; but on the judge's orders, they refused any payment for their use.

Early in the evening, Max called Senor Reitmann and gave him a shortened version of the happenings. The senor in conjunction with his wife invited the team to dine with him the next evening at a restaurant in town where he was a partner to feast on his famous freshwater shrimp. He also said he would personally invite the ambassador and his wife and daughter and, if acceptable, that he would invite the judge and his wife. Of course, it was. Max asked if he could also personally invite the colonel, JJ, and their wives. Senor Reitmann said he would be glad to and would bring the wife of his absent son as well. It would be quite a party. Max offered to split the bill with him since he asked that others be included. The senor would have none of it. The party was to be on him.

Then Max checked with Chuck and asked if he could sponsor a buffet luncheon at Chuck's the next day at noon for all the helpers, that is, the marines, the guards, et al. Of course, the team, JJ, and the colonel would be there as well. He forewarned Chuck of Senor Reitmann's upcoming invitation to dinner the next evening.

Night was on them, and they were tired. The second shift, not so much. Max generously tipped and thanked the cook at Chuck's for the many meals and snacks that she'd laid out for them, some uneaten. He left a note for Chuck telling him that he had tipped the cook and stated the amount. When he arrived at his quarters, he similarly tipped and thanked the cook there, where again there were meals laid out that went uneaten. Again, he left a note for Senor Reitmann that he had tipped the cook and stated the amount.

He then set about making an envelope with a thank-you note and tip for each of the six marines, the two guards who had driven the K-Van, the guard who had gone with the colonel in VW-1 when they rescued the girls, and Alto, the guard who had been born in El Gato and was of so much help. Then he left a little note and tip for the housemaid and other servants at their quarters. He duly noted all these and others as expense items for later accounting purposes. Then he took a shower and went to bed early.

The next morning at breakfast, Max suggested that they should spend the morning preparing for the buffet lunch at Chuck's house at noon. They each volunteered for different items to fetch, prepare, and serve.

Afterward, Max told them of the dinner by Senor Reitmann that evening. They all promptly cleaned up and set out for the store and then Chuck's.

The buffet was laid out and none too soon. The first guests were beginning to arrive. There was much to do about nothing as all arrived and began to eat and drink from the layout. Mostly a boy's celebration, some bawdy stories were exchanged among a few. There was much laughing, and finally, it was time to finish.

Max took the podium, though there was none. He congratulated all, naming each—with a little help—and their individual contribution to their successes of the past two days. As a final gesture, he handed each a sealed thank-you note and tip in an envelope with their name inscribed on the outside as he shook their hands as they left.

"OK, guys, the staff will take care of the leftovers and see to the cleanup. It's now one o'clock, and we've got dinner at seven downtown. We really should go to our quarters and begin or continue our reports." They were all shuttled back to their quarters.

As they arrived, they found Max had beat them there and was in his swimsuit, saying, "Last one in is a chicken," as he dived into the pool. After an hour or a little more of pool play, exhausted, they all went to their rooms, cleaned up, and had a little nap. Max awoke at about five thirty and fished around in his luggage for clean and hopefully appropriate attire for the dinner party. They all had little else than khaki pants and pullovers, but they cleaned up fine. They all donned their bright red rescue caps and left for dinner about six twenty.

At the Azure Lago Restaurant, the red team was welcomed by a nicely dressed gentleman and escorted directly to a special dining area set aside from the regular guests. They arrived just after Senor Reitmann, who introduced his wife and daughter-in-law. The judge was there early as well, and he introduced his wife and met most of the team for the first time himself. Shortly, everyone was there. As they arrived in couples, they were introduced by Senor Reitmann, with some help from Max, to the red team members and those whom they did not already know.

Senor Reitmann took Max, JJ, and the colonel aside and told them of a late afternoon announcement by the government. "It seems that the deputy director of defense, General Sandoval, and his aide, Major Duserte, had been killed while leading a heroic raid on the headquarters of FARN in the small town of El Gato, where many FARN and their leaders were killed as well." He gave a copy of the dispatch to the three of them and said it contained many other details, including the announced funerals of the general and his major.

Then when all were in place, Senor Reitmann signaled a waiter, and the serving began. There was no ordering. The senor had picked everything and had individually asked each, as they arrived, if they had any food allergies or distastes. Apparently, no one did. The senor made the opening toast to the team as soon as a light wine was served. The food followed and followed and followed. There was a light dinner salad, followed by a small light soup. Then the main course was served—a full platter of fried, boiled, and coconut-encrusted shrimp or *camarones*.

Senor Reitmann explained that these shrimp were freshwater shrimp, very tender and very big. He explained that the ocean saltwater shrimp swam up a stream at the bottom of his mountain and spawned in the fresh water there. After their parents returned to the sea, the little shrimp hatched and spent a while in the fresh water feeding and gaining size to better adapt to the harsher saltwater environment they were to live in. However, before they could go downstream to the ocean, they were seined out of the stream, placed into a freshwater lake on his property on nutrients found in dry dog foods, and seined back out of the lake at a level of sixteen to the pound, or one ounce each. The tenderness of the shrimp was due to the fact that the shrimp had never reached salt water. The salt water was the agent that caused the skin beneath their shells to toughen. So they became the famed freshwater shrimp.

Of course, there were other courses, but the shrimp was the one that did it for the members of the red team and most everyone else. They seemed to eat for hours. Finally, a cleansing wine and fattening dessert were served. After that, over more wine, the accolades began.

First, the three hostages—Julie and Sally, the ambassador's wife and daughter, and Anita, Chuck's wife—thanked the team with a tear in their eyes for their rescue. More than one of the guests and the red team dabbed at their eyes as well. Finally, the girls, as Max called them, ended, saying in unison, "Thank you for saving our lives." Boy, what an ending.

Then Chuck stood and thanked the red team. He went on to say that his weekly report would be as standard and dry as ever this week. There would be no mention of the red team or the things they'd accomplished to his chain of command. But he added, "I will pen a separate note to the Exlite top men extolling the virtues of the red team."

Then the ambassador stood and thanked the team. He said that his report to Washington would praise the forethought, planning, and sense of the current administration in putting together a plan and an avenue to accomplish the rescue of their loved ones. He added that he would praise the aid of the Salvadoran Embassy staff and marine guard force. And he said at the very end that he would add a simple expression of his thanks to the red team.

Finally and surprisingly, the colonel rose and presented Max and the rest of the red team with bright chromium-plated machetes engraved full width and color filled along their blades with the emblems of the five countries of Central America. El Salvador's emblem was prominently placed in the center.

Clearly, it was the red team's time for a response. Again, surprisingly, number 2 rose and said that the members of the red team were doers, not speakers and that they would leave the closing speech to Max, number 1, their leader. Max rose and thanked Senor Reitmann for the sumptuous feast and his hospitality and the use of his daughter's home during her absence as the red team's quarters. Then he thanked Judge Santos for the fleet of VWs used by the team during their stay. Finally, he thanked Colonel Marin, a special aide to President Marcos, for the thoughtful gift and his ever-present aid and help during the trying period just past.

Finally, Max said, "We want to leave you all with this sailor's farewell." And he signaled his red team to stand.

They stood and donned their bright red caps, and as a hush came over the room, the red team spoke in unison.

> "May the Lord bless thee and keep thee.
> May he guide thee on a true and just course.
> And may his ever-freshening wind be at thy back
> to hasten thee on thy way."

Those assembled clapped vigorously, and again, there was eye dabbing. A few recognized this as Max's oft-offered parting comment of "May the wind be at your back."

With this, they broke up into little groups; and "the girls" approached each of the red team, gave them a kiss on the cheek and a hug, and whispered, "Thank you." The youngest of the red team—number 5, George Rendell, single and just twenty-two—blushed bright red when the ambassador's pretty young daughter, Sally, kissed his cheek while crying. He took much kidding from the others about that later, and they called him Georgie Porgie ("pudding and pie, kissed the girls and made them cry").

The ambassador gave Max a strong handshake and bear hug and whispered, "Thank you."

Back at the quarters, Max directed all to pack up and be ready to go to the airport at 7:00 a.m. Two had agreed to shuttle them, the colonel and Chuck. A guard would drive the van load of equipment and personal baggage.

After a restless night, broken by several with an early morning swim, they were transported to the airport, where a Learjet with tip tanks was waiting, freshly fueled. Max was the last to board and shook hands with Chuck and the colonel, who spoke quietly to Max. "May the wind be at your back." Max melted as he boarded, and they flew uneventfully to Dallas and a welcome home to their wives and families.

29

HOME SWEET HOME AGAIN

Max and the rest of the red team lay off through the weekend, but when they went into the office on Monday morning, they were greeted by all the staff with, as Max said, a million questions and comments about the heroism.

First thing, Max called Russ and the boys in DC and cancelled himself out of the self-defense training they were to start later that day. They all listened in on a speaker phone as Max related the events of the past week in El Salvador. Russ commented that Max had stolen his team and come home a hero. "His team, imagine that." They all had a great laugh at that.

Next, Max spoke with Bob, who promptly summoned him to a meeting with the chairman and CEO, the president, and the executive vice president of Exlite. They wanted to hear of the red team's exploits of the past week personally. Max asked red team number 2 to accompany him, and they spent some four hours regaling the upper brass with their story. The only break taken was when lunch was brought in. Otherwise, it had been a "do not disturb" session. Finally, they broke away amid congratulations and thanks and went back to the KPP campus.

Finally, Max called Marvin and was once again ordered to DC to tell his story in person to the director and staff. Max left early on Tuesday morning and met with the director, the deputy director, Ops, and Marvin. Same story, second verse. He had planned to spend the rest of the day with Marvin, but the director butted in and took him off to repeat the story to the president, vice president, and their two security advisers.

He spent the next day with Marvin, where they discussed many things, including the necessary increase in the original funding from $10 to $20 million. Marvin said the director had insisted on the increase to fund all this recent El Salvador adventure and to pay for some additional equipment that Marvin felt would be necessary to accomplish the upcoming but yet unexplained tasks.

At the end of the day, Max and Marvin went out to dinner, where Marvin got a call from the director. He asked that they return to the CIA and meet him in his office for a quick talk since Max was leaving early the next morning. They finished dinner quickly and went directly to the director's office without dessert.

The director greeted them both and said, when he phoned them, that he had just then returned from a second meeting with the president and his security council. He said he had been required to repeat Max's story of the day before and that the security council was mightily impressed with both the president's action and directive that had created the ability for such a response to this type of need, the actual response that had been taken, and the results accomplished. Accordingly, the president directed that aggressive action of this type be taken in every case of this sort at the discretion of the CIA director and that he be kept informed discreetly of all such action taken and the pursuant results. He said that all concerned ratified the decision of the president to make the directive and to continue this good work "in the national interest" to protect the American people and their economic base.

"In short, Max, the president said, 'This experiment, with earlier promising results, has reinforced those results dramatically, and we are justified in our actions and the continuation of this policy.' Thank you, my boy, thank you."

"Thank you, Mr. Director. We'll continue to do our best."

"Good. And, Max, tell your company people that we will cover all the costs to date, including those of your man in El Salvador earlier. I have directed Marvin to increase your budget accordingly."

"Yes, sir, thank you again."

"No thank-you is necessary. You've earned it and our trust of your judgment. And yours too, Marvin. And oh, by the way, Marvin, you are promoted effective immediately to CIA deputy director of special operations. Congratulations, Marvin, for a job well done."

"Yes, sir. Thank you, sir."

"OK, that's all. It's getting late, and I know you leave first thing in the morning, Max. I promise in the future not to jerk you up here with every happening. It's just that this first thing was so important for us and the president."

"No problem, sir, anytime." With that, the meeting ended. Marvin returned Max to the private quarters he had stayed in previously and, in the morning, flew home.

Max landed before noon, phoned Bob, and told him the good news. And then he met with the red team to review their actions since coming home. They were good guys, all of them. They had finished their reports more than Max could say, cleaned and inspected their gear, and made preparations to replace missing inventory. Max suggested that they each send personal thank-you notes to the people they had worked with in El Salvador and that Georgie Porgie might want to write a note to Miss Sally. They all had a laugh at that, and George's blush returned once again.

They then sat and had a lengthy session on equipment needed or not and any suggestions or additions they could think of in light of their recent experience. It seemed that everyone had an item or two in mind. They decided to table this and reconsider it in a week to give their heads time to clear. When the boys got home from camp, there would be plenty of time to go over all this again and get inputs from their most recent experiences.

Max called Kathy in, and they sat down with all his notes, recordings, and computer entries; her time line attempt from the recent endeavor; and last but not least Max's cherished pictograms, which told the story of the operation in simplistic stick figure/picture fashion with notes. Then they meticulously organized and wrote a detailed report for Marvin, Bob, and the file. Kathy wrote a summary for him. With spelling and grammar checked and corrected, it was sent by secure e-mail to both Bob and Marvin.

At week's end, Max received a report from the "boys at camp" regarding their week's instruction in weapons. In short, Russ reported that it was interesting and informative because they learned the ins and outs of the various weapons they might use or encounter. He said that it appeared to him that they could use the underslung portion of the M16 over and under. The under was a 20 mm launcher. Also, he spoke highly of the desirability of having access to a new mini-claymore-mine.

They signed off saying that they would miss Max at next week's defensive fight training. And of course, Russ added, "Don't steal my team off and be a hero again." This time, it was Max who laughed the most.

DEFENSIVE FIGHT SCHOOL

The FBI defensive fight school at Quantico, Virginia, was mostly composed of rigorous physical training. It was not that the boys didn't profit from this, but the actual fight training was nothing more than simplistic things like how to hold your gun so that it isn't taken from you, how to get out of a sudden headlock, and the typical judo, aikido, and karate stances and moves. All this was simply balance and deflection techniques, with a few countermoves and chops included. By midweek, the boys were bored. They talked to their CIA counterparts, who had taken side-by-side training with them the prior two weeks.

"This is not good enough. I've learned more and better moves from Max than these. There's a plethora of defensive moves that have been taught, and that's good, but we need a more aggressive program. When we're in the field and are attacked, it's a deadly attack. And I'm sure it's the same with you, CIA guys. We don't need a gentlemanly defensive move to keep from being overcome. We need aggressive moves that immediately disable or even kill our assailant. True, some attacks may be less than others, but we need the ability to immediately disable our opponent or face imminent death or capture and torture and eventual death. Our counter, be it a reaction to an attack or otherwise, must be effective." The CIA guys agreed. They had been taught that their first rule was "Do not get captured."

Russ offered them a proposition. "Come to Dallas with us for a couple of days, and we'll get Max to show us his moves and come up with a few others ourselves." They immediately agreed but didn't have the faintest idea how to get permission. Russ said, "I'll call Max, and he'll work it out."

Russ called Max and told him the problem. Max protested that he was no fight instructor. Russ countered that he'd learned more from Max than he'd learned in the FBI school. He explained that it would be a good chance for the CIA guys to bond with KPPS and vice versa. It would strengthen the friendships they had already made and, except for airfare, needn't cost much. The CIA guys could stay in the dorm and eat their meals in the cafeteria. Max finally relented and phoned Marvin.

"Marvin, it's Max. I've a favor to ask of you. Our guys and the recent CIA graduates who are training with our guys in bomb, weapons, and defense schools are quite disappointed in the defense school. They want extra defense training that Russ thinks they can get here. We can teach them our techniques, and they can coordinate and drum up some more at our facility here if you could get it approved for them to come down for about three days . . . OK, a week, counting coming and going. If you can arrange it, I'll do my best with them. They could come down this Sunday; we can meet with them and give them all we can in a couple of days, Monday and Tuesday; and they can cobble together their own ideas Wednesday. Then they could return home Thursday or Friday." Marvin said he didn't know their schedule, but would check.

"We can house them in our dorm, feed them their meals in our cafeteria, and shuttle them from and to the airport."

"Sounds good, Max. Can I come too?"

"Sure, glad to have you. You do understand that this is sixteen of your new guys, right?"

"Yes, I understand. With me, it will be seventeen. If this works out well, maybe we could use you guys about once a year to do this type of training."

"Hey, this is just a trial. Maybe it'll serve a purpose, maybe not."

"OK, I'll get back to you."

Max called Barry in and related the possibilities. "Will our quarters be ready?"

"You bet. This sounds like a good reason to hurry the last furniture and fixtures up. And Lisa will be delighted to have a captive group to feed for a week."

"OK, warn her. But it's not certain yet. Marvin will get back to me. If it's OK, they'll be here Sunday evening."

"Gotcha, boss." And Barry hurried off to talk to Lisa and then Max's wife, Gina, to hurry up the decorations and others.

Max called in his admin, Rick. "Rick, the red team has just done a hell of a job in El Salvador. I told them to take it easy this week to catch up. They're on duty and all, but I don't want them overworked. There's a possibility that we'll have sixteen or seventeen visitors staying here and doing some training with us next week. The week after, I'd like to give them a little vacation. Would you look into getting rooms at Mount Magazine Lodge in Arkansas? I'd like for you and me and our wives to transport them and their wives there on our bus for the week, say, Sunday through Friday of week after next. We'll cover all cost, including meals and activities. The team and I and our wives would stay in the lodge, and you and your wife would stay in a cabin. That way, the team would have their privacy as would you. However, I'd expect you to arrange some activities for us like parasailing, cliff rappelling, etc. You guys in the cabin could have us over Monday and Wednesday nights for drinks, hot tub, dinner, etc. Your contribution would be helping me drive the bus going and coming and you and your wife hosting us on Monday and Wednesday evenings, plus arranging the whole week for us. It's a good time of the year, and I don't think you'll have any trouble with reservations. Trust me, it's a wonderful remote place."

"Max, that sounds wonderful. I'm sure my wife would be delighted at a free trip to a nice lodge. I'll check with her first to be sure there's no conflict."

"Good. As soon as you get back to me about the reservations, I'll tell the red team. And, Rick, thanks for the enthusiasm."

Kathy came in and checked a number of things with Max, including his proposed schedule for the remainder of this month, two weeks, and next month. She attempted to keep his calendar and plans on a three-month basis, but lately, that had been impossible. This time, she just shot for six weeks. Then Max called in his staff one at a time and looked at their schedules, commented on them, and went on to other things.

Rick was back to Max in less than an hour and said his wife was delighted to hear about the trip and would gladly host the team at their cabin on Monday and Wednesday evenings. Rick said the reservations were welcome, and he would see to bus provisioning and the activity calendar at the lodge tomorrow. He was jubilant at the prospect.

Max called the red team to his office. He told them the news of the little trip to Arkansas and asked all to check with their wives immediately. If they had problems with baby sitters and others, he said to let him know. He'd get Kathy to find someone to house-sit or babysit. Within an hour, all five had reported back that their wives loved the idea and that they'd each arrange for their own house and sitter needs.

Last but certainly not least, he phoned Gina and told her the plan. She jumped at the idea. They had talked of visiting that lodge, and this was a perfect opportunity. He told of the arrangements, where she had no duties. It would be a perfect respite. There were a few activities to be offered but nothing that was required.

Lisa came in and said she would call Rick's wife, Jan, and Max's wife, Gina, and offer to help with Monday and Wednesday nights. Max told her it was not necessary, but she insisted. Gina told Max that she would be at the campus all Friday helping Barry with the last-minute details for the sixteen or seventeen guests who were coming on Sunday evening.

Marvin phoned and said the visit for the CIA recruits was approved but that he would not be able to attend. Marvin said all costs would be covered and to just bill them through him. Max got the coming and going airline schedules and arranged to pick up the bus just before dinner on Sunday. Then he called Lisa and firmed up the arrangements for meals and other things for sixteen, Sunday supper through Friday breakfast. Then he dialed Barry and told him the visitors would arrive Sunday at suppertime. Finally, Max called the team hut on the speakerphone and described the next week to them. They agreed to get out the mats and others for the gym.

Max had Kathy called the wives of the boys at camp and invited them on the trip to Arkansas. It would be a surprise for the boys and a nice thing for their wives, from whom they'd been absent for three weeks. Kathy got back to Max and said all welcomed the opportunity and could easily arrange for house or babysitters. Max noted that the bus was nearly full. It carried twenty-four, and his count was twenty, so they had plenty of additional space for their luggage and others.

On Friday evening, Max had reservations at the pool for supper, and Gina met him late in the afternoon for a swim before dinner was served. Lisa joined them for dessert and a glass of wine. They had a lovely early evening.

Late Saturday, Russ phoned Max at home on his cell. First, he thanked Max for arranging the fight school for the CIA guys. Second, he thanked Max for the surprise trip to Arkansas a week later. Third, he asked if he could pick up the guys at the airport on Sunday. "Of course, take them directly to the campus. Supper will be waiting, and their dormitory is ready as well. Barry will be there to help you get them all through supper and arranged in the dorm. Tell them to use the pool if they like. I'll plan to be there promptly at eight Monday morning in the gym. I hope you know what you want me to do. See you then. Goodbye."

30

KPP FIGHT SCHOOL

When Max arrived on Monday morning, all the guys were there, his thirteen and the sixteen CIA visitors. Russ introduced Max to the visitors, and Max welcomed them to the KPP campus. "I hope the accommodations are adequate."

The self-appointed CIA recruit team leader, Jeff, stood and replied that they really had not expected to be able to respond to Russ's invitation of a week earlier but were delighted that it had worked out. He said, "You must have some pull to have gotten this added to our schedule." Max replied that he didn't have any pull that he was aware of but that he did have some friends in high places.

Max expressed his concern about leading a training session such as the one that Russ had outlined. "I'm not sure that I'm at all qualified to speak about such a matter other than personally."

Russ said, "That's exactly what we want, Max, personally. And, Max, I'm having these sessions videotaped for our later use."

"OK by me," said Max. "Good idea. OK then, let me start by stating my personal opinion on what is needed for my men to accomplish their jobs. And likely, that's exactly what you'll need to accomplish your jobs on into the future, assuming you are to be active field agents.

"Most important, as I understand the nature and complexities of your future field assignments, it will be imperative that you not be detected and caught as you go about clandestine assignments. Note I said 'detected and caught.' To accomplish this, I believe that there are two significant issues here: equipment and responsive technique.

"Let me address equipment first. Often, we must enter a location when we have no knowledge of its level of protection. Of course, doing your homework is the first issue, but sometimes there is no opportunity because of time or other constraints. Accordingly and because even the best homework cannot prepare you for everything, you must have a modicum of equipment. We provide our teams with a kit of equipment pieces for their use in the field. It is contained in a day pack, like the one I have here."

After a little searching through the kit, Max produced a small, pager-sized device. "This first item is an ultrasonic and infrared detector. It is used to help determine if an area is guarded by an active ultrasonic or infrared system. And yes, it can see through doorways because of the inevitable cracks. A simple device, but it can warn you if an area is protected or armed against you. In the extreme, it might keep you from activating a small bomb set as a defense against your entry. But more likely, an opponent's entry detection system will be set to warn someone somewhere of any attempted entry. Whether you enter in such a circumstance is a decision you'll have to make, maybe based on the importance of the information you are seeking or that is worth entering, even if a remote alarm is sounded. At least it will speed up your operation if you decide to enter so that you might exit quickly before any response can arrive.

"This second device is PIDRA, portable intrusion detector and remote alarm. It's a two-piece device. The first is a passive infrared motion detector. It is gum backed and can be easily and quickly attached to most anything. It is used to watch your back when you must enter an area to warn you if someone comes behind you. Fastened beneath a bedside table or elsewhere, it will warn you if and when an intruder in a protected quarters is detected. The second unit is a small pager that is carried with you that has a warning light whenever anyone enters the protected area and also vibrates during the entire period of their presence there.

"A third device is a small entry alarm used to protect the area you are occupying. It alarms audibly to warn of an entry or approach."

Russ chimed in, "They are well aware of this item, Max. They tripped it first thing on our initial meeting at the Point."

"Yes," Jeff said. "And we were very impressed with the simple effectiveness of such a small unit, not to mention scared shitless by its alarm."

"Well, there are a plethora of other items we use, and I'll go through them all a little later with you, but now I think we should get into the basic defensive fighting techniques that I use. However, first, I'd like you to demonstrate in simple form the things you learned last week."

Russ and Jeff got up and went through the motions of a number of martial art maneuvers that they had been taught last week at the FBI academy fight school. "OK, enough. I see what the problem is. Jeff, you be the assailant, and I'll be the defender. Russ, please stand close to us, and use the foam protective shield to keep any blows from actually landing. Please, Jeff, don't try to outdo me. At your age and state of physical readiness, I'll concede up front that you can take me. Let's keep it simple and move in slow motion to show a few moves that are more in keeping with the nature of not getting caught. The intention is not to outscore or outpoint your opponent but to disable him, even if it means his death. The ultimate here is to *not get caught* or *taken*, if discovered, or when attacked, *you must win*.

"First, when mano a mano, face-to-face, you must assume that your attacker might well be superior to you in size or have a better knowledge and capability of the techniques of martial arts that you might employ. Accordingly, you should cheat. That means to employ first the Indiana Jones technique—club him, knife him, or shoot him according to the implements at hand. The old ploy of not making any noise that might attract others is baloney. Do what is necessary to survive. You've been taught the techniques to use when approached from the front or rear to defend yourself. Practice and employ those, but don't stop there. Disable or kill your opponent without favoring one or the other. To pause and think it out is to lose. You cannot and must not lose. Survive.

"Second, when facing a weapon—be it a club, knife, or gun—don't hesitate except to deflect your opponent's attention. If armed, shoot him instantly without regard to him. You must survive. If otherwise or likewise armed, don't engage in a fair fight—cheat. Use anything and everything against your opponent. If he has a weapon, the goal is obvious—kill him. I know you must have learned the art of disarming an opponent by grabbing the cylinder of a revolver or disabling the slide of an automatic, but don't stop there. He has a weapon. He was going to kill you, so kill him without hesitation. His pause is your weapon. Even if you don't have a weapon, kill him instantly. Survive.

"Now let's practice this. Let's practice how to disable or kill your opponent. The disabling techniques include kicking an opponent in the side of the knee, thereby partially disabling him by breaking the knee. There's popping his ears by slamming the palms of your hands over his two ears simultaneously. That's a painful and partially disabling technique. There are other partial or temporary disablers, like stomping the instep, thumb knuckling his thumb back, eye gouging, etc."

Max and Jeff demonstrated each of the above in slow motion, and several were called for as repeats so that the class might better understand them.

Then suddenly, it was time for lunch. They all decided to eat in their gym clothes as no one had worked up a sweat. Lisa had a light, nutritious lunch prepared and served to them on the pool patio. To a man, they all were having a great time, although some mumbled that they hadn't seen any action yet and hoped the afternoon would be more enlightening.

In the afternoon, back in the gym, Max began, "I hope to be able to answer any questions you have on nondeadly fight tactics that disable."

Jeff asked about the heart stab, that is, a quick jab to the middle of the chest affecting the heart muscle. Max's response was that the heart jab or stab was indeed an effective stunning blow and that, with some, it might be debilitating but with others only temporary.

Another asked about the deadly liver stab or jab. Max's response was that it was indeed deadly and often very painful but that it was no more painful typically than any other well-delivered blow. The deadly effect of bursting the liver did not have an effect for several hours, and by then, you might be caught or dead. Others asked similar questions and were quickly answered that the blow might indeed be effective but not instantly disabling or deadly.

All questions answered, Max then proceeded to demonstrate instantly disabling blows or those that set up a sequence that was disabling or deadly. The first such blow was one directed to the solar plexus. Everyone recognized it as temporarily disabling, but Max went on to point out that the blow caused an adversary to double over forward. This he and Russ simulated in slow motion. As Max delivered the simulated blow, he instantly went into a deep knee bend toward the floor. As Russ doubled over, Max came up from that low position, delivering a simulated blow from the open and upturned heel of his hand to Russ's chin. "Notice," he said, "that the follow-up blow with the heel of the hand was delivered with the added power of his legs from squat position to standing. This blow usually snapped the opponent's head back so sharply that it rendered him unconscious, if not breaking his neck."

They repeated the sequence, only this time the neck-snapping blow itself was delivered to the brow, or forehead, just above the eyes. Max noted that this blow could be equally fatal, and either blow could be delivered without needing to aim it; one place or the other would be equally effective.

Finally, they repeated it a third time; and this time, the blow was delivered at the base of the nose. Max explained that, if delivered correctly, this blow would break the nose bone where it joined the brow and drive it beneath the brow directly into the brain. Almost always, it was instantly fatal.

Max explained that there were two other blows that set up such a sequence. First was the more familiar "clothesline," where the blow was with the side or edge of the hand to the throat. He demonstrated how it was best delivered as he swung around and stretched his arm out, palm down, and simulated hitting Russ in the windpipe. This was a setup blow because it caused immediate choking and disabled the opponent instantly. From here, any number of other blows could easily be aimed. But again, the best of these was the heel of hand to chin, nose, or brow.

Max's last blow was similar to the clothesline, but that landed instead on the bridge of Russ's nose. He explained that this caused much pain and blood, broke the nose bone, and made it much easier to drive into the brain with an upward hand-heel-to-nose blow from below.

Finally, he added another set. "If you can deliver a blow of any kind—that is, crotch kick, plexus stab, etc.—that causes your opponent to double over forward, then you can deliver a knockout punch with your knee to the front part of his face as he drops to cover himself."

One other and final blow was with the thumb to the temple area. "This blow is equally disabling and at least momentarily debilitating and sometimes fatal. If not adequate in and of itself, a follow-up hand heel blow to chin, nose, or brow would finish the sequence."

The class was mesmerized through his whole demonstration and lecture. One asked when he or others had last used these blows and found them to be effective. Russ replied that he had delivered such a blow, hand heel to brow, about a month ago; and the opponent, who was armed, was instantly disabled and rendered unconscious. Later, it was determined that he had been killed on the spot. Max said that he had used the clothesline to the throat, followed by a hand-to-brow blow, just a week ago and rendered the adversary immediately unconscious. Later, it was determined that his neck had been broken.

It was four thirty, and Max called a halt. He suggested a dip in the pool to cool off. They would come back to the gym tomorrow and go through the motions and learn the blows. Russ jumped up and said, "Last one in buys the ice cream." With that, led by the home teams, all headed for their trunks and the pool.

After a brief swim, Max got his ice cream and returned to his office. He asked Russ to join him. "Russ, do you think today was effective or what you had in mind?"

"Yes, I do. It was nothing like we were taught at Quantico. There, all they taught were enhanced judo techniques, good for self-defense but not good enough to assure survival. Today in the beginning, I think the guys thought that this was just another lecture. But this afternoon, things popped. If you like, I'll take over tomorrow morning and put them through the drill."

"Thanks. That would be nice. What do you plan for the afternoon and Wednesday?"

"I think I'd like to see if any of the guys can come up with anything else in the order of what you taught us today. And thanks, boss. That's exactly what I had in mind. Our guys and the CIA guys both needed that. Why don't you plan to join us again at about 3:00 p.m. Wednesday and see if we've come up with anything new or useful and again end it with a swim and ice cream?"

"Sounds good. So I'll abandon you tomorrow. Are they happy with the quarters and food? Or should we provide them with some nightlife or something?"

"Yes, I think they are quite satisfied. No nightlife needed. But if we've some time Wednesday evening, we might plan a drive around just for familiarity with Dallas."

"OK, you're in charge, Russ."

Tuesday was eaten up quickly. Bob visited, and he and Max went over a plethora of things, including budget and funding. After lunch, Max took Bob into the gym and introduced him to the visitors. They were appropriately appreciative of a visit by an executive. And Bob was impressed with the aspect of them providing the CIA with a laboratory to test new training techniques. "Was this your idea, Max?" Bob asked.

"No, it was Russ's baby, and it seemed to be working. We'll be able to tell from the comments at the end of the session and the comments that come back from DC after they return."

Again, Wednesday morning was filled with administrative tasks, including a review of production, with Barry on the EAS side of the house. Max didn't recognize how much he was looking forward to the afternoon session with Russ and his guys. He could hardly wait for 3:00 p.m.

Max entered the gym just moments after that and was greeted by all. Russ said the guys had something to say. Of course, Jeff was the spokesman. "Max, we'd like to thank you for getting us out of DC for a while. It's been like a vacation staying here in your dorm. The food was great, and please relay that to the staff. But most of all, the training you gave us was great. You taught us to think in the right manner. Our handlers to date have not approached things on a survival basis. In the back of our heads, we knew that our jobs might just be mundane, but we also knew that when we were put to task, it might well be that we would be in danger as our axiom 'Don't get caught' suggests. However, we never had it brought home so well as when you described that we must act instantly, intensely, and with ferocity to assure that axiom. Your techniques are not new but have never been so appropriately demonstrated and explained. You might well have saved our lives with this training sometime when challenged in the future. Many thanks from us all. If in the future you need something from any of us, do not hesitate to ask. If it can be done, it will be done. Again, thanks for the hospitality and insights." With that, Jeff sat down, and they all clapped.

Max thanked them for their cooperation and overblown appreciation. And he said he had a little something for them. With that, he handed out his personal laminated business cards to each. On the back, it had the KPPS farewell. He had his three teams stand, and they recited it in unison.

> "May the Lord bless thee and keep thee.
> May he guide thee on a true and just course.
> And may his ever-freshening wind be at thy back
> to hasten thee on thy way."

He then called them each by name and handed each a silver coin with "KPPS" engraved on the front and the words "Wind at your back" on the rear. Also, neatly engraved in a small size at the bottom of the front side was an individualized number to designate each individual as C-1,

C-2 through C-16. Max told them that the card was theirs to use if ever they needed it, and the coin was theirs to ID them, if ever needed.

Russ said they had not come up with anything else as appropriate as the things he had taught. And then he said, "Last one in the pool pays for the ice cream." This time, it was Max who laughed and paid again.

That evening, Russ took them all for a ride around Dallas for familiarity. Next morning, he took them to the airport and waved them off.

31

A WELL-DESERVED BREAK

Saturday was a rest day for all. Max took Gina out to eat every meal that day. That evening, they packed their bags for the trip to Arkansas. Sunday morning, they rose early and went to breakfast at their favorite spot. Gina said she felt like she already had a vacation with no cooking.

They proceeded for rendezvous with the others at the KPP campus at nine. Some had come earlier and had breakfast biscuits at the cafeteria; others arrived at the last minute, plus a few. But all were there in plenty of time. They packed up the bus and picked out their bus seats. "Last one's a rotten egg" (gets the worst seats) was the sequence followed.

At nine thirty, Rick called all aboard. They all clambered aboard and were chatting like magpies when Max stood at the front of the bus and declared he was going to make a going-away speech. They all groaned in unison. His speech was "Let's go." With that, Rick drove the bus out of the campus toward Central Expressway and thence northward to LBJ. From there, they proceeded east around town to I-30. From there, it was pedal to the metal, that is, 70 mph northeastward to Texarkana and the state line of Arkansas.

It took just three and a half hours to reach Texarkana at 1:00 p.m. They exited there for lunch at Bryce's Cafeteria, a well-known location with excellent food. They paused there for an hour. It was plenty of time to overeat and rest up before the next leg. Fort Smith was north on US-71, where they made their turn on AR-22 eastward to Mount Magazine State Park, some three and a half hours from Texarkana. They arrived at their destination at five thirty. Max had taken over and driven the bus from Fort Smith to the park since he was more familiar with the terrain and roads through these mountains, a beautiful ride.

Everyone, especially the women, were atwitter; it was beautiful. There perched on a cliff some thousand feet above the Petit Jean River and Valley was a modern lodge styled after the great lodges of the U.S. Western Rockies. And off to either side, also perched on this cliff, were a dozen beautiful cabins.

Max let everyone off the bus at the door of the lodge, and bellboys got their luggage. All went into the lobby. Max checked them all in and got the keys to Rick and Jan's cabin, cabin 1. Rick and Jan then proceeded to drive the bus to the cabin and take their things in. Gina later said that she heard Jan's screams of delight all the way to the lodge when she saw the inside of the cabin.

Everyone scampered up to their rooms after Max said they were on their own. All meals and other things were covered, so they were free to eat whenever. He said that they might join in the activities offered, if desired. Max declared that he was going to go up, take a shower, and then go down to the dining room for supper. Later, he and Gina enjoyed the panoramic view from the back porch literally on the cliff's edge until the darkness enveloped them. They saw a few of the others at supper and on the porch, but most simply disappeared.

The next morning, Monday, Max talked to Rick and ordered large breakfasts to go for four. He and Gina crossed the hundred or so yards between the lodge and cabin 1 hurriedly with the best-smelling stuff in bags. They could hardly wait to get to the cabin and share it with Rick and Jan. Both couples chatted away as they made it through every morsel of breakfast. Jan and Gina went in the kitchen and planned the evening repast without any concern or comment from the two guys.

The day passed uneventfully, and the couples saw little of one another except at different times in the indoor pool or hot tub at the lodge, the nearby short walking trails, and the restaurant. They all took this opportunity to rest and be with their spouses. Incidentally, Georgie Porgie brought along a female companion whom he had been dating, Alice Crumby. He claimed she didn't appreciate having to sleep on the floor while he took the bed. No one believed that, not for one minute, and they just laughed it off.

Early evening at around six, they all convened at Rick and Jan's cabin. They brought suits and went in the hot tub on the deck. Jan, Gina, and Lisa had prepared and set out a buffet fit for a king. It had chicken salad, tuna salad, greens, tomatoes, cucumbers, carrots, cauliflower, squash, etc. Then there were chips and three different dips. Of course, there were white and wheat bread, French loaf, and buns. And for the diehards, there were hamburger patties and hot dogs with all the fixings. There were beer, wine, and a wonderful margarita mix that was finished off by each individually in a blender full of ice to make it frozen. A lot of food it was, but there were sixteen of them and all hungry like they'd not eaten all day.

A good time was had by all, and as night came, they settled down in small groups on the porch and in the hot tub again. Max, Rick, and Dave helped Gina, Jan, and Lisa clean up and put away in Ziplocs and Tupperware, which Jan had brought, all the leftovers. It sort of looked like the loaves and fishes story from the Bible. The leftovers seemed to be more than the buffet. What a swell night it was.

At about nine thirty, the couples started strolling back to the lodge. Max and Gina were the last to leave and thanked Rick and Jan for hosting the affair. Max described it as a beautiful night with a beautiful lady as they held hands and returned to the lodge and their room, all smiles.

On Tuesday at breakfast, most were there at about the same time. Max had gotten the schedule and announced that there would be cliff-rappelling classes at 10:30 a.m. and any and all were invited, including the women. About half the women decided to participate as did all the men. The other half of the women opted out and decided instead to visit the gift shop and see what else was there to the lodge and its environs.

Sure enough, the instruction was held right on time. The men whose wives were there rappelled first, and their women followed them. Then the rest of the men followed. The rappel was down about two hundred feet of cliff to an outcrop area from which the parasailing was done. Everyone did well rappelling, but all three number 1s and Max did it like professionals because they were. This was a skill they had all developed at different times and places in their careers. Of course, Russ and Max raced down, each touching rock only about four times in the two-hundred-foot descent. At the bottom, the others clapped to celebrate their fast descent. The path back up was fairly steep but not too much so. By the time they got back to the lodge, they were sweaty, and they decided to take a quick dip in the pool before lunch.

The afternoon was uneventful, though some went back to the pool, others took a hike, and Max took a nap. Again, that evening, they were on their own. Gina showed Max the things she had gotten at the visitor's shop and insisted on showing him a couple of things she thought he might like there. All in all, it was a very good day.

Mostly, they had an early supper because the parasailers were due out at about six thirty. They all looked down on the outcropping some two hundred feet below, where the parasailers were preparing their sails. Soon one went off and then another. In all, three launched that evening. In short order, the first, second, and third had worked the strong winds up from the valley until they were even with the lodge's back porch. Eventually, they worked the wind until they soared some three hundred feet above them. They circled and orbited above the porch, from which the guests all stared until their necks hurt from looking upward. Eventually, someone noticed that the chairs on the porch tilted backward and would support their heads as they looked up at this angle. Oh well, too soon old, too late smart. Well before dark at this time of year and at this elevation, at about a quarter to nine, those parasailing returned to their roost as though drawn there by a magnet. It looked awfully easy.

Next morning, Wednesday, although some were lazy sleep-ins, Max and Russ were up with the rooster. They ate breakfast together while their spouses took their good time rising and getting themselves ready for the day; after all, this was a holiday for them.

Russ and Max strolled over to Rick's cabin to see if he was up, and they found him drinking coffee and eating toasted buns left over from their Monday night feast. Max buttered and popped more cut buns into the oven while Russ fixed their coffee. The three assumed the most restful positions they could on the porch chairs, snacked on the buns, drank large mugs of coffee, and simply enjoyed the view, company, and fresh morning air in silence.

Sometime later, Russ asked Rick if he had been able to arrange for them to parasail off the cliff. Rick replied affirmatively but that he had scheduled the lessons and actual parasailing for Thursday morning at about ten thirty. He said that he had planned their actual activities—rappelling and parasailing—on alternate days with a free day in between. Max congratulated him for an excellent plan.

Finally, Jan joined them and suggested some eggs and ham. Since Max and Russ had already eaten twice, they deferred and excused themselves to return to their wives. Rick quickly took Jan up on her offer. They said their goodbyes and strode quickly to the lodge.

They found others and their wives eating breakfast in the restaurant. They sat next to their wives and picked at their leftover bits of food. They joined the others in conversation and told them of the plans to parasail tomorrow morning. It was clear that the two of them were becoming jumpy because of the lack of activity. Their wives suggested a vigorous hike in the mountains that they had heard of. They both jumped at it as did a couple of the others.

Checking at the desk for information about the trail, they learned it was a four-hour round-trip climb. Accordingly, they ordered a lunch packed for the four of them and, while it was being prepared, fashioned a small pack for each to carry out of bits and pieces of cloth (mainly cloth table napkins from the restaurant) and some cord they found in the maintenance area. Also, they each took two standard bottles of water and, looping a cord about the necks, fashioned a way to carry those as well. A small stand in the lobby held trail maps, and in short order, they set off on the four-hour climb and picnic.

Along the way, they spotted eagles flying overhead. At first, they mistook them for buzzards, common in Texas, but discovered they were indeed eagles. They flew very high and swooped down in steep dives once in a while. Once, an eagle that disappeared in a dive into the forested side of the mountain came close by them on his return to the heights. He clearly had prey in his talons. It was an amazing sight, and they all reveled in it.

About an hour in, it was clear they were at a halfway point, so they stopped for lunch. They had only finished about a bottle of water apiece when they started the homeward turn. About an hour later, another half bottle of water was gone, and they were back at the lodge. The desk manager on duty questioned if they had done the entire trail and was amazed that they had completed it in two hours. Normally, their guests took at least four to do the same. Of course, he had no idea how good a shape they were in. They all did a gymnastic workout daily and sometimes hit the pool as much as three times a day.

They found the rest of their group and their wives in the restaurant finishing a light lunch. These four did not have a light lunch. They ate double portions as they were famished after their trek. Most opted for a two-hour nap and then a dip in the pool until time to go to Rick's cabin for their every-other-evening dinner.

This evening, as they arrived, Rick was putting the finishing touches on barbecue ribs on the outside grill provided with the cabin. The smell hurried them all across the way from the lodge. When they arrived, they found a complete array of barbecue meats with beans, coleslaw, and buns. The drink array was as before, but most took to the margaritas. They had music from a boom box Rick had brought for the occasion and CDs of the current popular country-western entertainers. The music spilled out into the evening as they slowly ate everything in sight. A few of the wives who had helped with the setup cleaned up. As the day ended, they clasped hands with their sweeties and strolled in the moonlight back toward the lodge. Fine Wednesday.

On Thursday, everyone was looking forward to parasailing. All the guys tried it and none of the wives. While sailing, Max got an idea. Floating up there, up high, he watched the eagles look down, spot their prey, and swoop down. All the wives watched the antics from the back porch of the lodge. There were much oohing and aahing and a little bit of anxiety expressed. But that calmed as each new flier stabilized and swooped back and forth to take the wind again and gain altitude. Afterward, they all ate lunch together in the restaurant and wiled away the rest of the day and evening.

First thing Friday morning, everyone breakfasted, packed, and got their stuff on the bus. Max began the drive home at about nine. They should make it home by about five; this time, they stopped just short of Texarkana at a Burger Doodle, and all indulged in burgers and Cokes. Somewhere between Texarkana and Dallas, George announced the he and Alice were engaged. This set the bus all atwitter. Alice said they would visit both their parents soon and make it official. George whispered to Max that he already had a ring and would give it to Alice once he had met her family and obtained her father's permission.

Soon enough, they were home. The staff was just leaving as they unpacked the bus. Most came by and welcomed the team home. Two couples opted to stay and eat at the campus cafeteria, but most headed home after many farewells. The trip had been a success in ways Max had not anticipated. The wives had bonded, and the guys and wives had gotten along extraordinarily well. The wives might well need one another at a later time when their men were in the field.

32

A NEW DAY, A NEW IDEA

Monday morning, Marvin phoned. "Max, I didn't want to interrupt your R & R but wanted to tell you the recruits got back last week and are singing your praises. They brought back a video that Russ gave them of your first day's lecture and demonstrations, and I've just finished viewing it. We have nothing else like it. It needs some editing, but we'd like to use it to train future recruit classes. Would that be OK?"

"Sure, Marvin. I'm surprised because it's hardly professional."

"Yes, but it's right on the mark for our needs. Think you could come up here and maybe make some inserts for the edit?"

"Sure, whatever you want, but I think future classes might rather come down here."

"I'm sure they would. Apparently, you treated them very well, and they enjoyed themselves immensely."

"Well, maybe you should consider letting them come here as a break from their regular training up there. You know, all those Yankees can get on your nerves."

"Ha ha! Yes, you're right. They do. We'll see."

"Oh, and, Max, the trouble we talked about earlier brewing in Italy? Well, it looks really serious. If anything happens there, we're sure to need your help."

Other than the call from Marvin, Max had a full schedule to follow up on from the prior week's absence; but first thing on Tuesday, he got Jimmy into his office and went over the idea he had while parasailing.

But that was an idea and a story for another day. Until then,

"MAY THE WIND BE AT YOUR BACK."